WRONG NUMBER, RIGHT GUY

ALSO BY ELLE CASEY

WRONG NUMBER, RIGHT GUY

Bourbon Street Boys: Book 1

Elle Casey

Montlake
Romance

Published by Montlake Romance Publishing, Seattle

www.apub.com

Amazon, the Amazon logo, and Montlake Romance Publishing are trademarks of Amazon.com, Inc., or its affiliates.

ISBN-13: 978-1503947450
ISBN-10: 1503947459

Cover design by Sarah Hansen

Printed in the United States of America

For my momma, my biggest fan

CHAPTER ONE

My sister is at her wit's end, but that's nothing new. Her three kids are always making her crazy. I pick up my phone to take a look at her latest text.

Sis: *I need a frign break. Taking the butt strings to the arcade.*

I frown. Since when are we calling her kids butt strings? I mean, they *are* up her butt all the time, but still . . .

Me: *Butt strings?*

A few seconds later her response comes in.

Sis: *I meant to say breast sling. Effing autocorrect.*

Then two seconds later this comes in:

Sis: *Argh! Not breast sling! I'm going to kill the dick who shit on my ass because it's going all jello.*

I'm laughing too hard to stop at this point.

Sis (again): *Shit storm! Epic shit storm of autocorrect madness! I'm taking the butt HEADS to the arcade and I'm going to kill the dog who shit on my grass because it's going all yellow. Please just shit me cow.*
Sis (once more): *SHOOT ME NOW, NOT SHIT ME COW. WHAT IS WRONG WITH YOU AUTOCORRECT??? WHY ARE YOU SO FILTHY???*

I can barely press the right keys, I'm laughing so hard.

Me: *Call their daddy and take a pill. I'll be over later.*
Sis: *I need a new phone. I'm going to the slut to buy one.*
Me: *That should be an interesting transaction. Does she take credit cards?*
Sis: *STORE NOT SLUT. And I'm going to go ride off the autocorrect too.*
Me: *lol. Ride that mother, big sis. Ride it hard.*
Sis: *Shut up. I'm going to get rid of it, not ride it. Frigging automobiles.*

She must have given up, because that's the last I hear from her or her out-of-control automobile . . . errr, autocorrect.

I chuckle my way back to my home screen, clicking away from the text messages as I lie down on my couch, reveling in my single, childless adulthood.

My sister Jenny started early in life; like me she was in a rush to leave home, anxious to leave the unhappy mess our father had created with his lies and unfaithfulness to our mother. Jenny had her first kid at twenty-two and finished with the third one by the time she was twenty-eight. Now, at thirty-two, she's divorced and mostly insane, trying to play the role of both parents while holding down a full-time job, all while her ex pretends to be eighteen again with women way too young to be doing anything but going to college. It's pitiful.

No way in a million years am I going down that path. I've seen the mess it leaves behind. Whoo-hoo, no thank you. Commitment's great when it's with the right guy; I've seen that with friends. Some people get lucky. But so far I'm not even sure there's a guy out there for me. When I get a hint of a lie or even just a shaded truth, I'm outta there. Good-bye, so long, don't let the door hit you on the butt on the way out. Liar, liar, I will set your pants on fire.

I'm single and loving it, twenty-nine, working as a freelance wedding and portrait photographer, and absolutely not in the market for a relationship. I just ended a long-term affair that should have been a short-term one and have sworn off dating for a while. As far as I'm concerned, it's better to have not loved at all than to have loved and been lied to. I need a little me-time, and since my schedule is pretty much empty, it's going to work out perfectly. My plan consists of being in the studio or on location whenever I can book some work, napping, gardening, going to the river in the evenings for glorious, relaxing walks, and drinking copious amounts of wine in between all those things. Nothing is going to get in the way of me enjoying the last year of my twenties. Nothing, not even the little butt strings and their crazy momma.

I've been planning this self-imposed get-back-to-the-real-May-Wexler program for a while. Ever since I graduated from NYU with a major in photography, I've been focusing on getting past the things that drove me away from my family and across the country to get my degree. But even though it's been over five years, I'm still really no closer to reaching that elusive goal.

Heck, I knew I needed to exorcise my demons just a couple years after graduating, which is why I moved back South and took up residence a few miles from my older sister in New Orleans, the place she landed after college.

Jenny's my rock. The shoulder I can always lean on. But making the move of coming here to be near her didn't magically send the baggage I've been carrying around up to the attic. The specters of my family's past still follow me, still haunt me, still influence the way I feel about myself, my life, and every single guy I come into contact with in a romantic way. It's really pretty pitiful, actually.

Jenny's doing much better than I am in the self-help department. After dealing with her own failed relationship, destroyed by a lack of faithfulness on her ex's part, she's come to a place where she can be honest with herself about what happened and take responsibility for her own happiness without making excuses when she fails. Me, I'm still working on that part of it. I blame my father for everything; I'm not ready to forgive and let go.

So, yeah. I'm going to figure me out. *This* is my grand plan. Forget the fact that I have absolutely no idea how to do this for myself. I'm hoping several bottles of wine will help kick-start the process.

I'm going to decide once and for all who I want to be when I grow up, and then I'm somehow going to become that person, even if it means I'm not going to be taking pictures of happily married couples and families wearing matching white shirts and denim pants anymore. It's not like that was my life goal when I left college anyway; it's just what I fell into when I couldn't find a job doing anything else. I shouldn't complain, though. Until the economy fell into the dump a couple years ago, I was doing really well.

Another text comes in and lights up my screen. I blink a few times to clear the sleep from my eyes. I must have dozed off, because my clock says it's an hour later.

Unknown number: *You're going down.*
Me: *Oh really?*

I smile to myself. My sister is going to blame me for something that happened while I was sleeping. Apparently she has her new phone and a temporary number until her old one switches over, and her first text is to bitch at me. Excellent.

Me: *Says who?*

I take a moment to save her number.

Jen: *Says me, that's who. You need to get out here.*
Me: *No. I'm sleeping. Can't you hear me snoring? Zzzzzzzz*
Jen: *Screw that. Come here or I'm coming there and I won't be alone. You're my backup, remember?*

I picture the little monsters running all over my freshly cleaned floors, putting sticky goo on everything, and smile at her empty threat. I'll forgive those little beasts pretty much anything. They might be wild, but they sure are cute. I can say that because I only have them for a few hours at a time.

Me: *Bring it. I can handle whatever your butt strings throw at me.*
Jen: *Are you serious? Butt strings? Get your ass out here! I mean it, dick!*
Me: *Did you just call me a penis? That's harsh.*

I'm laughing all over again.

Jen: *I call it like I see it. Get here yesterday.*

I sit up on the couch and sigh. She sounds like she really needs a break. It's tempting to send her another text, but I decide against it. No more messing around. She's about to blow a gasket, and the last time that happened, I was stuck with the kids for a whole week while she went to our family cabin to find herself again. I need to head this one off at the pass.

Me: *Fine. Where are you exactly?*

Jen: *Frankie's Pub. Downtown at Lexington.*

I pull my phone in closer to see if I'm reading that right. Sure enough, it says Frankie's.

Me: *Isn't that a biker bar? Are you sure you should be bringing the kids in there?*

Jen: *If you call them my kids again I will shoot you.*

I stare at the screen for a while and then decide against a smart-ass answer. If my sister has reached the point of disowning her kids, Auntie May needs to swoop in and save the day, once again.

I stand up and sigh over the terrible burden of being so awe-some, typing out my response as I make my way across the room to the front door.

Me: *Fine. See you in 20.*

Jen: *Bring the Phoenix.*

I pause with my fingers on the door handle. *Phoenix?*

As if he can sense it, my half-Chihuahua/half-Pomeranian fur-ball perks up and rouses himself from his doggy bed to join me in the foyer. His tiny claws click across the tile floor. Felix is good for keeping the kids occupied so Jenny and I can talk. She often requests his presence when she needs to let off steam and doesn't want the kids listening in.

"I think she wants me to bring you, Felix." I grab my bigger purse off the rack at the door and throw my wallet, keys, and Taser into it. Even if I weren't going to a biker bar, I'd add that last item to my bag; I was mugged once in college, and I'm never going down easy again. And if I do go down, I'm electrocuting a bad guy on the way. "Come on, little guy—up you go."

He waits patiently for me to scoop him up and put him in the bag, back legs in first. Once settled, he pokes his head out of the top, and his tongue comes out to do a happy pant.

"Do not pee in my bag, Felix. I'm not kidding this time."

As I slide my feet into my pink espadrilles, I check my look in the window's reflection, smoothing down my shoulder-length brown hair, making sure it's tucked neatly behind the light blue plastic hair-band that had gone slightly askew as I slept. My tailored, blue-striped blouse and beige pants are still crisp and clean, no worse for the wear after my little nap and a day's work. Today was a studio job, so there was no need to wear a suit or dress, but I never wear jeans to work. I don't want my clients thinking I'm a hack. I take my work seriously, even if it's as boring as watching paint dry sometimes, so I need to look the part. I don't need any more makeup than I'm already wearing; a little lip gloss and some eyeliner and mascara to outline my light blue eyes, and I'm ready to go. I'll make sure nothing smeared during my nap out in the car, before anyone besides Felix sees me.

We walk out the door and get into my adorable cherry-red Chevy Sonic, heading downtown to a bar I'm absolutely sure my sister should not have gone into with her kids. Hopefully, I won't stand out too much in my casual uptown outfit. I've never been to Frankie's, but I have to assume it's not the type of place I'd go to regularly. It gets mentioned in the news from time to time, and never because there's something good happening there.

Me: *We're on our way. Hold tight. Don't kill anyone until I get there.*
Jen: *No promises.*

CHAPTER TWO

I'm parked in a lot mostly filled with old-school motorcycles and big sedans that probably should have been junked long ago. There are two pickup trucks, one of them new. Besides my car, it's the only vehicle here I'd be caught dead in, and it's a truck, for God's sake. I hate trucks. They're so . . . big and rednecky.

This has got to be the worst parenting decision my sister has ever made. What happened to her? It can't just be the autocorrect on her phone. Her ex-husband Miles must have pushed her too far this time.

Felix and I enter the bar and stop just inside the doorway, getting the lay of the land. I'm trying to talk myself out of being nervous—after all, I'm a grown woman who's been to plenty of bars, and I have no reason to fear anyone here—but it's not working. My palms are getting sweatier by the second. My gaze roams the room, searching for the figure of a desperate woman with her hair mostly pulled out and her three young children swinging from light fixtures.

Instead, I see barstools with large male butts on them, their wallets chained to their pockets; pool tables with groups of men standing around holding cue sticks, all of them wearing leather vests and chaps; and a couple of women who I'm pretty sure get paid by the hour to practice the oldest profession in the world, straddling barstools in the corner.

I wonder for the briefest of moments if any of them need a wedding photographer. That's my desperation talking, the part of me that is always thinking about my bank account and how little money I have in there. Then my rational brain takes over again, and I realize that if any of these people were to get married, they would more than likely do it in a city hall, followed by shots of whiskey to seal the deal. People who celebrate life events that way normally do not book photo sessions that involve clothed individuals.

Talk about being out of one's element. I look down at my feet. Maybe the pink espadrilles were a bad idea. The narrow-eyed looks I'm getting from the people in leather are not helping my sweaty-palm issue one bit.

There's an archway across the room from me that leads into another public space whose specifics I can't make out from here. Since I don't see my family members in this main room, I assume that must be where they are. I can only imagine what's back there. Probably drugs. Probably more leather and more chained wallets. Now my armpits have joined the sweat party. Fantastic.

What was my sister thinking? She came into this bar *and* went into the back room? Nothing good could possibly be happening back there. Best-case scenario? Poker game. Her ex would have a field day over that one. He's always more than happy to point out her failings as a mother. Adding *gambler* to the list would be bad. Now I feel terrible that I was messing with her on the phone. She was clearly walking a fine line between stressed momma and bat-poo crazy momma, and now I know she's crossed over that line into a very dark place. My poor sister. Her poor kids!

I've never had to confront Jenny over questionable parenting choices before. She's gotten stressed, sure, but she's never gone completely off the range like this. When it got really bad with her divorce, she took a time out, but she arranged everything with me and the kids ahead of time and made sure we were all good before she took off for a week.

I'm not sure, but I think I can stage a one-woman intervention without letting everyone in the place know that I think they're not the best of company for my sister—my poor, older but misguided sister who is *so* going to pay for dragging me into this place.

My feet are literally sticking to the floor. In order to move forward, I have to peel them off the . . . what is it . . . ? Carpet? Linoleum? It's impossible to tell. I shudder with the thought of how much bacteria I'm collecting on my person right now. I'm totally leaving my shoes outside my front door after this trip. I should probably just burn them to stop the spread of contagions. That makes me sad because I love my pink espadrilles.

Several heads swivel around to stare at me as I begin to walk again.

As I hitch Felix's bag up higher on my shoulder, his head pops out and he takes a look around.

"What do you think, Fee?" I ask softly, my voice a little too high. "Feel like having a brewski?" Instead of blazing into the back room demanding my sister leave at once, I decide that playing it cool is the best way to handle it. Sometimes she can be stubborn. I've seen her cut off her nose to spite her face on more than one occasion, and I don't want this to backfire on me and end up being one of those somebody-call-the-cops-another-divorcée-has-gone-rogue situations. I'll stand here at the bar for a minute or two and work up the courage to have the showdown that's sure to come.

Felix pants excitedly. I take that as a *maybe* to my beer question.

My phone buzzes as I make my way over to the bar, telling me I have a text waiting.

Jen: *Where the hell r u?*
Me: *Keep your bra on. I'm here.*
Jen: *Where? All I see is a bimbo with a purse dog.*

My jaw goes off center as I stare down at her message. Now she really has lost her mind. Bimbo? Since when am I a bimbo? She knows I graduated summa cum laude. My fingers fly over the keys.

Me: *U better chillax or ur rescue party's going to start some boob punching and yours r def on the kill list.*
Jen: *Consider yourself a dead man. I warned you about that boob thing.*

I snort. She must be wasted. I cancel my plans to order a beer and turn to head into the back room instead. Nervousness has taken a back seat to indignation. My loving sister just called me a bimbo and a dead man. She's obviously drunk in front of her kids, so forget nicey-nice, loving, younger sister interventions. Shit just got real. I crack my knuckles, getting ready for that boob punch I promised her.

The back room is darker than the front of the bar. There's no dance floor, no couples, and nothing resembling decor unless you consider broken beer signs and nicotine-stained walls interior design. The place is totally empty, but I see what might be bathroom doors near the farthest corner of the room. They must be in there.

I'm in the alcove between the front of the bar and the back room when a loud boom sounds behind me. I don't have time to even turn around before I'm being shoved in the spine.

"What the hell?!" The words fly out of me as I do a slight back-bend and trip, falling forward.

I smell smoke. Adrenaline surges into my veins as I gain my feet under me. Felix is barking like a very angry, devil-possessed half-Chihuahua. I feel like I'm going to have a heart attack.

The person who pushed me grabs me by the upper arms and practically lifts me off my feet, forcefully moving me into the back room, whether I like it or not.

"What are you doing?!" I yell, twisting to get out of his grip. Now I'm scared and pissed. I have no idea what's going on, but I don't like being manhandled. It reminds me too much of that mugging that left me with a black eye, a skinned knee, and a stolen purse.

When I can finally turn around, I see a mountain of a guy standing there behind me, sporting a big black beard and a pile of matching frizzy hair encircled by a folded-up blue bandana. He could be anywhere from thirty to sixty years old; it's impossible to tell with that much of his face and head obscured in . . . ugh . . . grizzly bear fur.

"Getting you out of here," he growls, shoving me sideways.

I lose a few feet of ground before I can dig my heels in. "I have to find my sister and her kids!" I struggle against his grip, trying to reach into my purse so I can get my Taser and teach this beast-man a thing or two about how to treat a lady. Forget being scared. My sister is here somewhere and she needs me. Crazy brain chemicals have turned me into some kind of superhero. I even have a sidekick named Felix. We should have matching capes.

"There're no kids in here—are you nuts?" He's not taking no for an answer. I'm halfway into the back room before I can even process what he's said. I give up on finding my Taser under Felix's fuzzy butt in favor of trying to control any further advancement.

He's right. I haven't seen my sister yet, but that doesn't mean she's not here. She could be in the bathroom or in another part of the bar I can't see from here. She texted me, and I came, and I'm not leaving here without her and those babies.

"Why are you pushing me?!" I try to grab the back of a high-top chair as I go by, but I lose my grip on it and it falls with a crash in our wake. The sounds of people yelling in the other room grow louder. Screams from the front bar area join the mix, and not all of them are female.

"Exit," he says. "You need to leave."

I grab the edge of a table that's thankfully nailed into the floor, stopping our progress.

"I'm not going anywhere," I grunt out, bending in half as he tries to pick me up by my waist. "I need to get my sister." I kick out at him, catching him in the shin.

"Oooph!" He bends over, surprised by the pain, letting me go.

I hear a crack and a ping. My eyes open wide as I notice a huge gouge in the wood next to me where there used to be a mostly smooth surface. When I look up, I see a man standing in the entrance of the back room with a gun raised in our direction. My hear stops beating for a second or two, and it feels as though my chest is caving in with fear.

I'm not ashamed to say that I screech pretty loudly at that point, and it isn't one of those really cute lady-screams either. More like a crazy chicken being unsuccessfully strangled.

The mountain man who'd been trying to get me out of the bar grabs me by the purse and yanks me down to the floor. I crumble to my knees, shaking uncontrollably.

Felix thanks him by biting his hand.

"Mother fu—!" The guy shoves his hand into his mouth for a second and then pulls it out. "Let's go!" Crouched in half, he takes me by the hand and drags me out of the room, using tables and chairs as cover. I'm half-tripping, half-running, trying to put more distance between me and the nut job who actually had the gall to shoot at me.

More cracks and a couple pings follow us, making bits of wood fly up and hit the side of my face. They immediately start stinging like a mofo.

"I've been hit!" My free hand flies up to my face, finding something wet and sticky. When I pull my hand away and look at it, I see something dark smeared there. Holy shit, is that *blood?* "Oh my god, I'm bleeding?!"

There's a roaring in my ears now, but it's not coming from outside my body. I think my heart's about to explode. This is the worst sister rescue ever!

"Just keep running!" my rescuer shouts, shoving me out a door.

I fall to my hands and knees out in a stinky, slimy, dirty alleyway, my purse landing next to me. Felix spills out and then gets to his feet, barking like he's possessed by the devil himself. I know exactly how he feels. I think I'm going to vomit.

The door slams shut behind me. "Shut that dog up," the guy yells.

"You're still here?!" I'm shouting. I'm not happy because I know for a fact those bullets were meant for him, not Felix and me. We've never inspired anyone to that level of hatred. Maybe a few strong words about tiny dog poops left on a neighbor's lawn, sure, but bullets? Never. This guy is dangerous. Anyone can see he's a motorcycle gangster guy or a drug dealer, and I don't want him anywhere near me.

One second I'm smelling what I'm pretty sure is someone else's stomach contents on the ground, and the next, I'm flying through the air. I'm only a little disoriented when my feet hit the ground and I'm right-side up.

"What just happened?" I whisper, my tone way too high for a normal human. A half-second later I realize I'm standing because he lifted me to my feet as easily as if I were just a piece of paper.

"Get your dog and let's go." He has his hand on the back door under a glowing exit sign, holding it shut. If I weren't so scared for my life, I'd be impressed with his chivalry. He probably could have been a mile gone from here if all he'd been worried about was his own hide.

My entire body, including my voice, is shaking. "Come here, Felix. Get in the bag."

Felix is barking at everyone and everything, real or imagined. His entire body is bouncing up and down with angry energy. "Get over here, Felix! We have to go!" When I finally get my hands on him, I'm almost impressed with how much his outrage is completely possessing him; he's humming like a recently twanged guitar string. I'm already moving, even before I have Felix situated. That beard guy is right; my sister's not in that bar. Why did I think she was? Maybe she's drinking at home and drunk-texting me. I'm going to kill her.

"Come on, Fee, get in. Stop messing around." I shove Felix into my bag headfirst and close it with my arm against my ribs. "Time to get the hell outta here." *And leave this gangster behind.* As I start fast-walking to the end of the alley, I'm once again grabbed by the elbow.

"What?!" I yell, spinning to face the man-beast who obviously doesn't believe in personal hygiene or basic manners. "What now?!" My heart is hammering away in my chest as my gaze darts between the door and my captor. I know that lunatic with the gun is going to reach that door any second, and I don't want to be hanging around here in the alley when he comes out.

"You can't go that way—they'll be waiting for you. Follow me."

I feel just the tiniest bit sorry that I was having bad thoughts about him, since he's obviously trying to help me out. But when he takes off at a jog, leaving me standing there, my guilt disappears. So much for chivalry. He doesn't even look back to see if I'm following, the jerk.

My feet start moving of their own volition. "Who's *they*? Why are they waiting for me?"

He doesn't answer. Instead, he turns a corner several yards ahead, leaving me alone in the garbage-strewn, vomit-y alley. When

I look in the opposite direction toward the street where my car is waiting, I swear I can see the outline of a bad man with a gun, so I take off running after the guy with the horrible beard, praying I'm not going to regret this decision as much as I regret coming to a rescue that was never needed in the first place.

CHAPTER THREE

After I catch up to the bearded gangster, he leaves me shaking in the shadows of a dumpster four streets over, promising to return. Felix isn't concerned anymore. He wanders around my feet, leaving p-mail for any dog who might come by in the next few days, while I text my drunk-ass sister and slowly get my respirations back to a normal rate. I can only imagine what his messages say. Something like: "Dude, you would not believe what happened to me tonight!" I know *I'm* pretty much shell-shocked over the whole thing and I'm not even a Chihuahua mix. I hunker down where no one will see me and keep a sharp ear out for footsteps. The only thing I can hear are my own heartbeats for a while, going like crazy, but then there are sirens too, and it's like music to my ears when I realize they're coming from the area by the bar.

I pray my sister is okay. I didn't see her or the kids, so that gives me some measure of comfort. She hasn't answered any of my latest texts, though. I check the screen again just to be sure. All the messages showing are still from me. No more of her crazy messages are coming anymore. She must have passed out on her couch. It's so unlike her to do anything like this. I need to get to her place as soon as possible and make sure everyone is okay.

Where are you?
Are you safe?
I hope you're not in that bar.
I'm going to kill you for dragging me out here.
Please text me back. I'm getting worried.

The big fancy truck from the same lot where I parked earlier pulls up to the curb, and its interior cab lights come on, revealing the bearded beast inside. Color me a little surprised that the grossest guy in the place has the most expensive ride. My phone beeps, alerting me to a received text message. As I bend over to retrieve Felix, I read it.

Jen: *We've been made. Don't go back. Meet up at the next drop point in thirty.*

I'm staring at the screen as I stop at the passenger door. It opens from the inside, and I look up to see my rescuer's face.

"Get in," he says. He glances down at his phone as he waits for me to comply.

"Uhhh, no thanks." I look over my shoulder. The dark cover of the dumpster is looking pretty good right now.

"You can't stay out here where you could be seen by someone driving by."

"But I *should* get into a car with a gangster drug dealer who's probably going to kill me and dump my body in the Mississippi River?"

He hisses out a sigh of annoyance. "I'm not a drug dealer or a gangster. Come on—stop messing around. I don't want to be seen here."

"Because you're a drug dealer."

His voice carries exaggerated patience. "No, because drug dealers will see me on their turf and probably not like it too much."

I look around me, new fear rushing into my body, making it feel like something is trying to suffocate me. "This is a drug dealer's turf?"

He gestures out the window. "Look around. What do you think?"

Random people on the street corners, drinking out of paper bags. Groups of men standing around looking at us. Yeah. Not good. I bite my lip as I consider my options. I could call the police and then wait around for who knows how long to be picked up—hours if my past experience is any measure—and in the meantime be a sitting duck. I could get in the car with this guy and maybe get raped and pillaged and then even murdered. What other choices do I have left? There are no businesses I'd consider safe nearby, and no way do I want to start walking the street. Talk about being between a rock and a hard place.

"I'll take my chances," I say, holding Felix more firmly under my arm.

The guy lifts up a butt cheek. "Here. Take a look at this."

I back away, sure I'm about to see the wrong end of a gun.

Instead he pulls out a wallet. From that wallet he takes a card and hands it to me.

I read the writing on the front of the white business card. There's just a company name and address on it, no name: "Bourbon Street Boys Security." Looking up at him, I squint my eyes. "Are you trying to tell me you're a good guy?"

"That's it. Now get in."

Holding the card out, I take a picture of it and type out an email to myself, attaching the photo.

"Okay, Mister Bourbon Street Boy person, I have just sent an email with your business address to my sister and myself, so if anything happens to me, you will be held responsible."

"Great. Get in."

I know my plan isn't foolproof, but it's the best I've got. I can still plainly see that shooter's face in my mind, and it gets more menacing by the second.

First I take my Taser out and slide it surreptitiously into my waistband. Then I put my purse and Felix inside the truck's cab, and with the help of the door itself and a handle inside, I climb up too. Once I'm settled, I buckle myself up and quickly tap out a response to my sister's message. I thought I'd calmed down, but my pulse is still pounding away. I can literally feel it hammering away in my neck.

Me: *You have got to be drunk. Where are the kids?*

I hear a beep beside me, a two-second pause as the beard-beast man checks his phone, and then he roars and punches his steering wheel.

I cringe, squeezing myself into the corner of the cab, as I realize that the business card he gave me means nothing. I've jumped out of the frying pan and landed right in the fire. Is he nuts? He has to be. Who punches their car when they get a text? And who is he so mad at? Must be a girlfriend or something, although I can't imagine what kind of woman would date a guy like this. Maybe one of those weight-lifter chicks with a really thick neck and beard hair from all the steroids she puts into her protein shakes. I slowly pull my Taser from my pants and hold it down at the side of my leg. If he makes a single move to hurt me, I'm going to light him up like a Christmas tree.

He throws his phone on the dashboard and hisses out a long breath, shifting into drive at the same time.

"Where do you live?" he asks. "I'll take you home."

I laugh as I tremble. I think maybe it's the pent-up stress or something, but whatever it is, it's powerful stuff. I can't stop. I'm about to pee my pants. Apparently, when faced with impending death, I completely lose my shit.

He stops at a red light. "I don't see what's so funny about asking for your address." His beard wiggles with every word, which only makes things worse. Or better. I can finally stop shaking, anyway.

I pause to try and breathe normally. "What's funny is you thinking I'm actually going to give you that information." A snort escapes my nose. "Yeah. Right. Here, Mister Crazy Mountain Man Grizzly Bear Person, why don't you come on over to my house and murder me in my living room? That sounds like fun." I cross my eyes with the ridiculousness of it as I stare out the front windshield. "You must think I'm the dumbest woman alive to fall for that crap." Forget the part where I actually got in his truck on the basis of a business card that probably isn't even his. Hell, for all I know, it could belong to the last guy he killed! I need to have my head examined. Being lost and confused about my life has made me completely stupid. Thank God, I have my Taser.

The light turns green and he steps on the gas. The engine roars, but we remain at the speed limit. I guess he's some kind of Boy Scout. Or maybe he's a murderer who doesn't want to get pulled over by the cops. That's probably the more likely scenario.

"Would I have bothered to rescue you from the bar if I planned to kill you?"

"How am I supposed to know? I'm not a crazy person."

"Neither am I."

"Could've fooled me," I mumble under my breath. I point to an all-night diner down the street. "Just drop me off over there. I'll get a ride back to the bar and get my car from there."

"Whatever you say." He changes lanes to be able to turn into the parking lot. The sense of relief that fills me is intoxicating. It's like being at the end of a really wild, really awful roller coaster ride as you pull into the station to get off. It's a little dizzying, actually.

My phone beeps as we pull into a space.

Sis: *Hey cutie. Feel like having a glass of wine? Got the buttheads to bed finally.*

I stare at the screen for a really long time. The rumble of the truck's engine kind of puts me in a trance as I try to figure out what the hell is wrong with my sister. Does she have a split personality now? Has the stress of being a single mother finally cracked her brain? Should I call her Sybil? Why is her phone showing the name "Sis" now? Did the number transfer over finally?

"What's the matter?" he asks. "Get some bad news?"

"Why would you say that?" I tear my gaze away from the phone to look at him.

"Because your face looks like it's melting, you're frowning so hard."

I go back to staring at the screen. "It's nothing. Just my sister losing her damn mind." Or me losing mine. None of this makes sense. I think all the stress of being shot at has made my brain go offline. I can't think straight. What the hell is happening here?

Felix climbs out of my bag enough to reach up and lick my chin.

"Thanks, buddy." I sigh. "Come on. Let's go." I place my hand on the door and feel around for the handle. I guess I'm not fast enough, because the mountain man reaches over both of us and opens the door for me.

I jump in surprise, thinking for a split second that he's going to whack me. Then, as soon as I realize he was just being polite, I expect to be repulsed by his closeness, but instead I find myself inhaling deeply, bringing the scent of his cologne deep into my brain. Wow. That was yummy.

This makes no sense at all, of course. He looks like a *Duck Dynasty* nut ball prepper off the range for a good long while now, but he smells like a metrosexual about to go clubbing. What?

Something is seriously going on with this guy, but I'm not interested enough to find out what it is. I just want to get over to my sister's house and collapse on her couch. Once I figure out what the hell happened, I'll decide whether I'm going to yell at her for a solid ten minutes for almost getting me killed.

"Thanks," I say, sliding down off the seat to the parking lot below, dragging Felix and my purse with me.

"Don't mention it."

I slam the door shut behind me and hitch Felix up higher on my shoulder. The passenger window rolls down with an electric whine. When I look inside the truck, all I can see is darkness.

"Take a cab home. Don't go back for your car until tomorrow."

"Why?"

"Because I said so, that's why."

I snort again. Tonight I am part human, part pig, apparently. "Whatever. Have a nice life." I walk away, headed for the brightly lit diner that I can see has pies on display just inside the front door.

My rescuer says nothing. His truck peels out in a cloud of dust and gravel, and I'm left alone in the lot with Felix once again barking his tiny head off.

"Come on, Fee. Let's go get some pie and then we'll get the car." My feet crunch over the graveled asphalt. I should probably call the police and report everything that just happened, but I know they're already there at the bar. I heard the sirens. Besides, I can tell them everything in the morning, right? After all I've been through, sitting in a police station all night is the very last thing I want to do. I know how the system works. After I was mugged, I was ignored, tied up for hours in interviews and reports, and in the end they never found the guy. It was a complete waste of time.

No. No cops. Not now anyway. I need to go see my sister. I need to talk to her and figure everything out in my head before I even try to explain it to a detective.

My conscience nags me about my plan, the grizzly man's words echoing around in my brain telling me not to go to my car. "That guy's not the boss of me," I say in a whisper as we approach the doors. I can get my car whenever I want; I don't have to wait until tomorrow. That's way too inconvenient.

Felix lets out a bark of understanding. I take it as his agreement that we should get our car and go home. Forget what that guy said.

"That's right, Fee. I'm a grown woman. You're a grown half-Chihuahua. We can take care of ourselves. We don't need some weirdo Wookie telling us what to do and when to do it, right?" Any bad people who were at Frankie's will be long gone by the time we're done with our pie. Shooters don't stick around after the fact, right? That would be suicide, and from what I've noticed of the world, bad people live forever.

Felix whines and disappears inside my bag.

"Punk." So much for loyalty from man's best friend. I step inside the diner and inhale the scent of recently fried bacon. "Mmmm, you smell that, Felix? That's bacon. Too bad you can't have any, on account of your digestion problems." I smile at my vengeful thoughts. That'll teach the little turd to not have my back.

I can feel him digging around in my bag.

My voice lowers to a growling whisper. "Felix, if you pee in my bag, you are a dead dog, you hear me?"

He growls. And then he pees. I can hear it hitting the little pee pad I keep in there for that eventuality.

So much for pie and bacon. I take five minutes to use the bathroom and then step outside the front doors, whipping out my phone and dialing Information. Before I can finish asking for a number for a taxi service, a cab pulls up to the curb behind me. I'm kind of stunned over the weird coincidence until the driver gets out and shouts over the roof of his car. "You the lady with the dog who needs a ride home?"

Okay, so my heart warms a little bit at the idea that my rescuer actually did a pretty good job of rescuing me and Felix. He could have just driven away and left us hanging out to dry, but he didn't. He called us a cab. Another surprise from the grizzly man who smells like a dream.

What? Did I just think that? Whoa.

"Yes, that's me." I make my way down the sidewalk and stop at the back door, pausing to put my bag inside before I climb in myself.

The driver gets in too and puts his seatbelt on. "Address?"

"Frankie's Bar," I say, "just a mile or two that way." I wave in the general direction I remember coming from.

"Sorry, lady, no can do. I was told to take you home, not bring you to the bar."

My ears start a slow burn. This taxi guy probably thinks I'm a drunk who's been cut off by her sponsor. *Dammit.* I wait a few precious seconds before speaking, to be sure I'm not about to let fly a few choice cuss words.

"I don't care what that Neanderthal said to you . . . I need to get my car, and it's at Frankie's. Take me to Frankie's."

The driver scratches at his head nervously. "He was real specific, though."

"I don't care how specific he was. If you want my fare, you'll go to Frankie's."

"He already paid the fare. Added a tip in too." The guy grins in the rearview mirror at me.

"How could he have paid the fare if he doesn't know where I live?"

The guy laughs, staring out the windshield again. "He figured it was somewhere uptown, based on how you were dressed. Gave me the fare to cover an entire round trip up and back." He turns around to face me. "Was he wrong?"

I roll my eyes, so pissed I'm that easy to read. I feel like maybe I should move downtown just to keep things interesting. Then I get pissed at myself for caring even one bit what a stupid grizzly beard thinks about my life.

"No, he wasn't wrong. But if you think I'm letting you keep that fare for not doing what I ask you to do, you'd better think again. Either take me to Frankie's or forfeit the fare. That's the deal." I glare at him.

The cabbie smiles. "He warned me you might give me trouble."

"How could he possibly have done that?!" I'm yelling, but I don't care. "He doesn't know jack poop about me!"

The guy has the nerve to chuckle. "You sure about that?" He turns back around and shifts the car into drive. "You gonna give me the address or what?" He's looking at me in the rearview mirror again.

I want to reach into the front seat and break it off, but instead, I decide to play dirty. Desperate times call for desperate measures. He's forced me into this. I have no other choice. It's time for the waterworks.

Great big blubbering sobs well up from deep inside me as my shoulders shake and my chest heaves. I'm fake-crying like I just watched the *Titanic* go down in person. I think of every sad thought or feeling I've ever had and own them completely. I could so win an Oscar right now if they gave them out for performances in the back seats of cabs.

"Ah, no, don't cry!" He sounds as distressed as I'm pretending to be. I have to battle not to smile with triumphant glee. "I hate when ladies cry! Come on, just relax, would ya? It's for your own good. He said that place ain't safe for you right now."

"But I need my car for work!" I sob. "I'm going to lose my job, and then I'll have to move, and I have nowhere to go, and no one will help me, and I'm down to my last twenty bucks, so I can't get a cab back in the morning, and my dog is sick, and he's probably going to have an accident in my purse because he ate some bacon, and bacon doesn't agree with him, and—"

"Hey! Hey! It's okay! I'm going to take you to your car, okay? And then I'll just . . . I'll just follow you home or whatever, and make sure you get there, okay? That'll work, right?" He twists around and drapes his arm over the back of the front seat. "Okay? That'll work for me. I can do that."

I nod, letting out a few more sobs so he doesn't suspect I'm not completely devastated over the idea of my dog pooping in my purse. Yes, it would be a tragedy, but not one I'd cry over. I have other bags. Besides, Felix's poops are about the size of Ikea pencils.

We pull out of the diner's parking lot, and I make a big show of wiping my tears away and sniffling. I don't stop until we get to Frankie's bar. There are cop cars parked at the curb, but no uniforms outside that I can see.

"Thanks," I say, patting the taxi driver on the shoulder as I slide across the seat to get out. "No need to follow me home. I'm sure I'll be fine. See?" I point out the window. "Cops are here."

"Yeah, okay. See you later." He sounds stressed. I'm not sure if it's because of my Oscar-worthy performance or the fact that he's not doing what he was paid to do, but I don't care; I've got my car back and I'm going home.

I shut the door behind me and open my purse so I can find my keys. The distinct odor of doggy pee hits me in the face.

"Oh, for chrissake, Felix. Did you have to?"

He licks my hand.

I sigh, wrapping my fingers around my keys. "I am so going to kill Jen when I see her." Glass of wine, my butt. I'm going to drive over there and give her a knuckle sandwich.

CHAPTER FOUR

I'm halfway to my sister's place before I take a sharp right and head over to my house instead. I'm tired, Felix stinks, and I have a big family coming in tomorrow for portraits and my studio isn't set up for them yet. I need to get to bed early. This is the only job I have booked for the entire month, so I can't flake out and be a no-show.

My mind wanders as I make my way through the neighborhood streets. Those texts I got from Jenny make no sense. How could she have gone from being completely off the range to saying, "Come have a glass of wine with me"? It's like she's two different people today. Or someone hijacked her phone.

Then it hits me. *Yes!* A hijacking! That's the only explanation that makes any sense. My sister's not a crazy alcoholic. She never endangers her kids, and she wouldn't be caught dead in a place like Frankie's. Someone else must have her phone, or the lines got crossed when she got that new one today.

I'm so happy I could cry. This is so much better than having her committed and taking her kids away from her.

Speak of the devil . . . my phone beeps again. I tilt the screen toward me as it rests on the console by my radio.

Jen: *I told you to leave your car in the lot.*

A split second after reading those words, it's like there are fireworks going off in my brain, explosions of light and sound, a jumble of thoughts and words and images. Nothing makes any sense. This message has to be from The Beard, but how is he using my sister's new phone to text me?

Then it hits me.

He's *not* using my sister's new phone to text me.

He's using *his* phone.

He's always been using his phone.

Oh my god. Ohmygod, ohmygod, ohmygod. It can't . . . it didn't . . . it . . . oh my.

Wrong number! Wrong number catastrophe! Ack!

The tires on my car screech to a halt as I pull over in a hurry. Grabbing my phone, I quickly scroll through the texts from start to finish. Understanding dawns clearly for the first time all day.

"Holy crud, Felix." I look over at my little buddy, who's staring at me from the passenger seat with his head tilted. He's as confused as I am, apparently. "I think I've been texting a complete stranger this entire time."

I'm almost relieved. This makes waaaay more sense than my sister taking her kids to a biker bar. It doesn't, however, make my situation any better.

As it is, I didn't escape unscathed. Glancing in the mirror confirms it; I have cuts on my face that are going to make me look like I was attacked by a herd of very small cats. I'm going to have to come up with a hell of an excuse for these clients tomorrow. My reflection in the rearview mirror tells me that no amount of foundation is going to erase my brush with death.

Lights fill the interior of my car, interrupting my thoughts. I frown in my mirror, trying to see what's going on behind me. I'm in the middle of a quiet neighborhood, but maybe I'm blocking someone's driveway or something.

When the headlights that were lighting up my car's interior go out, I can see a car parked a half a block behind me. I wait, but no one gets out. I know the car is occupied because there's the silhouette of a person inside. It looks like a man, based on his size.

"Huh." I shrug, almost convinced I'm imagining something sinister about the situation. "Oh well. Not my neighborhood. I don't have to be concerned about weirdos hanging out in parked cars, right?" Talking out loud to Felix makes me feel better, like I have nothing at all to worry about. I'm just a normal girl, driving around in a dark neighborhood with her purse puppy for fun. Nothing to see here, people—move along.

I put the car into first gear and ease back onto the road. I assume all is well until a glance in my rearview mirror has my heart stopping in fear. The car behind me has moved out too, but the driver doesn't put his headlights back on.

Whoa. It literally hurts, the way my heart muscle is spasming right now. It thumps really hard a few times and then picks up its pace. My ears are burning with the fear that's taking over. Should I call the police? What will I say? That there's a person *maybe* following me in a car? They'll probably just hang up on me. The New Orleans police department has murders and robberies to deal with on a daily basis, and they're going to get worried about a woman who's paranoid as she drives home from a bar she should have never gone to? Yeah, right. I'm not going to waste my time or theirs. I can handle this non-event. I'm just going to drive and stop thinking that everyone is out to get me. Just because one guy took a few shots at someone standing next to me, it doesn't mean I'm a target, now, right?

I try to calm myself down by talking to Felix. "There's no way anyone would follow me anywhere, Fee. Don't be silly." At least, I'm pretty sure that's the case. Let's face it: I'm nobody to ninety-nine point nine percent of the world. Totally not stalker worthy. The most valuable thing about me is my Canon Rebel, which I don't even have with me tonight.

My calming efforts are having little effect. Paranoia goes into overdrive, and I quickly become convinced that I am, in fact, being stalked. I can tell the car tailing me isn't that big truck I got a ride in earlier, so it's not Mister Grizzly Pants here to berate me for not listening to his orders. And who else would it be if not him?

No one.

I blow out a long breath, letting some of my stress go with it. Of course, it's no one. Ha-ha, this is so crazy! I'm just a photographer with a Chihuahua-mix riding shotgun in a pee-purse. Why would anyone want to follow me, right? I mean, all my ex-boyfriends are happily dating other women, and no stalker-type has made himself known to me before this. The entire idea is absurd. I am completely safe riding around in my cherry-red Chevy Sonic.

I continue on my way, my eyeballs sharing time between the road and my mirror. Instead of going straight to my address, though, I turn left four blocks away. Just in case. It doesn't hurt to be cautious, right? Even though I have nothing at all to worry about. My life is boring. Car chases only happen in the movies. Assassins go after presidents and drug cartel kingpins, and I'm about as far from being one of those as a girl can be.

The car behind me flicks its lights on and takes the turn as well.

A weird shiver moves up my entire body from my feet to the top of my head, making my hair stand up at the nape of my neck. Then I start sweating all over. I shiver with the sudden change in temperature that I'm pretty sure I'm imagining. I resist the urge to turn on the heater.

"Felix, I'm afraid we're being followed. Is that paranoid enough for ya?" I try to laugh it off, but Felix is not laughing with me.

He jumps into the back seat and up onto the platform over the hatchback's trunk. Several sharp barks tell me he agrees that something is up with this guy behind us.

"There's only one way to find out for sure." Feeling ridiculous, like I'm playacting in a really bad spy movie, I make a hard right onto a street that I know ends in a cul-de-sac.

My palms are sweaty and I'm having a hard time gripping the steering wheel. I wipe one hand off on my pants and then the other. It really doesn't help much. I can see the end of the street coming, and I feel like I'm going to vomit. This idea seemed great when I took the turn, but now it looks like a trap of my own making. How stupid can I possibly get tonight?

Apparently, *quite* stupid.

Landscape lights in one of the driveways make it look like the end of a runway, but I'm not coming in for a landing. *It's a trap, it's a trap, it's a trap!* My brain is racing, berating me for being so airbrained. Why did I turn onto a dead-end street? Am I insane? Do I *want* to be raped and pillaged? Jesus, I need to get my head examined when this is all over. I just hope it's still going to be attached to my body tomorrow.

As I reach the first part of the circle, I slow down, giving the car behind me enough time to catch up, hoping to catch a glimpse of him when I go in the opposite direction. This time he leaves his headlights on.

Slowly, slowly, I make my way around the circle, praying he'll turn into one of the driveways, stop his car, get out, and walk in his front door. I'll laugh all the way back to my place and go to sleep after a long bath filled with bubbles if that happens. I might even honk my horn as I drive by, thanking him for the tour of his lovely neighborhood.

The other car approaches. It doesn't pull into any driveways, it just keeps coming.

My headlights swing over, and I finally see the man behind the wheel through his windshield. *And* the gun he's holding up by his shoulder.

I scream and duck down below the level of the dashboard, slamming the accelerator to the floor and surging forward like a bat flying out of hell. The engine whines as the RPMs climb, so I slam the shifter into third gear, giving the car another few horses to run with as I race down the street in the other direction. I pray I'm going straight and not aimed for someone's mailbox.

A loud crack comes to my ears and then there's a bang against my door. It takes less than a second for me to put it all together. Felix starts barking at the same time I begin screaming. "Oh my god, he shot at me! He *actually* shot a gun at me, that asshole!"

I have to sit up so I can see to drive, but I hunch down as much as possible, praying my headrest will stop a bullet from entering my brain. I look like Quasimodo driving the getaway car in a bank robbery gone really wrong.

"If you shoot my dog, I will *destroy* you!" I roar, downshifting as I take a corner way too fast. Obviously this whole scenario has unbalanced me a bit. "Felix, get down out of that window, right now! Come here! *Come*, you mangy mutt!"

My tires squeal as I take the next turn that will get me out of this neighborhood and as far from my house as I can be. Felix's claws scramble for purchase. When I hear his little body hit the floor of the back seat, I know he's lost the battle. I'm happy he's out of the line of fire though, so I keep going, throwing the car into fourth when I hit a straightaway.

When I bought my Chevy Sonic hatchback a few months ago, I thought I was being practical and responsible, but now, as it hugs the next corner and shoots off like a rocket in second gear, I give my thanks to the gods of General Motors that they had the good sense to put so many strong horses under this hood.

The distance between me and the maniac grows rapidly. After three more turns and me driving like I'm trying out for the Formula One circuit, I feel like I have enough time to pull out my phone and press the green button. It's not the cops, but in my crazy panicked mind, it's the next best thing.

A gruff voice answers. "This better be good," it says.

"Are you the guy with the horrible beard?" I ask, my voice breathless and way too high. Felix whines. I'm probably hurting his sensitive ears, poor little guy.

"Come again?"

Good. He sounds confused. I'm happy to know I'm not the only idiot in the room.

"You're the Bourbon Street guy, right? Well, I'm the bimbo with the dog from the bar, who's not a bimbo by the way. I need your help. Again."

"What's going on?" He's all seriousness now.

"Some guy followed me in his car and shot at me. With a gun."

"Where are you?"

"I don't know. I was going home, but then I noticed him following me, so I didn't go home. I kind of got lost in this other neighborhood."

"Good girl. Hang up. I'll call you back."

And just like that he's gone. So much for my rescue party.

In between shifting from one gear to another and then one more, I glance at the phone a couple times. I don't know what the hell just happened with The Beard, but I'm pretty sure I'm screwed now. Stupid penny-pinching me, I didn't spring for the GPS when I bought my car, and so now I can't find my way out of this suburban maze. And the guy who I thought could help me just disconnected my call.

Dammit! Why is this happening to me?!

My phone rings, the sound cutting through the haze of my panic. I answer, almost dropping the phone in my haste to put it to my ear.

"Hello!" I scream.

"Take a left at the next main street." He's way calmer than I am.

"Take a left . . . ?" I hold the phone out and look at it for a second before putting it back to my ear. "What are you talking about?!"

"Take a left!" the voice roars.

I grab the wheel with both hands, the cell phone squashed against the leather wrapping, and yank to the left. A quick downshift has us powering down the street, now headed north if my dashboard's digital compass is accurate.

"How do you know I had to take a left?" I can barely see straight, I'm huffing and puffing so much. My frantic respirations are making me dizzy. I look in my rearview mirror but see nothing but blackness. There's a loud ringing in my ears. I think it's my blood pressure about to explode my veins.

"I'm tracking your cell signal," says the faint voice from my phone. "Take a right on Wilson Avenue." The roar in my ears calms just a little.

The glowing white letters on a green background appear on a street sign above me. I barely have time to slow before I have to take the turn. My tires leave a little rubber behind.

"Keep going about a half mile until you get to Lincoln," says my savior. "Take a left there."

"Where are you guiding me?" I'm not one hundred percent sure that following these directions are the best option for me, but it's the only option I can see clearly right now. My mind is in a blind panic.

"To my place. You'll be safe here."

When he says it in that slightly tired but soothing voice of his, I almost believe him, despite the beard.

CHAPTER FIVE

Twenty minutes later I'm driving up to a building in a somewhat questionable part of town, at the Port of New Orleans on the Mississippi River. Why am I not at a police station? Well, because I don't know where one is. And I'm obviously crazy. I keep thinking that if I continue to drive around aimlessly, I'm going to aim myself right into that murderer's arms. I need to find a safe haven. Why I think this bearded guy is my answer, I can't say for sure. It just feels right. Righter than going home, righter than calling the cops, and definitely righter than going to my sister's house.

"This can't be right," I say out loud.

I was talking to myself, but The Beard responds. "It's right. I can see you outside the window. Drive inside."

As he says that, a giant door attached to the warehouse in front of me starts to slide open. I don't think it's a person moving it manually, because it's sliding too smoothly and there's an electric whine coming from somewhere and making its way into my car through the crack in my window.

It's humid out tonight, and I'd normally be using my air conditioner, but I needed to be able to hear the instructions I was being given over my cell's speakerphone, so I left it off. Now I wish I'd just turned up the volume instead, because I'm sure there are sweat stains in my armpits and probably everywhere else too.

As I wait for the door to open wide enough to admit Felix and me, I wipe the sweat from my temples. I've probably lost about three pounds of water weight with all the freaking out I've done over the last half hour. I'm still not even sure I know what's going on, although I have my suspicions. I'm guessing I got caught up in a drug deal gone bad or something like that. I just pray this guy with the beard isn't the dealer. I don't think he is.

I'm really not sure why I've let myself believe he's one of the good guys. I should probably be more cautious and not just drive into his Batcave and let the door shut behind me. But he did try to save me when the bullets started flying. He could totally have left me there to be filled with holes. That has to mean something, right?

"I don't think I'm going to drive in," I say, looking to my left and right, trying to decide if I should just take off and find my way home. Or I could go to a hotel. That would be safe. Safer than this place, probably. This looks like a good spot to murder someone. No people around, relatively quiet. My murderer could start up a loud motor to cover the sound of my screams. Or maybe I wouldn't have time to scream. Maybe it'd all be over in an instant.

I start freaking out all over again. I swear I can smell B.O. now too. Ugh.

"You don't have to come in if you don't want to," he says, "but I would if I were you."

"Why?"

"Because your car is easy to spot by anyone who might be looking for it."

I bark out a quick laugh. This is getting ridiculous. "As if someone could find me way out here. I left that guy behind in suburbia twenty minutes ago." I look in my rearview mirror just to be sure.

"That guy doesn't work alone. He has associates all over the city. All he has to do is put the word out to look for your car, and you'll be found. That bright red is kind of hard to miss."

My heart sinks and my voice doesn't seem to want to work very well. It comes out as a squeak. "Are you serious? Who is he? And why does he want to find me? I'm no one. I don't even smoke pot. I don't even smoke *anything*, for God's sake."

"Drive in," says the voice, like it has lost patience with me.

Felix whines.

I reach over and scratch him under his tiny chin. "Just relax, buddy. Everything's going to be fine."

"Are you telling me to relax?" He sounds a little incredulous.

"No, I'm telling Felix to relax."

"Who's Felix? I thought you were alone."

"Felix is my dog. I'm coming in." I decide to do it for Fee. He doesn't deserve to be hunted down like a dog, even if he is a tiny angel wearing a canine costume.

Putting the car in first gear, I slowly roll past the large door that's finally finished opening. As soon as the rear bumper is past, it begins to close. As I watch it slide into place behind me, I try to keep my respirations at a normal level, but it's difficult. I'm afraid I've just sealed my doom by coming into this place. A quick look around my car confirms that I have no weapons at my disposal. The best I can hope for is that Felix will bite my attacker's ankle before he's sent heaven bound with me.

I quickly tap out a message to my sister.

Me: *Can't come for wine. I'm in a building at the port. If you don't hear from me tomorrow morning, call the cops.*

I'm about to press the "Send" button, but then I hesitate. I think about her and the kids and the fact that she really has no backup for babysitting purposes, and how she's barely hanging on to her sanity by a string sometimes. The last thing she needs in her life is me going off the rails.

I read my message again, wondering if I should send it off.

Nope. Can't do it. She'll see this text and freak out, guaranteed. No way can I launch it like this. I hit the backspace key and try again, thinking about what I can say that will not alert her to anything being wrong, but will also guarantee that someone will come looking for me sooner rather than later if I fail to make it back to the real world within a reasonable time.

Me: *Can't come for wine. With someone at the port of New Orleans. Will call tomorrow around 8am.*

There. That looks innocuous enough. And if I don't call, she'll know where to tell the cops to start looking. I send it off and turn the ignition key backward. My engine dies immediately, and I'm left with the tick-tick-ticking of my Swatch watch. It's going about half as fast as my heartbeat.

Felix jumps over onto my lap, puts his front paws on my chest, and starts licking my chin like crazy.

"Oh, God, your breath is horrible, Fee—stop." I pull him away so I can take the leash I keep in the glove compartment and attach it to his collar. Together, we wait for The Beard to arrive from wherever he was sending his instructions. I pray he's not going to show up with a gun in his hand and murder in his eyes.

CHAPTER SIX

I wait for ten full minutes before I finally unbuckle my seat belt.

"Are you going to come out here, or what?" I look down at my phone and remember that the call between us was disconnected a long time ago.

Okay, so I'm talking to myself now. Excellent.

I press the "Home" button and my latest call comes up. I hit the green button to dial it again.

"Yes?" says The Beard. I think it's him, anyway.

"So, what's next? Am I going to sleep in my car tonight or what?"

"If you want."

A heavy sigh expels on its own. I'm so tired of the cloak-and-dagger game. I mean, really. Can't we act like normal people now?

"Actually, what I *want* is to go home and sleep in my bed, but apparently your little drug deal or whatever that was at Frankie's went bust, and I got thrown in the middle of it, so now I'm stuck at the smelly port in a dingy warehouse, and my dog has to go to the bathroom."

He doesn't answer. I look down at my phone and see that the call has been disconnected again.

"Dammit!" Looking out the windshield tells me nothing. The room is lit up, but it's mostly empty, save for a scarred wood table with chairs around it, a punching bag in the corner that's hanging from an overhead beam, some weight-lifting equipment, a row of lockers, and a set of metal stairs. There's room for maybe six cars inside here, but mine's the only one around. Does this guy live here? It might explain the beard, but not much else.

As I'm contemplating my options, the big door behind me begins to open again. I put my hand on the ignition, ready to fire my Sonic up and get the hell out of here if necessary.

The big black pickup that I had a ride in earlier pulls into the space next to me. I can't see the driver because of the tinted windows.

Now I'm completely confused. The Beard said he could see me from the window, and I assumed he meant from the warehouse. Was he outside the whole time? And why would he wait out there and not be in here? And why is he in here now? And what's he been doing this whole time, just sitting in his car? Maybe he's afraid of me. Maybe that's why it took him so long to decide to come in. Maybe he thinks *I'm* the bad guy.

The rumbling engine cuts off and the door cracks open. It bounces a few times and then swings out wide. My brain cannot compute what I see getting out.

First of all, there's no beard. And he's missing about four inches of height. And half a foot of shoulder span. This is definitely not my rescuer.

The guy leans down and looks in my passenger window. "Hello, there," he says before flashing a grin at me. Perfect teeth. Of course. Why do guys like him have to have perfect teeth anyway? Shouldn't they have some kryptonite, like coffee stains or twisted incisors?

Okay, so if this guy is going to murder me, I'm not sure how I'm going to handle it. I always pictured killers as big, hairy, gross people. Kind of like The Beard. But this guy? No way. He could be a runway model. If he tries to kill me, I'll be bitter. To have been so wrong all my life will make me mad. Guys this good looking should not be criminals. It'll throw off the balance of the universe or something.

"Hi," I say, not sure what the rules are when it comes to greeting strange men in warehouses after running from gunshots at a biker bar.

"You going to come up?" he asks, gesturing toward the stairs.

I look where he's pointing and frown. Do I want to come up into their lair and offer myself up for killing? No, I think not.

"No, that's all right. I think I'll just stay right here."

He shrugs, pulling a bag of what looks like groceries out of the car after him. "Suit yourself."

I watch as he takes long strides across the space to the stairs and mounts the steps three at a time. His cargo shorts show off his muscled calves and rear end, giving me a hint of what the rest of him might look like under his T-shirt. He must be the one using the weight-lifting equipment.

Felix whines at me again.

"Fine. I'll let you out." If he poops, I have Baggies. Surely there's a dumpster around here somewhere. I open my door halfway and lower Felix to the ground, hoping he'll be content with just investigating the space.

I'm not paying attention to him and only realize he's given me the slip when I tug on the leash and it easily flies up and lands in my lap.

"What the . . . ? Felix!" I'm whisper-yelling. "Get back here, you little punk!" I see a tiny shadow flitting across the floor near the punching bag.

"Felix!" I pause, waiting for the sound of tiny footsteps rushing to my side. "Felix!" All I hear is a Chihuahua investigating a new place. He's gone adventure doggy on me at the worst possible time.

My little guy can be very inquisitive and busy when he puts his cashew-sized brain to it.

Dammit. Now I have to get out of the car. If they have radiator fluid lying around in puddles, Felix will think it's Gatorade and lick up every last drop. My sister calls him a mini-Hoover. He won't stand a chance.

It's way cooler out here in the warehouse than it is in my stuffy car. I use the few moments I have in the semi-fresh air to pull my shirt off my chest and shake it around a little. The smell that hits me in the face is not pleasant. *Great.*

"Felix, come on, stop futzing around."

He ignores me, of course. He's a Chihuahua on a mission, and I'm just the woman who feeds, bathes, cuddles, and fawns over him 24/7.

"No treat, Felix. No treats for a week. I'm not kidding." I stare into the bleak corner of the room, hoping to catch a glimpse of his sorry little butt.

I see a flash of his brown and cream fur near one of the weight machines and change my trajectory to intercept his next move. He's working his way toward the door we drove through earlier. If he gets out and starts running around the port, I'll cry. I swear to God, I'll cry like a big, blubbering baby. He'll surly get squashed by a forklift or something equally deadly out here. The port is no place for six-pound Chihuahua mutts.

He's busy sniffing the part of the machine where the black metal weights are stacked up, and I know exactly what he's thinking.

"No, Felix! No! Don't you *dare!*"

He lifts up his back leg and takes a wee on the metal.

I look over my shoulder in a panic, sure that someone's going to come down the stairs and bust my dog for having the worst manners a mutt can possibly have.

Strike that. Make that the *second* worst manners a dog can have. Felix is now squatting next to the place he peed. A two-fer! Hurray for Felix! I'm going to kill him as soon as I get my hands on him.

I run back to my car and grab my purse. Rummaging through it, I find a small bag and some baby wipes. Felix is just finishing up his business when I arrive on the scene of the crime.

I snatch him up before he can get away, and shove him into my purse. I trap it between my ankles as I take care of the other mess he left behind. When I'm all done, I look around for a garbage can.

Dammit. Where do they put their trash around here? I walk briskly over to the automatic door and put the plastic Baggie down near the edge of it, my purse clamped under my arm. When I leave, I'll take the evidence bag with me, but there's no way I'm storing it in my car before then.

I open my purse as I walk back to the car. "No more Houdini-ing tonight, Fee, you hear me? You stay with me. Stay. *Stay.*" I glare at him.

He smiles and tries to lick me. I hate when he does that. I can never stay mad at a smiling Chihuahua.

I stop outside my car door. It's so damn hot inside there, I really don't want to get back in. But what else am I supposed to do? Call the police? That seems kind of silly at this point. Sleep on the concrete floor? I look over at the weight-lifting equipment. I don't think I could sleep on the bench press. I'd roll over and fall off, probably breaking something in the process, like my nose. And I'm particularly attached to my nose keeping the same, small, straight shape it's had my whole life.

My watch says it's getting close to eleven o'clock. My clients are arriving at nine in the morning at my studio, and I'm going to need an hour to set up. That gives me seven hours to sleep, an hour to get home and shower, and then time to get to work. What in the hell am I going to do for seven hours? Because at this point, I'm starting to feel comfortable with the idea that I'm not going to be killed here, but that the guy who shot at me could still be roaming the neighborhood near my house. Surely The Beard and Hollywood would have already done the deed if that were their intention, right? I'm probably safe. I'm about sixty-five percent sure I am.

The big warehouse door begins to open again, and I immediately duck down, using the side of my car as a hiding spot. Who the heck is coming in now? Another hot guy? Another biker beast? Another murderer or another savior?

CHAPTER SEVEN

It's an SUV this time, black, with tinted windows. It reminds me of an FBI truck like they have in all the movies. Half the time they carry around the good guys, but the other half . . . not so much. I peek over the edge of my car door to see through its windows. The SUV parks on the other side of the truck. I'll have to wait until the people get out and move away before I'll be able to see anything.

I hear voices, one male and one female.

"I don't care what he says. I'm not on board with that," says the male voice.

"I'd love to see you tell him no," says the female.

"Just watch, then. Watch and learn, little grasshopper."

The woman laughs. "Yeah, okay. Got my phone all charged up. I'll run video for posterity's sake."

"Go to hell," he says in response.

"Been there, done that, got the T-shirt," she says. "Not going back. Not tonight, at least."

They both laugh.

And then she comes into view. She's petite, thin, and has long jet-black hair. I can't tell if her pants are denim or leather, but man, they're tight. Paired with her airy white spaghetti-strap blouse and high-heeled boots, they make her look about nineteen. I suppose if

I had a body like that I'd be in skinny-wear too. I can't hate her for making the most of things. She does make me feel kind of frumpy though, crouching down here in my Ann Taylor ensemble.

The man is behind her. He's on the short side as well, same color hair, maybe slightly lighter, and compact. He's in jeans and a black shirt, rolled up at the elbows. His shoes are black, something I'd expect to see on a guy going out clubbing. Both of them have Cajun accents, one of my favorite things in the world. It's part of what drew me here to New Orleans from New York two years ago. That and my sister. Our family home in Florida didn't interest me after I left it at eighteen.

I stand up a little as they climb the stairs, trying to get a better view and stop the circulation from backing up at my knees.

"You coming up?" the man asks me as he turns in my direction.

I look behind me.

Nope. No one there. There's just me and Felix, stinking up the joint.

"Who, me?" I ask, just in case.

"Yeah, you. Who else would I be talking to?" He laughs good-naturedly. I swear I can see his eyes twinkle from here. He must smile a lot.

I shrug, feeling colossally stupid. Beard guy must have called them and told them all about me.

He gestures, waving me to join them. "Come on. Dinner's on."

I frown. *Dinner?* My stomach growls in response, reminding me I haven't eaten since lunch.

The woman has reached the door at the top of the stairs and opened it. The man is waiting for my response.

"No thanks," I say, still not certain that I'm not the one on this evening's menu, although I realize the likelihood of that becomes less and less as more people join the party. Group murder plans went out in the seventies, right?

"If you change your mind, just bang on the door." He disappears behind the woman, and the heavy door slams shut behind him.

Felix whines at me again.

"What?" I ask him. "You want to go up there?"

Felix pants, his eyes bright and excited.

"You have no idea who they are. They could be criminals. This could be a Mafia hangout. If I go up and see too much, I'll have to join. Then I'll get a nickname like May 'the Meatball' Wexler. Or they'll force me to use some kind of crazy weapon in my initiation, and then they'll put it in my name like May 'the Axe' Wexler or May 'the Machete' Wexler. You know I can't stand the sight of blood. It'll never work. I'll fail their tryouts, and they'll throw me into the wet foundation of a new building, drowning me in new cement. My body will never be found. Jenny will die of a broken heart. My nieces and nephew won't have anywhere to go when they want to run away as teenagers."

Felix tilts his head and stares at me for a few seconds.

"Don't look at me like that. It could happen. And don't think you won't be lying right next to me in that cement too, buddy."

The door behind us had started to shut, but now it stops and goes in the other direction. Headlights tell me someone else is about to join the party. It can't be a murder party, right? Right?

I don't even duck down this time. I watch from the opening of my car door. I could get away pretty quickly from this position. I'm still relatively safe from immediate harm.

An old vehicle that should have been left in the seventies pulls in, sliding to a slow stop next to the SUV. It's an orange-gold color with whitewall tires. The man driving has his arm out, resting on the windowsill. He waves at me once before he disappears from view.

The brakes squeak as he pulls to a stop. I'm holding my breath as I wait to see what will happen next. Will he ignore me too, going up the stairs and leaving me to wonder what's for dinner? Or will he go on the attack, rushing me from behind the SUV? I glance over, just to be sure. There's no one there.

A car door slams shut.

Footsteps grind grit into the concrete floor.

And then the tallest man I have ever seen in my entire life comes around the corner of the SUV, heading right for me.

I take a step back, but it does me no good. All he needs is three strides with those stilts for legs, and he's right in front of me.

"Hey there," he says, holding out his hand to shake mine. "I'm Devon. You can call me Dev."

I stare first at his giant, dinner-plate-sized hand and then at his face. I want to say something, but no words come to mind. He's devoid of hair. Like, *any* hair. No eyebrows, no eyelashes, no beard, no five-o'clock shadow, even. Is he part of a religious cult? Am I about to initiated into the Hare Krishna movement?

He grins and points to his head. "Alopecia. No hair. I don't shave it off or pluck it out, if that's what you were wondering."

I shake my head, not even sure at this point what I was thinking. I go ahead and take his proffered hand, just because not doing it seems so rude now that he's shared his personal medical history with me.

"You coming up for dinner? Burgoo night. Otherwise known as Rundown Soup. You don't want to miss it, trust me. Ozzie's the best cook, and it's his night in the kitchen."

"I'm not sure I understand." It feels so good to confess to this complete stranger.

He lets go of my hand and gestures to follow him. "Come on. I'll introduce you to the group."

"Group?"

"Yeah, the group." He hesitates at the bottom of the stairs, turning to look at me. "You've met Ozzie already, right?"

"If you mean the giant beast with the beard, then yes."

Dev's eyes open wide. "Oh boy."

I'm worried now. "Oh boy? What's that mean?"

He laughs, his smile back in place. "Nothing. Nothing at all. Come on. I don't want to miss out on getting a second helping." He takes the stairs two at a time, obviously expecting me to follow.

"What about Felix?"

"Who's Felix?" he asks, not even looking at us.

"My dog." I take Felix out of my purse and hold him up for viewing.

Dev is at the top of the stairs. He punches in some numbers on a keypad and opens the door. "Bring him along. Does he like sausage?"

I walk over and put a foot on the first stair. "He likes sausage, but I'm not sure sausage likes him."

"We'll figure something out," Dev assures me. "His stomach can't be that big."

"Oh, you'd be surprised," I say, halfway up the stairs. "He ate an entire running shoe once."

"Just keep him away from Oz. He's not a fan."

"Not a fan? Of Felix?" I'm standing on the landing next to Dev. I look down at my tiny dog and wonder how anyone could not love him on sight.

"Of small dogs. He's a big dog kind of guy. You'll see what I mean."

I follow Dev inside, wondering what kind of trouble I'm about to get in. I really don't want to be called May "the Meatball" Wexler, and there's no way I'm touching a machete.

CHAPTER EIGHT

"Wow. Nice machete," I say, walking into what I think is a living room of sorts. There are couches, an area rug, and a coffee table, but that's where all resemblance to a home's interior stops. The heavy metal door clanks shut behind me.

Weapons are on display everywhere, some of them set up like artifacts and some that appear to be for everyday use. I have a hard time swallowing as my fear takes over again. Who uses weapons like these? Ninjas? Not the good guys, I know that. No way. I haven't seen any Asians around, though, so this has to be a Mafia lair. Looking behind me, I see that the door I just went through has a digital keypad on the inside wall. I'm locked in. *Trapped!*

I'm in such deep doo-doo right now, it's not even funny. Maybe I'll be able to excuse myself to the bathroom and send out an emergency text to Jenny or the police or the National Guard.

"It's not a machete," Dev clarifies. "It's a samurai sword."

May "the Samurai" Wexler. Hmmm . . . *No.* I still don't like the idea of joining their Mafia gang or whatever this is. Can I go home now? I hesitate in the entrance of the room, trying to decide what my next move should be. Nothing is coming to mind. Everything is scaring the crap out of me, with the exception of this guy. He makes me want to buy a box of popcorn and watch a movie, more like a brother-slash-friend kind of guy, not a murderer. That thought helps me get my breathing under control.

Felix apparently grows tired of waiting for me to make a decision about what to do, and makes it for me. He launches himself out of my purse and runs off, disappearing around a corner into what I can only assume is another room.

"Felix!" I yell, afraid for his tiny life.

"Oh, shit," Dev says. Then he cups his hands around his mouth and yells, "Incoming! Chihuahua on the loose!"

I hear furniture scraping, tiny barks, and then something that could possibly be the hounds of hell being unleashed to bring their murderous fury down upon our heads. I run past Dev, knocking him out of the way, heedless for my own safety as I rush to save my baby's life.

"Felix, noooooo!"

I round the corner, praying I'm not going to see my dog torn to bits all over the floor. I'm not sure what's going faster, my legs or my heartbeats.

What I see when I enter the next room stops me in my tracks, though. I think everyone is pretty much as stunned as I am.

There's a dog bigger than any domesticated animal I've ever seen, standing in the middle of a large commercial-style kitchen, stock still, its tail erect and pointed straight up. The people I saw coming in earlier are frozen nearby, staring at the dogs. There's a guy at the sink who's got his hands out in a calming gesture, a dishtowel over his shoulder.

Whoa, *he's* amazingly hot. I've never seen such nice muscles outside of a health magazine. I'll have to check them out better later. After I rescue my dog from certain peril.

Felix could care less about this guy's physique. He's dancing around the big dog, trying to lick its face, its ribs, its butt—anything he can get his little tongue on. He can't reach anything but the dog's ankles, though, so he quickly decides that's good enough for him.

The dog-beast's tail falls into a more natural position, and it tips its head down to Felix, licking him hard enough to send my little dog over sideways. Felix jumps right up, of course, and goes to town on the dog's legs again. Lick, lick, licklicklick. He's a lick-o-matic right now. I've never seen him so enthusiastic about cleaning ankles before.

"Holy shit, man," the small man who drove the SUV says to the man standing at the sink. "Your dog's a total pussy."

The guy throws the dishtowel lightning fast, hitting him right in the face. "Say that again and see what happens."

My heart skips a beat when I recognize the voice.

I stare at him, forgetting everything else around me. He must be related to my savior. Same voice, same eyes, same giant body, but everything else is different. The hair is short, buzzed in a military style. His face is clean-shaven, his eyebrows neatly trimmed, and there isn't a bandana or leather jacket in sight. He's wearing jeans and a black T-shirt like his friend across the room, and his biceps are stretching the sleeves enough that I'm worried for their seams. There's a small emblem printed over his left breast and some words: "BSB Security Specialists."

"Cute dog," says the woman, looking up at me.

She's gorgeous, like pretty much everyone else here is, making me wish I'd at least brushed my hair before I'd left the house tonight. I can only imagine what these people are thinking about me right now standing here in my espadrilles.

"Thanks." I turn my attention back to the dogs. "Come here, Felix. Stop being a pest." My pulse is calmer, now that I can see my dog is not going to die today.

The big dog flops down onto his elbows and rolls over onto his side. Then I realize it's not a *he*, it's a *she*. I don't know why my brain was telling me that *big* dog means *male* dog when I have a six-pounder who I carry around in my purse and who is definitely not a girl.

Felix climbs on top of the she-beast's rib cage, turns around several times, and then lies down, laying his head on his paws. Apparently, he has mistaken this giant man-eating wolf for a couch cushion.

"You've got to be kidding me," the cook says, sounding seriously offended. "Sahara, have a little pride, would you?"

She tips her head up to look at him but then lays it back down and groans loud and long. She blinks a few times, but doesn't otherwise move. It's like she wants Felix to be comfortable and is willing to be tortured as part of the deal.

My heart melts just watching her. Obviously she's a pretty amazing dog, even if her poops are probably as big as Felix himself.

"Let's eat!" Dev says enthusiastically.

The cook gestures at the stove with another towel. "Have at it. Bread's in the oven." He tosses the towel to the counter and walks out of the kitchen, leaving the room for parts unknown.

Everyone moves at the same time, walking to the sink to grab a bowl off the counter and then over to the pot on the stove. A line forms quickly.

"What's going on?" I ask anyone who might answer.

"Soup's on. Bon appétit," says the small Cajun with a grin.

I watch as each person fills a bowl, grabs a slice or two of bread out of the oven, off a tray, and then sits at a long metal table at the other end of the kitchen.

When they're all seated, someone says a quick prayer, and they dig in. It's possible they haven't eaten in a while; to say they're enthusiastic about the soup is a bit of an understatement.

"Mmmm, mmmm, so good," says Dev, his mouth full of something. I look away so I can't see the details.

"Never fails," says the woman.

"I get a second bowl," says the Hollywood-handsome guy. "I was on a detail all day."

"First come, first served," says the Cajun guy, "and Ozzie's friend hasn't eaten yet."

I think they're talking about me. "Is Ozzie the one with the horrible beard?" I ask before I think to come up with another adjective for his facial hair. *Oops.*

"Yep," says the woman. "The one and only."

"I thought Ozzie was the cook," I say, now thoroughly confused.

"He is. The best." Dev is busy shoveling soup into his mouth, so his words come out a little juicier than I think he intended.

"They have these things called napkins," the girl says, throwing one at Dev's face.

He grabs it just before it hits his forehead, without even breaking eye contact with his spoon. "I like to savor my soup and napkin my chin at the end."

I've never heard *napkin* used as a verb before, but I can see what he means. He's going to need some serious napkining when he's done. I'm not even sure he's caught a breath between bites. How is he not choking? I think I see a drop of soup on his cheek, just under his eye.

"Better get a bowl before you miss out," the Cajun says, pointing with his spoon at the sink. "Lucky would take out his own grandmother for the last bite."

I guess Hollywood's name is Lucky. He doesn't seem to disagree with the measure of his character.

I slowly walk over to the bowls, my mind whirling with confusion. Who are these people? Do they live here together? How is Ozzie both the cook and the guy with the beard? And who was the hot guy at the sink, if not Ozzie? Obviously the soup isn't poisoned, because they're all eating it. Why am I here? Why aren't they asking me questions? Why is Felix sleeping on a wolf?

None of this makes a single bit of sense, so I go ahead and spoon some soup into my bowl. Confused and starving is not a good combination. I leave the bread alone, though. I really want a piece, but I keep picturing someone attacking me when my back is turned, and reaching into the oven makes me too vulnerable. I wish Felix would stop acting so calm. This is still a semi-emergency situation as far as I'm concerned.

I approach the table with my bowl of soup and a head full of caution. There are four empty seats, but only one provides me a good getaway, being nearest the door. I start to sit and then nearly have a heart attack when everyone at the table yells at the same time.

"Not there!"

I stand up and jump back.

"That's Ozzie's seat. Take this one." Lucky pats the seat next to him. It will put me smack dab in between him and the girl. Her I can probably take. Him, I'm not so sure.

"I promise we don't bite," she says.

"Much," says Lucky.

She snorts but doesn't disagree.

My stomach makes the decision for me, growling like an angry bear. I put my bowl down first and then release my purse from my shoulder.

The girl scrunches up her nose as my purse is lowered to the floor. "I smell dog piss." She turns around and glares at the dogs. "You're supposed to be potty trained, Sahara."

"It's not her—it's me," I say.

Everyone stops eating at the same time and stares at me.

My face flames red. "Actually, it's my *purse*, not me. Felix peed in it earlier."

The girl stares at me for a couple seconds, her expression one of disgust. "Oh. That's much better than it being you."

My jaw drops open. I'm not sure if she's trying to be funny or completely rude.

The Cajun guy solves the mystery for me. "Don't be such a bitch, Toni. She's a little shell-shocked. Wouldn't you be?" He shakes his head, maybe in disappointment, and goes back to his soup. A loud slurping follows as the liquid is drawn up from his spoon into his mouth.

Toni doesn't say anything. She just bites into her bread like she didn't just beg me to whack her with my pee-purse.

Since I'm vastly outnumbered by the brawn around the table that I can only assume is her quasi-family, I decide to at least enjoy my meal. Who knows? It could be my last.

My first bite makes it perfectly clear why Lucky would be willing to take out his grandmother for another bowl of it.

"Wow." I say, savoring a chunk of spicy sausage. "This is amazing soup."

"Told ya." Dev smiles at me. "Wait 'til you have his jambalaya. Out of this world."

The Cajun rolls his eyes heavenward. "Oh là là, I'm going to make a special request for next week—you can count on that." He winks at me. "It's my birthday."

I nod, going back to my soup. Three bites and I'm even more in love with the man who cooked this meal. "So where is Ozzie, anyway?" I ask. "Isn't he going to eat?" I'm not looking forward to seeing that beard again anytime soon, but I would like to thank him. So far he hasn't killed me, and now he's saved me from a stalker and fed me. That deserves some gratitude at the very least.

"He probably already did. He doesn't eat with the group that much," says Lucky.

"How come?" I keep staring at his bread, wondering if he's going to eat it. I should have gotten a piece from the oven when I had a chance.

Dev gets up and goes over to the stove. I can hear him spooning out more soup behind me.

"He's got a lot of admin to do," Lucky says.

"He's a loner," says Toni. "Big time."

"Huh." I have nothing to say to that. All I know is, he's a great cook. I hope there aren't any beard hairs in here, though.

Dev drops a piece of toasted garlic bread on the table by my bowl. "Saw you eyeing Lucky's piece. Didn't want you to get your fingers bitten off."

"Shut up, dick, I'm hungry. You would be too, tailing that dirtbag for twelve hours." Dev opens his mouth to answer but is stopped by an angry voice from the doorway.

"Not a word," he says. "She's not staying."

I look up and see the man who threw the kitchen towel standing at the entrance to the room.

"Oh, come on, Oz, don't be such a hard-ass," says the Cajun. "She can stay for a little while. You said yourself she might be at risk."

It's then that I put it all together. This gorgeous hunk of man-meat standing there lording his muscles all over us is not Ozzie's brother. *He's* Ozzie. *He's* The Beard. *He's* the guy who told me to leave my car alone and then guided me here when I didn't listen. And *he's* the one looking hotter than a man should be allowed to look, with muscles bulging out of his shirt and his jaw twitching in annoyance as he glares at me. He looks totally and *completely* different.

"What happened to your horrible beard?" I ask, before I think to stop myself.

CHAPTER NINE

The Cajun laughs but says nothing, staring down into his soup as he swirls his spoon around in it.

Ozzie doesn't answer me. Instead, he walks across the room, grabs a bowl, and fills it to the top. I look around the table as he comes over to take his seat. No one seems to be in any hurry to explain this complete body makeover Ozzie has somehow accomplished in less than an hour.

"Good stuff, Oz," says Lucky, referencing the meal. "Outdid yourself again."

Ozzie grunts, taking a bite of some bread. He makes eye contact with no one.

"Listen, man, about tonight . . ." says Dev.

Ozzie drops his spoon with a clang into the bowl. "Let it go for now." He's staring at the middle of the table, clearly making an effort to contain his temper.

"I just wanted you to know I meant to be there."

"Sure you did," says Lucky. I can't tell if he's disgusted or amused. "Just like you meant to be at Roscoe's last week and Beat Street the week before."

"Hey, you guys know I have responsibilities."

Ozzie finally lifts his gaze. "We all have responsibilities, Dev. All of us. It's just that yours get in the way of you doing your job way more often than they should."

The stress floating over the table is too much. I can't take it.

"So what exactly *is* your job, anyway?" I'm shooting for a casual tone, but not quite getting there. My voice is too high, too strained.

Everyone looks at me, including Ozzie, forcing me to explain myself.

"I mean, I saw your business card, so obviously you're not murderers. Or I hope you aren't. I mean, would you feed me if you were?"

No one answers. They just stare at me.

"You're not the Mafia, I hope. Not that I'm any threat, okay? I won't say a word to anyone about your lair."

"Our *lair*?" Toni asks.

I look around. "Yeah. The Batcave or whatever you call this place."

The Cajun laughs quietly.

"Shut up, Thibault." Ozzie's cranky again, I guess.

I sigh. "Seriously, could someone please just tell me what this place is? Who you are? Because my imagination is running wild, and that's not a good thing."

"What do you think we are?" Lucky asks, putting his spoon down and sitting back to focus on me.

I look around the table. The emblem on Ozzie's shirt catches my eye again. "I guess, if I were to take the serial-group-murderer idea off the table, I'd say you're either some sort of private security company or a fan of one." Or they're drug dealers and they use those T-shirts and business cards to throw people off. I'm not going to say that thought aloud, though.

Lucky winks at me. "Good eye." He gives me a quick chin lift. "What else do you see?"

I feel like I've entered a televised trivia game. Putting down my spoon, I take a closer look at my surroundings, using my photographer's eye to soak up the details. It's easier now that I don't feel quite as threatened. So far, no one's pointed a gun or a knife at me, and it seems like there're probably plenty of those available around here.

"Well, I see a group of people who act like family but who aren't. Except maybe for you two." I point at Toni and the Cajun—Thibault I guess his name is. He nods, confirming my suspicion. "Obviously you're . . . uh . . . a health-conscious group. I suppose if you're into doing security things, that's important." I look down at the dog. "You have a guard dog who's supposed to be very scary but really isn't so much. She seems like a big softie to me." Felix stretches out, and she doesn't move a single hair on her body other than to blink.

A couple of people snicker, but when I look up to see who it was, no one's taking ownership. Ozzie looks like he's about to explode, his face is so red.

"There are cameras in all the corners, here and downstairs, so either you have something valuable in this place or you worry about someone getting in and coming after you. I saw lockers that could have something valuable in them. Maybe weapons, since I noticed that one looked like a gun safe, and you seem to have a collection going upstairs here too." I realize that I'm describing both a security company and a drug gang's lair with equal accuracy.

I realize I've probably said too much when Dev's eyebrow spots go up. There's no hair there, but that doesn't stop his brow from moving up toward what would be a hairline on a person without alopecia.

"And uh . . . you have swords all over the place, so I guess there's someone here with a ninja fetish."

Thibault starts laughing, placing his hand on his stomach. "Oh my god, I can't take it." He stands and walks around the table with his bowl, bringing it to the sink.

"What?" I ask, looking around. "What'd I say?"

"She's pretty observant," says Lucky, shrugging. "Most people miss the cameras."

I smile. "Well, I'm a photographer, so I tend to focus on those kinds of things."

"Focus, eh? No pun intended?" asks Toni. Her expression is kind of hard to read, but I think it might be a smile. I decide then and there that I'll always think twice before whacking her with my pee-purse.

My face flushes. "Yeah, no pun intended." I clasp my hands hard in my lap. "So, Ozzie, are you going to tell me what happened to that hairy mess you had on your face, or what?"

Someone lets out a low whistle—Lucky, I think.

I look around. "What? Did I say something wrong?" He couldn't possibly have liked that thing, could he?

Dev's non-eyebrows are still at his scalp.

I frown, worried I've upset the kingpin. "Oh, is he sensitive about his facial hair?" I look over at Ozzie, his expression unreadable. "Were you attached to it? I'm sorry. I didn't mean to offend you. It was kind of big, though, right? And . . . puffy?"

"That beard was keeping me in that bar with those people."

I smile. "Oh, okay. Well, then, you're welcome."

"No, I'm not welcome." He glares at me.

"Oh." My smile falls away. "So losing the beard and those people is a bad thing?" I look over at Toni. She's nodding. This, I don't get, because any woman in the entire world would have looked at that hairy mess and thought the same thing as I did: gross, unsanitary, and—well . . . gross. And those people back in that bar—well, one of them did shoot at us, so I can't really see as how the loss of their friendship is that big of a deal.

"Losing the beard means losing my cover and months of work. Now we're back to square one with the Sixth Ward."

Again I'm back to panicking, just like that. "The Sixth Ward? As in the Sixth Ward D-Block? Isn't that a gang?" My voice peters out at the end. I distinctly remember reading about a string of murders they were blamed for not that long ago.

"Only the most vicious one in New Orleans," Dev says, standing up with his bowl in hand. He sounds pretty proud of that fact.

I slowly sink down in my chair. "Oh, crap. I knew this was a lair." I wait for my sentence to be handed down. Looking at my soup causes a crazy thought to float through my head: *At least I had a decent last meal.*

"It's not a lair," says Ozzie, picking up his bread. "It's our place of business. And we're not gang members; we're a private security firm. That's all you need to know." He bites into his food, taking more bread than I would have imagined possible.

"You ever do any freelance work?" Thibault asks me, sitting back down at the table.

"That's all I ever do," I say. "I'm self-employed."

"Hmmm." He nods his head, glancing for a second at Ozzie before continuing. "Ever do any surveillance work?"

I open my mouth to answer, but Ozzie cuts me off.

"No. She's never done any surveillance work, and she's not going to start."

I sit up straighter. "Excuse me, but I'll have you know that I *have* done some surveillance work." Okay, so I'm exaggerating my history a little bit, but they'll never know.

"Really?" Thibault says. "What kind?" Now everyone at the table is looking at me.

My face is going pink again. "I . . . uh . . . took some photos of a man cheating on his wife." I hurry to add, "At the park," so they won't think I was perving out in someone's bedroom closet or something equally distasteful.

"You bust him?" Toni asks, like she has a personal stake in my answer.

"Yes, as a matter of fact, I did. Got some great stills. Caught him red-handed, as they say." I grin with pride. Yes, it was an embarrassing job, but sometimes when the wedding bookings and family portraits get fewer and farther between, I have to be less picky about the kind of work I do. I won't tell them about the sexy housewife shoot I did last winter. They probably won't get as excited about that one, and I still can't get some of the images out of my head. The last thing I want to do is start dredging those memories up.

"You didn't get caught?" asks Lucky.

"I find that hard to believe," Ozzie says, not even giving me a chance to answer.

My eyebrows draw together again as I glare at the cook. "As a matter of fact, I was able to take the pictures right in front of his face." My chin lifts with pride. "I pretended to be taking pictures of the flowers near where he was sitting. He didn't suspect a thing."

Lucky gestures at me with his bread. "If she was wearing that Little Bo Peep outfit, I wouldn't suspect anything either. You know that's our biggest problem with recruiting, Ozzie. We don't have a single Bo Peep in the group."

He's grinning at me, but I don't smile back.

"What's that supposed to mean?"

Ozzie stands, his voice booming across the table. "It means you don't belong here. Time to go."

Everyone looks up at him. Dev looks especially confused. "Where's she going to go? You said she was stuck here for a while."

"I changed my mind." Ozzie brings his half-full bowl to the sink, and I look at everyone around the table. "She can't stay."

"What's going on?" My voice comes out as a near whisper. No one answers me. They're all looking at Thibault.

"Time to take a vote," says Thibault, sounding resigned.

"What exactly are we voting on?" asks Toni, glancing at me before turning her attention back to the guy who looks like her brother.

He gestures at me with his chin. "On what to do with her. Does she stay or go?"

I have difficulty swallowing when I realize that I might be witnessing my own death sentence being handed down.

CHAPTER TEN

"We don't need a vote because I say she goes." Ozzie is back at the head of the table, but he remains standing.

"Dude, you must have been way more attached to that facial hair than you ever let on," says Toni, giving him a slight, teasing smile.

Her brother glares at her, but she acts like she doesn't care, shrugging and turning her back on him to face Ozzie.

"You know as well as anyone else here how long I worked to cultivate those connections. Now they're all blown, thanks to Little Bo Peep over there, and we're back to square one. You want to tell me how I'm going to get my hands on their list now?"

"Whose list?" I ask. The more they talk, the more interesting things are getting. So they're not the bad guys, and yet they're trying to infiltrate a gang? What's up with *that*?

"Never mind whose list," Ozzie says, glaring at me.

I don't have any idea why, but when he does that, it makes me smile. Instead of holding back, I just let the lights bounce off my pearly whites. He reminds me of his dog—all scary and blustery, but really just a giant couch pillow for a tiny dog when all's said and done. I'll bet his stomach would make a great headrest during a movie.

Say *what*? Did I just really think that?

I must be losing my mind. It's probably from lack of calories. I take a big spoonful of soup, just in case.

"It's a list of gang members with their contact info and stats," says Dev.

"Stats?" I look around the room, trying to pick up on some body language that would explain that little tidbit of info. No one's helping me out, though. They all keep trading glances with each other, but none of them are looking at me. All I can think of when someone says they're keeping "stats" is baseball scores and batting averages. Do gangsters rate each other?

"Yeah, stats," says Lucky. "Like kills, kilos moved, numbers on the street moving product, and so on."

I shake my head, feeling a little lost in the lingo. "I have no idea what you're talking about." A shudder moves through my body. "I hope you don't mean literally killing, like actual people or whatever." I take another bite of my soup. "Who would keep stats on that?"

The room is completely quiet. I look up in time to catch Thibault and Lucky exchanging meaningful glances.

"What?" I ask.

"You looking for work?" Thibault asks.

"No!" Ozzie yells before I can even open my mouth.

"She has experience," Lucky says, appealing to the man I can only assume is the boss, now that I see he's trying to lower the boom. "It's not a ton of experience, granted, but she's a professional photographer, and she can get past anyone." He gestures at me. "Just look at her."

"Taking pictures of a cheating deadbeat one day in the park does not equal surveillance experience." Ozzie's head looks like it's going to explode.

Not that I'm interested in surveillance work, but it's kind of offensive the way he keeps throwing up roadblocks in my face. He's way too bossy for his own good. I'd probably be pretty awesome at surveillance work. I'm discreet, I'm an excellent photographer, and I have the equipment, at least for the picture and video-taking part. My jaw sticks out a little as the expression on Ozzie's face gets darker.

Dev gestures at me. "She'd totally blend into the crowd. Not like Toni."

"Hey!" Toni throws a spoon at him.

He catches it in midair without blinking, saving himself from a thunk to the forehead.

"Are you calling me plain?" I ask, pretty sure I should be offended. I know I'm no supermodel, but I wouldn't go so far as to call myself ugly either.

"She's anything but plain—look at her!" Ozzie's pointing at me, making a spectacle of us both. "She might as well be wearing neon lights spelling out 'Look At Me' right now."

All the heads around the table swivel in my direction. Then they look at each other, obviously confused.

"Sorry, Oz, but I'm not seeing it," says Lucky. He leans over and puts his arm on the back of my chair as he talks next to my ear. "Feel like earning a little money taking some pictures? We pay on receipt of invoice."

He's too close for comfort. I lean as far away as I can without falling out of my chair or lying in Toni's lap. "That depends on what the pictures are of."

Lucky laughs, sitting up straight and giving me my space back. "I like your style."

I sit back up, not sure if that was a compliment.

"Well, I don't, and what I say goes." Ozzie crosses his arms, forcing his muscles to bulge out even more. He literally looks like he has boobs needing a bra, resting over the top of his forearms.

Dev smirks and points at Ozzie's chest, talking so only we can hear him. "Look. The kids."

Lucky tries not to smile, looking up at the ceiling instead of at Ozzie.

I think they're talking about Ozzie's pecs. They are pretty impressive. Then our text conversation comes back to me and more of it makes sense. When I said *kids*, I was talking about two nieces and a nephew; he thought I was talking about his boobs. No wonder he got so cranky. I try not to smile too.

"This ain't no dictatorship," says Thibault, his tone even. "We take a vote. That was the deal when we started five years ago, and it's still the deal today." He gently puts his fist on the table. "First thing's first . . . what do we do with her?" He points a finger unrolled from the fist at me. "Let her stay or make her go?"

"I think maybe you should ask me what I want to do first." I'm having a hard time keeping the annoyance out of my voice.

Thibault's eyebrow lifts up. "You want to go back to your house and be a sitting duck for a drug dealer who wants to shoot you in the head?"

My face blanches. "Uh. No. I don't want that."

"That's what we thought." He looks around the table. "She stays here; all in favor?" His hand goes up.

I look around the table as all the guys raise a hand—everyone except Ozzie, of course. And Toni. She's just staring at the table like she's not even aware of what's going on.

Ozzie's reaction pisses me off. "You want me to get shot in the head?" It's actually kind of hurtful that Ozzie's voting me off the island. I thought we'd had a moment in that alley together. He rescued me . . . I was rescued . . . that means something, right? Damn, he even called me a cab and paid for it, so why is he kicking me to the curb now?

His expression changes to one of chagrin. "Of course I don't want you to get shot in the head . . ."

Dev cuts him off before he can finish. "Excellent! So she stays. Now let's vote on giving her some work."

Ozzie and I both hold out our hands in front of us like stop signs.

"Now wait a minute . . ." he says.

"Hold on," I say.

We both stop and stare at each other. He glares. I narrow my eyes.

"Sure. Go ahead and vote," I say, flipping my hands around like I'm totally cool with everything happening right now. "I could use some extra work. Not a lot of weddings going on right now." I'm kind of serious and kind of just yanking Ozzie's chain. Some extra money would be nice, but I'm not sure taking pictures of drug dealers is the best career move for me.

Ozzie stares at me, his jaw clenching and unclenching. For some reason, it cheers me up to see him getting all pissed about me being here. Is he scared of me? Ha! He must be. I did do a pretty good job of evading that guy who tried to kill me, even before Ozzie was helping me out. Some might even call me brave. I did lead him down into a cul-de-sac.

Or maybe I hurt his feelings about his beard. My smile falters. I guess since I'll be staying at his place of business, I should probably apologize for that.

"Listen, Ozzie, I'm sorry for the horrible beard comments. It was just . . . way bigger than a beard has a right to be. I couldn't help myself."

Thibault speaks up as he laughs at me. "Oh my lord . . . all in favor of giving Little Bo Peep a trial run, say aye." He's still smiling at me.

"Aye." I hear the word three times. Then there's a long silence. I ignore Toni and turn to face Ozzie instead, smiling before I too say, "Aye."

He looks like he's about to say something, but he doesn't. Instead, he storms out of the room, yelling, "Sahara!" The giant dog slowly gets to her feet and ambles out of the kitchen, with Felix following closely at her heels.

CHAPTER ELEVEN

I'm given a camping cot, a sleeping bag, and the corner of the kitchen for my very own. It's either this or risk going home and being spotted by that guy who was following me in the neighborhood too close to mine for comfort. I stare at my setup, wondering if I'm going to get even a single minute of sleep tonight. Things are not looking very promising. I would never call myself the camping type. More like the rent-a-hotel-room-and-lie-by-the-pool type, actually. I'm itching to call my sister, but I know it'll send her into a tailspin of panic if I do that. She'll never be satisfied with half-explanations and excuses. I need to wait until I can sit down and tell her every last detail.

"You going to be okay?" Lucky asks. He doesn't look that concerned. More like amused.

"I guess." I look around the room. Besides Ozzie, who still hasn't shown his face since storming off, Lucky's the only one left here with me, but he's heading toward the exit now. "Aren't you staying?" I can't quite keep the neediness from my voice. This place is full of samurai swords. What if I trip over one in the middle of the night and cut off a limb? I absolutely need all my limbs, every single one of them.

"Nah. I've gotta go feed my goldfish. I'll catch you tomorrow." He walks to the door that leads into the ninja room.

"Is anyone staying here tonight, or will I be here alone?"

"Oz'll be here. He never leaves except to go to work. His bedroom is just down that hall there." He points to the place Ozzie stormed off to a half hour earlier. "If you need anything, just yell."

I pick up the sleeping bag and hold it against me, sighing. "Okay. Thanks."

"No problem. Welcome to the Bourbon Street Boys' bed and breakfast." He winks and leaves the room, flicking off the main light on his way out. I hear his chuckle and the digital beeps of the lock pad, followed by the sound of a heavy metal door closing.

"Bourbon Street Boys," I mumble to myself as I try to spread the sleeping bag over the cot, using the light from over the stove to guide me. "What kind of name is that for a security company? We're not even on Bourbon Street. It's miles from here."

I look at the entrance to the hallway where Ozzie sleeps. Felix hasn't emerged yet, and I'm starting to worry. Should I worry? Yes, I should. Felix could wee at any moment. His bladder's the size of a grape. I have to have him near me so I can read the signs of him needing to go out before it's too late.

"Felix," I whisper as loudly as I can.

No answer. Not a single clicking of a claw on tile comes to my ears.

"Felix!" I whisper more loudly, cocking my ear and focusing everything I have on the possible sounds of a Chihuahua on the move.

Nothing.

"Dammit, Felix! Get in here!" My voice is louder than I plan for it to be.

At first there's no response, but then I hear some swearing.

"Oops." I sit down on the edge of the cot and wait for the big bad Ozzie wolf to come out and scold me for waking him from his beauty sleep.

I snort out loud over that idea. Before, when he was sporting that horrible facial hair, I would have said he needed about six months of beauty sleep to get things right, but now I'd say he should probably stay awake for a few weeks. Months, maybe. He's prettier than a man should be allowed to be with that body of his. His face, as harsh and angry as it looked tonight, is enough to have me thinking thoughts I shouldn't be. I've always been a sucker for high cheekbones and a chiseled jaw. Even the scar he has on his right cheek isn't enough to make him anything less than ruggedly handsome. Damn. Just the memory of him is enough to heat up the room.

Never, ever would I have thought that the man-beast I met at Frankie's could have revealed himself to be the real Ozzie that lay underneath. That was one hell of a cover. I can kind of see why he's so pissed he had to get rid of it, because he really stands out now. Before he was just another big, hairy biker guy; today he's a dream come to life. One of these days I'm going to ask him if it was a press-on beard or if he actually grew it that way and shaved it off.

Suddenly he's in the entrance to the kitchen, scowling at me. "Are you calling me?"

"Not unless your name is Felix."

"Who's Felix?"

I shake my head. "For a security professional, you sure aren't very observant. For the third time, Felix is my *dog*. You know . . . the Chihuahua mix that's probably sleeping in your bed right now?"

He folds his arms across his chest. Not intimidating at all, by the way. *Kids.* I almost giggle.

"Dogs don't sleep in my bed," he says.

"Tell that to Felix. Trust me, he always finds a way." I gave up on kicking him out of bed long ago. Besides, he's awesome in the

73

winter as a foot warmer, preferring to sleep under the covers at the bottom of the bed to being anywhere else. I have no idea how the little guy gets enough oxygen to survive, but he wakes up just fine every morning, no worse for the wear.

Ozzie leaves, and a few seconds later there's yelling.

"Son of a bitch! Get out of my bed, you mutt!"

Then there's a low, horrific growl that I know didn't come from my little baby.

Ozzie's clearly offended. "Oh, you have got to be kidding me . . . Hey! Lady! Get in here, would you?!"

I guess that would be me. Lady. May "the Lady" Wexler. I sigh.

"Little Bo Peep! Need you in here for a second!"

I think I prefer "Lady" to this nickname.

I get up and go down the hall, passing framed photographs of the people I had dinner with and some letters behind glass too. I stop near one to skim it. It's a thank-you from the New Orleans chief of police, thanking Bourbon Street Boys for helping them catch a criminal.

Hmmmm. More evidence that I'm actually in the good-guys' lair. *Sweet.* This is a total Batcave. I feel much better about closing my eyes and trying to catch some sleep tonight. Maybe I won't have huge blue bags under them during my shoot tomorrow after all. A girl can dream.

I reach a room that has an open door and light spilling out of it. Two more steps has me in the entrance, where I can see the interior of Ozzie's bedroom. It's as one would expect of a guy like him—cold, sterile, lots of metal and a flat screen TV on the wall along with some big speakers, a computer on a glass desk, and a dock that holds a phone. The sheets on his bed are black. The fact that they're satin has me going a little warm. I didn't expect that at all. It makes me wonder how many women have enjoyed them with him. Then my face goes red as I realize the next scene in this fantasy film includes him being naked.

Whoa. Stop right there, brain. Don't take another step.

"What's up?" I ask, leaning on the doorframe pretending like I'm completely cool and not all flustered over the idea of being in his black satin–sheeted bedroom. Oy, those muscles . . . what they do to me!

Ozzie points to the mattress. "Your dog is in my bed."

I shrug. Felix is so bold. I'm actually a little jealous of him right now. I want to be in those satin sheets, rolling around, sliding across the top of that bed . . .

Ack! Stop that, brain! Stop that right now!

"So?" I shrug my shoulders. So cool. So not affected by all that satin. "Get him out."

"I tried." He glares at me for a second before moving toward the bed.

A big orange head pops up from the floor next to the mattress. Sahara. She growls, and when she does that, she really does look like one of those hellhounds. Yikes.

"Are you fucking kidding me?" Ozzie sounds shattered.

Poor Ozzie. I could only imagine what it would be like to have my little Felix turn on me. And it's partially my fault this is happening. Or it's Felix's fault for being so adorable, so I'm his accomplice for bringing him here in the first place.

This will never do. I can't be held responsible for coming between a man and his dog. Feelings of righteous indignation well up inside me and take over my good sense.

I shake my head and advance into the room. "Cut that out." I use a firm tone, barely giving the big beastly dog the time of day. "Felix, get your furry butt out of that bed *right* this second." Felix dips his head down and looks up at me with his tiny brown eyes, knowing he's in the wrong and using his I'm-too-cute-to-discipline maneuver.

Sahara keeps growling.

"Shut it!" I yell at her.

She goes silent instantly and lowers her head. Wow. I'm going to have a hard time disciplining her too. She's cute when she's feeling guilty.

"I'll be goddamned," Ozzie says in a low tone.

I sweep Felix off the top of the bed and tuck him under my arm. "I told you he likes to sleep in the bed. You should listen to me more often. I'm usually right, you know." I cut myself off when I realize I'm sounding like what Jenny calls "naggy." For some reason, having Ozzie consider me a nag makes me sad, and that just makes me confused. Why do I care what he thinks about me? Time to abandon ship.

I nod once, putting an end to the moment. "Have a good night." I leave the bedroom without a backward glance, refusing to give in to the instinct to run.

CHAPTER TWELVE

Settling Felix at the bottom of the cot, I do what I can to get comfortable. My shoes go under the bed, and my hair band goes under the tiny pillow I was given. I lie down on my back, placing the sleeping bag over me, and stare at the ceiling, considering my situation.

I should probably be more scared than I am, but I can't seem to muster the adrenaline or fear response from anywhere. Maybe my system is broken. I was pretty much scared witless for a solid hour or two tonight. I probably used all my fear juice earlier. Now all that's left is the power to analyze, so analyzing is what I'm going to do.

I chew a dry spot on my lip and contemplate the facts. These guys work with the police, so they're the good guys. They're on my side. If they have weapons here, it's probably just to do their jobs. I was the perfect target if killing innocent women is what they're into, but instead of shooting me, freezing my corpse, and putting it in a wood chipper, they fed me soup. And not just any soup . . . amazing soup.

And what's up with that? Ozzie is some kind of awesome chef? Ha. I never saw that coming. I smile at all the things that just don't make sense about that guy. He's a giant beast of a man, but no one is afraid of him, even when he's yelling. He has their respect, but not out of fear. Now that I think about it, I guess he has mine too. Even though he clearly doesn't want anything to do with me, he saved me. Not just once, but twice. And now he's given me a place to stay, so I can return home in the light of day without worrying about a stalker following me in his car. Bad guys lie low in the daytime, right? It's much riskier for them to come after me when people can see them. Maybe it's naive of me, but it's the darkness and the cover it offers them that I fear.

Heck, maybe I could get one of these Bourbon Street Boys to come and check my house before I go inside tomorrow, to make sure it's all safe. The idea makes me both warm and tired. Safety. Big muscular men to protect me. Yay. It's got to be past midnight, and the room is surprisingly comfortable. They have a great air conditioning unit in here—just cool enough to get rid of the humidity, but not so cold I can't fall asleep like a little baby being held in its momma's arms . . .

I'm just starting to drift off when the smell hits me.

"Oh my god," I whisper, inhaling to make sure it's not just a nightmare I'm having. "Felix, was that you?" My eyes fly open.

When I hear a groan, a sliding sound across the floor, and a grunt, I realize that Felix and I are not alone in the room. Turning my head to the side, I see the giant beast—Felix's girlfriend—lying there next to my cot.

"Holy crap, Sahara, does your owner have gas masks around here anywhere? Because he should. Damn." I put the sleeping bag over my face and try to breathe.

Forget comfortably warm and tired. I'm wide-awake now, living in the nightmare that is a hellhound's intestinal gas.

"Jesus, what do they feed you, anyway?"

I hear another noise and turn my head toward the doorway. The dim light from something in the kitchen illuminates Ozzie's head and shoulders.

"Can I help you with something?" I ask from under the sleeping bag that's acting as a not very effective gas mask. I really hope he doesn't think that smell came from me.

He sighs heavily. "Come get in my bed."

I blink a few times, not sure I heard him correctly. The stench could be affecting my hearing—it's that strong. I thought I heard an invitation to heaven leave his lips, but that can't be right.

"Excuse me?"

"I meant *take* my bed. I can't have you out here sleeping on that cot."

Flashes of those satin sheets have me breaking out in a cold sweat.

"Uhhhh, no thank you." No way. I'm no nympho, but I can only be expected to endure so much. Being in his bed, in those sheets, with him standing there with that chest and those arms. No. Just . . . no.

"I'll take the cot," he says, persistent rescuer that he is.

My voice goes up into a higher register in my effort to sound carefree. "No, that's okay. I love camping. This cot is awesome. Really. Keep the bed. I'll be fine."

He walks farther into the kitchen. "Thibault'll give me a ration of shit if I let you sleep out here. Come on—I promise I won't bother you. Just take the bed. The sheets were washed today."

I swallow with difficulty. I can see his naked body so clearly in my mind. The fact that he's wearing that tight shirt is not helping erase the images. Sometimes I hate that I'm a photographer. All I need is an outline of muscles, and my brain fills in all the rest.

"I'll tell Thibault I refused. Don't worry." I wait for Ozzie to leave. I've practically engraved an invitation for him to beat it out of here at this point.

He tilts his head, reminding me of a confused canine. "I don't get it."

"You don't get what?" I let the sleeping bag slide down from my face a little. Testing the air tells me I'm probably safe breathing it again, which is great because it was getting stiflingly hot under that thing.

"I'm offering you a real bed in a room with a door you can lock, and you're telling me you'd rather sleep on that hard cot out here in the kitchen?" He lifts his nose to the air. "It smells like sausages out here."

I sigh, knowing that as difficult as it may be to dispense it, a little dose of honesty will be very effective at making this guy go away. I'm getting the sense that Ozzie is a very cut and dried kind of person, so here goes nothing . . .

"Listen, Ozzie, I appreciate the hospitality, but I'm not going to sleep in your bed. It's not the sheets being dirty or the fact that the cot is comfy that's making me say no, okay? It's that they're satin. And they're yours. So just go to bed, okay? And take your smelly dog with you, because that's not sausages you smell in here; she's got gas."

He stands there and stares at me. The heat from his gaze starts seeping into my bones. The time for honesty is gone, gone, gone. Now I just have to lie to get rid of him.

"Honestly, Ozzie, you're kind of creeping me out right now."

"Is it the beard?"

He sounds so vulnerable, I can't help but giggle. I think I actually struck a nerve with that insult. Oops.

"No, it's not the beard, okay? Your beard was hideous, but it wasn't scary. It wouldn't keep me out of your bed."

Holy crap. I can't believe I said that. My ears are on fire. Go away, honesty!

"I'm sorry if I came off rude earlier."

Thank goodness he didn't pick up on that innuendo I slathered all over that last comment. I can breathe normally again. Almost normally.

"You weren't rude. Well, okay, maybe you were a little rude, but it didn't bother me."

"Why not?"

I shrug, not sure why myself. "I don't know. It just didn't."

Another long pause occurs before he speaks. "You're not like I expected you to be."

"Oh yeah?" I yawn really loudly, my eyes falling closed on their own. It's way past my bedtime, and now Ozzie's being nice. It makes me feel like snuggling down into this bed and going to sleep. Tomorrow I'll have the energy to spar with him some more. "Prob'ly 'cuz I'm Little Bo Peep. I totally blend."

My mind wanders to that day I took pictures of that philandering creep in the park, and I smile in my half-asleep state. So busted. I took over fifty shots of him with his arm draped around that girl half his age, kissing her neck, giving her a gift wrapped in a jewelry box. Maybe he's the guy who shot my car tonight. I frown a little as my mind wanders over that potential nightmare.

"I guess maybe you could blend a little," says a deep voice off to my right.

I'm too tired to place it.

"Go count your sheep then, Little Bo Peep," the voice says, soothing in timbre and pitch. "I'll see you in the morning."

I picture a bunch of fluffy white sheep jumping over a fence. Boing, boing, boing. So peaceful. So nice. So tiring. But then a giant black one with curly horns on its head comes up to the fence and just stands there, glaring at me.

"Well?" I mumble, annoyed that it's keeping me from sleep. "Get it over with. Jump already, you hairy beast."

Someone chuckles.

And that's the last thing I remember before waking up in someone's kitchen, completely confused and staring at the text from my sister that woke me out of a sound slumber.

Sis: *If you don't call me back in ten minutes, I'm calling the cops. I'm not kidding. Call me. Now.*

CHAPTER THIRTEEN

"Hi, Jenny." My cell phone is cool against my cheek.

"Hi, yourself. Where have you been? I've been calling you all morning."

I yawn, trying to stretch my back out a little. That cot was a bad idea. I have sore spots in the most uncomfortable places. "You wouldn't believe me if I told you. What time is it?" I squint at the stove but can't read the digital clock from where I'm sitting.

"It's eight forty-five. Don't you have a shoot today? Where are you? Home?"

"Holy shit! No, I'm not home. Not even close." I jump to my feet, spinning around, trying to locate my shoes. I find them shoved way under the cot.

"Oh, crap. Do you need me to go over there and cover for you?"

"Yes! Go now! I'll be there . . . I don't know. Soon." I'm trying to place where exactly I am. The Port. Okay. Now I remember. "I'll be there in twenty minutes."

My sister laughs. "One-night stands are a bitch, huh?"

"That's not what this is." I fall over trying to get my shoes on standing up. My words come out as grunts. "Why aren't you at work today, anyway, coding computer programs until your fingers fall off?"

"They're apps, May, apps. And I have this weekend off. Besides, Sammy's sick. I couldn't send him to day care if I wanted to."

I sit on the cot so I don't hurt myself, sliding my feet into my shoes and using my finger at the heel to get them to cooperate. "Okay, go to the studio and stall them."

"Stall them. Right. And how exactly do I go about doing that?"

"I don't know—hint around that their hair's a mess or something. Put them in the dressing room and tell them I'm picking up a new lens and will be there by nine-thirty."

"Ten-four. And I'll expect a full explanation of your evening when you're done for the day."

"You got it. All the dirty details, I promise. See you in thirty."

"See ya."

She hangs up, and I throw the phone down on the cot. "Felix!" *Sorry for waking you up, Ozzie, but I have to go, go.*

I have my shoes and hair band on and the sleeping bag folded up and placed on the cot before I realize that no one is responding to my yell.

"Felix! Come on, baby—time to go!"

Nothing.

I stare at the hallway leading to Ozzie's bedroom. Should I go in there? What if he's naked?

My feet move without conscious thought on my part. One minute I'm next to my cot, and the next I'm standing in the entrance to his bedroom, and there's no nakedness happening anywhere. Damn. The bed is made tight enough I could probably bounce a quarter on it, and there's no sign of either dogs or humans.

After a quick trip to the bathroom, I'm back in the kitchen, where I find a note on the counter.

Took the mutts for a walk. Be back soon. Will escort you home.

I look at the clock in the kitchen. It's already almost nine. I'm never going to make it to the studio in time if I have to wait for Felix, and I cannot afford to lose this job. "Dammit!"

I run back to my phone and send a text to Ozzie, but the beep of its receipt comes from his bedroom, telling me he left without his phone.

"Double dammit!"

I grab the pen used to leave me a note and scribble out a reply on the back of the paper.

Had to go, clients waiting, my studio's at 1001 Vet. Mem. Blvd., would appreciate you bringing Felix by, but I can come back and get him later today if necessary. Thanks for your hospitality. Tried to text, but you left your phone here.

I was hoping that Ozzie would come back as I was writing the message out, but no such luck. I'm about to walk away, but then something makes me go back and add to my note. I don't want him to have any hard feelings over what I said last night, not while he's babysitting my furbaby Felix.

Sorry about the beard thing. It wasn't too horrible, but you're much handsomer without it.

There. That should soothe any hurt feelings he has over it. I smile as I race through the ninja room, and keep on grinning when I see that he's left the door cracked enough for me to get out. There's no digital code to hold me back now. The garage door is wide open too. I spare only a glance at the bullet hole in my driver's side door before getting into my Sonic and speeding out of the Port like there's a drug dealer on my tail.

CHAPTER FOURTEEN

The very happy and well-photographed family isn't out the door thirty seconds before Jenny is all over me for details.

"Okay, spill it, sister. I want to know everything from start to finish. Leave nothing out."

I sit down on my stool and grab a bottle of water from the small fridge I keep nearby. Cracking the top, I sigh. "It was crazy. Completely and totally crazy." I gulp down half the bottle as my sister absorbs my intro.

My nephew Sammy pipes up from the play area in the corner. "Tota-wee cwazy." His sisters are at a birthday party, thank goodness. He's enough of a handful even just by himself. Thankfully, his naptime fell during the shoot, or Jenny and I would be wrecked right now.

I lower my voice, knowing anything he hears could get repeated in front of his father. "Remember yesterday how you went out to get a new phone?"

"Yes." She holds it up and wiggles it at me. "Like it?"

"Yes." I roll my eyes at the bright purple case on it. My sister is a freak for that color, has been all her life. "Anyway, I got a text yesterday evening, and I thought it was from your new phone."

She looks down at it. "I did text you."

"I know. But so did someone else." I pull my phone out of my pocket and show her. "See? Look."

She frowns as she reads through the texts. "I don't get it."

"I thought *that* person was you. I thought you had a temporary phone, and that was your temporary number. So when I thought you asked me to come to Frankie's, I went. I thought you were there with the kids, losing your mind or something."

I wait for that to sink in as she continues reading.

"Oh. Wow."

"Yeah."

She looks up at me. "So what happened? You went to Frankie's and I wasn't there, obviously. And by the way, I can't believe you would actually think I would go to Frankie's with the kids. That place is a dive."

"I wanna go to Fwankies!" Sammy yells. He's too busy pulling the head off a Barbie to look at us, but that doesn't mean his ears aren't completely tuned in.

"Oh, Jesus." My sister closes her eyes and inhales deeply, letting the breath out really slowly as she relaxes her body. She's doing the calming meditation thing that keeps her from blowing her stack. She used to do it about once a day. Now she does it at least once an hour.

"We didn't say 'Frankie's'; we said '*McDonald's*,'" I say loudly, winking at Jenny.

She rolls her eyes when Sammy jumps up and starts running around the studio.

"McDonawd's, McDonawd's, hoo-way, hoo-way, fo' McDonawd's!"

"Great." She throws up her free hand. "Let's go pump the kid full of trans fats and sodium. Excellent plan, May." She closes her eyes and shakes her drooping head.

I pat her leg. "Never mind. He can wait. Besides, I can't go anywhere until I get Felix."

Jenny looks around on the floor. "Why am I just realizing he's not here?" Her head jerks up. "Where is he?"

"He's where I was last night."

The gleam comes back to Jenny's eyes. "And where might that be?"

I point to the texts on my phone. "I went to that place mentioned there that's *not* McDonald's, and while I was looking for you in the back room, something happened—a gunshot went off or whatever, and this guy, this big hairy biker guy shoved me out the back door and into an alley."

"Whaaaat?!!" Jenny grabs me by the arms and shakes me. "Are you okay??!!" Her face is two inches from mine, her eyes full of sisterly concern.

I wiggle out of her grasp. "I'm fine, as you can see." I try to smooth some wrinkles out of my shirt as I finish my story. "Anyway, I tried to go home, but then, when I realized someone was following me from the bar, I took a detour and lost him. And then the guy I was texting gave me directions to this security company's address, and I spent the night there."

She narrows her eyes at me. "And why do I get the impression that I'm only getting a very small part of this story?"

I grin. "Because you are?"

She whacks me on the arm. "Tell me! You know how boring my life is." She glances at her son, who is now struggling to get into a dress. He already has some pink heels on. My studio is awesome for playing dress-up.

"I guess I stumbled into some sort of police sting or some undercover thing, and whoever was there shooting stuff, I guess thought I was worth following."

"Oh my god, that's awful!" Her eyes tear up.

"No, it's fine." I don't know why I think she's going to believe me. I don't even really believe me. It's not like this shooter is going to disappear. I guess I'm lucky he doesn't know my home address, at least.

"Of course it's not fine." She looks me over more carefully. "Were you hurt?"

"No, not a scratch."

She points at my face. "I see scratches."

"Okay, so some minor scratches. That was from some wood chips."

She waits for more, but I say nothing.

"Wood chips," she deadpans.

"Yes, wood chips. They flew up and hit my face. It's no big deal."

"I don't get how you were in a bar and ended up with that on your face."

She's getting mad now. I either have to tell her everything or get mad in response as a getaway tactic.

"Just tell me." She sighs heavily. "You know I have no life. You know if anything happens to you, it'll be me picking up the pieces."

"Those are two very compelling reasons not to say anything, actually."

"Fine. You want to play hardball? I can play hardball. How about this . . . if you don't tell me, I'll go away for a week to the cabin and leave you with my children."

Fear throws a lance into my heart. "Okay, fine. I'll tell you. But not because I don't love my nieces and nephew."

She smiles knowingly. "Agreed."

"All right, so I went to the bar, ran out into the alley after a gunshot splintered a table I was standing near . . ."

"A gunshot?!" My sister grabs my arm, her nails digging into me.

I hold up my free hand to stop her from freaking out. "Wait, just save your questions 'til the end."

"May, oh my god, you were *shot* at? How can you expect me to not react to that?"

I carefully peel her hand off my arm. "Just . . . give me a chance to tell you the whole story, and you can react all you want."

"Fine. But I reserve the right to completely freak out when you're finished."

When I'm done regaling her with the details, Jenny just stares at me. I remain quiet, giving her time to process. Then her gaze shifts to rest somewhere over my shoulder.

"Holy macaroni," she finally says, her voice a little breathless. She's staring out of the plate-glass windows at the front of my studio.

"Ho-whee macawoni," Sammy repeats. "Ho-whee macawoni on a thtick."

The bell on my studio door dings as it's pushed inward. I stand, suddenly nervous when I realize who's there. I pull on the bottom of my blouse, trying to stretch the wrinkles out of the cotton.

"Hey there," Ozzie says, his eyes scanning the space as his body fills the entire entrance.

CHAPTER FIFTEEN

Jenny stands in a hurry next to me. "Hey there," she says before I can respond. She pulls her shirt down over her love handles and then nervously brushes her hands off on her butt. "And who might you be? The dog sitter?"

He frowns briefly at my sister before turning his attention to me. "Brought your dog back."

"What's his name?" I ask, teasing him to get past the awkward moment.

"Mutt." Ozzie keeps a straight face, but I could swear I see a hint of a twinkle in his eye. He puts Felix on the ground and stands. Felix takes off running toward Sammy.

"Fee-Fee!" Sammy yells, bending down to hug the dog. He knows he's not supposed to pick him up, but that rule does not forbid strangling hugs. Felix does his duty and accepts the affection without biting.

"His name is not Mutt; it's Felix." I gesture to Jenny. "And this is my sister, Jennifer, and her son, Sammy. Jenny, this is Ozzie."

We all look over in time to see Sammy stuffing Felix into a sparkly purse and hiking it over his arm. Felix's butt and back legs are hanging out over the edge, his head nowhere to be seen.

I run over to intervene as my sister takes control of the conversation.

"So let me guess . . . you're the guy who rescued my little sister last night, is that right?"

"I gave her a place to stay."

She folds her arms over her chest and nods her head slowly. "Aaaand you babysat her dog for her."

"Actually, I *walked* her dog for her, and she took off before I got back."

I come back to the grown-ups. "I'm really sorry about that. I had a shoot scheduled, and I couldn't miss it. I didn't know where you went."

"Oh my god!" Jenny yells, her face a mask of horror, as she steps back a few paces while staring at the windows again.

A big orange head and a smear of drool are at my front door.

"Sahara!" Ozzie yells. "You were supposed to stay in the truck!"

Jenny runs over and grabs Sammy, lifting him up high in her arms.

"Hey! Put me down, Momma! I wanna pway!" He strains toward the floor, but she holds him with an iron grip.

"What *is* that thing?" she asks, clearly terrified.

I walk over to the door and open it up. "That *thing* is Sahara, Felix's new girlfriend."

The giant dog walks casually into the studio, looking around until she spies Felix licking his privates in front of the meadow background I had up for the family who was just here getting portraits done. Sahara walks over and flops down on the sheet Felix is on, resting her head on her paws.

"Oh my goodness. That's kind of cute, actually." Jenny slowly slides Sammy down her leg. "Is it safe?" She looks at Ozzie. "Is it kid friendly?"

"It's not an *it*, it's a *she*," I say. "And I would guess she is." I look at Ozzie for confirmation.

He's too busy frowning to confirm or deny. I get the impression he'd like to say she's a child-eating monster, but Sahara would probably just fart and fall asleep in response and make him look silly, so he says nothing. Smart man.

He sighs in defeat. "Come on, Sahara—time to go."

I grab my camera and walk over to where the dogs are. They're too cute not to grab a couple shots of while I have the chance. Felix is turning circles in the spot just next to Sahara's belly, trying to make the perfect doggie bed on the sheet. Once he's settled, I start pushing the button, making the shutter go off several times.

"Want me to turn on the lights?" Jenny asks.

"Yes." I'm moving to get a better angle. The expression on Sahara's face is priceless. She's in love.

"No. We have to go," Ozzie says.

"It'll just take a second," Jenny says in a hushed tone. "Just wait and see. My sister's a genius with the camera."

My cheek and nose are pressed up to the back of my Canon. "I like how you qualified that with the word *camera*." A snort escapes me.

"Well, you did pretty terrible in physics. I think to get a solid genius rating, you need to do better than that."

"That was high school, and I got a C, not an F." I pull the camera away and change over to another setting before putting the viewfinder to my eye again. "I got an A in college, so let it go already." She's never going to let me live down my one bad grade ever.

I look down at my screen and scroll through the last few shots I took. *Wow.* I could put these in a calendar. They're definitely going on my website.

"You don't mind if I use these for ad work, do you, Ozzie?"

He doesn't answer, but I keep on shooting. The lights come on, and it's even better. "Oh man. I'm in heaven right now."

Suddenly a big black thing comes into the frame, and then my autofocus kicks in, and I realize it's a butt. A very fine butt, actually. I take a couple shots just for the fun of it. Ozzie is bent over, trying to convince his dog it's time to go.

"Up, Sahara, up." He pulls on her collar, but she's not budging.

"Turn around for a second, would you?"

Ozzie stands to argue, and I catch him in the perfect light and get a few shots off before he steps out of the frame.

I pull the camera from my face. "What's wrong?"

"I didn't come here to get photographed, I came here to give you your dog back and escort you home!"

The room goes silent.

"The reluctant knight in shining armor. I like it." Jenny is grinning from ear to ear.

We both scowl at her. Me, because she's making it look like I've got goo-goo eyes for him or something, and him, I don't know. Maybe he's angry he's still stuck with me.

Jenny moves first. "Anyway, have fun, kids. I have to get Sammy some lunch before he goes all hypoglycemic on me." She scoops him up—dress, heels, and all—and heads for the door. She grabs her purse on her way out.

"I thought we were having lunch together," I yell as she exits.

"Better get your escort to take you. I have errands to run. Ciao!"

I'm about to open my mouth to respond to Ozzie's obvious displeasure over having to rescue me again, but I snap it shut in a hurry when the smell hits me.

"Oh my god." Grabbing a nearby shirt that Sammy got off the rack of clothing, I push it over my nose.

Ozzie's nose scrunches up as he realizes what's happened. "Oh, for Pete's sake, Sahara! What's gotten into you?"

"If I were to guess, I'd say sausage." I wink at Ozzie over the shirt.

He tries to stay mad, but he just can't. His face flushes just the slightest bit, and his expression relaxes. "It's impossible to stay cool when she does that."

I punch him playfully in the arm. "Don't worry about staying cool around me. It'll take a lot more than a dog fart to scare me off."

My entire body freezes up as I realize what I've just said. To Ozzie. With all his muscles. And his black shirt and tight jeans. Oh. My god.

It's only when he tips his head back and lets out a huge laugh that I can finally breathe again.

CHAPTER SIXTEEN

"So this is your place." Ozzie walks through the foyer just inside my townhouse's front door and into the living room with an assessing eye. I can't tell if he likes what he sees or not, his expression neutral. His offer to make sure things were copacetic at my place was too tempting to turn down. I'm going to pretend I said yes because I was worried about my home security and not because I wanted to see him stretch his T-shirt out some more with those muscles of his.

"Yep. Home sweet home." I pass through the living room and go into the kitchen, pulling out the dog food from one of the upper cabinets and pouring two bowls full—one large and one tiny. Sahara wolfs her portion down in about five seconds and lets out a large burp after as she collapses to the floor. Felix takes a few kibbles, carries them across the kitchen, and eats them in the corner of the room before returning for more.

"What's he doing?" Ozzie asks, staring at Felix with a bemused expression.

I watch with him, charmed by my baby's idiosyncrasies. "We call it doggie takeout. Felix never eats at his bowl. He considers it crass."

Sahara sits up on her haunches and watches Felix go back and forth, back and forth. It's almost comical the way her head moves like she's watching a tennis match in slow motion.

Ozzie scans the room behind him. "Anything look out of place?"

It takes a few seconds for his meaning to sink in. "What? Why would it be?" Where before I was entranced by our adorable dogs, now I'm afraid. The events of last night come rushing back to the front of my mind.

He shrugs. "You never know. Just being sure."

I rest my hand on the counter to keep from falling over. I feel a little dizzy. "Are you suggesting that the person who tried to shoot me could have come here?"

Ozzie leaves the kitchen and moves toward the stairs. "I'm just going to look around if you don't mind."

"No, of course. Look all you want." My mind is racing. I didn't come home last night, so how would the shooter know where I live? He wouldn't, right? I don't have any advertising for my business on my car. I was going to put something on, but then I couldn't bear to cover up the brilliant red paint. I figured when I got tired of the car a little, I'd put a sign on it. Now I'm glad I didn't. Anonymity has its benefits, especially when outrunning murderers.

Footsteps sound above my head. "Is everything okay up there?" I yell.

"I guess. No strange men lurking around."

"Ha-ha!" That wasn't funny at all. He should know better than to joke about me being attacked. What kind of security expert is he, anyway?

I go up the stairs in a hurry, wondering if I remembered to make my bed or not. Believe it or not, the fear that my lackluster housekeeping will be discovered is overtaking my fear of being stalked by a murderer, especially after seeing how pristine Ozzie's place was. Yes, I have problems, obviously. I'm going to blame it on Ozzie's muscles. He's wearing another one of those tight BSB Security shirts again. Don't they make them in his size?

When I get to my room, I'm disappointed. Of course I didn't make my bed. Now he knows that I'm messy, and I sleep on sheets covered in flowers. He probably hates that, being the black-satin type. For some reason, that bothers me. Then the realization hits me like a bus; I want him to like everything about me, even my sheets. I'm insane, or at the very least, sexually deprived enough to have become completely irrational.

He comes out of the bathroom that adjoins my bedroom and stops in the doorway. "You left some diamond earrings on the counter in here, and in my experience, even someone who's not normally a thief, but who comes into a home with bad intentions, will pocket something like that. I think you're okay."

The breath I was holding comes flying out in a long, loud stream of air. "Oh, thank God."

He frowns. "Are you seriously that worried?"

"Wouldn't you be?"

He shrugs. "No, but I live in a secured warehouse." He looks around my bedroom. "You don't have any security here, do you?"

I shake my head. My decision to save that money seems really stupid right now.

"I'll send someone over." He leaves my room without another word.

I rush out behind him, afraid to have him disappear so soon. "Someone? Who? Why?"

He's practically running down the stairs. "Thibault. Maybe Toni. They'll hook you up with some basics just to put your mind at ease." He turns his gaze to the kitchen when he reaches the bottom of the stairs. "Sahara! Let's go!"

Ozzie and I are both standing in the foyer. Awkward doesn't even begin to cover the atmosphere. He saw my bedroom. He saw my sheets. He went into my bathroom, and for sure there was a box of tampons on the counter. He's sending someone over to hook me up. He's so hot it makes me ache in dark places. Ack!

The dog ambles out of the kitchen and through the living room, meeting her owner by the front door.

"Is there anything else you need?" Ozzie asks, and for the first time he's looking me dead in the eye and waiting for my answer. Time stands still as I fall under the trance created by his bright green eyes. My blood starts to boil, but not with the angry kind of heat; it's something else entirely.

Yeah, Ozzie, I think to myself, *I need something.* Something I haven't had in a really long time. Sex, and lots of it.

Ozzie tilts his head. "You okay?"

I shake my head, trying to yank it out of the clouds. "Uh, yeah, I'm fine. Really." I put my hand on his arm in an effort to calm myself and distract him from my crazy reaction to a simple question.

Oopsy. Mistake.

I can feel the warmth there and the muscles moving under his skin. I have to clear my throat so I can talk normally. It only works a little. "Thanks for everything, Ozzie. Really. You're a prince among men."

He doesn't pull away from me. He should, but he doesn't. The heat grows between us in the spot where our skin is touching.

"That's what I do."

I laugh and smile. "Rescue damsels in distress?"

"No, the right thing. I do the right thing, much as it might pain me to do it."

Ouch. Talk about a cold shower. Wow, did I read that moment wrong or what?

My hand falls from his arm as I suffer the ache of embarrassment. "Sorry I was so much trouble."

His expression goes confused for a second, and then he reaches out for my hand, taking it in his huge one. The warmth kicks in again, double time. He's holding my hand! I'm sixteen again!

"No, no, I didn't mean *you're* a pain." He shakes his head and jiggles my hand a little. "Dammit, I'm screwing this up." He sighs heavily and starts again. "What I'm trying to say is that making sure you got home safe was the right thing to do. And even though I have about ten other things I should be doing right now, I'm happy to be here making sure your home is secure."

I grin. It's not a marriage proposal, but I don't want one of those anyway. "Wow, Ozzie. That was almost sweet."

He drops my hand and frowns. "Call me if you run into any trouble." He turns around and opens the door without another word.

I panic, thinking this is the last time I'm ever going to see him. Quick, Brain! Think of something charming and witty and interesting to say!

"Was it the flowered sheets?"

I have no idea why those words just burst out of my mouth. Sleep deprivation. It's a terrible thing. Terrible, terrible, awful.

He pauses on the front step and slowly turns his head. "Flowered sheets?"

"Is that why you're running away? Because my flowered sheets are so awful?"

Yep! That's me! I keep talking when I should shove a shoe down my throat. My face burns bright red as I realize there is no coming back from this one. It's like I've never been around a man before. How long has it been since I've had sex, anyway?

"I actually liked the sheets." He smiles awkwardly, as if he's just as confused about that as I am. As if he didn't just charm me from my toes to my nose by not mentioning how whack-a-doodle I am.

He walks down the steps and over the stepping-stones to the driveway, without another word. Sahara almost knocks me over when she bounds past me to catch up to him.

I watch him climb up into his truck and reverse out of my driveway after Sahara's safely in the bed, and I wonder if I'm ever going to see him again, all the while definitely hoping that I will.

CHAPTER SEVENTEEN

I've got popcorn on the stove when my doorbell rings. "It's open!" I yell over the sound of the kernels bursting.

The door shuts and footsteps follow. Only when I notice that they're heavy and coming fast do I realize that I probably shouldn't leave my door unlocked and just tell people to walk in when there could be a murderer on the loose. I grab a knife out of the block on the counter and turn around to confront my visitor.

"Smells good in here." When Thibault rounds the corner and takes my knife into consideration, he slows. "Whoa." His hands come up in surrender. "I come in peace."

My racing heart begins to calm in seconds. "Oh, hey. It's you." The knife goes down to waist level.

"Yeah, it's me. Who were you expecting? Ozzie?" He chuckles at his own joke, but I can't tell if he's hinting that I like Ozzie and was hoping he'd come by or I want to stab him. I put the knife back where it belongs before responding.

"I didn't know who to expect. Want some popcorn?"

"Definitely. After work, though. Work before pleasure." He looks around the kitchen. "Mind if I take a look around?"

"No, feel free. I'm on my computer in the living room, working on some photographs. Just shout if you need me." I'm not worried about being judged this time; I made sure to make my bed and clean up the bathroom counter after Ozzie left.

"I'm just going to count up all the points of entry and see what we'll need to get them secured and hooked into the network."

"Network?" I chew my lip, wondering how much this is going to cost me. I don't have a lot of savings left. My latest dry spell has been pretty desert-like.

"It's a monitored system. If it goes off, someone will be on the line for you within twenty seconds. It's state of the art. Wireless. You can use your cell phone to monitor it and change the settings if you want."

"Great." I don't sound as enthusiastic as I should, but Thibault doesn't notice. He leaves the living room to mount the stairs, and I get a small bowl and fill it with popcorn. When I'm in panic mode, I eat popcorn. I shove an entire handful in my mouth at once. Bits go flying everywhere.

I'm back at the computer, trying to concentrate on photoshopping errant hairs and pimples from the family portraits I shot earlier today, but I can't. My mind keeps straying to the alarm system I'm about to have installed. I'm not even sure I want it. Do I need it? The killer's had ample opportunity to come after me, and I've been safe all afternoon.

As rational as it is, that thought doesn't make me feel any safer. In the movies, killers are always very patient as they stalk their prey.

I lean back in my chair, rolling my eyes up to stare at the ceiling. Money, money, money. I need more of it. When the economy takes a dip, photographers are some of the first to feel it. People don't care about capturing precious moments when the moments suck. Look! Here's Dad with his hair graying from the loss of his job! And here's

Mom with an extra twenty pounds from all the stress eating she's been doing!

No. The portrait business goes bye-bye during a downturn in the economy, and it takes a long time for it to recover. In the meantime, I have to get creative. So far, I haven't found much to cover the holes in my cash flow. Even the wedding bookings are getting scarcer.

A movement outside catches my eye. Tilting my head, I watch as a car crawls down the street, passing by my townhouse. I sit up straighter. Is that the guy who was following me last night?

Panic seizes me. I stand up quickly and move back from the window. The driver keeps going, but he's definitely looking for something, his head swiveling left and right. He pauses when facing my direction, and I hold my breath. No, no, no, no, no! Do *not* shoot your gun at my house!

When he keeps on going, I let my breath out. Thank the stars I parked my car in the garage today. I often leave it in the driveway, but I was worried anyone coming to help me with the security stuff wouldn't have a place to park if I didn't leave the driveway empty. I'm starting to think I'm never going to feel safe parking out there again.

Thibault comes down the stairs, startling me.

"Jumpy." He walks up and stands next to me, looking out the window. "See something out there?"

"I'm not sure." I move closer to him. "I thought maybe I saw the car that followed me last night, but probably not."

"Make and model?"

My face scrunches up as I try to remember. "Big? Ford? Cadillac? Buick?" I look at him. "Sorry. I'm terrible with the older models. Ask me about the 2014 economy models, and I could give you everything."

"Special hobby of yours?" He's smiling.

"No, I had to do some car shopping a few months back. It included a lot of research before I made my decision."

"Ah, a car enthusiast."

"No, more like a budget enthusiast. I wanted to get the best bang for my small buck." I walk over and sit down at my computer again. Thibault's easy manner has lowered my stress level. Plus the car that was out there is gone now and the street is empty once again.

"We really could use your help if you're in the market for some work." He comes over and stands next to me, watching me manipulate a photo on the computer. "I'm good at setting things up, but terrible at anything that requires looking through a lens."

I look up at him and smile. "I don't imagine surveillance work requires all that much artistic talent."

"You'd be surprised." He gestures at my screen. "You're using some kind of program to fix the photographs?"

"Yes, I use Photoshop." I quickly erase a hair that's sticking up above the mother's head.

"I can't tell you how many times we shoot someone and the lighting is so bad, we can't see a thing on the film. You can fix that, right?"

I shrug. "To some degree. I can lighten or darken, remove things, add things in. But I can't fix everything. If you're not taking the shots from the right spot, there's not a lot that anyone can do."

"That's the thing. We're missing that talent. We've got most of our bases covered, but not that one."

My hand leaves the mouse, and I turn my chair a little to face him more. "What bases do you mean?"

Thibault grabs a chair from the nearby dining table and drags it over to sit near me. He starts counting off on his fingers. "Well, let's see . . . we've got Dev on martial arts. He does all our physical training stuff, with help from Toni. Lucky's the numbers guy. He can get into financials and find anything anyone tries to hide. He's not a bad shot either. I'm on security, and Ozzie's the brains behind everything. He's also the public face of the business. He works with the police or whoever hires us to get the scope of the job and put all the pieces together. He also writes up the report at the end. He hates doing that part, but no one else will do it, so he gets stuck with it."

It's on the tip of my tongue to say that I love writing up reports and essays and so on, but I keep it to myself. He doesn't care about that. Instead, I decide to question him about something I noticed last night and have been reminded of today.

"I get the impression you guys know each other from somewhere else." I hook my arm over the back of my chair and lean on my hand, waiting for his answer.

"We grew up together. Got into a little trouble together over on Bourbon Street from time to time when we were younger." He grins. "Ozzie went into the military, and when he got out, he rounded us all up and made us an offer we couldn't refuse."

"And that was . . . ?"

"Get on board or get your ass beat down. He made the decision real easy."

I smile, picturing those exact words coming from Ozzie's mouth. "He tries to be so hardcore."

"Tries?" Thibault's eyebrows go up. "And you think he doesn't succeed?"

I shrug, my vision going fuzzy as I picture Ozzie in my mind, trying to stay serious, but smiling when his dog does something goofy. "I don't know. I guess so. But he's not as scary to me as I think he wants to be."

"Most people think he's the meanest bastard they've ever met."

I snort. "Yeah, right. As if."

Thibault stares at me, a vague smile on his lips.

"What?" I'm worried I have popcorn shrapnel on my face or something.

"Nothing." He immediately shifts his attention to the pad of paper he threw down on the table after his review of my townhouse. "So, here we go . . . my assessment of your security needs."

I lean over to see what he's written, but his handwriting is undecipherable. I wait for him to translate.

"You have five windows upstairs, two in each bedroom and one in the bathroom. There are three downstairs and two entrances, one in the front and one in the back, plus the one from the garage. That's a total of eleven entry points that need to be fitted."

"Fitted?"

"Fitted with security devices. I'd also recommend a glass-break sensor at these front windows and the sliders on the back patio, motion detectors in the hallway and this room, and you also need pet immunity." He makes a few notes on his pad.

"What's that?"

"Just a device that makes sure your dog doesn't set off the motion detectors." He looks up and catches my expression. "What's wrong?"

I look down at the floor, trying to ease my embarrassment. "I'm just worrying about how much this is going to cost me."

He claps me on the back, throwing me forward a little. "Not a penny!" He stands and picks up the chair, swinging it around to put it back where it came from.

"What?" I get to my feet, not sure what he's talking about.

"It's not going to cost you a penny. It's a perk."

"A perk? A perk for what?"

"Anybody who works for Bourbon Street Boys Security gets a home security system as part of the deal."

"Wow. That's . . . generous. I guess." I don't remember telling anyone I was going to work for them, although I guess I did argue pretty forcefully in favor of my qualifications. Why in the heck did I do that?

"Nope, not generous. Smart. In our line of work, you can never be too careful."

My face falls. "That's really not the best way to sell me on the idea of working with you guys, you know."

He scratches his head. "Probably not. But hey, taking pictures? That's nothing. It's practically no risk. None of the people we're dealing with will ever even see you. You'll be like the invisible man."

"Invisible man . . ." I'm thinking about how much risk there might be for the invisible man when Thibault interrupts my thoughts.

"The job pays three hundred bucks an hour, plus expenses. Most jobs have a minimum of five hours of surveillance, give or take, and we do an average of five jobs a month. At least that's what Lucky tells me."

My eyeballs almost fall out of my head. I'm still stuck on the first part of his explanation. Surely I've heard that pay rate wrong. "Say *what*?"

He grins. "Three hundred bucks plus expenses."

"And I'm supposed to believe there's no risk?" My blood pressure is spiking. I could really use three hundred bucks an hour, even if it's just one hour a month, but not if I'm going to get killed doing it.

"Not for the surveillance team. But their role is critical. Without them, we're going into situations blind and deaf. We charge a lot when surveillance is part of the job." He starts walking toward the door. "You should come see the equipment we have. See if you need to order anything else."

"Order? What do you mean?"

"If you're going to be doing the job, you need the right equipment, right?"

"I have cameras."

"Ozzie wants all the equipment to be owned by the company, so if he doesn't already have what you need, he'll buy it."

I stand at the front door as Thibault goes down the steps toward his SUV. "Is he expecting me to call him or something?"

"Maybe." Thibault opens up his back door and pulls out a big case. A second one follows in his other hand. He puts them on the ground and then reaches inside the car once more, taking out a large cardboard box.

I run out to help him.

"What's all this?" I ask, hefting one of the very heavy duffle bags over my shoulder.

"The stuff I need to install your system."

"But I haven't even agreed to take the job yet."

"You will. Trust me. No one says no to Ozzie."

CHAPTER EIGHTEEN

A text makes my phone beep. I'm standing at the alarm panel near my front door, trying to remember all the instructions Thibault gave me an hour ago. If someone comes in the door and insists I turn off the alarm so he can rob or murder me, I'm supposed to type in what four numbers?

Ozzie: *Mind if I stop by around seven?*

I guess he plans to make me that offer I can't refuse tonight. I've already decided, though. I'm not going to work with them. I'm not a spy girl; I'm just a photographer with a special talent for catching a moment on film. Plus I'm not all that excited about being in danger. One night of being followed and sleeping in a warehouse is enough for me.

Me: *If u want. I don't want u to waste ur time though.*
Ozzie: *See you at 7.*

He didn't take the hint. *Sigh.* I look around the room and decide if he's going to come over, I might as well pick up a few things. Like the socks I left on the floor by my desk, for one. I should probably also get a bottle of wine. Not that we're going to wine and dine or whatever, but it would be rude not to have beverages, right? I walk quickly to the door, slide my feet into my sandals, and grab my purse from the floor in the foyer.

The door beeps, reminding me I have to set the alarm. I close the door again and stare at the keypad. Thibault used his own birthday as my code so I wouldn't forget either one. It's only a week away, he said.

I push in the four numbers I think I remember and leave the house, locking the door behind me. Waiting a few seconds, I hear nothing, so I assume it's safe to leave.

The corner store doesn't have the best wine selection in the world, but it's all I have time for. The big store will be too busy to allow me to get me in and out in less than fifteen minutes.

I start with one bottle of merlot and then decide I should buy two, just in case. Just in case what? I have no idea. Just in case he brings a friend, maybe. Not that I expect him to stay for two bottles. That would suggest I'm thinking about getting tipsy and possibly a little handsy. And I'm not doing that, of course. No way. Just the idea makes me feel antsy in a sexy kind of way.

I pull my car into the garage and enter the house through the inside door. The alarm starts beeping immediately. I know I have a few seconds to turn it off, but does that stop me from panicking? No. I feel like I've broken and entered my own home.

"What was that code?" I mumble, staring at the keypad. The loud beeping is too distracting. I can't remember! I yank my phone out of my purse, pressing on the calendar button. "When is your birthday, Thibault?!" I stare at the days of the week, but I can't recall if it's on Saturday or Sunday. I take a wild guess and press in the numbers.

Sirens start going off.

"Dammit!"

Felix comes running around the corner, barking his head off. Better late than never, I guess.

A voice comes out over a loudspeaker somewhere. "BSB Security. Please enter your pass code."

"I don't remember my pass code!" I yell.

My phone rings.

"Hello!" I'm yelling to be heard over the sirens.

"Hello, this is Amy from Bourbon Street Boys Security Home Monitoring Service. Who am I speaking with?"

"This is May. I'm May. I'm the owner of this house." I press in a few more buttons on the keypad, trying the other date, but nothing happens. My eardrums are aching from the sirens and Felix's freak-out.

"Are you okay?"

"I'm fine! I just can't remember the stupid code to put in this thing, dammit!"

"Do you remember your secret password to tell me over the phone?"

My mind races. Thibault told me not to use the dog's name. Too easy to guess, he said. A former pet was okay and a friend's name was fine too. A Disney character was a popular choice. Which one did I choose? I thought of so many options when he was here, but I can't remember which one I finally settled on . . .

"Sahara!" I shout. "Sahara is the secret code!"

"Great. I'm going to shut the siren off and cancel the call that went out to law enforcement."

The siren goes silent and I lean on the wall for support.

"Is there anything else you need?" Amy asks.

"Yes. A shot of tequila."

She laughs. "Maybe some tea might be a better choice."

"If you say so. Thanks."

"You're welcome. Have a great night."

"You too. Bye." I hang up and slide my phone into my purse before bending over to get Felix and calm him down. He's vibrating with energy.

Kissing his head makes him twist around to try and lick me. "Easy, little man. Everything's fine. No bad guys coming in the house today." Now that I've seen the system in action, I'm kind of impressed. Not that I really believe there's a killer still looking for me, but still . . . better safe than sorry, right? At the very least, that siren would make him deaf.

My doorbell rings, sending Felix into spasms of outrage. I put him down so he can run to the door and scare the hell out of whoever is there. I check my watch. It's probably Ozzie, even though it's still ten minutes to seven.

I put the bottles of wine on the counter and go to the door. The peephole confirms my visitor is early. I unlock the door and pull it open.

"Hey."

"Hey," he says, his arms wrapped around two paper bags. Sahara pushes past both of us and goes into the living room, her tail wagging. Felix begins his welcome-to-my-bachelor-pad dance as she turns in small circles, trying to get her nose on his butt.

"You brought gifts," I say, trying to peek into the closest bag.

"I brought dinner. Hope you're hungry."

I hold the door open until he's through and then shut it. He continues through the living room and into the kitchen like he owns the place.

Huh. Not sure how I feel about this impromptu dinner thing. Did he mention it in the text? I verify that he did not.

"How's the security system working out for you?" he asks, unpacking the paper bags. White boxes of various sizes come out and get stacked up on the counter.

Both dogs are at our feet, hoping something will drop.

"Great. Had my first incident already."

He pauses to look at me. "Incident? You had a break-in?"

I laugh a little self-consciously. "Not unless you count me try-ing to get into my own house and forgetting the code as a break-in."

His expression goes a little dark. "You were supposed to choose a code that was easy for you to remember."

"It was easy. Kind of."

"What was it?"

"Thibault's birthday."

Ozzie sighs in disgust. "Figures." He continues with his unpack-ing. At one point he glares at Sahara and motions to the corner of the room. "Go lie down." She immediately moves to do his bidding. Felix follows and curls up next to her.

I'm kind of amazed not only with how well he controls our dogs, but also with how much food he's brought. Is the rest of the team joining us, or what?

"You pick four numbers you can remember, and I'll program them in for you tonight."

I'm feeling a little saucy or something, because I respond with, "What makes you think I want *you* knowing my secret code?"

He just keeps on moving boxes, without even blinking. "I'm no threat to you."

"Yeah, right." It pops out of my mouth before I can stop it. I was imagining his hand touching my body and how I'd completely lose all self-control if that happened, but thank God, he doesn't know that.

He takes the last box out and crushes the bag down. "What's that supposed to mean?"

I shrug. "Nothing." I actually meant that he's a potential threat to my good sense, but if he wants to take it to mean I find him scary, I'm not going to disabuse him of that notion. Maybe it'll give him a nice ego pump. Plus there's no way in hell I'm going to admit to having a crush on him when he's not interested in anything of the sort from me.

He turns to face me, and it looks like he's having trouble selecting the right words. His mouth opens, but nothing comes out. He looks around the room a little and tries again.

"I . . . uh . . . uh . . . I wanted to say that . . . uh . . ." I grab a bottle of wine off the counter and hold it up between us. "Wine anyone?"

"Yeah, sure. One glass." He sounds relieved.

Now who's the superhero? I grin as I open the bottle, take out two glasses, and fill them halfway.

"I can't promise it's any good, but it has alcohol in it." I hand him a glass and hold mine up.

He pauses, staring at me. Then he brings his glass up and touches his to mine. "Cheers."

I can't think of anything more prosaic to say, so instead I do what's expected of me. "Cheers." I take a serious gulp, draining half my glass in one go. I turn so he won't notice my eyes bugging out of my head as I suffer the burn of alcohol in my throat.

"Plates?" he asks.

I open a cupboard and pull two out. Then I pause before shutting the door. "How many will be joining us?"

"No one. It's just the two of us." His voice is gruff.

My heart is skipping beats all over the place. I somehow manage to pull out the correct amount of silverware and napkins, even though my mind is elsewhere. I set the table in my tiny kitchen on autopilot.

Why did he bring dinner? Is this a date, or is he just buttering me up to take the job? I'm not taking that job, no matter how much butter is involved.

"I hope you like lobster," he says.

"What the hell, man." I drop the last silverware on the table with a clang and a crash.

His hand freezes over one of the boxes. "Are you allergic?"

"No, I'm not allergic. I'm pissed."

He steps back away from the food, his arms falling to his sides. I can actually picture him in a military uniform getting ready to salute. "You're angry."

I pout a little. That lobster is calling to me with all its rich, buttery goodness. "No, not angry. Frustrated. I've been checked."

"Checked?"

"Yes. Checked. As in the game of chess. You've out-flanked me."

His mask slips a little. "You like lobster, I take it."

"I don't like lobster, you fool—I love lobster. I'd eat lobster every day if I had the money." I flop down into my chair. "I'm not going to work for you, though. No matter how much clarified butter you have in those little cups." There are several of them. *Dammit.* But what the hell? He expects me to just come work for him because he buys me lobster? It could be a dangerous job. That's what the security system is for, right?

He brings boxes over to the table and starts opening them up. "I have fresh lemon too."

"Of course you do. Jerk."

He chuckles. "I think this is the first time I've ticked a woman off by buying her lobster." He's mixing up some rice pilaf before scooping out a couple helpings, one for each plate.

"I'm not sure why that makes you so happy," I grumble.

"Me neither."

Out comes a huge lobster that floats down onto my plate. Its fire engine–red shell is still glistening from whatever steam did it in. Felix leaves his spot by Sahara and settles in by my feet. The little beast knows me well; he will end up having a taste of everything

that's on my plate, but not because I feed him tidbits on purpose. I have a tendency to drop things.

"Where did you get these monsters?" I ask when the second one comes out and lands on his plate.

"I get them flown in every once in a while from Maine. I have a friend up there."

"Wow. Nice friend." I take another long sip from my wine glass. It's almost empty, so I help myself to some more.

"He owes me."

I wonder what he'd demand of me if I owed him a favor. Just the idea makes me get all antsy again. I know what I'd like to offer.

Whoa! Slow down, nympho! He just walked in the door. Jesus.

Ozzie sits down and pulls his chair in. "Bon appétit." He rips a claw off before I can lift a fork.

CHAPTER NINETEEN

We eat in companionable silence for a few minutes, enough time for me to dip a chunk of lobster in some butter and close my eyes, sighing with happiness. I haven't had this kind of food in a loooong time. I think the last time I had lobster was when I was dating this lawyer named Alfred. He was a putz, but he did love fancy restaurants. I had to break up with him when he refused to eat my baked ziti, though. Food snobbery is not tolerated in my household. Just ask Felix.

Ozzie's voice breaks into my thoughts, cutting them short. "Thibault says you two talked today. About the job."

The last bite of lobster gets stuck in my throat. I have to guzzle the rest of my wine to move it along.

"Yeah," I say, my voice strained. I'm sweating now. Dammit again. Too nervous to tell him straight off the bat that I'm not interested.

Ozzie fills my glass with more dark red wine. I'm dizzy, watching the liquid pour in. Maybe if I drink more, it'll be easier to turn him down. To never see him again. *Ugh.* Who am I trying to kid? I know that it'll never be easy to do that.

"He says you're concerned about your personal safety."

I nod. This is an easy one. Anyone would be concerned in my shoes. That's totally normal. "Yep. Very. I don't wanna die before I'm at least eighty if I can help it. Especially not with bullets involved."

He drinks his wine and watches me over his glass.

"What?" I'm getting paranoid again. "Do I have something on my face?"

He reaches over with a napkin. "Just some butter on your chin." He swipes at me before I can move away. Even though there was a piece of cloth between his hand and my face, I can still feel the heat there. How pitiful am I?

A tiny bit of outrage takes over. It might be the wine talking. "Hey! You're not supposed to do that."

"Do what?" he asks.

"Say there's something on my face." I wipe at my chin several times, making it burn in the process. How embarrassing. How long have I been sitting here with a shiny chin? What a weirdo.

He shrugs. "Okay."

"Okay what?" His unquestioning acquiescence bugs me. I don't think it's a normal reaction for him. Is he mocking me?

"Okay, I won't tell you when you have something like rice on your face."

"Rice too?!" Ack! I wipe my entire lower jaw, praying the grain isn't any higher. *What? Am I throwing food into my eyebrows now too?*

He's laughing.

"You're an idiot." I throw my napkin at him. Then the lobster catches my eye, and I decide I'd rather be eating it than worrying about a piece of rice on my lip. If I'm going to be a weirdo around him, then so be it. It's not like he's ever going to come over here again, and that lobster is too damn good to go to waste.

He goes back to eating his meal, this time smiling.

I revel in the corn muffins that I discover in another box. So sweet. So . . . corny.

"Listen," he says a couple minutes later, "I know I was pretty adamant before that I didn't want you on board, but I've changed my mind. I want you to come to work for us." He pauses. "I can guarantee your safety."

"Why me? And why the change of heart?" I take a bite of my muffin and chew while I watch him, searching his face for any deception. I'm immediately distracted, though, when a new taste hits my tongue. My god, someone put chives in these things. Some genius! Wow. I chew twice as fast, looking forward to my next bite. I might also be humming a little.

"I checked out your work online. Made some inquiries, background checks and so forth. And after talking to Thibault, whose opinion I trust more than anyone's, I think he's right. You'd be good for the team. I'd have to put you on a probationary period, but it shouldn't be a problem. I think you could hack it."

My half-eaten muffin falls from my hand and lands with a clank on my fork and plate. "Hack it?" A few crumbs fly from my mouth, necessitating a quick chewing and a swallow before I can finish. "Of course I could hack it. The question is whether I *want* to hack it." There are bits of cornmeal all around the inside of my mouth. I try not to look like a total psycho corralling all of them together with my tongue.

"Well, you'd need some training first. It's not like you could just step out tomorrow and be ready, but you could get there." He looks me up and down, leaning over to see my bottom half under the table.

I lean back and put my hands in my lap, suddenly nervous. "What are you looking at?"

"Your physique."

"What's my physique have to do with anything?" I can feel my ears starting to burn. I reach up and smooth my hair down, then immediately stop. He's not assessing my hairdo, for God's sake. What's wrong with me? When did I become so self-conscious?

"Everyone on the team is job ready, always. We don't take any slackers."

I wipe my hands together over my plate to get the crumbs off me. "And job ready means . . . ?"

"Means you get trained by Dev, just like the rest of us."

"Because sitting in a car taking pictures is so physically demanding." I don't admit to him that it is actually difficult to stand all day long taking pictures of people you sometimes want to slap. I don't want him to think I'm soft.

"You won't be just sitting in a car." He puts his fork down, wipes his face, and then drops his napkin on the table. "The job comes with full benefits: insurance, 401k, home security, company car, all the equipment you'll need, and references if you want to do side work."

I swallow with difficulty. He's already said the magic word, but he's not done.

"We pay for a complete physical once a year, three weeks of vacation, paid travel when it's a job out of the area, travel expense account, and day care for kids."

"What about dogs?"

He lifts an eyebrow. "We can negotiate."

I chew my lip as I contemplate the offer. It's really kind of silly to stall like this because I already know what I'm going to say.

"So, what do you think?" he prompts. "You want to come work with us at Bourbon Street Boys Security?"

I lift my glass toward him and smile. "You had me at *insurance*."

CHAPTER TWENTY

By the time dinner and dessert are over, I've consumed about two too many glasses of wine. When I stand, the room tilts. Luckily, Ozzie's at the sink, rinsing off dishes, so he doesn't catch me being a drunken lush.

"I'm just going to go freshen up," I say, trying like hell to walk a straight line to the bathroom. Felix is at my heels, making sure to sneak in past the door before I can shut him out.

I stare at my reflection in the mirror and lean my hands on the counter. "Get. Your shit. Together, May Wexler." I splash some water on my face and then freak when I see my mascara making a black trail down my cheek. "Ack! Stop that!"

Felix whines, putting his feet on my leg.

There's a tapping at the door. "You okay in there?"

Oh my god! Oh my god! He thinks I need a toilet rescue!

"I'm fine!" I say with all the fake and casual cheer I can muster. "Couldn't be finer, actually!" Shut up! Shut up! Shut up, idiot! "Be right out!"

Felix barks. I bend down and pet his tiny head, ears, and neck. He goes into a happy trance as I try to get my brain back online.

I need to give myself a pep talk before I leave the bathroom and face Ozzie again.

"Breathe, May. Just breathe. He's your employer now, so you have to stop thinking about dropping your panties every time you look at him. It'll make stakeouts really awkward."

I stand up in a hurry, whispering, "Stakeouts?" I think it's a whisper, anyway. "Will we be doing stakeouts together?"

I pee really quickly, wash my hands, and remove any remaining mascara from my face before leaving the bathroom. I find Ozzie in the living room, looking at some family photos I took before my grandmother died.

"Will I be doing stakeouts?" I ask.

"Maybe."

"Cool. With *whom*?" I hope to impress him with my awesome command of the English language. Even though the room is spinning, I can still manage to keep my subjects and objects straight. *Boom.* Take that, Grammar Girl. Try not to envy me too much.

"Depends. We all take turns."

I nod, like I know what we're talking about. I don't. I really, really don't. I can't remember now why I accepted his job proposal. I think it was the muscles.

"You live alone?" he asks.

I blush like a young girl. "If you're asking if I'm seeing someone, the answer is no."

He turns to look at me. "I was asking if you have a roommate."

"Oh." I have to look away so I can remove my foot from my mouth. There I go again, assuming this is a two-way crush. Idiot. "In that case, the answer is no. I live alone." I turn to face the windows so he won't see my expression, best described as "humiliated."

His voice is suddenly closer. "Are you seeing anyone?"

I freeze, my back to him. Is he behind me? Is he going to touch me? Kiss me? Ravish my body?

"No." My voice is barely a whisper.

"Good." I can tell from his voice he's near the front door now. "That makes it easier."

I spin to face him, not quite losing my balance, but coming close. "Easier for what?"

He opens the door, jingling his keys in his hand. "Easier to make demands on your time. We work late hours sometimes."

He and Sahara are through the entrance and going down the front porch stairs before I realize what's happening.

He's leaving! Why so soon?! I'm still buzzing! This party's just getting started, yo!

I race to the door and throw it open wide. "Hey! You! You can't just wine me and dine me and not . . . and not . . ." Oh my god! I almost said "sixty-nine me"! Ack! Alert, alert! Send the fire engines! I'm on fire!

"And not what?" he's standing at his door, smiling at me. Sahara's already in the bed of the truck.

"Say good-bye!" I shout before slamming the door shut. Holy shit.

I run back into my living room and grab my hair on both sides. "Oh my god! What did I just do?!" Snatching a pillow off the nearby couch, I fling it across the room. But just one won't do; I'm too embarrassed. I grab another and another, winging them as far and as fast as I can. Felix runs for cover, hiding under the coffee table.

The couch cushions are next, those bastards. I flip them upside down and sideways. *Ugh*, it's so not satisfying to mess up a couch cushion. I want to break something, but I hate breaking things because then I have to clean them up, so instead I mess up my hair. When I'm done, I'm certain my hair looks like it got caught in a blender. Phew. Using all that energy to destroy my hairdo and my surroundings has actually helped me calm down a notch.

"Okay. It's okay." I'm trying to convince myself as I breathe like an angry bull. "I didn't say, 'sixty-nine me.' I said, 'say good-bye.' Totally reasonable. Totally normal, right? People should say good-bye when they leave after sharing lobster and wine. Wine me, dine me, say good-bye to me. That's the polite thing to do."

The doorbell distracts me from my rationalizing. I walk to the foyer, tripping over one of my pillows on the way. I land on the door and barely get it open. I'm half bent over, huffing and puffing like I just ran a mile or five. When I see who it is, I pull the door open wider.

Ozzie is standing there, a giant mountain of muscles and cool. One of his eyebrows goes up when he takes in my appearance.

I stand up straight and lift my chin. I have to try and salvage what little pride I have left with some fake bravado. "Did you forget something?"

He glances first at my hair and then my mouth.

"Yeah. I forgot to say good-bye."

And then something crazy happens.

He reaches out and takes me by the waist, easily drawing me to him.

My lips part as his face gets closer and closer. I can't breathe. I can't talk. I can't even think straight.

"Good-bye," he whispers against my mouth, just before he presses his lips against mine.

Melting. I'm melting, just like that lobster butter, into his arms, inside my body. Everything is going hot and boneless.

He, on the other hand, is as solid as a rock. *Everywhere.*

What is happening?!

I've barely tasted any of him, and he's pulling away again.

When I realize I'm looking a little too wasted, I get control of myself and stand on my own. His hand falls away, and I want to cry with loneliness. Holy drunk girl going on here.

My hands are shaking when I reach up to push my hair back from my face. I can be cool. I can handle this . . . whatever it is. Maybe he kisses all his new employees. I'm not going to be the first one to make a big deal out of it, if that's the case.

"Well . . . good-bye then," I say, staring at his shoulder. I can't bring my gaze any higher.

He walks backward two steps before he turns around and walks to his truck. "See you around, Little Bo Peep." He climbs up into the vehicle and shuts the door, reversing out of the driveway in mere seconds.

I wait until he's out of sight before I close the door and fall to the floor in a puddle of goo.

"Oh my god, *he kissed me!!*"

CHAPTER TWENTY-ONE

After receiving instructions from Ozzie via text again, I show up for my first day of work two days later on Monday at the warehouse, leaving Felix to fend for himself at home. He's used to it. I've had plenty of full days at the studio. I'm pretty sure he naps the entire time I'm gone.

I'm kind of surprised I'm able to find the warehouse, even though I was just here not that long ago. It seems like everything passed by in a blur. I'm completely over Ozzie kissing me already. It was nothing more than just too much wine. I'm not even going to look at him funny when I see him again. He's my boss now, and because he's my boss, I will not ever be touching his lips or his gorgeous body again.

When I pull up to the warehouse, Thibault motions for me to bring my car inside. Everyone else has parked outside.

"Is there something wrong?" I ask after rolling down my window.

"Just helping you keep a low profile. Park it over there." He gestures to a dark corner on the far right of the building. I didn't even notice it existed when I was here before. This place is huge.

When I emerge from my car, everyone but Ozzie is standing around in the middle of the big space. He's nowhere to be seen.

Sunlight streams through the open wall of the warehouse, but it's slowly cut off as the big door rolls closed.

"Welcome, everyone," Thibault says. "Today is May's first day with us, so I thought we'd give her a little primer about what we do before we have our morning meeting."

I nod at everyone, receiving nods in return. Dev gives me a smile, as does Lucky. Toni's more serious. I kind of respect her for that. She looks all business, and from what I can tell, she's doing well in a man's kind of world. I wonder how high she can kick in those black leather boots she's wearing.

"Who's first?" asks Dev.

"You are." Thibault nods at him. "Just give her the basics."

Dev rubs his hands together. "Okay, batter up." He makes a quick bow. "Consider me your PE teacher."

I smile, remembering the chubby balding man who always wore puffy sweat pants and carried a basketball under his arm at my high school. Mr. Pritchard was so nice.

Dev's expression goes dark. "Only not like any PE teacher you've ever had before."

"You can say that again," mumbles Toni.

"Let's see what you got." He gestures for me to move closer. "Come on over here and hit me."

I laugh for a second before I realize he's serious. So is everyone else.

"Hit you?" I hug my purse to my side, glad I left Felix home today. Felix doesn't like violence of any kind, and I can't say as I blame him.

"Yes. Hit me." He gestures at his chest. "Give it your best shot."

I frown. "I'm not going to hit you."

"Why not?" He bends at the waist a little, getting his head more level with mine.

"Because . . . I don't like hitting people."

"What about people who are getting ready to hit you?" He reaches over and grabs a stick from a nearby table and holds it up. "You like to hit them?"

"If you hit me with that stick, you're going to be very sorry." My hand slides slowly down into my purse. I'm not exactly panicked right now, because I feel confident that Dev is a nice guy and he's just messing around, but that doesn't mean I won't taze his stupid ass if he hits me with that weapon. What kind of welcoming committee is this, anyway? I was kind of expecting coffee and donuts, not whacks with a stick.

He smiles. "Good. She's got attitude. I like it." He moves forward.

"I'm not kidding, Dev." I take a step back. He looks serious, but he can't be, right? I look around at everyone else, and they're watching us closely. None of them looks distressed or amused. This is business to them.

He moves quicker than I expect; two strides has him right in front of me. The stick goes up.

I cower down as it descends, closing my eyes and bracing for impact. *Please don't hit me, please don't hit me, please don't hit me.*

It stops just next to my arm, and I open one eye first to make sure it's okay.

"You're not moving," he says. He looks frustrated.

Now both of my eyes are open, and I'm standing straight. "No, I'm not. I'm hoping this is all going to stop very soon."

Toni snorts.

I catch the mocking expression on her face, and it instantly gets me all fired up.

Forget this cowardly lion act. What the hell, man. I didn't come here to get hit with a stick. Who does he think he is, standing there threatening me like that? Does he know I had lobster with the boss two days ago *and* shared a hot kiss on my doorstep?

Dev moves in closer. "This isn't going to stop until you see how serious it is."

"Okaaaay." I look up into his eyes, my finger flipping the safety button off on my Taser inside my purse. Bastard. Making me use my Taser. These cartridges are expensive. I know because I had to replace one when I accidentally shot myself in the foot one time. Getting tazed is also painful as all hell, so he's definitely not going to be happy with me after.

"Now listen up, Little Bo Peep . . . I'm going to hit you with this stick unless you do something to defend yourself." He's looking down at me with pity in his eyes. Everyone else is dead silent. "This isn't a game. We play to live. That's how it works. Slackers get injured, and I won't have that happening when I'm in charge."

"I really wish you wouldn't do this," I say, sounding as weak as possible. Part of it is an act, and part of it is really how I feel. Being a badass has never been part of my repertoire. I hate that I'm being pushed into this. Why is this happening on my first day? This is the worst orientation day I've ever had.

"I'll try not to leave too big of a bruise." The stick goes up, almost above his head and starts its descent. This time I'm sure he's not going to stop.

I jerk my hand out of my purse and shove the Taser toward his chest. Some kind of crazy war cry leaves my lips as I cringe and wait for the pain to come from the stick. "Awwwoooooahhh!"

My whole body clenches up and my finger squeezes the trigger on the Taser. The prongs fire out of the end of it, and all hell breaks loose.

Dev's eyes bug out of his head.

He drops the stick and it clatters on the ground near our feet.

The rat-tat-tat-tat-tat of several thousand volts of electricity makes a nice beat for the convulsions that start to rack his body a few seconds later.

"What the hell is going on down here!" yells Ozzie from the top of the stairs.

"Holy shit, she tazed him!" Lucky's stuck in a daze of confusion.

Dev grunts, his eyes roll back in his head, and he starts to go down.

I jump to the side to avoid getting squashed. The wires coming out of the end of my Taser stretch right along with me.

Lucky leans over and grabs Dev's arm to slow his descent.

Both of them fall into a heap on the ground, Dev on top of his stupid stick, Lucky on top of Dev, who's groaning like a wounded elephant, and my wires tangled up with both of them.

I hug my purse to my chest, my Taser in one hand, my keys in the other.

"Oh my god, I can't believe it! She actually tazed his ass!" Toni starts to laugh.

"That ain't funny, man." Thibault is shaking his head, first looking at Dev and then at me.

"I'm sorry. I'm really sorry." I can barely get the words out, I'm so embarrassed. I feel terrible. "The trigger was way more sensitive than I expected it to be." I should probably get it checked. Two accidental Taserings can't be good. I swear I wasn't really going to taze him. I was planning to just scare him into not hitting me. *Dammit.*

Lucky gets up and rolls Dev onto his back. The wires are still connecting him to my gun. Yep, the barbs are definitely in his skin, not just his clothes. Oops.

"Why in the hell is Dev lying on the ground with Taser barbs in his chest?" Ozzie is standing a few feet away with his hands on his hips.

"We were giving her an intro," Toni says, "just like you told us to."

"I'm pretty sure I didn't tell anyone to get her so fired up she'd shoot Dev." He scrubs at the back of his head. "You all right, man?"

Dev tries to answer, but the only things that will come out are grunts and groans. His eyes roll up into his head.

"Ozzie, I'm sorry." I can look at his chin. Not his eyes, but his chin. It's close enough that probably no one will notice I'm a chicken. "I didn't mean to hurt him."

His words come out as a growl. "Don't you apologize." He glares at Thibault. "You're the one who should be talking right now."

"All right, fine, fine. I take full responsibility." Thibault has his hands up in surrender. "We talked about it before she got here and decided we'd just see if she had any self-defense instincts."

"And what have you decided after your little experiment?" Ozzie looks at each person individually.

Toni shrugs. "I'd say she passed." She turns away so Ozzie won't see her smiling.

"I think we probably should have come at this from another angle," says Lucky.

"Oh, you think?" Ozzie gestures at Dev. "Get him up, and get those damn barbs out of his chest. And if he whines, slap him in the head."

"You got it, boss." Lucky braces his legs to help Dev to his feet. After a few stumbles, they're both standing, Lucky with his arm under Dev's shoulder to give him support. After I remove the cartridge from my Taser and give it to Lucky, they begin to walk away, but stop after a few steps. Dev turns his head and speaks over his shoulder. His words are a little slurred.

"I wanna re-mash. She trick't me."

Ozzie growls. "Bullshit, she tricked you. She got one over on you. Big difference."

I could swear I hear pride in Ozzie's voice, but I'm not going to let it go to my head. I feel terrible. I can't think of a worse way to start off my new job. Dev is never going to forgive me.

Ozzie jabs his thumb at the stairs. "When you're done goofing around out here, we have a meeting upstairs that needs to happen."

"No better time than the present." Toni holds up her hand as she walks by. "High-five, sister. Well played."

I reach up and slap her hand delicately. I don't want to look too enthusiastic about putting holes in Dev's chest and shooting him up with all those volts.

Thibault comes over and stops in front of me. "You mind if I take that from you?" He holds out his hand and looks down at my cartridgeless weapon.

I put the Taser in his palm. "Sure. Sorry about shooting your friend."

Thibault smiles. "Don't apologize. He got what he had coming to him. Next time he'll think twice about lifting a stick to you."

"I'm hoping there won't be a next time."

"Oh, there will be—you can trust me on that." He walks away to climb the stairs.

What the hell? He's going to try to hit me again? I'm going to need my Taser back. I wonder if the cartridges are a legitimate business expense. I don't think I should have to pay out of my paycheck for protection against nutty colleagues.

Ozzie and I are left on the ground floor together, standing a few feet apart.

"I guess this is where I welcome you to Bourbon Street Boys and tell you where to hang your coat."

I laugh a little. "And I think this is where I'm supposed to say I'm glad to be here and can't wait to get started."

He smiles. "How about we start over and do this thing the right way this time?"

"Sounds good to me."

He points to the exercise machines. "You can hang your coat anywhere over there you can find a hook. Welcome to Bourbon Street Boys. Follow me. We have a meeting in five."

I walk behind him, my face on fire. He's being nice, and he's not mad I tazed his employee. Maybe today won't suck after all.

"I'm really glad to be here. Can't wait to get started."

He chuckles but says nothing in response. We climb the stairs together and enter the room full of ninja swords.

CHAPTER TWENTY-TWO

Everyone has a spot around the table where we had soup the other night. There are a few folders in front of each person and a pitcher with ice water in the center of it all. My glass is already full, courtesy of Dev.

"Peace offering," he says, placing it in front of me and giving me a wink.

"Peace offering accepted," I say, taking a sip and winking back. My stress level drops down a few notches. Maybe he's not going to hold a grudge against me after all.

"Okay, so let's take a look at the Harley file," Ozzie says, turning the cover back on the folder in front of him.

I open my copy and see a memo there. A quick scan of the paper tells me that the New Orleans Police Department has retained these consultants—the Bourbon Street Boys Security firm—to help them infiltrate a local gang and try to gather data that might lead to some arrests. The operation is termed the Harley Op because that was Ozzie's nickname when he wore the beard and leather.

I have to bite my lip to keep from giggling. That beard was so awful. I steal a quick glance at him to see if I can picture him wearing it again, but I can't. He's too cute now to be that ugly man who saved my life last week.

"As you all know, due to unforeseen circumstances"—everyone but Ozzie looks at me—"we had to take me out of the picture. Thibault and I were talking about pulling out entirely, but we decided that might not need to happen." He looks up. "If we can save this project, I'd like to do that. We have a lot invested."

I make a mental note to ask someone exactly how it was that I screwed things up. Just by me being in that bar everything went south? I doubt it. It was probably that beard. Even criminals know something that ugly can't be right.

Lucky speaks up. "We've got nobody on the inside, though. How are we going to get any info at all?"

Ozzie closes the folder and looks up at me, putting his hands down flat on the table in front of him. "I was hoping we could try again to gather some info via surveillance. I know the detectives on the case tried before, but I think we should budget some of our own work in on this one."

Oh, poo. I think this is where I come in. Is this going to be my penance for screwing up his silly beard costume? I squirm in my chair, with all the attention on me.

"It's possible," Lucky says. "What'd you have in mind?"

"The night you were supposed to show up and be my backup,"—Ozzie glares at Dev—"I learned the location of one of their big runners. It's over off Burgundy. I swung by this weekend. It has possibilities."

"You thinking stills or video?" Thibault asks.

"Both. And maybe some ears too. We'll see. I need Toni's opinion."

She nods. "You got it. When?"

"You and Bo Peep can head over there today if you can manage it." He's looking at Toni, not me.

I raise my hand.

Everyone looks at me like I'm crazy.

"You have something you want to add?" Ozzie asks.

"Actually, I have a question. And feel free to call me May, by the way." I smile. "I'm just wondering, if I were to go with Toni today, what exactly would we be doing?" I draw an invisible letter M on the table in front of me, trying to act as cool as possible. If it requires that I carry a weapon, I'm not doing this thing he's talking about, whatever it is.

"Just a quick drive-by," Toni says. "It's no big deal. It's just to get the lay of the land, see what kind of property it is, best places to set up to watch things going down, stuff like that."

"And by going down, you mean . . . ?" I draw an invisible A and a Y on the tabletop to complete my little distraction. I will not freak out. I will not let my face burn bright red.

She shrugs. "Whatever. If they have people stopping by, business going on, birthday parties—whatever."

I nod, wondering if she's purposely glossing over the more dangerous situations or if there just aren't any. It sounds innocent enough. Driving by. What would that take? Five seconds?

"I can probably manage that," I say, nodding with confidence.

Ozzie slides a second folder out from under the first. "Good. Moving on. We got a new project, this one from a private party. It's the Blue Marine Operation folder there in front of you. Lucky, I'm going to put you on it for now. Let me know if we need to hire outsiders."

"Outsiders?" I ask.

"People who have skills we don't," Thibault explains.

"Like what?"

"Mainly computer experts," Lucky says. "I can manage the financials, but when it comes to . . . getting inside things . . ."—he wiggles his eyebrows—"I'm still at basic level."

I nod. My sister is a computer guru, but she's so busy at work, she never has time for side jobs. She's always threatening to quit and go freelance, but I know she never will because she's too afraid of not making enough money to support the kids. Her ex can't always be counted on for his part of the bills. Not because he's not in town, but because he's a lowlife asshole who'd rather spend the money on his new girlfriend than his old ex wife and kids.

"What's the job?" Dev asks.

"Corporate embezzlement. Marine accessories company. Not a lot of money involved from the initial look of things, but you never know."

They all nod, like there's some inside story that goes with that comment.

"Anything else?" Thibault asks, pushing out his chair.

"Just Bo Peep. You all know who she is. She's on a ninety-day probationary period, so make sure you do what you can as soon as possible to get her up to speed."

"I'll show her the equipment," Toni says, nodding at me.

I nod back, leaving the Bo Peep comment on the table for later. I think I like May "the Meatball" Wexler better. It's less insulting. Kind of.

Everyone stands. I quickly follow suit.

Ozzie speaks again. "May, stay behind for a minute."

"Okay. Sure thing." No, I'm not freaking out about being alone with him up here while everyone else leaves and goes downstairs.

I act like it's critically important that my folders are lined up on all four sides while the team files out. Thibault is the last one to leave, and he closes the kitchen door behind him.

Ozzie clears his throat, so I look up.

"Listen, I don't want to keep you, but I just needed to . . . uh . . . apologize."

He regrets what he did. I know he does. A sharp pain stabs me in the heart. Ouch.

"Apologize?" My tone is completely casual. "For what?"

"For the other night." His expression is darker than I'd like. Yuck, it hurts.

"Don't be silly; there's nothing to apologize for." I wave my hand between us and scrunch up my face, acting like he's crazy.

"I was out of line, and I shouldn't have done what I did."

"The lobster was a little over the top, but I forgive you. Can I get going now? I'm anxious to do this drive-by thing with Toni. I think she and I are going to get along great." I leave my folders on the table and start walking toward the door. I'm going to save my tears of regret for later tonight when I'm drinking wine alone.

"I'm not talking about the lobster."

"Lobster, wine, a kiss good-bye—whatever. It's all the same to me." I get through the door and shut it behind me before he can see my face crumple.

By the time I'm at the door with the digital lock, I'm almost able to hold it together. I've been through this before, where a guy messes around with me and then regrets it later. I guess I can be irresistible sometimes, and this is the price I pay. Dammit. I really kind of liked him too.

The door opens before I can start to panic about the code I don't know.

Dev is standing there, startled by seeing me. "You're not going to shoot me again, are you?"

"Not unless you're about to hit me with a stick." I gesture at the door lock. "Am I allowed to know the code?"

"Oh, yeah, sorry about that. I guess you need this one and the one outside the door here. You'll also need one to open the big door outside, the gun safe, and the camera locker."

I dig around in my purse, looking for a pen.

"Can't write 'em down. You have to memorize 'em." He points to the pad. "This one is my door, because I'm the one who collects the swords you see in this room. So the code for this door is Dev 1. Letters are on the number keys." He shuts the door and gestures at the pad. "Go ahead and give it a shot."

I push in the keys, and the door clicks.

He claps me on the back, throwing me forward. "Well done, Bo Peep. The other side of the door is Thibault's domain. The code for the main warehouse room is T-B-O-1. Get it?"

I nod. We go outside and shut the door behind us. "Try it," Dev orders.

I type in T-B-O-1, and the lock clicks.

"You're on a roll, baby." Dev opens the door but lets it shut. He points from up where we are to a keypad down near the big door that lets the cars in. "Keypad over there belongs to Toni. Why? I don't know. The code is T-O-N-1. You can close up when you leave. The rest of us have automatic openers. You won't get one until you're out of your probationary period."

"What about the gun safe and those other places?" I ask as we go downstairs.

"Toni can give you those. I have to beat it out of here."

"Someone waiting on a stick to the forehead out there?" I laugh at my own lame joke.

"Yeah, my son. My mom could only watch him for two hours today, so I've gotta get over there and take him back."

I pause, surprised at his answer. "You have a son? How old?"

"He's four, and a handful and a half." He grins with pride. "But I wouldn't have it any other way."

A lightbulb pops on in my head. So that's what he meant when he was complaining to Ozzie that he has responsibilities. As I recall, Ozzie wasn't very understanding about that excuse. Surely he knows Dev meant his son . . .

"Good luck out there." Dev holds up a hand, and I try to high-five him, but miss.

He punches me lightly on the upper arm twice. "Two for missing. Try again."

I do better this time, and he winks. "You'll get there." He's jogging across the floor before I can respond.

"Don't make me taze you again!"

He laughs as he climbs into his car, and I smile all the way across the room to where Toni is waiting with a scowl on her face.

CHAPTER TWENTY-THREE

"Whenever you're done playing grabass, I can show you the lockers you'll need access to."

I'm too stunned to answer. I thought we were going to be friends. I guess I thought wrong. Poo. I hate chick drama, especially at work.

She points to the gun safe I noticed on my last trip here. "These are the weapons we use from time to time. I don't always carry, but when I do, I get my piece from in here. The code is C-O-L-T-4-5."

"Original." I'm too cranky to play nice now. Why was she so rude to me? Was she only being nice before because everyone was watching? That's going to suck if that's the case. I'm about to be stuck in a car with her for I don't know how long. Too long, probably.

She pulls the door open to reveal more weapons than I've ever seen in one place, outside of an action flick.

"Wow. That's a lot of firepower."

She points, giving me a tour. "Handguns there; rifles and shotguns there. That one's not exactly legal, so don't get that one out without talking to Ozzie first."

"Oh, don't worry, I won't be taking any of these out *ever*."

"Sure you will. Everyone here gets firearm training. We do refresher shooting once a month after we're certified."

"Certified?"

"Certified marksmen. Ozzie insists on it. He doesn't want any of us shooting the wrong guy."

Most of the energy is missing from my voice. "That's nice. I guess."

"Grenades there . . . they're not live until that pin is pulled out, but I don't recommend you touch them."

"Don't worry, I won't." My eyes roll up into my head. These people are crazy. Why am I here again? Oh yeah. The money.

"Bullets there. The boxes are labeled, so make sure you grab the right box for the right gun."

"Yeah, okay." This is a complete joke. As if I'd know what the right bullet for a gun would be. Ha. Not gonna happen. The only thing I'm shooting is a camera.

"Knives, nunchucks, singlesticks there, brass knuckles in that small drawer." She turns partway to face me. "Any questions?"

"Yeah. Where are the rocket launchers?"

"We keep those in a separate location."

She leaves me standing there with my mouth hanging open like an idiot, talking as she walks. I have no idea if she was serious or not.

"Other gear is in these lockers over here." She throws the doors of one open. "Gas masks, Kevlar vests, gloves, helmets, boots." She closes that door and opens another. "Camping gear for stakeouts that aren't in the city." That door closes, and she moves over to a locked closet. "And inside here is your domain. Lucky already changed the code on it." She gestures at the lock and smiles deviously. "Guess what it is."

I walk up slowly, eyeing the stupid lock, wondering what the big joke is. "How many digits?"

143

"Four."

I sigh heavily. Her face is giving everything away. I press on the alpha keys, one at a time: P-E-E-P. The lock clicks open, and Toni's smile falls away.

"Ha-ha, very funny." I pull the door open, gasping when I see the contents.

"You like?" she asks. She's back to smiling again.

"I like a *lot*." I reach in and pick up a camera I've wanted to own for the last five years but haven't been able to afford. "Holy mother of camera gods . . ."

"Yeah. Ozzie doesn't skimp. He says we're only as effective as our tools."

I smile, thinking about Dev. "What's up with Dev's car, then?"

"The Phoenix?" she grins. "You can put like ten dead bodies in the trunk. We've used it a ton since he bought it last year."

I almost drop the camera.

She takes it away from me gently and puts it back on the shelf. "Easy, Bo Peep, I was just kidding. Kind of." She shuts the door and makes sure the lock is engaged. "I'll let you play in there later. Now we have to go before all the bad guys wake up."

She leaves me standing at the locker. "Bad guys?"

She's climbing up into Thibault's SUV, expecting me to go around to the passenger side. The motor is already running.

"Shouldn't we bring a camera or something?"

"Nope." She answers me through her open window. "This is just eyes-on recon, nothing more."

I hold onto the handle above the door to get inside. The SUV is higher off the ground than it looks. "Eyes-on recon. Eyes-on recon." I'm repeating the expression so I can use it later in conversation. I'm starting to hate the fact that I stick out like a stupid Bo Peep in this group. Seeing all that camera and video equipment makes me want to give this thing a serious whirl.

"Buckle up," she says, adjusting the rearview mirror.

I just get the belt clicked into place when she throws the car into reverse and tears out of the warehouse. Grabbing the handle is the only thing that keeps me from falling into her lap.

"Holy crap, where's the fire?"

The tires screech a little as she swings the car around to go forward. "No fire. I just don't see the need to drive like a grandma."

I frown as I sink down into my seat. Great. I'm a grandma Bo Peep. How much farther out of my element can I get?

CHAPTER TWENTY-FOUR

Turns out, pretty far. I can get really, really far out of my element, hanging out with Toni for half a day.

We started out in a seriously scary part of town I never want to go back to and ended up in something worse. What do you call a place where you see people actually dealing drugs in broad daylight? Hell?

This is the place, believe it or not, where I'm supposed to set up some surveillance—with Toni's help—so we can try to gather some information from the scumbags who live here. Or deal their crack here or whatever it is they're doing. Ha! Crazy town! All I know is I've seen way too many pants hanging down past way too many butts today. Don't any of these guys own belts?

"So, what do you think?" Toni asks as we head back to the BSB lair, making her way through the Port, through the maze of commercial buildings and warehouses. "Doable?"

I shrug. "I suppose. I didn't really see what you have for equipment, but in theory, sure." Anyplace can be photographed, watched, spied on. Whether you can do it without getting killed is the question. I have my doubts about the locations we scouted today, but

Ozzie guaranteed my safety, so I'm going to focus on that and not the handguns I saw in people's waistbands.

"Wait 'til you see our van." She's grinning and squeezing the steering wheel. Two seconds later she jerks it to the right, and we take a corner way too fast. The tires complain. Again. She must go through a new set every couple months, the way she leaves rubber behind wherever she goes.

"What van?" I ask.

"Eyeballs on wheels. It's where we monitor everything when we don't have feet on the ground."

"Feet on the ground?"

She pulls up to the warehouse door and grabs a small black remote that she taps a number into. "When we're on foot and not in the van." She sighs, like she's tired of dealing with the lady on the short bus.

It's very disheartening to know I'm such a disappointment. I'm pretty sure I failed my trial today with her. It should be telling that I gain a point electrocuting her friend and lose a point not being a crazy driver with a death wish. I should probably not hang out with her too much.

"Who does that work?" I ask, trying to keep the conversation going. "The being-on-foot stuff?" I don't see anyone in the warehouse, and I'm afraid we're going to be stuck with each other for another two hours. Gotta keep things flowing.

"Sometimes Thibault, sometimes me. Maybe you one day."

"Me?" I can't keep the panic from my voice.

"Not now. Not until you get some serious training." She drives into the warehouse, shifts into park, and shuts the engine off. "Maybe after about six months you'll be ready." She opens her door and gets out.

"Six months?" I get out too, a little offended. "I'm not that out of shape." I pinch my side just to be sure. There can't be more than an extra inch there. Inch and a half maybe, if I've recently been on a Ben & Jerry's splurge.

She's walking up the stairs. "You won't know how out of shape you are until you start working with Dev. Trust me. None of us did."

I flex my bicep and smile with pride at the little lump that comes up to say hello. Toni has no idea what she's talking about. I lift cameras all day long without complaining. I stand on my feet for hours at a time. Three months. That's all it'll take me to become a badass. *Ka-chow*, baby—look out!

A badass? Where did that idea come from? I don't want to be a badass, do I? I let my arm fall back down to my side as I picture that man coming after me in his car and shooting at me again, and I nod. Yes. I want to be a badass. I want to be someone who won't be afraid when she walks out the front door of her house, when she sees someone just drive by her house slowly, for God's sake. I want to be the kind of badass that Ozzie finds attractive.

"Oh my god," I say out loud to myself. "Seriously, May, you need to get laid."

"What's that?" says a voice off to my right.

I look to the left instead. Nope. I'm not even going to acknowledge this person who might have just heard me. This isn't happening.

"Were you talking to me?" Ozzie comes out of the dark shadows and walks in my direction.

I jerk my head over to see him. "Who me? No, I didn't say anything. Just reminding myself of some chores I have to do later." Namely, talk to a therapist because I'm crazy.

"I thought I heard you say you need to get paid."

I point at him in a hurry. "I did! I *did* say that. Wow, you have great hearing." Thank you, God!

"I just need you to fill out a form with all your details, and then Lucky can get you on the payroll. Remember to keep all your receipts. He'll show you the format for turning them in at the end of the month."

I nod, using my very serious expression. Keeping this all business will erase all those sexy thoughts that continue to try to pop into my head when he's around. My inner poet takes over:

Muscles, muscles, hard butts and pecs,
Why must I keep my libido in check?

Ack! Go away, sexy thoughts!

"How'd your first day go?" he asks.

This is good. Focus on work. "Good, I guess. Am I done?" I've only been here a total of three hours. I can't imagine he considers that full-time.

"You just have one more thing to do, and then you can go."

I hitch my purse up on my shoulder. "Great. What is it?"

"A workout."

"A workout as in . . . like at the gym?"

Ozzie nods over at the equipment on the other side of the room. "Our gym, yeah."

"Okay." I rub my hands together and look around. "Where's Dev? He's my trainer, right?"

"Normally he would be, but today he's recuperating from a Taser strike."

"Oh." Aaaand the guilt is back.

"So you get me as your trainer instead."

Aaaaand the sexy is back.

He pulls off his sweatshirt to reveal a very tight sleeveless T-shirt underneath. It goes way too perfectly with his very revealing gym shorts.

Quick! Evasion tactics, engage!

"I, uh, didn't bring my workout clothes."

"That's all right. We have some for you." He points to a locker. "In there. Get changed. I'll be back in five."

And with that, he leaves me in the warehouse alone to work myself up into a righteous panic. I don't know how I'm going to watch his muscles bulge and not throw myself at him. This is going to be a total test of willpower.

CHAPTER TWENTY-FIVE

Turns out, it's not such a hard test of my willpower to keep my hands off Ozzie while we work out together. The minute he starts making me strain and grunt to press things with my legs and lift some stupid dumbbells up into the air, all his attractive qualities take a back seat to his military hardheaded *un*attractiveness. I'm surprised he didn't trade his beard in for a tiny, square mustache.

"Give me one more!" he yells. "Come on! Push it out!"

"Errrrrgh!" I know someone who won't be invited to the birth of my first child. Push it out, my ass.

"One more. Come on—you can do it. Push it!"

"I already did one more!" I huff and puff as the weights dangle from my limp arms. Everything burns. Everything. Even my butt muscles are on fire.

"You aren't tapped out. Come on—I see one more in your eyes. Lift."

"What you see in my eyes is a death threat." I try to lift the weights anyway. Mainly because the door at the top of the stairs just opened, and Dev is coming down. I'm afraid if he sees any weakness in me, he'll come after me twice as hard once he's recuperated, which rumor says will be tomorrow. He has a decidedly springy step right now.

"Come on, *lift*!" Ozzie shouts in my face.

"Get away from me!" I shout-grunt as my arms start to go up. I'd kick him if I could, but I need to focus all my potential energy on my biceps. My body is slowly bending backward, trying to compensate for my lack of arm strength.

"Bad form! Stand up straight!"

More sweat droplets pop out on my face as I stop bending and try to use just my arms to get the twenty pounds up past my belly button.

"I can't . . . I can't . . ."

He puts a single finger under each dumbbell. "Here, I'll help."

I want to scream at his ridiculous offer of so-called help, but I can't. I have no extra energy for anything. I'm so afraid I'm going to toot; I have my butt cheeks squeezed together as tight as they'll go, and that leaves very little extra strength for lifting these twenty-pound weights up to my shoulders for the twelfth time.

"Eeeerrrrrr!"

"That's it!" he yells. "You got this!"

Dev stops when he's next to Ozzie and nods. "You got this. You got it."

My muscles are crying, begging me to stop, but I keep forcing them to perform anyway, because if I don't, I'll leave here with my head hung in shame. I know everyone at BSB gives this training everything they've got, and I can't be Bo Peep forever. My arms are trembling with my effort. *Please don't let me toot, please don't let me toot.*

The weights finally obey my command and reach the apex of the upper swing. Ozzie grabs them from my hands and lifts them away from me like they're made of feathers, releasing me from the prison that is his workout. My arms feel like they're going to float right up into the atmosphere with all the heaviness gone. Then when I drop them to my sides they feel like they have fifty-pound weights tied to the wrists.

"That's good for your first day," he says, placing the weights on a rack with several others of various poundage.

Thank God, I can finally unclench my butt cheeks now that the threat of accidental tootage has passed. Bending over, I rest my hands on my knees. Sweat follows the law of gravity and drips *up* my face and goes into my eyes. Wow, that stings. I stand and try to blink the pain away. I'm sure it looks like I'm crying, but I'm too tired to wipe the sweat away.

"Tough workout?" Dev asks. He looks like he's barely holding in his laughter.

"Pretty tough." I shrug, noticing how much effort it takes to lift shoulders that no longer have any strength left in them. I eye my car, wondering if I'm going to be able to drive it now. That stick shift is going to be a problem. Maybe I can call a cab without anyone noticing. I wish I hadn't bought such a brightly painted car. No way are they going to miss it being left overnight in the corner of their warehouse.

Ozzie pats me on the shoulder. "We'll give you one day off and then start again Wednesday."

I flick some sweat off my temple with a trembling finger. "No need to wait. I can go again tomorrow." This whole badass thing is coming from deep down inside my most primitive self. I'm pretty sure there's a bucketload of adrenaline coursing through my veins, released from the feelings I was just having a few minutes ago that I was going to die from weight lifting.

"We'll see how you feel tomorrow." Dev claps me on the back and then pulls his hand away in disgust when he realizes how wet it is now.

Ozzie's all business again. "Tomorrow I need you to go in the van with Toni and Thibault and see what you can do about setting up over there."

"Operation Ugly Beard?" I ask.

Dev laughs and then stops immediately when Ozzie glares at him.

"Harley," Ozzie says. "It's Harley, not ugly beard."

I mumble under my breath as I pick up my sweaty towel. "Could've fooled me."

"Oh man." Dev is smiling, rubbing his hands together. "I can't wait for our next workout."

His happiness is infectious. "Oh, yeah?" I wipe my face and neck off with the towel, trying not to cringe at how gross it is. It smells like metal. "How come?"

"Because, you've got a lot of piss and vinegar. I think I'm going to enjoy breaking you."

I snort. "Yeah, right. Whatever." I'm talking tough, but I'm actually on the verge of crying. Why am I setting myself up as a challenge to the team's personal trainer? I never saw myself as a glutton for punishment before, but now I'm starting to wonder how well I actually know myself. This place has either revealed my true self or turned me into someone else altogether. In one day. What the hell.

My phone beeps and I pick it up off the weight bench to see who it is. Jenny. She's left me a text that I can't ignore.

Sis: *Please call asap. Sammy sick and I'm stuck.*

Stuck could mean anything with her; she could be without a babysitter or locked in the bathroom, knowing my sister.

"Am I done here, or is there something else you want me to do?" I ask Ozzie.

"Nah, you're good. Just come back tomorrow by seven if you can. You need time to go through the equipment before you guys take off for the job."

I nod, hoping if I come in that early, it also means I can leave earlier. Not that I'll complain if I can't. This place isn't like any job I've ever had before. It's much too . . . different. Casual. Like hanging out with a crazy family in a way. Family who likes to work out and do hand-to-hand combat. Crazy people. I find I kind of like crazy.

"Can I talk to you for a minute?" Dev asks me as we all start walking toward the stairs.

"Sure, what's up?"

He stops and waits for Ozzie to get farther ahead. Turning to face me, his volume level drops. "Listen, I know you gave it your all today, so if you're not up to another workout for a few days, all you have to do is say the word. You won't lose any cred with any of us. We can see how hard you're trying."

I frown, wondering if this is a trick. "Okay."

"You're going to be sore tomorrow. Make sure you do some stretches now, some more tonight, and some tomorrow morning too. You ever do yoga?"

I shake my head. "That's my sister's domain, not mine."

"You should start. It'll help with your flexibility. Maybe she can show you some of the poses."

"Okay, noted. Stretching and yoga."

Dev stops at the wood table and rearranges some of the weaponry resting on top of it. I'm not even worried he might decide to use one of them on me. If he does, I'll just take a nice nap on the ground and be thankful for it. Just standing here is sapping the last bit of energy I have left.

I was never much of a gym person before, so having someone force me into it is probably a good thing. I suppose I could stand to be a little more flexible. I'm going to be thirty soon, and my sister's already told me about a hundred times that thirty was when her body started falling apart.

Thoughts of her remind me of her text. I quickly tap out a response.

Me: *On my way.*

"See you tomorrow?" Dev asks, holding up a hand.

I give him a solid high five. No two punches for missing this time. "Yep. Tomorrow."

"Welcome to the team," he says, walking over to the stairs, grabbing the railing, and launching himself up the first three stairs.

"Thanks. It's good to be here."

As he's entering the door upstairs, Ozzie comes out. I walk over to my car real slowly in case he wants to say good-bye. I'm sitting inside it, pretending like I have to organize my glove box, when I hear his voice at my window.

He leans in a little and smiles. "Good first day?"

I smile too, suddenly nervous. Gone is the military butt-head, and in his place is the charming Ozzie, just inches away from my sweaty body. The guy who saved my life and gave me a pretty cool job. My heart warms at the events that brought me here. Maybe getting shot at wasn't the worst thing that ever happened to me.

"You're not going to quit, are you?" he asks.

"Are you kidding? Just when things are getting interesting?" I didn't mean for my words to have a double meaning, but the slight lift to his right eyebrow makes me fully aware that they do.

"Got plans tonight?" he asks, his casual tone giving nothing away.

"I think I do, actually." I look at my phone, sad that my sister is having a crisis. Maybe Ozzie was going to ask me out.

"Good for you. Stay safe." He bangs his hand on my windowsill twice and backs away.

I watch him go, wondering if I should tell him what my plans are. Would that look too desperate? *Ozzie, don't worry! My plans aren't with a guy!* Oh my god, yes. Totally desperate. Maybe it's better to let him think whatever he wants about it. It's better to play hard-to-get, right? And since when does *that* matter? He's my boss! I'm not going to sleep with him, dammit!

I jam the key into the ignition with more force than I mean to, breaking my fingernail in the process. I suck on it for a couple seconds before shifting into first gear. I hate that I'm such a slave to my easy libido.

Ozzie's watching me like a hawk as I turn around inside the big warehouse and point my car toward the open door.

"See you tomorrow," I say as I glide by, cool as can be.

"See you tomorrow." He walks next to my car as it's rolling and hands me my Taser. "Park your car in your garage tonight."

I put the Taser in my purse and salute as I drive out the doors. My car bucks and shimmies when I accidentally let too much clutch out. I quickly slam the pedal back in and grab the shifter, trying to get it to go into second. Things all come together a couple seconds later, but not until after I've made a complete fool of myself right in front of the one person I wanted to think of me as cool. Typical. I don't know why I even bother trying.

I let out a long sigh as I grind another gear going past the big door leading outside. Good-bye, Bourbon Street Boys and hello, New Orleans night.

CHAPTER TWENTY-SIX

I hear the yelling before I even get into the house, which makes me wonder if I should have come straight here instead of stopping off to get Felix. I frown when my sister's door opens without the use of the key I keep on my ring. She really should be more careful about her home security. I make a mental note to check how many entrances she has. Maybe I'll be able to afford a security system for her one of these days. Maybe BSB gives a family discount of some sort.

Felix takes off into the back of the house as my sister's voice comes like a boom to my eardrums, a slightly unhinged quality coloring its timbre.

"Get your butt *back* on that toilet seat, and do *not* get up until you've pooped! I'm not kidding! I have work to get done and dinner to make!"

A wail follows. I can't tell if it's one of the girls or Sammy. My money's on the boy. Being the youngest and the only male in the house has somehow given him license to whine pretty much all the time. I've mostly learned to tune it out, but it makes my sister get gray hairs.

I lean into the downstairs bathroom, determining with a quick scan that it is indeed Sammy there on the potty and the two girls in the tub together. Mounds of bubbles go multicolored anywhere there's a toy floating nearby.

Jenny is standing with her hands in her back pockets and her hair going everywhere. Her blouse is buttoned up all askew, leaving one half hanging lower in the front. She has wet splotches on both legs and only one sock on. The other foot is sporting toenail polish that I'm pretty sure was applied at least six months ago.

"Took you long enough," she says, huffing her bangs from her eyes as she glares at me.

The absolute wrongest thing to do in a situation like this is to meet her attitude with one of my own. I know this from prior experience, so I keep my reply breezy and simple. "I was at work. What's going on?"

"Work? What work? I called your studio, and you didn't pick up."

"My new job." I sidle in behind her, kneeling down so I can play with the toys in the tub with the girls. I sink my head down into my shoulders as I wait for the yelling to start.

Sophie and Melody look at me with wide-open eyes. They know it's coming too.

"New job? *What* new job? What the hell, May? You have this whole other life you're keeping secret from me now?"

Aaaand now we know why I waited to say anything. I turn my head and look up at her, using my soothing-therapist voice. "You've had a bad day, Jenny-Boo. Go get a glass of wine and sit on the couch. I'm going to bathe the girls, convince Sammy to give it up to the potty gods, and then, after they're settled down with dinner that I will cook them, I will join you. Consider this your night off."

She glowers at me for only about a half a second before her face crumbles. "Okay," she says weakly, leaving the bathroom before anyone can see her cry.

I hate to see how her feet shuffle, barely leaving the ground. She's wasted already, and she hasn't even had a drop of alcohol. I love my nieces and nephew more than anything in the world, but they are *the* most effective birth control I've ever encountered. High school girls should be required to babysit them before they can go out on their first dates.

"What's wrong with Mommy?" Melody, the middle child, asks when she's gone. We call her Melody-in-the-middle sometimes. She's still young enough at six not to hate it.

"Shhhhh," Sophie, the eight-year-old, breaks in before I can respond. "She's stressed out. Just be good until she feels better. Then you can be bad again."

Melody splashes her sister. "I'm *not* bad!"

"Hey!" I hold up the time-out signal, not able to keep it there for longer than two seconds on account of my spaghetti-arm muscles that no longer want to work. "Chillax, you two. Can't you see Sammy is in crisis?"

We all look over at him and his sad expression.

"Constipated again?" I ask.

He nods. "Conthapated again. My bummy and my tummy hurt-th."

"Don't strain. Just relax."

"Yeah, just relax," Melody says, giggling.

"Hey,"—I point at her face—"no mocking your brother. Being constipated sucks."

"Yeah, being conthapated thuckth." Sammy grabs a toothbrush off the counter and launches it at his sister.

I stand up as fast and I can in an effort to distract Melody from certain retaliation. "Okay, smallish people, listen up!"

All the kids tilt their heads to look up at me. The bathroom goes quiet enough that we all hear the cork popping out of a wine bottle around the corner in the kitchen.

I make a sweeping gesture with my very sore arms. "Auntie May is here!" I lower my arms so I can count on my fingers. It's much easier on my muscles this way. "And that means there will be no throwing things, no spitting, no potty talking, no farting, no barfing, no calling each other names, and no complaining about what I cook—you got it?" I stare each of them down in turn, lowering myself back into a seated position because the muscles in my legs aren't very happy right now.

They exchange silent looks among themselves.

A squeak comes from the toilet. Sammy tries not to grin when I glower at him.

"Oopth. I fahted. Thowwy."

They all giggle.

Melody points at her brother. "He broke the farting rule!" She grips her elbows against her ribs, strains, and forces three little bubbles to come up out of the water.

Sophie looks at her aghast. "You just farted too! Ew! Not in the tub!" She jumps up and tries to scramble out of the bathtub, but she's too covered in bubbles to make it happen. She slides back in with a tumble of arms, legs, elbows, and knees. Bubbly water flies up everywhere.

By the time I can see again, all three kids are laughing hysterically.

"Auntie May, you have bubbles all over your head!" Melody yells.

"Ow! I have a bruise on my knee now," Sophie whines.

"Hey! Geth what, evewybody?!" Sammy screams.

We all look at him, waiting for the big news.

"I pooped!"

CHAPTER TWENTY-SEVEN

The kids are eating their spaghetti at the kitchen table, with Felix underneath, ready for things to drop. They're being extra quiet in exchange for an ice-cream dessert, and I'm pouring myself a glass of wine from the bottle my sister has already half-finished.

When I drop into the armchair next to her couch, she stares at me over her glass.

I stare back as I take a sip.

"So? Are you going to tell me about this new job or what?"

I consider folding my legs up under me, but when I try, it hurts too much, so I just let them drop to the floor instead.

"It's no big deal, really. I'm just taking some pictures for these people."

"Why do I get the impression that it's a lot more than just taking some pictures? Is this some kind of porn thing?" She glances over her shoulder at the kitchen and then lowers her voice. "You know you can't get involved in the porn industry. They'll recruit you into the acting part!"

I laugh. It's so nice to be sitting here in her family room with her. I love my sister and her nutty mind. "You're crazy. And you can relax, because it has nothing at all to do with the porn industry. It's a security company." It sounds so much safer when I say it that way. No risk. It's better for my sister to hear it this way; otherwise, she'll go all mother hen on me and make me start doubting myself.

She blinks a few times as she mulls it over in her head.

"Remember that guy who helped me out when I accidentally ended up in Frankie's bar?"

"The one with all the muscles?" She smiles for the first time since I arrived.

"Yeah, that one. He offered me a job." I try not to smile, but it's tough.

"So he works at a security firm, and he offered you a job to take pictures? Of what?"

I shrug, trying to think of a way to minimize the danger. Jenny has always been my self-assigned protector. "I don't know. People. Places. Things."

"A job of nouns." She narrows her eyes at me. "Don't play, little sister. What aren't you telling me?"

I fiddle with a loose thread on my new workout shorts. "Nothing much. Just that it's basically kind of like—a little bit of this sort of thing that's kind of hard to explain."

She takes a long sip of her wine, almost emptying her glass.

I jump up to get the bottle, hoping it will distract her from my horrible attempts at downplaying my job's negative points.

"You are the worst liar who ever walked planet Earth," she says, laughing into her glass as she finishes it off.

"Better than being the best liar, right?" I lean over and fill up her glass, topping off my own while I'm at it, before setting the bottle down on the coffee table.

"Maybe. So what's the deal? Straight up. Just tell me. I won't get mad."

"Straight up? Fine. It's a surveillance gig. I take pictures of bad guys doing bad things."

She rolls her eyes to the ceiling and lets out a long, loud growl. "Eeeeeerrrrrhhhhh!" Then she glares at me. "May, how *could* you?!"

"How could I what?" I'm playing innocent. "Get a job so I can pay my bills?"

"How many times have I asked you to move in with me? We could both save so much money." Her eyes get teary.

"Aw, babe . . ." I get up and sit next to her on the couch, leaving my wine on the table, "you know I can't do that. I need my space. You guys need your space to be a family. I don't want the kids getting mad at me because I'm cranky all the time."

"You're not cranky all the time." She's crying now. "You're always happy."

"That's because I have my own place."

"Are you saying being at my place or living with me would make you unhappy?"

It's a fair question. I have kind of been saying that for the last year. "No, I'm saying that I'm a young, single girl who likes to walk around her house naked sometimes and take long baths with a glass of wine once in a while."

Jenny sighs, leaning her head on mine. "That sounds nice, actually."

"Anytime you need that, just call me. Or text me like you did today, and I'll come running. I'm here for you; you know that."

"I do know that." She pats me on the leg and sips more wine. "I'm just feeling sorry for myself. Ignore me."

"What happened? Was it Miles?" The ex. The arrogant asshole who refuses to step up to the plate and be a real father to these kids.

"Of course it was Miles—who else would it be? The child-support check he gave me bounced, once again, so several payments I made to other places aren't going to go through now."

I chew my lip, knowing I'm treading on dangerous ground. Moving in with her could save her from a lot of these problems, but

I also worry that if I did that, Miles would stop doing the little he does do. He'd see me as his kids' stand-in dad and disappear forever. Forget the bouncing check problems; we'd be moving into three hundred and sixty-five days of continuous child care on my sister's part instead of her getting the two weeks of vacation when he takes them for some of the summer and the one weekend a month he still manages to put on his schedule.

Nope. I can't move in with Jenny. Much as it would ease some problems, I'm sure it would create worse ones. The last thing I want is something coming between us. I love her and her babies too much for that.

"I'm getting paid pretty well at this new place. Maybe I can help out with some bills."

"That's not fair to you." She sniffs and smiles at me. "How will you be able to afford all that bubble bath?"

I nudge her with my elbow. "I can make my own. I'll just run the bathwater over a bar of soap."

She snorts. "Sure you will." She moves a little away from me so she can see me. "So tell me about this guy."

"What guy?" I'm trying to act like I really have no clue what she's talking about, but I can tell from her expression she's not buying it.

"As if. Come on, you know who I'm talking about. Tall, dark, and built like a tank."

"Who, Ozzie?"

"Don't make me strangle you. I'm mad enough at Miles to take it out on an innocent bystander."

"Fine. Ozzie is the guy who saved my life, basically." I pick at the thread on my shorts again. "And, as you might recall, he watched Felix that one day and brought him back to me, which was really nice." I sip my wine as I remember that kiss. "Anyway, there's nothing going on with us. He's just my new boss, that's all."

"Mmm-hmmm." Jenny drinks more wine. "And your face getting all red right now and you pulling your shorts apart is all just . . . what? The flu? You coming down with something?"

I close my eyes and tip my head back on the couch. "We kissed, okay? We kissed."

She whacks me on the shoulder. "When?!" She sounds suddenly very happy.

"Saturday night. At my place. When he brought dinner over."

"Oh my god! All this happened, and you didn't say anything?! Now I understand why you don't want to move in."

"Shut up." I look at her, keeping my head on the couch. "Nothing else can happen. We work together now. He's my boss. He apologized."

"Ouch."

"Yeah. Ouch. So it's nothing, okay? Just . . . let it drop."

"Is it hard working with him?"

I sigh, thinking about my day. "Not really. Sure, I'm sweating him the whole time, but I don't think he can tell."

"Oh, yeah," she says in her mocking tone, "you're always so cool about that kind of thing."

I have to smile. She knows me too well. "I'm trying to be cool, okay? And today it got a lot easier when he was in charge of my stupid workout."

"Workout? Is that code for something?"

"No. Like at the gym—a workout. I lifted weights with every muscle in my body for an hour today."

She reaches over and squeezes my bicep.

"Ow." I flinch with the pain but find I can't move very well. The longer I sit on her couch, the stiffer I get.

"You need to stretch."

"That's what Dev said."

"Dev?"

"A coworker. The trainer."

"I thought you said Ozzie trained you."

"He did. But next time it'll be Dev."

"So you're getting all sweaty at work with a bunch of guys. Is Dev as hot as Ozzie is?"

I laugh. "Perv. It's not like that."

"Just let me dream. Is he?"

"If you like guys who are six and a half feet tall and totally bald, then sure. He's cute."

"You're kidding."

"No, trust me, I'm not."

"Hmmm." She rubs the rim of her glass. "Maybe I'll get to meet him someday."

"Maybe you will." I sit up and moan as my muscles complain.

"You okay?" Jenny asks, resting her hand on my back.

"Sore muscles." I breathe through the pain.

"Better get home and take one of those baths you were talking about."

I twist a little to look at her. "Will you be okay?" I glance at the kitchen were I can hear the kids whispering. Plotting a takeover or a coup, probably.

"Yeah, we'll be fine. The wine helped."

"I promised them ice cream."

"I heard that. Don't worry. I'll cover for you." She stands and holds out a hand to help me up.

I take it and get to my feet with difficulty.

"Thanks for coming over and saving me from going insane."

I hug her close and kiss her cheek. "Any time, any place. I'm there."

"Same for you, you know." She pats me on the back. "If you ever need me, I'm there too."

"I know." I pull away and walk carefully around the furniture. One wrong move and I could trip, and if I end up on the ground, I'm probably going to have to stay there for the night. I have about enough juice left in my body to get me home, and that's it.

"Call me tomorrow after work, so you can tell me all the details." Jenny opens the front door for me.

"I will." I lift my chin and talk louder. "See you later, kids!"

"Bye, Auntie May!" comes a chorus of tiny voices.

"Thankth for the ithe cweam!" adds Sammy.

"Thank your mom!" I yell back before walking outside. I pick Felix up and hold him under my arm. The night is balmy, with just enough humidity to make my shirt start sticking to me again.

"Gotta love this N' Orleans weather," Jenny says, gesturing with her glass like she's saying cheers to the night.

"There's nowhere I'd rather be." Blowing her a kiss, I get into my car, putting Felix on the passenger seat before I gently shift into reverse and leave her and her crazy kids behind. I'm exhausted, but happy. Happier than I remember being in a long time. I've got a new job, a great family, an adorable dog, and a group of people who call themselves a team, who've welcomed me into their fold. Life is good.

CHAPTER TWENTY-EIGHT

My life completely sucks. My body is broken. It's Tuesday morning and my alarm has gone off, so I should be getting into the shower. But instead I'm lying in my bed, paralyzed. Felix licks my cheek, and I don't have the energy to stop him.

I moan as I try to roll over toward my phone. He follows me, knowing I have no fight in me, licking my ear now.

"Oooooooohhh my god, what the hellllll." Every muscle in my body aches. I think I tore them all. This can't be just regular muscle pain; it's too severe.

The only thing that doesn't hurt is my thumb. After nudging Felix away, I use it to type out a text message, resting the phone on my mattress so I won't have to use any arm muscles to hold it up.

Me: *Ozzie, I'm dying.*

A few seconds later, my phone rings.

"Hello?" I groan, putting the phone to my doggie-licked, wet ear.

"What's going on? Talk to me." Ozzie's all business. Does he know it's only six in the morning?

"I'm sore. I think I'm dying."

A long hiss of breath hits my ear before he speaks again. "Are you dying because of your workout or because you've been shot?"

I hold the phone out and look at it. I guess 6:00 a.m. is crazy-talk time.

"No, don't be silly. Who would shoot me in my own house?"

"How am I supposed to know where you are?!" He's yelling as if he's genuinely mad at me.

"Excuse me, Mister Angry Pants, but I thought you had a phone-tracker thingy!" Now I'm mad too. I was expecting pity and I'm getting scolded? What's up with that?

"Which I don't turn on unless I think someone's in trouble, May!"

I blink a few times, letting that sink in. Makes sense now that I've been awake for more than three minutes.

"Okay, fine. I'm sorry if I caused you any distress by telling you I'm dying."

He says nothing for a while.

"Ozzie? Are you still there?"

"Yeah, just give me a minute."

As the seconds tick by, I become more and more convinced that I never should have picked up my phone this morning. He's not my boyfriend; he's my boss. He doesn't want to hear about my sore muscles; he just wants me to walk into work by seven and get going with my assignment. Why do I keep defaulting back to this boyfriend role for him? What is wrong with my brain?

"Listen, do you want the day off? Are you that sore?"

I sit up with effort. "No." The word comes out sounding like it was uttered by an eighty-year-old woman. "No." The second time is better. I feel stronger. Humiliation is giving me wings. "I don't want a day off; don't be ridiculous. It's only my second day." Felix climbs into my lap, and I absently play with his ears.

"But if you're too sore . . ."

"I'm not. I'm totally not. I'm fine. I'll see you in an hour. Sorry I called you. I won't do it again."

He says nothing.

"Okay, so see you later. Bye."

"See you later . . ."—he pauses—"Bo Peep."

I press the red button and fling my phone into the covers. "Bo Peep. Bo *Peep*. I'll give you Bo Peep." I lift Felix off me and swing my legs out of the bed, groaning the entire way. I never knew before how many of my abdominal muscles, back muscles, arm muscles, and neck muscles are necessary to complete that small motion. Wow.

A ten-minute shower and liberal coating of my body in lotion to facilitate a quick self-massage go a long way toward getting me more mobile. I can actually walk with only a small limp now. But every step down my staircase brings a whimper to my lips. By the time I'm at the bottom, I'm basically just falling down the stairs. I grab the railing at the bottom to keep from collapsing on the floor. Felix runs next to me, I think concerned for my welfare. He keeps looking up at me and whining.

"Don't worry, Fee. I'm not going to die today."

I let him out in my small yard to do his business, fill his bowl with kibble, and leave him there to play doggie takeout.

Four anti-inflammatories have me singing about walking on sunshine when I drive into the warehouse a half hour later. I lose a little of my good cheer when I see Dev standing in the middle of the floor with a singlestick in his hand. When his eyes lock on me, he grins real evil-like and smacks his palm with the weapon.

Fine. He wants to play it that way? Fine. Finer than fine. I pull into the corner of the warehouse and park, grab my Taser out of my purse, and climb out of my car. I'm headed in his direction before the door is even shut.

171

"You even think about touching me with that stick and I'll shoot you up with so much electricity, you'll be able to power this entire block with your finger in a socket." I hold it out in front of me with two hands, since one arm is too weak to do the job on its own. I could possibly look like an FBI badass.

Everyone starts laughing, including Dev.

He puts the stick on the table and opens his arms. "Come to Papa, Bo Peep. I knew you had it in you."

I sigh with relief and lower my weapon, limping forward to join my team.

CHAPTER TWENTY-NINE

"I gotta give you props," Toni says, turning the wheel of the van slowly so we can park on the side of the street half a block up from our surveillance target. "That was a great approach with Dev this morning."

"It's not like he gave me any choice." I tuck my hair behind my ear and swivel in my seat to watch her as she moves around in the back of the van. It's a tiny command center, with two short stools set up in front of a bank of screens and two laptops on a very narrow shelf built into the side of the van. I was relieved to learn that the entire thing is bulletproof.

"You had plenty of choices. I had money on you turning around and leaving."

My smile falls. "Oh."

"Buuut you'll be happy to know everyone else thought you'd stick." She's messing with wires under the shelf, frowning when something isn't doing what she wants it to do.

I don't want to dwell on her lack of faith in me, so I change the subject. "What are you doing down there?"

"Trying"—she grimaces—"to find"—she yanks on some cords really hard—"the power supply"—a cord comes flying out and hits her head—"for the computers." She sits up and smiles at it. "There we go. You can run, but you can't hide, you little bastard." She plugs the laptops in and opens the one in front of her.

"So what exactly are we doing here today?" I shift in my seat so my leg muscles aren't quite as cramped. Pretty much any position I pick isn't going to work, though. My body is in full broke-down mode.

"First we need to assess which type of surveillance is going to work with what we have here on this street, and then we need to get it set up. Deadline to finish is tooo-day." She looks out the front windshield. "You should come back here with me and pull that curtain." She gestures at a spot behind the front seats.

I move to the back part of the van and unhook the black curtain from its tieback behind the passenger seat. It runs from right to left via a metal track imbedded in the ceiling. Once it's in place, the back room goes dark except for the laptop's screen. Toni leans forward and presses a button on the panel in front of her, and a dim overhead light goes on.

"This is so super spy," I say in a whisper.

"If you say so." She's too busy tapping on her keyboard to look up at me.

I turn around and drag the hard plastic case full of equipment closer to me. "I guess I'll go through this stuff."

"Good idea. Try a couple lenses out. See if any of them can get into the house." She pauses and reaches over me to get to the curtain. "You can pull down this little flap and put the lens up there. Try not to let it down until you're ready to fill the hole with the lens."

The black curtain has a camera spy hole. Cool.

The first lens I select does the trick, as much as any camera lens can, anyway; when I place it up to the hole in the curtain, I can pick up the small mailbox attached next to the front door. The faded nameplate says "Juarez." It looks like our targets haven't done any housekeeping since the house was built in the sixties, though, so seeing into any of the interior probably isn't going to happen.

"I'm not sure how much I'm going to see through those brown windows," I say. "Reminds me of *My Cousin Vinny*."

She surprises me when she jumps right in. "Love that movie. One of my favorites. The two 'yoots.'" She laughs, shaking her head with a sigh.

I try not to get too excited over the fact that we share the same taste in cinema. Whenever I start thinking she and I can be friends, she throws me a curveball. Like betting against me this morning. I wonder what it's going to take to earn her respect. I hope it won't involve me getting shot.

The front door of the house opens. "Someone's coming out!" My pulse starts beating hard, and suddenly it's difficult to breathe. I'm both excited and scared to death. What if they see us? What if they know exactly what we're doing? Is a bulletproof van bombproof too?

"Take some shots!"

"Oh, right." My finger presses the shutter button. I quickly focus on the subject and do my best to catch him in profile and full on. He turns in our direction to get to his car, parked just a few vehicles down from where we are.

"Oh my god, I'm getting some great shots right now."

"Keep going. You can never have too many."

"Thank goodness for digital, right?"

"Yeah." Toni's moving around behind me, but I can't stop to figure out what she's doing.

"Listen, if he gets closer, you should back off the curtain and close it up."

"How close?" I'm still taking shots.

"Within ten feet."

I take a few more pictures and back up, pulling the camera out of the hole and shutting the flap.

The entire van is pitch-black inside. Toni must have shut off the light when I was busy taking a hundred pictures in ten seconds.

"Next time, warn me when you're going to do that," Toni says.

"Why?"

"Because it's better if it's dark inside here when you pull out, so they don't see a square of light in the curtain."

"Oh. Sorry."

"No worries. I figured you were about to do it, so I shut the light off. Next time, just give me a signal first."

"What's the signal?"

"Lights."

"Oh. That's easy."

"We try to keep everything as simple as possible, so in the heat of the moment we don't forget."

"Good plan." I can picture myself forgetting a code word more complicated than *lights*. I am secretly appreciative of the genius in charge of passwords and signals, whoever that person is. Is it Ozzie? Seems like it would be. He strikes me as both a thoughtful and practical person.

"Get anything good?" she asks.

I switch the camera into play mode and buzz through the photographs. "Yes. Several." I hold the camera over by her. "You know this guy?"

"No. But that doesn't mean anything. We'll run it through our facial recognition program and see what we come up with."

"You have that? That program, I mean?"

"Yeah." She sounds defensive.

"Sorry, it's just . . . kind of hard to believe you'd have something that sophisticated in a security firm. It's not like you're the police or anything."

"First of all, we're not just any security firm. Ozzie only runs top-of-the-line operations. And second, we work with the police department. They give us access to all kinds of databases. We can't do our job very well without it."

I nod, thinking it through. "That makes sense." I'm even more impressed with Ozzie than I was before. If I'm not careful, pretty soon I'll be drooling whenever he walks into the room.

"This is interesting," Toni says, staring at her screen.

"What?"

She leans a little to the right so I can look at her laptop screen. There's an aerial photograph of a neighborhood, showing houses, driveways, and even cars.

"What's that?"

"We're right here," she says, pointing to a spot on the map.

"I don't see our van."

"This picture was taken awhile ago. It's not a live feed. Anyway, do you see that?" She points to a house on the street behind the one we've been watching.

"Yes."

"Did it look vacant to you yesterday when we drove past it?"

"I don't know. I can't remember."

"You're supposed to remember these things." She shuts her laptop and starts to climb over me.

"I'm confused." I'm afraid I've failed another test with her.

Toni peeks around the corner of the curtain for a few seconds before she pushes it back enough to take the driver's seat. "Let's go take a look."

"Can I come up there with you?"

"If you want." She fires up the engine and pulls out of our parking spot.

I climb into the front with her and buckle myself in. "What did you mean, I'm supposed to remember that other house?"

"Your job when we're out surveilling is to take in the details and file them away in your brain for future use."

"Oh. And which details do I file and which ones do I disregard?"

"Disregard nothing."

I don't answer with the obvious response to that, which is, *Oh, so I'll just see about booting up my photographic memory.*

"If you don't have a good mind for details, you'd better take a lot of pictures," she adds.

I lean into the back and pull a smaller camera with a more manageable lens out of the hard case that holds all the equipment I'm supposed to be using.

"Fine. I can take pictures." No big deal. That won't look suspicious at all, a woman driving down the street taking photos of every single detail.

"You'll learn eventually what things are important and what aren't." She turns onto the road that runs behind the target house. "You want to take photos of the street here from this angle, the houses that connect to the target house, unusual things that look out of place . . ."

"Like what, for example?"

"Like a woman who's sitting in a chair on her front porch. You don't see that much around here, but when you do, it either means you have an old-school granny who likes to keep an eye on her neighborhood or you have someone employed by a dealer to watch out for the po-po."

"Grannies do that?"

"Grannies gotta eat." Toni slows when she gets near the house she pointed out on the satellite photo. "That's what I thought," she says, smiling.

I take a few pictures, although I'm not sure why.

"What's going on?" I ask, leaning over to see the house better as she drives by.

"It's vacant, I'm pretty sure. And part of the fence connects to the fence of our target. We could get eyes on the back of the target if we can get into that backyard."

"Is it worth the risk?"

"I'm betting yes. Come on—let's go see."

Now our faded blue jumpsuits are starting to make sense. "You mean we're going to get out of the van?"

"Yes. Put your hair up and your hat on. Sunglasses are optional."

I'm too shocked to argue. My hands move to my hair and follow her instructions, using the rubber band I had on my wrist. I'm afraid, but I can do this. I don't want Toni being disgusted with my cowardice, even though I know that emotion is in place to keep me from getting in trouble with the wrong kind of people.

Ego. It's a terrible thing sometimes.

I slide the baseball cap onto my head as Toni's getting out. I have to count to ten before I can make my fingers take the door handle and pull on it. My muscles scream with agony as I drop to the ground from the elevated passenger seat.

"Bring your camera, but keep it hidden."

I take the equipment and put it inside the roomy leg compartments of my jumpsuit, securing it inside with the Velcro flaps.

"Here, take this." Toni hands me a toolbox.

"What's in it?"

"Nothing you need to worry about. Just act like you're supposed to be here, and everything will be just fine."

I'm already sweating. It's not that hot out yet, but does that matter? No. Because this jumpsuit, turning into a sauna designed to poach my body, is not hot because of the outside temperature; it's hot because I'm panicking. I'm not bulletproof!

"We'll go around the back. We're meter readers."

"Oh. Okay. We're meter readers." Nothing at all suspicious about two chick meter readers. Ha.

I follow Toni around the side of the house, noticing the windows here are broken or at least cracked. The smell of mildew is strong. I wonder if this is one of those houses that never recovered after Hurricane Katrina. I'd heard that there were still some around.

Toni walks right by the meter. I follow closely behind. The box I'm carrying bangs against my leg, and something heavy and metal rattles around inside.

"Being real quiet is a good idea right now," Toni says in a low voice.

My heart skips a beat. I try to tiptoe through the grass, mostly unsuccessfully.

She stops at the far left corner of the backyard. I realize as I step up next to her that we're also at the back fence of the target house. I'm afraid I'm going to pee my pants.

CHAPTER THIRTY

Toni bends down and opens up the toolbox she had under her arm. Inside is a drill and various bits mixed in with some other tools.

"Open yours up," she says, taking the drill out. She unscrews the end and puts a bit inside, screwing it back tight again when she's got it where she wants it.

I undo the latch on my toolbox, and my heart leaps into my throat when I see a handgun inside. "Oh my god," I whisper.

Toni reaches inside and takes the gun out, placing it in the weeds at her feet. The next thing out of the toolbox is a small black box.

"What's that?" I whisper.

"Watch and learn, Bo Peep."

She drills a hole at the bottom of the fence separating the two properties. Even though the drill is completely quiet, with some kind of crazy silencer on it, and she goes slowly enough that the wood hardly makes a whisper, sweat flows down my face in tiny rivers. I'm trying to decide if I should pick the weapon up and have it ready for Toni if she needs it. No way am I going to use the stupid thing myself.

The black box attaches to the wood fence with four tiny screws. Toni puts those in manually. She pushes a button on it, and a tiny green light comes on.

"Find me some brush."

I blink a few times, wondering what the hell she's talking about.

"Or some garbage or something. I need to cover this thing."

The lightbulb goes on above my head, and I quickly stand to gather bits of garbage and dead weeds. Toni takes them from me and adds them to the things she assembled, covering the camera so neither it nor its green light is visible.

"Sweet." Toni stands and smiles. "You ready to get out of here?"

"Sure." I'm proud of myself that I was able to keep my cool. What I really want to do is sprint to the van, but I follow Toni's casual pace and cringe as sweat trickles down my spine.

When we're in the van again, Toni goes to the back, opening up the laptop. She clicks the touch pad a few times and turns the screen to face me. "Lookie, lookie." She's smiling.

The camera inside the black box has a fish-eye lens, allowing it to pick up almost the entire back side of the house and the yard. The only thing we can't see is the yard on the north side and the back corner, parallel with the camera.

"Not bad." I nod in appreciation. "How much battery does that camera have?"

"Forty-eight hours, give or take."

"Wow. That's impressive."

"Lithium ion. Waterproof too. I love gadgets." She closes the laptop and stands to go to the front of the van. I swivel to the front so she doesn't have to climb over my legs.

"Where to now?" I ask.

"Last part. And this is my favorite part, by the way."

"I'm almost afraid to ask."

She laughs. "You're going to love it, I promise." She pulls out of the driveway of the abandoned house and goes back to the other street we were on before. She stops at the corner and parks on the side of the road behind another car.

Once she's done, with the engine off, she goes into the back. She's all the way in the rear of the van, so I can't see anything that she's doing.

Her voice sounds muffled. "Come out and play, Polly. Polly want a cracker?"

"Please tell me you don't have a parrot back there." I twist around farther to see better.

"Oh, but I *do* have a parrot back here." She giggles like a mad scientist.

She comes to the front of the van and holds something black out in front of her. "Behold: Polly."

"What is that?" It looks like a small black X with helicopter blades on it in four places.

"This is a drone. She's my Parrot." She cackles with glee. "And today she's going to go sit on a pole and spy for us."

I reach out to touch it, but Toni stops me with a sharp slap to the back of my hand.

"Ow!"

"Don't touch. She's mine."

I lift an eyebrow. "She has a camera on her. I think that makes her mine too."

Toni's eyes narrow. "Keep your paws off her or else."

My jaw drops open in surprise. Is she threatening me?

Then her expression changes and she smiles. "Gotcha." She motions for me to join her. "Come on back here and help me fly this bitch."

I feel like a kid in a toy store. I'm so excited. I never outgrew getting gadgets for Christmas and my birthday, and this is one hell of a gadget. I've never seen anything like it before. I thought all those stories in the news about drones were science fiction.

Toni clicks on a program on her computer, and a black window opens. She presses a button on the drone, and in a couple seconds, the window on the computer flickers. I can barely make out the interior of the van, where the drone is pointing.

"Whoa."

She hands it to me. "Here. Be careful with it. In a minute I'm going to send you outside with it."

My enthusiasm is tempered by the reality of our situation. "Outside the van, you mean?"

She pauses in her keystrokes to look at me. "Where else would I mean?" She shakes her head in disappointment and then starts clicking her keys again. "As soon as I have this ready, you're going to go outside the van and put Polly on the ground. I'll launch her up, and then my goal is to get her on that light pole just behind the van."

"Why are you doing that?"

"Because. The bird's-eye view is awesome for catching daily activity and vehicles and sometimes people too." She frowns. "Not always great at getting faces, but still, valuable intel worth getting."

She leans over and grabs a big black box. It has hand controls on it, joysticks and buttons. She flicks a switch and it goes on.

"Okay, so, hold Polly from underneath and away from your face. I'm going to check her props."

I do as I'm told and hold the thing as far from me as I can. My arm muscles ache with the effort, even though it weighs not much more than a feather.

It vibrates as the propellers start to buzz. They're going so fast, they're a blur.

"Good. We're all set. Go outside and put it on the curb behind the van. Take this with you." She hands me a walkie-talkie. "I want you to let me know of any problems that you see."

"Problems?" I'm picturing bad guys with guns.

"Yeah, like power lines I might not see in the monitor or whatever."

"Oh. Okay. I can do that." I think. Being almost a whole block down from the target house makes me feel a little safer than I did in the backyard behind it, but not much.

"Go. We have to get back soon."

A glance at my watch tells me that time flies when you're scared shitless that you're going to get discovered on a surveillance run. I'm not unhappy about that. It sure beats time crawling.

I step outside the van with the drone in one hand and my walkie-talkie in the other. Behind the vehicle in two seconds, I put the drone down on the curb.

A voice comes out from the two-way radio, so low I can barely hear it.

"We good?" Toni asks.

I look all over the device for a button, pressing one on the side experimentally. The static that was there is gone. "Um, yeah. We're all good." I let go of the button.

"Good. Now step back a little. I don't want to hit you with this thing."

I walk back a couple strides, but it's not enough. The drone takes off straight up about one foot and then veers to the side, slamming into my thigh.

"Ow, shit, mother fu . . ." I hop around on one leg, trying to keep the shout from leaving my lungs.

"What just happened?" comes a voice over the speaker.

I grab it and press the button. "You ran the thing into my leg!" There's going to be a bruise, I know it.

"Oh. Sorry. Let's try this again."

Again?! What am I, the crash test dummy?

I grumble as I pick up the drone that's fallen to its side in the street. I put it down on the curb again and go around the back of the van until I'm at its side. This way I can peek around the corner and watch from a safe distance.

The propellers start up again, and the device rocks back and forth. It rises slowly from the ground and hovers near the back of the van. I move farther toward the side of the vehicle. Now I can hear it, but I can't see it. The whir of the blades is whisper soft. I'm sure none of the neighbors will notice a thing.

Suddenly, it appears around the side of the van.

"Ack!" I run backward, but it follows me.

I scramble for my walkie-talkie. "Stop chasing me with that thing!"

It surges forward at me and then at the last second goes backward and sideways, banging into the side of the van before hitting the street.

I'm nearly out of breath with the panic of my near miss. I press the button on my radio. "What the hell, Toni, is this some kind of weird initiation?"

Her voice comes out as a growl. "Just get the damn thing and come back inside."

I approach it carefully, nudging it with my toe first. It doesn't move. Flipping it over onto its back, I bend down to retrieve it. It buzzes once, but I shake it really hard, and it stops. "Not this time, Polly, you little asshole."

I get into the van as quickly as I can, holding the drone out at arm's length.

Toni's glowering in the driver's seat, staring out the windshield. I wait for her explanation. Apparently, she doesn't feel the need to give me one, though. Instead she turns the key and starts reversing out of our parallel parking space.

WRONG NUMBER, RIGHT GUY

"What the hell, Toni?"

"What the hell, what?" She shifts into drive.

"I thought we were going to put this up on the pole."

"Yeah, so did I, but it didn't work out, did it?" She glares at me for a second before going back to her gearshift.

I put my hand on hers to stop her. There's a vulnerability to her that I've never noticed. "What's going on?"

She takes a deep breath in and then lets it all out. "I totally suck at flying that thing."

I look at it in my hand and frown. "You didn't totally suck. You got liftoff."

"Liftoff is a long way from implantation."

"Maybe we should practice somewhere else and come back."

She pulls out onto the street. "Ozzie's going to want us back for a briefing soon."

"It probably won't take longer than thirty minutes." I check my watch. "We have time."

She chews her lip as she drives to the next block. "Where?"

I point to an abandoned-looking lot, one that's obviously been used as a garbage dump by the local population if all the empty bottles and plastic bags spread around is any indicator. "There."

She pulls up onto the sidewalk, the entire van bouncing side to side when she gets back out on the street.

"Great parking job."

"Shut up." She puts the van in park and turns off the engine. She looks at me, strangely expressionless. "You sure you want to do this? I almost cut your leg off earlier."

I smile. "Not even close. I have reflexes like a ninja."

She snorts.

"Here," I say, handing her the drone. "You go put Polly down, and I'm going to try to fly her."

She stares at the drone sitting in her hand. "You think you can fly it?"

"I've had radio-controlled toys before. Can't be too hard, right?"

"Tell that to your leg." She points to my jumpsuit. There's a spot of red on it where the drone hit my leg.

"Oh my god. You cut me!"

She smiles, but there's a hint of regret to it. "I told you I suck at it."

I open the door. "Come on. Bring the controller. I'm going to make this happen."

She follows me outside, and we stand together at the edge of the lot.

CHAPTER THIRTY-ONE

"You completely suck, you know that?" Toni's glaring at me with her arms crossed over her chest.

I maneuver the drone so it's level with her eyes, a couple feet away. "Say it again and see what happens." I giggle with maniacal glee.

"How is it you can control that thing after ten minutes of trying, and I can't get it to do anything but cut people after hours of practice?"

"I'm a ninja pilot. Live with it." I lower the drone to a smooth stop at her feet. "Can we go now? I'm starving." It's nearly three o'clock, and I haven't eaten anything since the bagel with cream cheese provided by our employer this morning.

"Yes, we can go after you've placed the drone."

My bravado simmers to a dull roar. "Place it? You really think I can do that?"

"Well, either you're going to do it, or you're going to crash and burn one of our best pieces of surveillance equipment." She snorts.

"No pressure."

"Listen, if you want Thibault to come out and do our jobs for us, fine. I'll call him." She lifts up her phone.

"No! Don't call him. We can do this." I climb into the van next to her. "Girl power, right?"

"Sure," she says, turning the engine on and driving out onto the street. "Whatever you say."

There's a definite chill to her tone. I chew my lip as we make our way back to the target, wondering if I should say something. My misgivings about what her reaction might be last all of three seconds.

"So what's the deal, Toni? Did I do something to piss you off, or is it just that you don't like me on principle?"

She doesn't answer right away. She waits so long to reply, I'm convinced she's just going to ignore my question. That's not awkward at all. Just as I'm about to apologize, she responds.

"I don't dislike you at all. I'm just not . . . a warm and fuzzy person."

"Oh."

"I don't get along with women very well."

I consider that for a few seconds. "Do you have any sisters?"

"No. Three brothers. Thibault is one of them."

"Female cousins?"

"Nope. Thirteen male cousins."

"Wow. That's a lot of testosterone."

She shrugs. "I'm used to it. I never played with dolls; I played with soldiers. I prefer boots to sandals."

I look at her and smile. She's petite, with tiny little features that would look right at home on a china doll.

"What?" She glances at me before looking back at the road. "What are you looking at?"

"I'm looking at a tomboy who looks like a girly girl."

She snorts. "Yeah, right. Girly girl. That'll be the day."

"You wear heels. Those boots I saw you in the first day I met you had heels."

"Good for poking holes in bad guys."

I cringe inwardly. "Oh. Gross."

"And they make my legs look longer. I hate being short."

At five-seven I can't really commiserate on that one.

"In our business you have to be tough to get respect."

I frown. This isn't sounding so good for me right now.

She looks over and winks. "Don't worry, Bo Peep. You don't need to start wearing boots anytime soon."

My chin goes up. "I have boots." I don't mention the part about the sparkles.

She says nothing, and we drive on. My heart starts beating faster when we arrive at our destination. The target house. All those tricky moves I was making with the drone take on new meaning here.

"You ready?" she asks. She sits very still in her seat, waiting for me to answer.

"As ready as I'm going to be."

She opens her mouth to speak, but then shakes her head and starts to open her door.

"What?" I put my hand on her arm to stop her. "You were going to say something."

She sighs, not looking at me as she speaks. "I was just going to say that you'll be fine. And that I'm glad you're here with me. On the team."

I punch her in the arm, knowing how much it took for her to say that and also that anything more affectionate, like a hug, would freak her out.

"Me too," I say, really meaning it. "Come on. Let's go put this mother on that pole."

She slides to the ground, but I see her smile in the side mirror. My heart soars with the idea that I could have just earned a friend with my mad drone-flying skills.

I move to the back seat and take up a position in front of the computer, with the joysticks on my lap.

"Okay," she says, talking to me through the walkie-talkie. "Easy does it. Can you see through the drone's camera?"

"Yep." I put the radio down so I can use both hands. I'm staring at the computer screen in front of me. The drone has a camera on the front that takes in all the scenery around it, almost in a three-hundred-and-sixty-degree radius. It's impressive.

"We have liftoff," she says as I bring the drone above the van.

"Easy, easy," I mumble to myself.

The pole is in sight.

"Watch the power line to your left."

I can just imagine how angry Ozzie would be if I electrocuted his drone. I'd forever be known as The Executioner, I'm sure of it. And as much as I'd like to get rid of the Bo Peep moniker, I'd prefer it be for something less . . . harsh. Seems like there should be something halfway between a fairy tale character and a murderer.

"Okay, to the right, you see that little platform? You can land it there and deploy the hooks." This little drone comes with equipment to hook it onto things like this pole, to keep it from being blown down by the wind.

I get the drone on the platform, using a maneuver that proves to be a little tricky in the tiny space available. I'm looking for the button to get the hooks in place, when Toni's voice comes over the line.

"Uh-oh."

"What's 'uh-oh'?" I ask out into the van. I can't turn and respond to her because I'm focusing on using both hands for the drone.

"Potential bad guy, twelve o'clock. Be cool."

I press the button to hook the drone to the pole and then sit back, hiding behind the front seat, not that I need to for security purposes, because the curtain is drawn. What is she talking about?

Then I look at the computer screen, and the drone lets me see exactly what she means. A guy is walking down the sidewalk toward us, a pit bull on a leash straining in front of him. Did he come from the target house? I try to swallow, but it's hard to do on account of the lump in my throat.

I can hear their voices through the back door of the van.

"Hey, what's up?" the guy says.

"Nothin' much. What's up with you? Nice dog."

"Thanks. Just out for a walk. What're you doing here?" He gestures up at the pole. "Electric company?"

Our van has no markings on it that are permanent, but there's a magnetic sign I was told is used by contractors who work for the phone company.

"Nah. Phones." Toni gestures over at a junction box not far away. "Connecting some new lines. Economy's picking up."

"Good news."

"Yeah. Well, I'm outta here. Have a good one." She waves as she goes around the side of the van and gets inside.

"Just stay put," she says in a low voice.

I watch on the screen as we pull away. The man turns to watch us drive away and down the street.

"I think he made us," she says.

I watch as he turns back around and continues away from the target house.

"I don't think so. He's still walking his dog, and he's not looking at the drone."

Toni lets out a long breath. "Thank Jesus."

My heart fills with pride. "We did it."

"Yes, we did."

Both of us are on cloud nine, all the way back to the warehouse. When we arrive, Thibault is waiting with his hands on his hips.

"Well?" he asks before the engine's even off.

Toni and I get out of the van, and she walks over to give him a high five. "Done deal, thanks to Bo Peep over there."

I approach, feeling shy about taking all the credit. "I didn't do anything, really. Toni got the camera in place for the entire back side of the house."

"And she flew the drone up to the pole and secured it," Toni adds.

"She did?" Thibault looks at me with a questioning expression. "How come *you* did it?"

"I, uh . . ." I look over at Toni. She's staring at the ground. "I wanted to try it out. I like radio-controlled cars, so I figured the drone would be fun."

"What happened to your leg?" he asks, gesturing to the spot of blood above my knee.

I look down. "Huh. I don't know?" Even I don't believe me. I obviously need to practice my lying skills.

Thibault smiles. "You didn't have a run-in with a drone by any chance, did you?"

"Oh, for crying out loud, Thibault—again?!" Toni storms off, yelling loud enough for anyone in the Port to hear. "One time, okay? *One* time I hit you!"

I can't *not* laugh when he lifts up his leg and shows me a small scar on his calf. "She nailed me. She's a fucking maniac with that thing."

I lift up my pant leg too, revealing a small cut on my thigh. "Tell me about it."

Thibault tips his head back and roars with laughter.

CHAPTER THIRTY-TWO

W hat's so funny?" Ozzie asks, coming out of the shadows near the weight equipment. He's sweating. Oh my. Sahara is walking behind him, and she looks as wiped out as I feel. Has he been making her work out too? I wouldn't be surprised.

"Toni tried to take her out with the drone." Thibault points at my leg as I let the pants drop into place.

"Again?" Ozzie shakes his head. "Man, she's dangerous."

"Bo Peep got the drone up, though. Girl's got skills, can't deny."

Ozzie gives me an assessing look that has my face going pink. "Let me take a look at that cut before you go upstairs," he says.

"Oh, it's no big deal, really. She barely tapped me."

"Regardless . . . go on over to the table there. I'll join you in a minute."

I limp over to the chair, not because of my drone accident, but because now that all the adrenaline is fading from my system, I'm feeling my aching muscles again. Holy shit, when is my body going to be back to normal?

Sahara and Thibault climb the stairs together and disappear into the samurai room. I take advantage of the alone time to give my arms and legs a massage while I wait for Ozzie to come over and assess my wound or whatever he's going to do.

I'm trying to keep my brain from imagining that his concern for my body is above and beyond that of a boss to an employee, but I lose that battle when he comes back downstairs, sits down next to me, and slowly rolls my pant leg up, putting his warm hand under my calf and lifting my leg to rest on his thigh.

"Does it hurt?"

He's concerned, that much is evident in the seriousness of his expression, not to mention his tone. He touches the skin around the wound very softly. I really wish he'd quit messing around and put those big hands of his on my chest instead.

Oh my god, did I just think that?!

"Not as much as the rest of me," I say jokingly, trying to act with a casualness I do not feel.

He looks up at me, confused. It's the first time I notice the flecks of amber in his green eyes. I try not to stare like a crazy person, but they're beautiful.

"I'm still sore from our workout."

"Ah. Sorry about that." He unscrews some disinfectant and puts some on a cotton ball. "Maybe I overdid it a little."

"No, it's fine. I don't want you to do anything special for me. Just treat me like everyone else."

He dabs at the cut on my leg with the cotton. "You know that's not going to be possible, right?"

He's not looking at me, but does that stop my blood pressure from shooting up into the stars? No, of course not. My whole body goes hot with just that one sentence.

I probably shouldn't assume he means anything special by it, though. I'm sure he's saying I'm weaker than any of his other recruits, so I'm going to need a special, more relaxed program for getting in shape.

"Why can't you treat me the same?" I ask. "I promise, I'll work as hard as I need to in order to make the team." After today I'm sure I want to be here. I want to be part of the Bourbon Street Boys family. This is the most fun I've had at work ever. Plus there's Ozzie. Getting to see him at work is like getting a Christmas bonus every day.

"I have no doubt you will. You've already given a hundred and ten percent. I can't ask for any more than that."

"So what's the problem then?" I hold my breath as I wait for his answer.

He stares at my leg, running a hand from my ankle to my knee as he leans down to examine the cut more closely.

With just that one movement, his fingers dragging along my sensitive skin like that, he sets me on fire. He's tilting my leg left and right, looking at my wound, but the gentleness of his touch is not normal for someone just playing concerned employer. I can't be imagining all of this, can I?

He looks up at me, his eyes darker than before. "I can't treat you like everyone else because you're not like everyone else."

Does he mean . . . ? No. Of course not. He means I'm a weakling. And let's face it: compared to Toni, I am.

"You're saying I'm weak, aren't you? Bo Peep. Some girl who walks around with a hook running after sheep all day long." I'm disgusted with myself. Why haven't I gone to the gym? Why do I eat so much cheesecake?

His smile is faint, but it's there. "No, that's not what I'm saying." He reaches up and squeezes my bicep.

I try not to flinch, but I'm only partially successful. Wow, those muscles are *so* sore.

"You've got strength. We're just going to build on what you already have. I know you can hack it. Otherwise, I would never have hired you."

"Really?" So many alternative meanings to our words are flying around my head. Are we talking about me being a suitable employee or a woman he has feelings for? Because I know I have feelings for him. There's no denying it any more. Every time I'm in his company, I feel closer to him. I want to get to know him better. I wonder if that's even possible; he seems like such a private person.

He shrugs and sits up. "I don't know."

"You don't know?"

What? What just happened? He was all soft before, and now he's back to being regular Ozzie. Is he regretting asking me to work with him?

"No, I don't know." He picks up my leg at the ankle and slowly lowers it to the ground. When he sits up again, he sighs, leans back, and rests his hands on his thighs. "I admit to being a little confused where you're concerned."

I smile. Now I finally feel like we're on even playing ground. Maybe.

"You seem happy about that." He frowns.

"I am, because now I don't feel like the only one."

"You're confused about me?"

"You could say that." No way in hell am I going to be the first one to admit there might be some chemistry between us. For all I know he could be talking about something completely different.

"So, we're mutually confused," he says. A smile starts to turn up the corners of his mouth.

I nudge him with my foot. "Stop."

"Stop what?"

"Smiling."

His eyebrows go up. "Stop smiling?"

My face gets hot. "Yes. You're making me nervous."

His grin goes decidedly devious. "Nervous? Why nervous?"

I kick him again on his boot, harder this time. "Seriously, stop." I stand, unable to take the pressure anymore.

He takes one of my hands and looks up at me. "Where are you going?" His fingers are so warm. Too warm. Oh my god.

"I have to . . . go. I can't handle this . . . whatever it is."

He waits for me to explain.

Ergh! I can't take it! I was never good at playing the game. It's time for some honesty. Someone has to break the ice, right? "It's just . . . been awhile for me, and I was never that experienced before anyway, so . . ." I shrug and stare at the ground.

He doesn't answer right away, so I look up at him.

He's frowning. "What exactly are you talking about?"

I blow out a big frustrated breath of air and then let the words just fly out of my mouth. They can't be contained any longer. "Sex, duh. What are you talking about?"

He stands, still hanging onto my hand. "I was talking about your workouts."

My face blanches and it's suddenly very difficult to breathe. My voice comes out like a croak. "Oh my god. I'm so embarrassed. I have to go." I try to yank my hand from his and move around him, but he won't let go.

He's smiling again.

What in the hell?! Why is he grinning at me like that?!

"Would you *quit* that?!"

His smile turns into chuckles.

I stare at him and realize then that he's been messing with me. This whole time. Maybe since the moment I met him.

"Oh my god, you are so incredibly bad." I can feel the red coming back to my face, crawling up my chest, to my neck, all the way to my forehead. No man has ever made me blush like he has.

"I am?" He moves closer to me.

"You've been completely messing with me. This entire time." I can't decide whether to sing with joy or kick him in the crotch. I still don't know what's going on, but now I *know* there's chemistry between us, on *both* sides. I cannot possibly be imagining everything.

"Don't be mad." He's trying to be cute now.

"Mad? Me? Please." I step away from him to put some distance between us. Mostly because I can think better when he's not so close. "It's going to take a lot more than a guy yanking my chain to piss me off." I start to walk away.

"Where are you going?" he asks, letting my hand slide from his.

"I'm going to go eat some late lunch."

He leans over, grabs my hand, and yanks me back, catching me off guard. I stumble and fall into him. He catches me in his arms as if we were just performing a swing-dancing move.

"You forgot to say good-bye." He's leaning over me, a twinkle in his eye.

CHAPTER THIRTY-THREE

Memories of our lobster dinner and him at my door saying good-bye with a kiss come rushing back. He liked it too! He wants a repeat performance just like I do! I'm going to have a heart attack right here at work!

A door opens above us. I panic, standing quickly and pulling myself out of his grip. Stealing a kiss now and again is one thing; letting other employees know something's going on is another. No way, José. I'll lose every ounce of credibility I have with my coworkers, and when that respect only comes in half-ounces at a time, every drop counts.

"Good-bye, Ozzie. Have a nice afternoon." I walk away with my chin up and my cheeks blazing red, flicking my hair over my shoulder as I go. I can do this. I can be completely cool when my insides are melting like a bar of chocolate left in the hot Louisiana summer sun.

Lucky is coming down the stairs in my direction, when I reach the first step. He has a singlestick in his right hand.

"I hear you're on the injured list," he says, pausing when we're at the same level. The weapon hangs at his side. He doesn't even act like it's there, as if it's just a part of his outfit, like a belt or a watch.

Hmmm, strange. Do they use those upstairs? They must or why would it be there? I don't say anything, because maybe that's normal for them. Maybe they just walk around with weapons for no reason.

"Nah, no injured list for me," I say, ignoring the pain that still racks my every muscle. "I'm fine."

"You got the surveillance equipment up?"

"Yes, we did." I grin with pride, glad to have something to talk about other than my injuries or lack of sex and the desire to have lots of it with Ozzie.

"Well done." He gives me a fist bump. I think it's the first one I've ever executed in my life. "Catch you tomorrow?"

"You're done for the day?"

"Gotta go to the police station and talk to some detectives, so I'm going to miss the afternoon excitement."

I glance back over my shoulder. Ozzie is watching us. "Excitement?" I face Lucky again, not sure I understand. I thought I was going upstairs for a meeting. The last one was interesting, but I don't know that I'd call it *exciting*, per se.

Lucky glances at Ozzie and frowns for a second before turning his attention back to me. "Yeah. The progress briefing. We usually have them every couple days."

I nod. "Oh. Okay. Well, I guess I'll see you tomorrow, then."

"Hey, do you mind?" He holds out the singlestick.

"Mind . . . ?"

"Taking this upstairs for me. I meant to leave it up there, but I guess I was distracted and kept it in my hand instead."

I smile. "Oh, sure. No problem. Where do you want me to put it?"

He starts to grin and then stops immediately. "Give it to Dev."

"Okaaaaay." I narrow my eyes at him, trying to figure out why he's trying so hard to appear serious when he clearly wants to smile. Examining the stick tells me nothing; it looks like it always does, about three feet long and an inch in diameter, thicker at the end where Lucky was holding it. I find it balances better if I hold it at that wider end too. It's kind of heavy, but not so much that I can't wield it. Maybe later I'll ask Ozzie how to actually use it.

He hops down the last few stairs. "See you later."

"Yeah, okay. Later."

I continue up the stairs, stopping at the digital keypad by the door. Whose name was on this side of the door for the code? Was it Toni? I press in T-O-N-I, but nothing happens. Okay, so it's not Toni's door. That makes it . . . Thibault's door? I press in T-B-O-I and hear a click. Even though I know Ozzie's down there watching me screw up, I smile. I did finally get it done, right? I'm not a complete nincompoop when it comes to this security stuff.

I pull the door open, and a flash of movement catches my eye.

"Hooraaaaaaaaahhhhhhhh!" screams a loud voice, a definite war cry.

Something silver flashes in front of my face, and a giant, white beast surges toward me.

I scream bloody murder and jump back, closing my eyes and swinging the singlestick out in front of me with all my frightened might, sore muscles be damned. I make solid contact with something.

"Oooph!" says a loud voice as the singlestick hits its mark.

I open my eyes and see Dev bent over, holding his middle. In his other hand he's gripping a big sword that now dangles down by his leg.

"Did you . . . ? Did you . . . ?" I can't even process what I'm seeing right away. Then I can and I'm *pissed*. "Did you just come at me with a *samurai* sword?!"

"I tried," he says, grunting the words out.

I lift the stick up and whack him on the back of his shoulder with it.

"Aaaawwww, shit!" he yells. "What was that for?!" His back is arched and leaning on a diagonal as he twists away from the pain.

"That was for scaring the shit out of me, you idiot!" I drop the singlestick at his feet with a clatter and shove past him. "Here's your stupid stick, dummy. Don't ever do that to me again!"

He falls to the right when I push him, landing against the doorjamb and sliding down to the floor onto his side.

"Your reflexes are much better than I thought they'd be," he grunts out, pain lacing his voice.

I'm almost through the room and into the kitchen when I answer him. "You just got your ass handed to you by someone you like to call Bo Peep. If I were you, I'd start questioning my ability to read people."

Toni and Thibault are sitting at the table, grinning from ear to ear, when I enter the kitchen.

"You knocked him out, didn't you?" Toni asks. She's still smiling as she bites into a sandwich.

"No. I just tapped him."

"Sounded like more than a tap."

Dev comes limping into the kitchen, his shirt off. There's a red welt on his stomach. "Do I have a bruise?" he asks, turning his back to the table.

I lower myself into a seat, trying not to feel bad about the welt that's there too. It's definitely going to hurt for a while.

"Not yet, but you will," Thibault says. "I warned you not to sneak up on her."

Pride fills my soul. Thibault believes I can't be taken down with a samurai sword sneak attack? Cool. Maybe I am a badass after all. I take a napkin from the stack and select a sandwich from a tray of them in the middle of the table. I have no idea what it is, but I'm going to eat it anyway. I'm that starving. Something about having someone come at me with a sword, and yet living through it, makes me especially hungry.

"She needs training," Dev says.

"I suggest you do some other kind of training," I say, chewing a bite of what I've determined is a turkey sandwich. "Not sneak attacks."

"Gotta keep your reflexes sharp." Dev sits down and helps himself to six sandwiches. No one bats an eyelash at his appetite.

"Seems like your own reflexes might be getting a little rusty," Thibault says.

"Nah. I had a sword. I didn't want to use it on her. She's not ready."

I swallow a bit of sandwich that's pretty much turned to sawdust in my mouth at his words. "Ready? You actually think I'll be ready someday to be attacked by someone with a sword?"

"If I'm doing my job right, yeah." Dev winks at me, his mouth full of food. "You'll be all right. Trust the process."

I shake my head while I take another bite. "You're crazy." I'm very rudely talking around some tomato, but I don't care. Anyone who sneak-attacks me forfeits the right to enjoy my good manners. I have to admit, though, I am kind of excited about the idea of being that highly trained, but there's nothing in me that wants to face a sword being used against me for real. I joined this team to take pictures, not fight ninjas, for God's sake.

Ozzie enters the room and takes his seat at the head of the table. "How'd it go today?" He's looking at Toni, so I keep my mouth shut. I'm glad she's his focus, because I'm kind of worried about him addressing me directly. I don't trust myself not to go all goo-goo eyes on him.

"Good," she says, oblivious to my discomfort. "Got eyes on the back of the house. We'll need to change the battery in a couple days on that one. The Parrot's on the pole, so we have bird's-eye. Bo Peep got some shots of someone who came outside while we were there."

I pause my chewing. I probably should have brought that camera upstairs to the meeting so they could review the pictures I took. Dammit. Rookie mistake. Grrr, I hate that.

"I can show you the pictures if you want. I just have to go downstairs . . ."

Ozzie waves a hand at me. "Later. What happened with the guy?"

Toni shrugs. "He was walking his dog."

"Who'd he see? Both of you?"

"No, just me."

"All right, I don't want you going back there for the time being."

Toni drops her sandwich onto her napkin. "What the hell, man? He didn't make me."

Ozzie goes rigid. "We lost Harley. We have no solid confirm they made me, but if they did, we can't have them seeing the same person twice in the 'hood, you got it?"

She scowls, but nods all the same. "Yeah, I got it."

"You can run through the images once they come in and see what there is to see."

She nods once and goes back to her sandwich. She's definitely not happy.

"What do you think?" he asks, looking at me.

I scan the faces waiting expectantly for my answer, hoping to glean a possible direction from them, but they give me nothing. I sigh in defeat. The rookie hot seat. I already hate being on this thing, and it's only been my place for two days.

CHAPTER THIRTY-FOUR

W̲hat do I think about what?" I ask. I hate being put on the spot. I wasn't prepared. What if I sound stupid? I haven't had any spy training yet. I don't even know the right lingo.

"What do you think about the work you did today?" Ozzie explains. "Any thoughts?"

"Well . . ." I think about it for a few seconds before continuing. "It went well, I guess. One person did see us, but he thought we were with the electric company. Toni said we were with the phone company. We watched him; he didn't look up at the drone at all."

"Good. Anything else?"

"Mmmm . . . well, I was just wondering . . . it doesn't have anything to do with what we did today, but how did they discover your Harley identity? Back in the bar, when I was there with Felix. You said it was my fault."

"The guy who took a shot at us was part of their group. If he shot at me, it means he knew something was up. I have to assume it had something to do with you walking in with your dog in that bag, because before that happened, everything seemed fine. Maybe I'm wrong about that, but I was looking at you and when he noticed, he got suspicious. When I went to help you, it just confirmed for him that I wasn't who I was supposed to be. You aren't exactly Harley's type."

"What he means is, he was acting like a good guy and not a bad guy," Toni says, probably noticing the confusion on my face.

"Yeah." Ozzie nods. "Right. I stepped out of character. Bad idea in a crowd like that. They tend to be very paranoid."

I'm trying to picture the scene. I can't remember the guy Harley was standing with. Was it the man who shot at us? "You're talking about that bald guy with the mustache and the giant mole on his cheek?"

"You saw all that?" Ozzie's gone all intense on me again. Man, his moods shift like the wind.

"Sure. He was looking right at me right after he fired that gun. You were trying to pull me off the table, but I thought my sister was there, so I was hanging on pretty tight. I was facing him the whole time."

Thibault lets out a long stream of air.

"What?" I look around at everyone exchanging glances. They're obviously worried.

"You said she was followed home," Thibault says to Ozzie. "That's not good."

"I have my security system now, though, and no one's bothered me at all." I'm not sure what I'm arguing against, but clearly they're making some kind of plan among them. Everyone gets it but me.

"She should stay here," Thibault says. Then he jumps in surprise and turns to glare at his sister.

I look at her, trying to figure out why she'd kick him under the table for that. Does she not want me to be here? Is she worried about Ozzie and me? Does she like him? Oh, God, that would be terrible. And Toni and I were becoming friends, I'm sure of it!

Love triangle. Dammit.

I decide to watch them closer. The last thing I want to do is horn in on some other woman's territory, even if it is Ozzie on the line.

"You're right." Ozzie looks at me, a very determined expression taking over. "I'll bring you home so you can pack a bag."

"You want backup?" Toni asks, her chin a little higher than normal.

"No, we got it."

I raise a finger.

Ozzie lifts a brow. "Yes? You have a question?"

I smile politely, lowering my arm. "More like a comment. I don't want to sleep here."

"She doesn't like the cot," Thibault says. "You should give her your bed."

"It's not the cot." The words rush out of me in an effort to stop that conversation as quickly as possible. Just the idea of being in Ozzie's bed makes me break out in a cold sweat. "It's just that I have Felix and I can't leave him behind, and it's my home, so it has all my things in it." The excuse sounds lame even to my own ears.

"It's the same as going on vacation," Toni says, not sounding very impressed. "Your house can survive without you for a few days until we assess the threat. What are you worried about over there? Plants?"

"I do have plants, as a matter of fact." Not that they'll miss me. They only need to be watered once a week, since they're all in the shade. I'm just worried about the stupid things I'll say and be tempted to do living in Ozzie's space with him for several days. My willpower can only manage so much.

"We'll take care of the plants, if necessary." Ozzie motions for Thibault to hand him something. Thibault gives him a folder.

"But . . ."

Ozzie looks up from the file he was opening. "You're an employee of this company. I can't send you back home if it's a dangerous place to be. I'm sorry. Hopefully, we'll neutralize any issues in a matter of days, and your plants won't have time to dry out."

My jaw drops open. I'm being railroaded into this, and while the idea of living with Ozzie is not entirely unpleasant, I don't like the feeling that I don't have a choice in the matter.

"I appreciate what you've said, and I thank you for your concern, but I'm afraid I'm going to decline your offer." I nod so they can see how serious I am. I'll sleep with my door locked and a big kitchen knife under my pillow. I'll be fine. Maybe Dev will loan me that singlestick. I seem to have a knack for it.

Thibault and Toni look at Ozzie. He nods at them. They get up and leave the table, going into the sword room to the outer stairs. I hear the main door close behind them. I guess that nod from Ozzie was code for *Leave, so I can talk some sense into her.*

"I'm not staying here, Ozzie, and that's final."

His eyes are storming but his expression remains impassive. "I'll stay somewhere else if being around me makes you that uncomfortable."

"It's not that." I chew my lip after the lie leaves my mouth. I cannot think of an excuse that will make any sense. I like my own shower? Your dog has gas? I'll miss my hibiscus bush?

"Whatever it is, I'm sure I can manage it."

"Okay, fine!" I say way too loudly. "It's you! There—are you happy now?"

"No."

I'm not sure, but from the look on his face, it kind of seems like I hurt his feelings. I try begging instead of being frustrated. "Ozzie, come on, you must be able to understand how this is for me."

"No, not really. Explain it."

"I just met you not even a week ago, and you were wearing the most hideous beard that ever was on a man's face."

"It wasn't that bad."

"Yes, it was that bad, trust me. There were probably small birds living inside it. But then you saved me, and you shaved it off, and you cooked amazing food, and you kissed me! And I'm not immune to those charms, okay? I'm just not. And as I embarrassingly admitted to you earlier, it's been awhile for me, so I'm kind of on a hair trigger where you're concerned, and that's not a good place for me to be when you're sleeping down the hall from me."

He sits there just staring at me for the longest time. It's making me crazy, but I refuse to say another word until he does. No one can do stubborn like I can do stubborn when I set my mind to it. Besides, I've already humiliated myself enough for one day.

"So, if I understand you correctly, what you're saying is . . . I'm irresistible." His expression doesn't change.

"Your words, not mine."

"If I promise to give you your own space, where you can lock the door against me and do your own thing, you'll be okay with it?"

"No, I never said that. I said I want to sleep in my own bed, in my own house."

"And risk having someone come there to make sure you can't describe him to the police?"

When he puts it that way, I have a harder time answering. But I do it anyway. "Yes. I can handle it."

He shrugs. "Fine. You have two bedrooms. I'll come stay with you in the second one."

"No!"

"Okay, I'll have Thibault come stay with you."

"No, not Thibault!" It's getting worse, not better. Since when did I become such a horrible negotiator?

"Lucky? He could bring his goldfish to your house without too much trouble."

"No, absolutely not." I cannot inconvenience my colleagues like that. How embarrassing! My nickname will never change if I need a babysitter my first week. Besides, I really don't think I'm in trouble at all. If that guy were going to come for me, he already would have.

"Dev can't do it," Ozzie explains, "and I'm pretty sure Toni would be a pain in the ass about it, so that leaves you with me."

I lift my chin. "I'll take Toni." I could manage it if it were a woman and not one of the guys. I don't know why. It makes no sense; babysitting is babysitting. But at least with a woman I'd feel like it was more a temporary roommate thing than a bodyguard thing.

"You'd rather have Toni watching your back than me?"

Is it my imagination or does he sound hurt by that? Maybe he's just offended. She is pretty puny.

"No, it's not that. It's just that with Toni, I can be myself. And I want to be able to be myself when I'm at home." My tone goes into a pleading mode. "You can understand that, can't you?" I think I've almost got him convinced. He's on the ropes. I can see him caving . . .

"No," he says. "That makes no sense whatsoever. I'm staying with you tonight and into the foreseeable future until we've assessed the threat and determined it doesn't exist anymore or have removed it."

I stand. "What if I say no?"

"I know the code to your alarm." He looks like he's about to smile, but lucky for him, he's smart enough to hold it in.

"No, you don't." He never did change it for me when he was at my house.

"Thibault's birthday."

The loss of my almost won victory deflates me like a balloon. "Dammit."

He loses some of his bravado too. "Would it really be that bad to have me around after hours?"

I cross my arms over my chest. "I don't know. Can you keep your hands to yourself?"

He shrugs. "I can if you can."

I roll my eyes. "Please. Check your ego at the door, Oswald, because I'm not going to be falling for any of that charm you like to spread around like peanut butter."

He chuckles. "Like peanut butter, huh?"

I throw a pencil at him. "Oh, shut up." Knowing that anything I say from here on out is only going to be defensive and stupid, I leave the room. His voice follows me out.

"Don't leave without me!"

"I'm leaving in five minutes, so you'd better be ready!" I mean it too. I'm taking off whether he's with me or not. He can't make me wait for him. Stupid, egotistical, bossy . . . boss person.

My feet slow down, even though I'm telling myself I need to hurry up and go. It takes me forever to get to my car. I hate it when my body defies my brain like that. It seems to be a big problem for me whenever Ozzie's around. So how in the hell am I going to listen to my brain telling me to stay the heck away from him when my body is constantly wanting to reach out and touch his glorious muscles?

Ugh, this is a mistake. This is going to be awful.

CHAPTER THIRTY-FIVE

Okay, so it's not as bad as I thought it was going to be. Ozzie follows me in his truck, Sahara tied up in the back, but calls me on my cell and tells me to turn into a plaza on the way. When we park next to one another, he explains that they have a great organic grocery here with ingredients he needs to make a chicken curry dinner for us. When I told him before I didn't want him to stay with me, I'd temporarily forgotten how well he cooks.

Ninety minutes later I'm eating the last bite of the most delicious meal I've ever had. I groan with the pain of my stretching stomach, but I don't regret a single calorie of it.

"Good?" he asks, sipping a bottle of beer. It's his second. I've stuck to water, because I don't trust myself not to be an idiot in his presence. Sobriety is my only hope.

"Good? No. Not good at all. Excellent. Amazing. Delicious." I rub my stomach. "You can cook for me anytime."

"So you don't mind me being here, then?"

His question is a challenge. I stand and gather plates, wondering whether I should jump into the game or just be real. I vote in favor of being up front about things. Playing games with Ozzie can be dangerous. I have a feeling I'll lose every time.

"I guess I never minded that you be here. That's not the right way to explain it. I just don't like being considered weak."

"Just because someone might have it in for you, doesn't make you weak. In your case it's a matter of being in the wrong place at the wrong time. It's no reflection of who you are or whether you're strong or not."

I let the water from the faucet wash away the remnants of our dinner as I contemplate those words.

"I don't know . . ." Sometimes things are really clear for me, and other times they're murky. This is one of those less-clear situations. Whenever The Fates seem to be interfering in my life, I wonder how much of it I have control of. "Um, I guess I'm having a hard time rationalizing those words with what's happened." It feels like a confession to tell him that.

"In what way?"

"Well, I started talking to you because you were a wrong number."

"Another one of those wrong place, wrong time situations," he says.

"No, not really."

He takes some dishes from the table and joins me in the kitchen. He stands at the dishwasher and takes plates and silverware from me, loading them carefully in the available slots.

"I was thinking that even though it seemed wrong at the start, and you seemed wrong at the start with that horrible beard and all, things turned out pretty good in retrospect."

"You mean you're happy I had the wrong number."

"Yes. Wrong number, right guy." I grin. "You're a good boss."

He grunts, leaning over the dishwasher as he puts a plate near the back. "Is that so."

"Yes, it is. You have a nice workplace for your employees, you provide lots of benefits, and you care about their safety. You're here at my house, in fact, making sure I'm okay. Not many bosses would do that."

He stands up and takes the next plate from me. But he doesn't bend over and put it in the dishwasher. "You're right. Not many would."

I grin. "See? Great boss."

He gives me a wry look. "I have to be honest, though. I'm not sure I'd do it for Lucky and his goldfish."

I force the butterflies to go away and not take up residence in my chest or my stomach. He's just being funny.

"Well, he's a guy. And he's been highly trained." I take the plate from Ozzie's hands and put it in the dishwasher myself. I'm not going to let this thing turn into a flirtation. We can be adults sharing the same living space without things getting silly.

"I'm not sure I'd do it for Toni either," he says.

Now I'm not as certain he isn't saying something about *us*. I try to laugh it off anyway.

"She's highly trained too."

"Yeah, she is." He puts the next plate in the washer. Then he leans over and grabs my sponge from the edge of the sink and leaves the kitchen to wipe down the table. The scent of him lingers, and I breathe it in quietly.

I'm sad he's left the conversation, but happy to have a moment to gather myself. Wow. He's saying I'm special. He didn't go so far as to say he likes me, but I'm definitely getting that impression.

So what do I do? Ignore it? Play it off? Send him signals that I'm not interested? Send him signals that I am? I really need to talk to my sister. She'll know what to do.

"Do you mind if I go upstairs to make a phone call?" I ask, wiping my hands dry on a dishtowel. "My sister gets kind of freaky when she doesn't hear from me in the evening."

"Yeah, sure. I'll finish up down here. Then I'm going to get on my computer in the living room, if that's okay."

I wave my hand around. "Oh, sure, no problem. My password's stuck to the front of my computer over by the window. Do whatever you want." I put the dishtowel down and try to walk casually over to the staircase. What I really want to do is run, pounding up the stairs as I dial my sister's number and give her a blow-by-blow recounting of my entire day, gushing like a schoolgirl. But I need to act like the adult I am and have some control. It's not that big a deal if Ozzie wants to sleep with me. We're both consenting adults. It's not like I'm going to fall in love with him.

I lock my bedroom door and put on some music, just in case he has plans to try and listen in. My sister picks up on the third ring.

CHAPTER THIRTY-SIX

"You were supposed to call me earlier," she says in a scolding tone.

"I know. I've been crazy busy with work." Felix jumps up on the bed and curls up in my lap. I stroke his tiny head and ears absently as I focus on my sister.

"I guess that's good news. You're talking about your new job, right?"

"Yes. How are the kids?" I need time to figure out how to broach the subject with Jenny about Ozzie being here. I'll distract her with talk about the children while I do that.

"Good." She sighs. "Miles is coming to get them next weekend, or so he says."

"That'll be nice for you."

"If he shows."

"What will you do with two whole days to yourself?"

"Oh, I don't know. Take a bath with a bottle of wine. See a movie. Get my nails done. Sleep for twelve hours straight."

"Call me if you want company for any of that. Except the bath. I'm done taking baths with you."

"You could sit on the toilet and keep my wineglass full."

"Yeah, I suppose I could do that." I smile. I would totally be my sister's bath-time wine filler-upper. It's the least I can do for the girl who taught me how to ride a bike and tie my shoes.

"So, what's up with you?" she asks. "How's the new job going?"

"Pretty good. I'm getting some training." I decide not to tell her about the surveillance stuff in detail. She'd worry too much. "Took some pictures. Did a little hand-to-hand combat." *Oops.* Probably should have held that back too.

"What, *what*? Did you say *combat*?"

I laugh, thinking about Dev crumpling to the floor. I hope it doesn't make me a sadist that I find that so amusing. "Yeah, there's this guy Dev, the one I told you about before, the really tall one . . . he tried to sneak-attack me today, but I had a weapon ready, so he lost."

There's a long silence before Jenny responds.

"Babe, I'm worried."

My mood falters. "Why?"

"Actually, I'm not sure whether to be more worried about the fact that your colleagues are attacking you or that you think it's no big deal. They're both very disturbing situations to any normal person. You used to be normal. What has that place done to you?"

A picture of Ozzie standing there with his arms crossed over his chest pops into my head. *Ozzie happened to me, sister. It was Ozzie.*

"I'm totally fine, really—I promise. Actually, though, I do need your advice about something."

"Does it relate to this crazy workplace?"

Now I'm nervous. Maybe this was a mistake calling her. She's already being kind of judge-y. "Yyyeeeesss."

"I'm listening."

It's too late to do anything but confess. I try to keep my tone light so she won't panic overly much. "Ozzie's staying at my place temporarily." Yay, good plan; yay, me! Jump right into the deep end without any warm-up!

"Oh my god! Are you serious?!" At least she doesn't sound too angry.

"It's kind of complicated."

"Do you like him? Does he like you? Have you guys had sex yet?"

"Ack, no! Stop! Just listen."

"Okay, I'm listening. Just remember, though, that I have no life, so anything you have going on is going to seem way more exciting to me than it probably is."

I laugh. "Okay, good. Thanks for the warning not to take your enthusiasm to heart."

"That's not what I meant, but go ahead. I can't wait to hear the details."

"Remember that night I was texting him, and I thought I was texting you?"

"Yes."

"Well, that guy who was shooting a gun that night in the bar—I can identify him. And Ozzie's worried that the guy might be able to figure out who I am, so he's moved in here just until they can assess the threat."

"Threat."

"Don't say it like that, Jen. Seriously, it's no big deal."

"I'm preeeeetty sure it's a *really* big deal, actually."

"No, it's not. I promise. I have a great security system, I have Ozzie and his giant dog here, I have Felix . . ."

"Who'd be really good at maybe puncturing the skin around a murderer's ankles, assuming he isn't kicked into a wall first."

"Now you're being mean."

"This isn't meanness, May; it's called sisterly concern. And like I said before, I think this new job has twisted your sense of reality.

When a gunman comes after you to find you, he kills you. He uses bullets. He doesn't walk up to the door, ring the bell, and have a conversation with you first. He can get you through a window or a wall, even. It's true. I've seen it on real-crime TV."

Her voice reminds me of my conscience. They have the same tone and everything.

"Well, this is my life, Jenny. I saw what I saw when I was out rescuing you and the kids, and I can't undo that."

"That's totally unfair, blaming this on me!"

"I'm not, I'm not." I take a breath to calm myself down. "Or I don't mean to. I'm just saying, it's fate. That wrong-number text coming to my phone when you were buying a new phone, me going to Frankie's where Ozzie was working undercover, me being a photographer when they need a photographer—it's all fate. It's meant to be."

"And you think Ozzie being in your house right now on a sleepover is fate too?"

"I don't know. That's why I called you."

"You want me to tell you if Ozzie being there is fate?"

"Kind of."

"You're thinking about sleeping with him, aren't you?" Her tone loses some of its angry edge. "You little slut."

"Stop. This isn't funny."

"No, you're right, it's not. He's your boss. He's there to make sure no one hurts you."

"So, you're saying I shouldn't sleep with him, then."

"No, I'm not saying that. I'm just saying what I'm saying."

"You're saying what you're saying. That makes no sense at all."

"I'm saying that it's complicated."

My hand flies up and waves around the room. "Hence my phone call to you!"

Felix looks up at me, concerned. I pat him on the back, and he goes back to napping, resting his head on my thigh.

"Okay. Fine. Let's analyze."

"Yes." I'm filled with relief. "Let's."

"He's your boss."

My eyes roll to the ceiling. "We already covered that."

"He's hot."

"Very." I smile. He is so, so, so, so cute. If I were sixteen again, I'd write his name all over my notebooks.

"He's willing, I assume?"

"He's already kissed me twice. Or did once and almost did a second time."

"Who stopped the second attempt?"

"I did."

"Good."

"Why is that good?"

"It gives you the upper hand in his mind. Okay, so what else?"

"I don't know." I'm depressed now. This is so messed up. "I can't think straight where he's concerned. Yes, he's my boss, and yes, he's here for professional reasons, and no, I don't want to get my heart broken. That's all I can think of."

"What about the sex? Have you thought about that?"

"Not really." My face flushes at the very idea. "I mean, I'm completely attracted to him, but every time I get near him, I get so flustered I say stupid things, and then I have to get away so I can think straight."

"Wow. Geez. You've got it bad."

"I know!" I whine, collapsing back onto my bed. I stare at the ceiling while Felix climbs up to lie down on my chest. "He's smart and tough and hot and sexy, and he cooks like a professional chef, and . . ."

"And he's your boss."

I fall down to earth, crashing from my high to a very low low. "Yes. And he's my boss."

"So what's the worst thing that could happen? If you slept with him, I mean."

I think about it for a few seconds. "I guess we could end up not working out and then it would be awkward, and I'd have to quit my new job."

"And you'd be right back where you were before: no harm, no foul."

"But I like my new job."

"Sure, but I'm just saying, the worst-case scenario doesn't make you worse off than you were before you met him."

"Except for the broken heart part."

"Meh, hearts heal. Trust me."

"I could also lose the respect of my coworkers."

"Who you don't even really know, and once they get to know you, they'll forgive you. Besides, maybe they'd like to see their boss in a relationship."

"What do you mean?"

"Everyone knows bosses who are getting laid regularly are much more reasonable."

"Everyone knows that?"

"Yes."

"I didn't."

"Well, you're young."

"You're only thirty-two!"

"I'm wise beyond my years."

"Okay, so are you telling me I should have sex with him, then?"

"I'm saying you should follow your heart, because if it doesn't work out, you'll be fine, and if it does work out, you'll be finer."

I grin from ear to ear. "I love you, Jenny. You're so smart."

She sighs. "You were going to sleep with him anyway, no matter what I said."

"That's not true. I value your opinion."

"Yeah, but you're hot for him. No amount of common sense is going to stop that train from running down the sexy track. Just go and get it over with. I predict you'll be glad you did."

I'm suddenly filled with the urge to see Ozzie. "Okay. I've gotta go."

She laughs. "So quickly? Don't you want to discuss the new computer program I'm working on? It's very exciting."

"Sure it is." She works for a company that makes calorie-counting applications for phones. "I'll hear about it this weekend."

"We'll be seeing you this weekend? Sure you won't be too busy having all kinds of dirty sex with your new boyfriend?"

"He's not my boyfriend."

"Not yet."

"Jen, stop! You're putting pressure on it now!"

"Okay, fine. I'll stop. I love you. Don't do anything I wouldn't do."

"But you're a total ho-bag."

"Once upon a time, I was! Have fun!" she trills before disconnecting the call.

I sigh with happiness as I let the phone fall to my side. My sister has green-lighted this affair. My sister and The Fates have spoken. It's time to tell Ozzie how I feel.

CHAPTER THIRTY-SEVEN

I find Ozzie in my living room, hovering over his computer. He's put a blanket that used to be on the back of my couch up over the windows. Sahara is sleeping in the hallway. Felix joins her there, taking up residence on her paws. She makes room for him to settle in, and my heart melts just a little more toward her. She is now permitted to toot in my living room.

"What's going on?" I ask, taking a seat near Ozzie. I pick up a magazine to show how cool and relaxed I am. He'll never know I'm burning up inside, imagining telling him that I want his body against mine. I hate that Britney Spears is singing in my head right now.

To distract my overly busy brain, I practice casual pickup lines in my head as I wait for his answer:

You look hot in that shirt. Maybe you should take it off.
Do you have a girlfriend? Do you want one?
I was wrong, Ozzie. So wrong. Take me to bed now.
Do you come here often?
Sex. I want some. Rawr.

"Nothing much," he says, oblivious to my mania, "just checking various cameras we have set up around town." He swivels the laptop in my direction. There are several windows open on his screen. When I recognize the houses in one of them, I point.

"Hey! That's our target from today!"

"Yeah." He makes the window bigger. "Looks like we're getting some activity."

There are two cars parked outside and one just arriving. The images aren't great quality, the individuals walking around lit by streetlights only, but they're good enough for one thing.

"That's that guy!" I say, getting up so I can kneel by the computer. "Right there. That's baldie." I point to the screen.

"Yes, it is," Ozzie says, typing something out really fast on his keyboard. The image gets bigger, as if the camera on the drone is focusing.

"Whoa," I say. "That's seriously cool."

"Not nearly as cool as what you're about to see." He shares a quick gleeful smile with me and then flicks over to another screen. To his right on my desk is a joystick I hadn't noticed before, plugged into the USB slot of his computer.

The fingers of his left hand type on the keyboard. His right hand is on the joystick. Suddenly, we're looking at another view of the house, but this one is moving, and it's going a lot faster than the Parrot I had in my hands today.

I feel a little dizzy, watching from this perspective. "What's happening?" It's as if he's taken the drone from the pole and moved it.

"Another bug we have."

"Bug?"

"Bugs. Electronics used to listen in on conversations and so forth." His tone is distracted as he concentrates on what he's doing. The bug that was heading toward the house now flies over to the side of it.

"Where's it going?"

"Just watch and see." When it reaches a dilapidated wood fence leading to the backyard, it stops. There are several people there, enjoying what looks like a barbecue. Ozzie presses one of the F-keys on his laptop, and suddenly sounds are coming out of his computer. Party sounds.

"Oh my god! It's a bug! Like in the movies!" I clap my hands together like a small child. When I realize I look like Sammy congratulating himself on the toilet, I stop.

"Yeah, except this one is the real deal." He pushes another button. "So now we record everything and analyze the data later."

"Can I help with that part?"

"I'm counting on it."

I go a little warm inside. He's counting on me. Cool. Hopefully, this bug will pick up something good. Assuming it doesn't get discovered, of course. I'm not sure how it could be missed, though. I mean, I can hear them partying it up, but that doesn't make them blind.

"Aren't they going to notice a drone sitting on their fence?"

"Not this one. It's the size of a dragon fly and looks a lot like one."

"Whoa. That's kind of spooky, actually." I look around my room, wondering if there are any bugs hiding around here.

He turns his head to look at me, removing his hands from the joystick and computer at the same time. "Did you want to talk to me about something a minute ago?"

Suddenly the conversation with my sister comes flooding back, and I go from being fascinated and impressed to nervous again. "Uhhh, heh-heh . . ." Ack! My brain and my mouth have disconnected!

"Are you okay?" Ozzie asks, frowning at my expression.

"Yeah, sure, I'm fine." Phew, thank goodness, the brain is back online. Now if I could just get my blood pressure to calm down I'd be stellar.

I get to my feet and back away from him, stopping when my calves hit the edge of a chair. I sink down into it, hoping I don't look as nervous as I feel. "Just had a chat with my sister. Thought I'd come down to see what you're up to." I glance at the clock. "I normally don't go to bed until after ten."

"Me neither." He leans back in the office chair, making it squeak in time with his slight rocking moves. "I guess we have a couple hours to kill." He looks me up and down. The way he's rocking makes it look like he's nodding his approval.

Whoa. Powerful stuff.

I can't hold his gaze. My eyes wander the room. "Yep, couple hours or so. We could watch TV." I shrug. I'm cool. I'm casual. I can watch television with a hot guy for two hours and keep my hands to myself. I'd better pop some popcorn, though. Keep the hands busy.

"We could." He nods slowly. The chair has stopped moving, so I know he's doing it on purpose this time. I think he might be holding back a smile; it's hard to tell.

"We could . . . play cards," I offer.

He stops nodding. "We *could* do that, or . . ."

I shrug and my mouth opens, words spilling out. "Or we could just sleep together. Get it over with."

Oh my god! I just said that out loud! Help! I'm going down like a clown to Crazy Town!

"That's always an option," he says just as calmly as he said we could play cards.

What. The. Hell!

I turn my gaze toward him and find him smiling.

"Stop looking at me like that," I say, a little breathless from my nerves being shattered. I'm sweating too, of course. Hopefully not enough to be noticeable.

"How am I *supposed* to be looking at you right now? You just propositioned me."

"No, I didn't." I frown like he's the crazy one and not me. I doubt it's very convincing since I'm pretty much wearing a name tag that says, "Hello, my name is CRAZY." I look off to the side, convinced there's something very interesting that needs my attention on the bookshelves.

"I might be a little rusty in this area, but I'm pretty sure you did."

"What area?" He has my full attention now. Is he confessing that he hasn't had sex in a long time too? Just like me? Are we both coming off a long, dry spell?

"The area of having women throw themselves at me."

I stand, outrage pouring out of my every pore. "I did no such thing! How dare you!" I'm so embarrassed! Humiliated! This is awful! My worst-case scenario was nothing this disastrous! Run away!

He jumps up too and lunges for me, grabbing me in a bear hug before I can escape. He's laughing, the bastard.

"I'm just kidding!" He buries his face in my neck as I struggle to get away. "Calm down, Bo Peep, before you hurt someone."

"I'm going to hurt *you* as soon as you let me go." The sting of his earlier tease is easing, quickly being replaced by the warmth of his touch. Our bodies are connected from toes to nose. I'm still going to slap him, of course, but then I just might do something else after.

"Aw, you don't want to do that, do you?"

My struggles mostly cease. "Kind of."

He kisses the delicate skin of my neck, ending my resistance completely. "Are you sure about that?" he asks in a whispery voice.

I sigh with delight and defeat. "I'm not sure about anything where you're concerned, Ozzie. Seriously. You're confusing the hell out of me right now." He's a complete stranger, but he's not. A big mountain man with a horrible beard, but not. Dangerous, but not. Ack! Something better start making sense around here . . .

"Good. I like confused." He growls and takes a small bite of my neck.

"Ow! Watch it." I push on his chest, pretending I want to get away.

He knows it's all an act, though. We both do. Besides, I'm not going to get away from this cage made of pure muscle until he wants to let me go. Hopefully, that won't be happening for a long time. The word *forever* flits through my mind.

He's kissing me again, slowly sucking the spot he nipped. Shivers go up and down my spine and everything feels like it's catching on fire. My system is going haywire. His kisses continue up my neck, where he licks the skin near my ear, before reversing direction and going down to my shoulder. My pulse is racing and my breath coming faster. My nipples grow hard under my bra, and other parts of me down below start to ache.

He groans. "Mmmm, you taste so good. I wonder . . . do you taste this good everywhere?"

Now my crotch is on fire too. Great. How am I going to say no to him now?

His left hand slides down my back and grabs my butt, squeezing and then using it to pull me against him. He's as hard as a rock. I can feel his arousal through all our layers of clothing, and he's just as big there as he is everywhere else. Oh my god.

A weird beep I've never heard before sounds out in my front foyer.

Ozzie freezes in place for two seconds, and then his hands drop away from my body. He steps back, every fiber of his body screaming the fact that he's on alert.

I stand there like a mannequin posed in a sex-shop window. My eyes remain half shut for a few seconds until I realize that he's walking away.

"Wha . . . ?"

"Shhhh." He holds a finger to his lips as he walks over to the foyer.

I cease the sex-mannequin act and follow him to the keypad at my front door. The number 8 is lit with a red light. It's ominous, as crazy as that sounds. I think my impression is aided by the fact that Ozzie has gone from being my sexy maybe-going-to-be lover to being an army commando ready to strike. It's both scary and hot as hell to see in action.

"Stay right here," Ozzie says, pulling me by the wrist over to the bathroom by the front door. "Get in, lock the door, don't come out until I tell you to."

"But . . . ?" Okay, this isn't sexy. This is scary. I don't want to play anymore.

"Do it. Tell me you understand." He takes me by the chin and holds my face still. He's staring at me so intensely, I have no choice but to nod.

"I hear you and I understand you," I say as best I can with him still controlling my jaw. "What did that light on the keypad mean?"

"It's a possible intruder alert."

My heart spasms in my chest. Am I going to get shot? I'd better not. Ozzie and I were just getting started. "Why didn't the siren go off?" I whisper-squeal.

"Because they haven't breached any entrances to the home yet. It's marking someone crossing the border onto your property."

I notice for the first time that an exterior light has come on in the front yard. When did that thing get installed? I don't remember having one of those before.

"When did . . . ? Since when do I have . . . ?"

"It was installed this afternoon. I asked Thibault to come over here and put the system in." He leans down and kisses me on the mouth before letting my chin go and leaving me alone in the bathroom.

I lean outside the door after he's gone.

"Felix!" I whisper. "Get in here!"

Felix comes over dutifully and enters the bathroom, his tiny toenails clicking on the tile like itsy-bitsy tap shoes. Once I've shut the door, locking us both inside, I sink down to the rug and commence panicking at level ten.

CHAPTER THIRTY-EIGHT

It seems like forever that we hear nothing. Then the alarm siren goes off, and I nearly squeeze Felix to death in surprised fright. He yips in pain and bites me on the arm.

"Ouch, you little punk!" I pick him up and climb into the bathtub, closing the shower curtain behind us. Felix feels bad about biting me, so now he's trying to make it up to me by giving my arm a tongue bath. Great. Curling up into the smallest human I can, over by the faucets, I pray that Ozzie doesn't get hurt trying to keep me and my little furbaby safe. I can hear every one of my heartbeats. Felix's too.

Sahara's deep, threatening barks come through the door next. Felix perks up and starts barking too. I hold his mouth closed, and his anger comes out muffled.

"Berf! Erf! Eerf, berf, berf!"

Little man's pissed, but no way in hell am I going to let him out there to get kicked into the wall. Jenny was right; Felix would go for the ankles and pay dearly for it.

After what seems like a really long time, long enough for me to sweat through my shirt, Ozzie's voice can now be heard over the din of Sahara's discontent. He's telling someone at the alarm company that everything is fine. Then he's at the bathroom door.

"What's your password?" he asks.

"Who's there?!" I want Ozzie to know I would at least check before trusting just a voice. I'm practically a security specialist already.

"It's me, Ozzie. I need the code, or they're going to send the cops."

"Are you alone or are you being held at gunpoint?"

"Open the door and see for yourself."

Ozzie would never tell me to do that if there was a real bad guy out there. I don't know him very well, but I know this. I honestly could picture him taking a bullet for anyone on his team, me included. I get out of the tub and crack open the door. "It's Sahara," I say as quietly as I can and still be heard over the sirens.

Ozzie is talking into my cell. "Sahara." He glances down at me, his eyes full of meaning, but one I cannot discern. It could be stress at dealing with whatever happened or something else. I don't know him well enough to read him, and now I'm not sure that I *could* ever know him that well.

He's like no man I've ever met before. Just now, when he thought an intruder was here, he didn't hesitate; he threw me in the bathroom and headed out to take care of it. I've never felt so safe in my entire life, so cared for. I thought I had the maximum-level hots for him before, but I was wrong. I'd have sex with him on the bathroom floor right this second if he asked.

"Okay, thanks," he says to the person on the phone. "I'm resetting now. Don't assume it's not a real call if you get another one tonight." He nods a few times. "Thanks. Later."

He shuts the call down and hands me my phone.

"What the hell was that?" I emerge from my hideout on shaky legs. Felix wants to get down, but I'm not letting him do that yet. Sahara is there at my feet, sniffing his legs from below.

"Someone came onto your property, but the alarm that I tripped scared them off."

"Did you see anyone?"

"No, but I'm going to assume it was the man who saw you in the bar."

"Why would you do that? It could have been a cat or dog or a raccoon." I don't want it to be a bad guy; I want it to be a false alarm. I'm sure there's a perfectly good explanation for that stupid alert to go off.

"You have raccoons that stand four feet tall in this neighborhood? Because that's the minimum height that'll set off the device."

We're standing in the middle of the living room now. My outrage has turned to fear. "No."

"The alarm only triggers when a person-sized object crosses over the edge of your property. Unfortunately, whoever it was—assuming they know anything about security systems—now knows that you have a perimeter warning system up."

"And that's bad because . . . ?"

"Because now they can disable it, and it won't help you anymore."

"But I thought this system is state of the art." I'm whining. I can't help it.

"Nothing is state of the art for someone knowledgeable and determined enough."

My face falls. "Oh. That sucks."

"I'd really like it if you would come stay at my place."

I chew my lip, considering my options.

Plan A: Stay here and fear for my life and possibly put Ozzie's life in danger too . . . or

Plan B: Go to his place and have that giant warehouse around us for protection. And the guns. And the swords. And the singlesticks. And that bed with the black satin sheets . . .

"Fine. I'll stay at your place." Yeah, that was an easy one.

"Thank you." He steps closer and puts his arms around my waist.

"On one condition," I say, putting my finger on his chest to stop him from getting any closer.

"What's that?"

I can't even think of a condition. I want to say that he can't trick me into sleeping with him, but then I'd be putting myself in sexual purgatory. Seeing Ozzie every day, but not being able to touch him? No thanks. Besides, it's not like he needs to trick me to sleep with him. I already propositioned him, as he so indelicately pointed out earlier.

"You have to cook," I say, quickly rescuing myself from being a total fool. "I can't cook worth anything, and you're great at it."

"Done."

"And . . . !" I hold up my finger near his chin.

His eyes are sparkling. "And?"

"And . . . you have to teach me how to use that singlestick."

"Dev could show you."

"But I want *you* to do it."

"Okay, fine. I'll show you how to use the singlestick."

"And . . . !" I place my hand gently on his cheek.

His voice is barely above a whisper. "And?" He's smiling.

"And I don't want you to get your hopes up." There. I said it. My worst fear is now out there in the air between us. I suck in bed. I've been told that by three different guys, so I believe it. And I never get those sensations that women describe in magazines and on sexy blogs, so I have all the self-confirmation I need. Some women are tigers in bed, but I'm more like a small, weak kitten. It's not that I don't try; it's just that I fail regardless.

The truth is that the scariest thing in my life is not a potential murderer who might be out there looking to gun me down; it's that I'm doomed to mediocre sex for the rest of my life, and I'll have to find a man who's okay with that for the rest of his life. Yes, it's possible I might have my priorities a little screwed up, but being bad at sex can be pretty devastating.

I continue with my confession. "I'm not good in bed, and I don't want you to be disappointed in me later, so I'm telling you now. Full disclosure."

He's still smiling.

"It's not a joke, Ozzie. I'm serious. I suck in bed."

"That's good."

My face gets hot as the double meaning sinks in. "I don't mean I suck, like *literally* . . ."

He play-pouts.

I giggle and it sounds crazy leaving my lips, so I cut it off immediately. "Of course I do that . . . I suck literally . . ." As soon as the words are out, I hate myself. Stupid much, May?!

Recover! Quick! "Ha-ha! I mean, that in *bed*, I'm not talented. Skilled. I'm lame in bed. But I try. I do try." My face falls as I realize that I've pretty much just guaranteed myself an empty bed whenever he's in town. No way will he want to be with someone as goofy as I am.

He leans down without saying anything and kisses me.

Slowly at first, and then with more urgency, his lips move against mine. Somehow we fit together perfectly. When he moves right to deepen the connection, I tilt my head left, and it works like magic. His tongue comes out to touch mine. It's big, just like the rest of him. Hot. Wet. Slippery. Oh my . . .

Little shivers zing around inside me like they're electrified. I kind of melt into him, wanting to be closer. He pulls me against him, and I love how his hard muscles press into my softer parts. This was meant to be. It has to be. It feels too good to be anything else.

His hands drop to my waist and rest there for a few moments while we play with each other's tongues. He grabs mine gently with his teeth and I giggle, taking it back. Then he presses his hips into mine, and I can feel his hard length again. He pulls his head back and smiles down at me. "Anyone who can kiss like you can't possibly suck in bed. And when I say *suck*, I mean not be good."

I smile shyly, practically drowning in the kindness and promises I see in his eyes. "You're just being nice."

"No, I'm just being turned on as hell and really looking forward to being inside you." He smacks me hard on the butt and steps away. "Not now, though. Business before pleasure."

I stand there in the middle of my living room, stunned. My panties are damp, my body is ringing with unspent passion, and my brain is spinning circles around itself. What just happened? He wants to be inside me? Hallelujah, baby, I'm gonna get laid tonight!

Just the thought has me panicking all over again.

He, of course, is oblivious to my mental anguish, probably never suffering a single nanosecond of self-doubt in his life.

His voice comes out like a drill sergeant's. "Come on! Chop-chop! Get the lead out! We've got some packing to do!" He's already halfway up my staircase.

I look over at the dogs. Both of them are asleep. Neither of them knows that my world just got turned upside down and inside out by a guy who used to have the most horrible beard on the planet but who now looks like he stepped out of my hottest, sexiest, wettest dream ever.

In my next life, I want to come back as a dog. I think everything will be a lot simpler than the stuff going on in this crazy world I'm living in right now.

I sigh and follow in Ozzie's trail. Before I even reach my room, I can hear him opening up drawers. I feel like I've lost control of everything when I see a suitcase open on the bed and it's already half full of my clothing.

"Are you sure this is the right thing to do?" I ask, leaning on the doorframe. Now that I'm not in his arms, I have a better perspective for what I'm getting into. This could end really badly for both of us. When he kissed me this time, I felt it in my heart. And while Jenny is right—hearts do heal—it sure hurts like hell when they get broken.

"I'm sure. Get whatever you need out of your bathroom. I'll hit the closet next. We leave after I let the dogs out for a quick run around the yard."

I wander into the bathroom, hoping The Fates have everything under control, because I know I sure don't.

CHAPTER THIRTY-NINE

The port is quiet, or as quiet as the Port of New Orleans can ever be. Even in the dead of night, there're things going on, with people moving around, shipments arriving or leaving, business to be attended to. We pull into the warehouse, and I don't get out of my car until the door shuts behind us with a solid *boom*.

Ozzie sets an alarm at a keypad near the main door before coming over to my car and unloading my suitcases. There are three, including a small bag for Felix's toys and bowls. My furbaby hops out of my car and joins Sahara. They climb the stairs to Ozzie's home ahead of us.

"You'll take my bedroom and I'll set up the cot for myself in the kitchen."

I sigh, battling in my head over the whole plan. Having to stay here really complicates an already overly complicated situation. I hate that it's my fault.

"You should take your bed. I don't mind the cot."

"Sorry, no can do. I get my way on this one."

"On this one? Are we taking turns?" We reach the top of the stairs and I press in the code Ozzie gives me to enter. The door clicks and I pull it open. Felix and Sahara push in first. I hold it in place for Ozzie, who's loaded down with all my bags. Those muscles really do come in handy sometimes. It's pretty impressive, actually, to see that they're not just for show. I think he could bench-press me. I'm kind of fascinated to see if it makes any difference in the bedroom. The last guy I was with weighed almost the same as me. Jenny called him The Twig.

"No, we're not taking turns," Ozzie says, moving through the sword room. "You can have your way all the time unless I decide I need to have my way."

I smile. "I guess I can handle that. As long as you don't decide you need to have your way more than half the time."

His response is a grunt.

Moving down the hallway, I feel my steps slowing. This is his domain, not mine. His business, his home, his kitchen, even. What am I doing here? Is he going to hate me when he wakes up with a sore back from that cot? Am I taking advantage of his hospitality, of his need to care for his employees?

He puts my cases down on the floor by the bed. "I can clear a couple drawers out for you here so you don't have to live out of your suitcases." He moves over to a bureau. "I know two's not enough, but I can move a rack in here for your hanging things."

I walk over and put my hand on his arm. "Ozzie, stop." I look up at him, pleading with my eyes.

His hands drop to his sides. "Stop what?"

"Stop . . . doing all this. Taking care of me while throwing yourself out of your own room."

His voice goes very soft, very calm. "I'm not going to stop, May, I'm sorry. It's not who I am."

I stomp my foot, frustrated with our situation. "Why?" This is going to doom our relationship or any chance at a relationship that we might have had. It's so unfair!

He takes one of my hands by the fingers and shakes it a little. "You're getting really worked up over nothing. I've slept more nights on the ground than I care to remember. That cot's a big step up." He looks over his shoulder at the bed. "That mattress is way too soft, anyway. You'll be doing me a favor."

"You're just saying that so I'll sleep there."

He moves closer and pulls me into a hug, resting his chin on my head. I try to wrap my arms around his upper back, but I can't. He's too big. I settle for his waist, which is much narrower. Now I can reach my hands around the other side of him the right way. I squeeze with as much appreciation as I have in me.

"You're too nice," I say, sadness tingeing my voice. "I'm afraid it's going to ruin everything."

"Nothing's going to get ruined by me treating you the way you deserve to be treated." He pulls back and looks down at me. "Are you one of those women who's been treated bad, told she's worthless or something?"

I shake my head. "No. I've had just a few boyfriends, and they were all nice enough. Just . . ."—I shrug—"not the right one for me."

He holds me again, like he's enjoying just standing there in the middle of his room doing nothing but trying to make me feel better. I love the strength of him I can feel, not just through his muscles, but in the way his mind works and his heart is. Ozzie being in charge of security makes all the sense in the world. I can't feel anything less than totally safe in his arms. Protected. Cared for, even.

"I can't make you any promises, except to say that I'll keep you safe," he says, his voice gruff.

He assumes my only fear is of the man who tried to shoot us back at Frankie's. He's right about that partially; I am afraid of that man. But that's not the only thing worrying me. Jenny calls me tenderhearted, and I wouldn't disagree with her on that.

"But what if the danger is coming from you?" I whisper back. My heart twists inside my chest as I imagine falling in love with him and then being cast aside. Committing to a real relationship is hard enough, but to take the risk and then get burned for it? I'd have to move in with my sister so she could take care of me for the rest of my life; I'd be that devastated.

"You have nothing to fear from me, I promise."

"I don't fear being hurt," I say in a small voice. "I fear being shattered."

He lets me go. The pain starts to come from what I assume is his rejection, but then it's swept away when he picks me up in his arms like a baby.

"How about we go to bed right now and worry about all the things that might never happen, tomorrow?"

He uses his elbow to shut the light off. One lamp remains lit next to the bed, casting a faint glow around the room. It's the sexy kind of lighting that makes me look really good naked, or as good as I can look without my clothes on. *Score.*

I reach up to slide my hand over his chest. "That sounds good to me." My head rises as his falls so we can meet in the middle for a kiss.

It's over much quicker than I anticipated, though. I have no time to figure out why that is before I'm lost and confused, flying through the air as he launches me right out of his arms and toward the bed.

I'm airborne! Oh my god! Will I die?!

Boof! I land on the mattress on my back and bounce high once before coming to a halt in the middle of the covers. I stare at the ceiling while my brain computes what just happened.

Oh my god . . . he actually *threw* me!

"Wait here for me. I'll be right back." He grins at me and takes off jogging from the room.

"Ozzie!" I screech, trying to get my breath back from that near-death experience. My head turns right and then left. I am still alive. Nothing's broken. My breath was stolen from me a bit, but it's back.

I literally flew four feet up into the air on the first bounce off that too-soft bed. What the hell.

"I'm going to kill you for that!" I scan the room for a weapon. I swear I'll use it too. He's trained. He can fight back. If he chooses to let me win, well, that's his problem.

His warm chuckles come down the hall from the kitchen, and instead of making up plans for retribution, I scooch back a bit and recline against the pillows, wondering what he's up to now. I have a feeling I'm going to like it a lot, and I can't help grinning about it. Being with him is like being at a crazy amusement park. I never know what's going to happen next, but it's always fun.

CHAPTER FORTY

I hear a tinkling of glass before he rounds the corner. He has a bottle in one hand and two tall champagne flutes in the other.

"I was saving this for the next birthday but figured we could have some now."

I sit up slowly, a little stunned by what I'm seeing. Ozzie is usually so reserved. This enthusiastic, happy person is not someone I've met before. I have a hard time believing anyone else on the team has seen him either. To think he might only act this way in my presence makes me go warm inside. I think he really likes me. A goofy smile takes over my face.

He puts the glasses down on his nightstand and twists the wire cage off the top of the cork. "I hope you like champagne."

I slide my legs over until they're hanging off the side of the bed. "I do like champagne. I don't have it very often."

"I have a friend with a vineyard in France. He sends me a few cases every year."

"Nice friend."

"We've done some work for him."

"What kind of work does a vineyard owner need from a security company?"

"Oh, they had some rare vintage stuff that was sent over for the president. We made sure it got where it was supposed to go in the condition it was supposed to be in."

"The president? As in the *president of the United States?*"

"The one and only."

"Wow. That's just . . . crazy."

The cork flies off and zooms across the room, distracting me from Ozzie's impressive client list. I only see it again when it bounces off the wall and lands on the floor. Felix pokes his head around the corner of the door, and within seconds his eyes lock on that cork. He grabs it and disappears again. This means there will be shredded champagne cork somewhere in Ozzie's house for me to clean up later. *Sigh.* At least the little bugger will be happy and occupied for a while.

Ozzie pours one glass full and hands it to me when the foam is halfway calmed down. When the second glass is full, he puts the bottle on the side table and lifts the flute. "Here's to new beginnings."

I lift my glass, wondering if we're toasting my new employment or my status as his roommate. "New beginnings," I say softly, making sure not to hit his glass too hard. With my nerves being what they are right now, I could easily shatter them both.

My first sip sends bubbles up my nose. I sneeze, and not very delicately.

He smiles. "You like it."

"I do, I do." I wipe my nose to keep it from tickling any more. My eyes are watering trying to hold in the next sneeze.

"This one isn't very sweet."

I take another sip and nod. "No, it's dry, but I like it." Now that I'm no longer sneezing, I can appreciate the taste. "It's like drinking firecrackers," I say, smiling.

"Never thought about it that way." He finishes off his glass, holding the liquid in his mouth for a few seconds. He tilts his head left to right, swallows, and nods. "You're right. Just like firecrackers."

We continue with another glass each, the whole time just looking around. The more time that passes, the more awkward it gets between us.

"So," he says, putting his glass down on the side table. "Feel like watching some television?"

The way he says it tells me he's not really asking me if I want to watch TV. He's asking me if I want to do that other thing we discussed before that intruder set off the yard alarm.

I put my glass down carefully, hoping the tremor in my hand isn't showing too much. "I don't know. Maybe. Is there anything good on?"

He shakes his head really slowly. "No. There's nothing good on."

"We could rent a movie," I say, kind of teasing. I want to see what he'll say to that.

"We could. But there aren't any good movies right now."

"There aren't?" I'm trying not to smile.

"No. None." He steps back a couple feet and slowly undoes his belt.

Panic rises up into my chest, into my throat, cutting off my air.

"What are you doing?" I say in a choked whisper. It's all I'm capable of right now.

"Taking my belt off."

"Oh." I nod. Of course that's what he's doing. Silly me.

After he drops his belt onto the floor, he pulls the bottom of his shirt out of his waistband.

I swallow the lump in my throat. "What are you doing now?"

"Taking off my shirt." He lifts it up over his head and down one arm with practiced ease, letting it fall to the floor to join his belt.

I gasp with admiration at all the muscles I see there. Holy shit, that shirt was covering waaay more than I thought possible. His body is beyond sculpted. It's like a Mr. Potato Head workout body. Clip-on abs, clip-on pecs, clip on triangle-shaped muscle thingies that go down into the front of his pants.

Oh my god, he's taking those pants off!

"Wait!" I yell, holding out a hand like a stop sign.

His hands pause on his button. "You want me to stop?" His right eyebrow goes up, and half his mouth moves up in a devious grin.

"Yes. Stop. Stop right there."

His hands fall away from his pants and hang at his sides. His grin slowly falls away too.

I fold my hands in my lap and press my lips together. I have to make sure I don't say the wrong thing. I need to get it all organized in my head before I start. It's not that I don't want to see him naked; it's just that I'm not sure I'm ready to do anything other than see him naked. And it doesn't seem fair to ogle him and then not offer him the payoff.

"Am I moving too fast for you?" he asks.

"You could say that."

"Do you want me to put my shirt back on?"

"No, not really." I cringe at my own honesty. How creepy I am. I'm an ogler.

He smiles. "But you want me to keep my pants on."

"For now, I think that would be a good idea."

He nods. "Okay. I can handle it." He walks over to his desk.

"What are you doing now?" My nerves are frayed. I want him, but I'm afraid to sleep with him. Madonna's most famous hit runs through my head, a little off tune. *"Like a virgin . . ."* Yeah. That's what I feel like. A virgin. How that can happen when I've had sex at least twenty times, probably more, I don't know. But it is. *"Touched for the very first tiiiimmme . . ."*

He opens up a drawer in the desk and pulls something small enough to fit in his hand out.

It has to be a condom. What else would he be bringing over here to the bed where I'm waiting like a non-virgin virgin?

"Can't watch TV, can't have sex, might as well play cards," he says, climbing up onto the bed on hands and knees, stopping when he gets to the center. He sits, drawing his legs up, bent at the knees.

I watch as he opens up a deck of cards and starts shuffling them on his leg.

I can't help but laugh. "You can't be serious."

"Why not?" He looks up at me and winks. "You afraid?"

"Who me? May 'Card Shark' Wexler? I think not." I turn around and get to the middle of the bed near the pillows. I cross my legs and tuck my feet under them. This, I can handle. "What's your poison? Poker? Blackjack?"

"We'll start with poker."

"Excellent." I rub my hands together, thankful that the pressure has temporarily been removed. Maybe after we play for a while and joke around a bit, I'll feel more comfortable about sleeping with him.

His grin is decidedly sly. "Seven card draw, jokers wild. You lose, you take off an article of clothing."

Ooooor maybe I won't feel more comfortable. I guess we're going to find out.

CHAPTER FORTY-ONE

I lose the first hand and my shoes. He loses the next three hands, which has him down to his underpants. He wears boxer briefs, in black, of course. His arms rest on his knees, and his poker hand hovers between them. He's looking at me. "What's it going to be, May 'Card Shark' Wexler? You want any cards?"

I'm holding a pair of threes. That's it. I'm sweating too, because if I lose this one, I'm taking off my top or my pants. He already put the kibosh on me taking off earrings. Clothing only, that's the rule.

"Hmmm, yeah. I'll take four."

He chuckles as he pulls four cards off the top of the deck. "Oh my, May. I think you're in a little bit of trouble."

I look at the cards he selected for me and smile. "Maybe. Maybe not." I'm completely bluffing. I know this pair of threes with a ten high isn't going to do jack diddly for me. My only hope is to get him to fold. Folding is a forfeit but without clothing removal.

"I'm going to take one card," he says, removing one from his hand and taking a new one from the deck.

One card. Oh, crap.

"What's it going to be?" he asks me. "You ready to go down?"

My face heats up. Go down? Not quite yet.

"I'm not folding, I know that. Maybe you should, though. You're going to be starkers if you lose another hand."

"Maybe I want to be starkers." He winks at me.

I frown. "Have you been losing on purpose?"

"Who, me?" He frowns a little too hard. "Don't be ridiculous. I'm too competitive to lose on purpose."

Or too chivalrous. I try to replay our earlier hands back in my head. Did he forfeit good cards for bad? I wasn't paying attention then, and it's too late now to figure it out. Dammit. And here I thought I was being a card shark for real when what I was probably being was a non-virgin virgin wannabe card shark. *Double dammit.*

He puts his cards on the bed. "Read 'em and weep." He has a full house.

I slowly put my cards on the bed in front of me. "Pair of threes, otherwise known as total suckage."

He leans over and takes my top button in his fingers.

"What are you doing?"

"Helping you." He unbuttons the first one.

I slap his hand away. "Hey! What if I was planning on taking my pants off first?" I feel like I'm going to have a heart attack right here over this stupid deck of cards. We are going to be naked together, and I'm not ready!

He leans back. "Take your pants off then, if you prefer." He leans back on his hands and grins. "I'll just wait over here. Your turn to deal, you know."

"I know." I say it with my annoyed voice. Standing, I first button my shirt up, all the way to my neck, and then I undo the top button of my pants.

"You nervous?" he asks. He's not smiling anymore.

"No."

"Liar."

I sigh. "Yeah, I'm lying. I am nervous." I push my pants down to my ankles anyway. Fair is fair; I lost the hand.

"We can quit anytime you want." He falls onto his back and talks at the ceiling. "I'm kind of tired of cards now anyway."

I step out of my pants, now wondering if he's still being a gentleman or if really doesn't care if he sees me naked. That thought should bring relief, but instead it makes me kind of sad. I hope I didn't blow it with him.

"What do you want to do instead?" I ask.

"We could watch TV."

"You said there was nothing good on!" I act outraged when, really, I'm happy. I'm glad he wanted to play strip poker with me. That's a compliment, right? And he's smiling, so it can't be all bad between us.

"I lied. Come on." He does a back flip off the end of the bed and leaves the room.

"Wait for me!" I run out of the room in just my shirt and underwear.

He's waiting for me on the couch, the television already on. The dogs are curled up together in a giant dog bed on the floor next to the far side of the couch. Sahara is snoring. Felix is crashed out on his back, his feet in the air. I'm tempted to go pick him up, but I don't. He'll sleep all night like that, and I want to be with Ozzie right now anyway.

"*Modern Family.* Cracks me up." He points the remote to the wall-mounted television set, and the channel changes. I see the familiar faces of Claire and Phil.

"You don't seem like the *Modern Family* type," I say, lowering myself onto the couch one cushion away from him. I'm near the end, he's in the middle. The thing is big enough for six people, probably.

He flips himself around and lies on the couch, putting his head in my lap like it's the most normal thing in the world—the two of us watching a sitcom, half naked, in the sword room. I'm obviously living in Crazy Town.

Instead of overanalyzing something that defies analysis, I sit back and watch the show. My hands find their way to his head where I massage his scalp, lightly drag my hands over his temple and cheek, and play with his ears. They're soft, where other parts of him are decidedly hard. When he laughs, the entire couch moves. He's adorable and charming when he's watching this silly show. It's definitely my new favorite.

At some point during the first half of the program, one of his hands goes under my thigh. Then a little while later, the other one reaches up and goes behind my back. It doesn't look very comfortable, but when a commercial comes on, I see how well it can work for both of us. He flips over onto his back and the arm that was under my thigh comes out. His hand floats up to my shirt button, the one I closed at the top of my neck.

I pretend to be enthralled with the excellent cleaning features of the Tide Stick that's being advertised, while he unbuttons three buttons, revealing the edges of my bra. I laugh at a commercial that has a small dog chasing a cat who took his toy, but can't keep up the charade when his fingers pull the top of my bra down and he cups my breast.

I tilt my head down and stare into his eyes. He's all seriousness now.

"I like you on my couch," he says.

"Aren't you worried someone from the team is going to come in?"

"No. I have security, remember?" He glances over at the hallway leading to the outer door. "I disabled the lock. No one can get in."

"Even with the code?"

"Even with the code. You could run around here naked, and no one would ever know."

The idea makes my ears burn. "You would know."

"But I'd never tell." He pulls me down and kisses me on the mouth, his tongue coming out and reaching up for mine. It's not the most comfortable position in the world, but it's hot. He's managed to get me half naked and not self-conscious about it. I can see his hard-on in his boxer briefs, so I know if I just said the word, he'd be all over me. But instead, he lets me go and just looks at me. Watches me for a reaction.

"I'm not as nervous as I was earlier," I say. I need him to know I appreciate what he's doing.

"Good. You want some popcorn?" He sits up.

I frown. "Do you?"

He shrugs. "Not really. But if you want some, I'll make it."

I shake my head. "No, it's late. I think I'll pass."

He sits up with his back against the cushions and pulls me into him. The skin of his thigh is warm against mine. I'm so glad I shaved today. The dark wiry hair of his legs tickles the delicate skin of mine. It makes me think of him and me in bed together, touching everywhere, no clothing getting in the way . . .

He squeezes me tight and kisses me on the top of the head as the show comes back on. "Wait until you see this part," he says, his mood lightening as he switches into television viewer mode.

So much for a raging hard-on. I sneak glances at it as it shrinks down to regular size, which, for the record, is still big enough to tell me that he must have a hard time finding pants that will fit properly. Wowza.

The longer I sit with him as he gently strokes my arm with his fingers, touches my hair, pulls me into him, the more comfortable I feel. And with this comfort comes a frustration. We are so close to getting sexual, but we're just not doing it. He's being a total gentleman, and it's driving me crazy.

Something needs to be done about this. Something needs to be done about this *now*.

CHAPTER FORTY-TWO

I pick up the remote and turn the television off.

Ozzie's hand freezes in the middle of stroking my arm.

I wait for him to make the next move.

"You turned off the show."

"Yes, I did." My heart is going wild.

"Does that mean you're ready for bed?"

Easy, May, easy. You can do this. "Not exactly."

He lets out a long breath of air. For a second, I think he's angry. But then he speaks.

"Stand up, May."

"Stand up?" I'm confused.

"Yes, stand up. Here in front of me." He leans back harder into the cushions and moves his butt forward a little, sinking down into the couch.

I don't know what's going to happen next, but I stand anyway.

"Face me."

I turn around.

He takes my left hand and pulls me to the left until I'm standing between his knees.

"Take your shirt off."

I swallow with difficulty. We're totally going to do this. We're going to have sex right now. In this room. On this couch. Holy shit.

I reach up with trembling fingers and undo my remaining buttons. It's all I have strength for, though. When I'm done, my hands fall to my sides. I'm chickening out and I'm not even naked yet. I hate myself! My head drops to my chest.

Ozzie sits up and pulls on my sleeve, making my blouse fall over to one side. "Take this off," he says in a calm voice. The fact that he's not sounding angry or scary is freaking me out. It's like he's my boss again, doing some sort of training exercise. "Take off your shirt, May. Don't make me say it again."

A shiver moves down my spine and right into the spot between my legs, *ka-zow*!

I do what he says because I'm not an idiot.

"Good girl," he says, his voice low, almost dangerous sounding.

I'm there in my matching bra and panties, a set I splurged for last year when the wedding bookings were plenty. I'm so glad I put them on today. Did I know I was going to be stripping in front of Ozzie? Maybe. I guess I'd hoped so. God, I'm so easy.

"Take off your bra." He's leaning back on the couch again, his eyes running up and down my body. The television is back on again, but the sound is off. Light flickers behind me. I hope it's making me look mysterious and sexy and not fat.

I lower the straps from my shoulders first, thrilled to see his bulge move in his boxers. He reaches over and squeezes it as his pelvis moves up. That sends a shock running through my body. I never thought a guy touching himself would turn me on, but I was wrong. Wrong, wrong, wrong-wrong-wrong.

As my straps hang loose over my upper arms, I reach behind me and undo the clasp. Crossing my arms across my chest, I hold the loose material against me. Revealing my upper body in its utter nakedness while he sits there below me is too much. It's going to take a lot more confidence than I have right now to pull that off.

"Let it go, May."

"I can't." I'm trembling again. I'm not sure if it's fear or anticipation in charge.

"You can and you will."

I shake my head no but can't speak. Fear and nerves have my tongue, and they're not letting it go.

He leans forward and reaches up to put his hands on my thighs. His fingers are hot on my air-cooled skin. Slowly they climb over my hips and waist to my elbows.

"Give yourself to me, May."

Tears make my eyes bright. "I can't."

"Of course you can." He takes the edge of my bra and gently tugs it out from under my arms.

I let it go because the bigger part of me wants to do this, wants to be naked with him. The smaller part of me that's self-conscious and finds me lacking wants to run for the hills and never look back. A fall from this height is going to be really, really painful, and we haven't even had sex yet.

Now the only thing covering my chest is my arms. Why do they have to be so skinny? My breasts are falling out everywhere.

He leans back onto the couch again, bringing the bra up to his face. He closes his eyes as he inhales. "Smells like your skin." His eyes open and he smiles.

I almost laugh. "Creepy."

He tosses the bra aside and sits up again. His hands start at my calves and slowly draw upward, both tickling me and setting me aflame. Goose bumps rise up everywhere.

"I love the way you smell, the way your skin feels, the way you stare at me with that wrinkle between your eyes."

"Wrinkle? What wrinkle?"

I'm too distracted to realize what he's up to until his fingers are at the edge of my panties, near the top.

I grab my chest with one arm, while the other hand goes over my panties. "What are you doing?"

"You want to keep them on?" He shrugs. "Okay by me." He leans in and puts his face on the front of me, over my panties.

Holy crap, what's he . . . ? Oh my god, that's . . . niiiice.

My hand is in the way, but he moves his face around until he can get his mouth between my fingers. His hot breath comes through the light, silky material, heating up my most sensitive area. I think that's about as sexy as this thing can get, and then he starts moving his mouth around and I realize I was waaaay wrong about that.

I moan when the feelings start to get out of control. How is he doing this to me? He's moaning too, and moving his mouth and breathing hot air everywhere, and it's making me feel like I'm going to have an orgasm with my panties still on. What the hell? I don't even have orgasms. My orgasm maker is broken or something. I figured that out a long time ago, and it's been confirmed by every boyfriend I've ever had. I'm just one of those women who never gets them.

The hand of mine that was trying to guard against his invasion moves back up to my chest. Pretending I don't want him doing what he's doing is ridiculous. I'm not fooling anyone.

He takes advantage of my surrender by pulling my panties down and burying his face in my mound. I was totally not expecting that.

I gasp and drop my hands, putting them first on his head and then his shoulders. I need to hold on to something so I don't collapse. His tongue is sliding into my hot, wet folds and I cry out with delight. Maybe I should be self-conscious about being so free and open to him, but I'm too turned on to worry about anything right now.

I feel him moving around as he continues to lick me, but I don't realize until his hands are on my waist and he's pulling away that he was taking off his boxers and putting on protection.

I look down and see his hard-on angled up at me. My panties are at my thighs. He's looking up at me with a mouth covered in my wetness. I let my panties drop to the floor and step out of them.

"Come here," he says, guiding me to sit on him.

I put one knee next to his left thigh and the other to his right.

"Put it in," he says, this time with more of a growl to his tone.

My heart is racing, but I need to feel him inside me. That tongue of his really got me amped up. Forget being embarrassed, forget being naked at work. I need this, and I need it now.

When our bodies first make contact, I'm not sure it's going to work. He's too big and I'm too swollen from what he's done to excite me already. But when he pushes up into me, he proves that I'm wrong, wrong, wrong. Again. He fits, but just barely. I lower myself onto him, groaning the whole way as I'm stretched to the max.

"Mmmmm . . ." He obviously enjoys it too. I smile at the look on his face when I lift myself up and come down for another stroke. "May, you're amazing . . ."

I lean forward and rest my hands on the couch, making it easier to move like I need to. My breasts touch his face.

He takes them in his hands and sucks first one and then the other nipple. The sensation of feeling him inside me, and also his hands and mouth fondling my breasts, is unreal. I move faster to keep up with the need building. He squeezes and kneads. My nipples get harder than they've ever been before.

"Kiss me," he says in a whisper.

I lean down as best I can, but it's not easy to reach him. I'm about to give up when he grabs me by the waist and flips me over onto my back. He's above me, positioning one knee in the couch cushion and the other leg on the floor.

"What are you doing?" I ask breathlessly.

He sinks all the way into me, even farther than he'd been before. "I'm fucking you, May."

The hard words and the dangerous look on his face send a rush of sexual energy through me. My muscles spasm and grip him from the inside. His eyes widen as he feels it and then he bites his bottom lip, pushing into me until he can't go any more.

"Oh my god . . ." I lift my legs and wrap them around him. "Ozzie . . ." It's a plea. I'm not sure what I'm begging for, but I hope he gives it to me soon.

His thrusts start slow and easy. We kiss, tongues tangling, lips mashing, his late evening beard scratching my chin. I can feel the muscles move beneath the skin of his back. Massive muscles, tense and corded, undulate with the in and out strokes that are slowly building a tension in me that begs to be released. My hands slide down to his hips and his butt where I can push him harder against me. He reads my signals perfectly, slowing at the deepest part, rubbing, drawing away only to bury himself again.

I can feel when he starts to lose control. His sweat begins to drip down onto my belly, where it mingles with mine. His breath comes in pants. His face is an expression of both pain and pleasure.

"Oh, Ozzie," I cry, feeling like I'm about to explode. I'm not sure where we go from here; I just know I don't ever want this to stop.

"Come on, baby," he says, urging me toward something.

I have to move faster. My body demands it. The core of me insists. It's the only way. The only way to end this sweet torture.

And then he just stops. He freezes. Buried to the hilt, he stops and breathes heavily above me.

"What are you doing?"

"You move now. It's your turn," he says.

I lay there under him in confusion. "How can I move when you're on top?"

He half-shrugs. "I don't know. See if you can figure it out."

If this will make him happy, I'm going to do it. Besides, the feeling of his huge hard length inside me is driving me wild. I couldn't sit still if I wanted to. My hips are already moving.

I tense my pelvis up toward him. With that tiny movement, I feel a sharp but amazing sensation in my core. Pulling away and doing it again makes it happen a second time. I spread my legs farther apart.

"That's it, baby . . ."

I don't need his encouragement, but when he speaks to me while I grind up against him, I feel wild. Feral. A little bit savage. I move against him with more urgency, answering to the demand that's coming from my more primal self. With every thrust up toward him, I take him into me more fully, until the most sensitive part of me is rubbing on his body while his rod stretches me to the fullest.

"Oh my god," I say as a slow burn starts to build.

"Oh, yeah. Come on, beautiful, come on." He pushes against me when I come up to him. Together we meet in the middle and I feel him grow even larger inside me.

And then I feel like I'm drowning. An intense fire rages between my legs. He feels it and starts pushing harder, faster. I meet him stroke for stroke, every thrust sending me closer to the edge.

"Ozzie! Ozzie!" I'm clinging to him, afraid I'll be lost forever if I let go.

"Come for me, baby, *come!*" he yells.

He pushes into me up to the limit, and then his body starts jerking inside me. I can't take it anymore. I cry out and hold on to him for dear life. I'm falling over the edge of a very dark cliff and I can't hold back. It's finally come for me: the orgasm I never had before but always read about in romance novels.

CHAPTER FORTY-THREE

When Ozzie is done and I've stopped yelling like a crazy person, he collapses on top of me.

"Urph." It's about all I can manage. My throat is sore. I think I might have busted a vocal chord or something.

He rolls off both me and the couch and lands on the floor on his back.

"Ow." He sounds as exhausted as I feel.

I giggle. "Are you okay?"

"I'll survive. As long as you don't try to do that to me again anytime soon."

I lean over and tap him with my fingers. "You did it, not me."

He reaches up and takes my fingers to kiss them. "Time for bed, Bo Peep. We have work in the morning."

"What time is it?" I roll onto my side and look for a clock.

"Midnight."

I sigh and stare up at the ceiling. He lets my hand go, and I slide it up to rest on my chest.

"Happy?" he asks me.

I grin and nod. "Happy."

"Tired?"

I shake my head. "Not in the least. I feel like I could fly right now."

"You're dangerous."

I love being dangerous. "You're the one who tricks perfectly nice girls into taking their clothes off and having crazy sex on the couch at work."

"I didn't trick you. You tricked me."

I roll over and stare down at him. "How so?" I pretend to be indignant over his accusation.

"You walked into that bar last week looking all hotsy-totsy in those pants and that shirt, with your little dog, making me think you were a bored housewife looking for a little action . . . come to find out you're a ruthless, Taser-wielding, singlestick master with a taste for ex-grunts in beards."

I can't stop laughing. His characterization of me couldn't be more ridiculous.

"Why are you laughing? You know I speak the truth."

"I know you speak nonsense."

"Name one thing that wasn't accurate."

"I hate beards."

He jumps up off the floor, and before I know what he's planning, I've been swept up into his arms.

"What are you doing?!" I yell. I sound way too happy for him to mistake my reaction for anger.

"I'm bringing you to bed to give you a spanking."

"Ohhh, a spanking. I'd like to see you try." I left my Taser in my purse in his bedroom. If he even thinks about spanking my butt, I'm going to light him on fire.

We fly out of the room and down the hall, with me laughing all the way. I feel like I've been tazed or something the way I can't control myself. It's like all my life the light switch that is the real me has been turned off, and Ozzie somehow figured out how to turn it on. This is me, the real May Wexler, running through a house naked with Ozzie. So, so Crazy Town right now. I am May "the Orgasm Queen" Wexler.

I'm not one bit surprised this time when he launches me into the air and onto the bed. I am, however, when he flips me over and smacks me on the butt.

"You . . . !" I scream. "You're going to pay for that!" I twist my body over and make a grab for his arm, but he's too sweaty to hang onto.

He pushes me back down onto the bed, face first. "You stay there, girl. I'm going to teach you a lesson in manners. Saying my beard was horrible. How dare you."

I'm lifting my head to defy him, when his hands come to my waist and yank my hips up.

"What are you . . . ?"

Suddenly he's there, behind me. "Surprise," he says, an evil grin on his face. He's pressing his hardness against me. It easily slides into the wetness there between my legs.

"Again?" I ask, my voice barely coming out. "Already?"

He smacks me on the butt, lightly this time. "Here I come, baby. Ready or not."

Oh, I'm so ready for him. He puts on a condom and I lift my butt as high as I can, sighing with pleasure as he fills me once again.

He goes slow this time, building the passion, mindful of my sensitivity. His fingers find their way around to the front of me, stroking me in time with his rhythm.

"You like that?" he asks, pulling me against him hard as he swivels his hips against me.

"Mmmm . . ." My eyes are closed, but I'm smiling. I stretch my arms out to the sides and hang onto the sheets. His rhythm is picking up, pushing me into the mattress.

"That's it," I say, encouraging him. "Harder."

And harder he comes, thrusting in and out, faster and faster. I push into him, letting him know I need even more.

He leans forward, putting his fingers on me again. "Come on, babe."

"Fuck me, Ozzie." The words slip out, but I don't regret them.

"Say that again," he growls.

"Fuck me . . ." I have to pause for breath, ". . .Ozzie."

He roars like a wounded lion, and shoves into me so hard we both collapse. His body jerks above me like he's being electrocuted and I can feel him come inside me.

His hand is still below me and now it moves again. Knowing I drove him over the edge with my body and my words is all I need. I cry and struggle with the orgasm that racks my body. I've lost complete control of myself, and I don't care.

When it's finally over, what seems like several minutes later, I feel as though I've died, or at the very least, run a marathon. I cannot move.

"I'm glad you decided to come over," he says in my ear.

I giggle like a schoolgirl and then snort lazily. "Me too."

He rolls off me and lies on his back next to me. I turn my head to look at him.

"Happy?" he asks.

I grin as best I can. My face doesn't really want to work. "Happy."

"Good." He leans over and kisses me before getting up.

"Where are you going?" I ask.

"Bathroom."

"'Kay." I rearrange myself on the bed, getting under the covers and resting my head on the pillow. This bed is so comfy. I'm just going to relax here until he comes back. Maybe he'll want to talk or something. We probably should discuss how we're going to handle working together tomorrow. I don't want things to be awkward, and I'm sure he doesn't want that either.

That's the last thought I remember having before an alarm is going off next to my head and I see a clock reading seven-thirty in the morning.

CHAPTER FORTY-FOUR

Oh my god! I slept here! With him! In his bed! And I have to get up for work! And Felix has to go outside! Ack!

The spot next to me looks slept in. Was Ozzie there all night and I never even noticed? Wow. That sex really knocked me out or something.

I throw my legs over the side of the bed and look around. Hopefully, Ozzie's taken Felix out with Sahara. Otherwise I'm going to have some cleaning up to do.

There's a door ahead of me that isn't the one that leads out into the hallway. It had better be the bathroom door, because there's no way I want to walk out into the kitchen area and have my coworkers catch me looking like I just rolled in the hay. Twice.

I grin as I collect some clothing from the drawers I was given and go through that door and into the bathroom.

Whoa. Now *that's* a bathroom. Marble, glass, and metal work together in the big space to create a spa-like oasis. I brush my teeth first, just in case Ozzie comes in and gets near me. I don't want to get dumped for having dragon breath.

The shower, big enough for several people, has three separate nozzles with various spray patterns. I use Ozzie's products for my body and hair, skipping the conditioner, since I guess he doesn't use it on the spikes he calls hair. I'm surprised he doesn't have any left over from when he had that beard. Surely he conditioned that mess?

A sound behind me distracts me from the memory of the bird's nest that used to decorate his face. I spin around and find Ozzie himself standing there, dressed and ready for work. He's even wearing his combat boots already.

I cross my arms over my chest self-consciously. For sure I'm going to use this scenario for a fantasy when I'm bored and alone one night. Me, naked and wet. Him being my boss standing there all muscled up. Talk about sexy.

"Good morning," he says.

"Good morning." I'm shy, which is ridiculous, considering what we did last night, but I can't control how I feel. Why did he just go to sleep last night without waking me up? Did he even sleep with me in the bed? Maybe he slept on the cot. That idea makes me sad. It feels like rejection.

"Meeting in fifteen minutes."

"Fifteen?" I move to rinse my hair out. "Okay." I hope he doesn't expect me to be gorgeous. I'm not exactly high maintenance, but fifteen minutes isn't enough time to pull off a miracle.

"Is Felix okay? I should have taken him out already."

"He's fine. He went out with his girlfriend."

I smile but don't say anything. I don't want Ozzie thinking I'm pressuring him into calling me *his* girlfriend, even though nothing would make me happier. I shut the water off and step out of the shower area. Ozzie hands me a towel, warm from being on a heating rack.

I hold it against me and blink the water out of my eyes. The heat from the towel seeps into my skin, relaxing me. I have nothing to be nervous about, right? We might not be a couple, but we've been intimate. And I'm an adult. I have enough confidence to move past this, whatever it is, whether it's for better or for worse.

Ack! Why are wedding vows swimming around in my brain?! Have I lost my mind completely?!

"Is there something else?" I ask, wondering why he's just standing there staring at me. God help me if he can read minds.

He leans toward me and kisses me on the cheek. "Nope." He turns and starts walking out of the bathroom.

My body is warming from not just the towel, but his touch too, even though it was as chaste as a kiss next to a shower can be.

"Ozzie?"

He pauses with his hand on the door. "Yeah?"

I have no idea what to say, but I feel like I should say something. Anything.

"Thanks. For everything."

He turns just his head to look at me. "Everything?"

I can't stop the smile that comes over me. I'm that non-virgin virgin again. Ridiculous, since we had sex not just once, but twice last night. "Yes, everything. For letting me stay here, for worrying about me, for Felix, for . . . the television show. All that stuff."

He lets the door go and comes back to stand in front of me.

I look up at him, freaking out because he's so close and fully clothed while I'm naked and wet. Are we going to have sex again? Make everyone wait for the meeting as we sigh, moan, and yell out in ecstasy?

He pulls me against him, trapping my arms against my chest, the towel there between us keeping things from getting too real.

"You're welcome for everything." He grins for a second. "For all that stuff."

"Is this going to be weird?" I ask, the first slivers of doubt sneaking in. What will the team think? Will they hate me on principle because I slept with the boss on my first week of work?

He shakes his head slowly. "Doesn't need to be." His green eyes are clear and kind. He seems very sure of himself.

"What do you think the others are going to say?"

"I don't think they're going to say anything. Why would they? You stayed the night for security reasons. Thibault suggested it."

"Oh. Okay." He means he's not going to act differently around me in front of the others, even though we slept together. I shouldn't be unhappy because it's better that no one knows what we're doing after hours. I just have to suppress the silly schoolgirl in me who wants to walk the halls holding hands. "Good."

"Don't worry," he says, his face expressionless.

"I'm not worried."

"You look worried."

"I'm not."

"You sound worried."

I frown. "No, I don't. I sound fine."

"I made you an omelet."

"You did?" I'm getting warm again. "Did you make one for everyone?"

"No, just for you."

He stands there, letting his words sink in. The way he's looking at me, I swear I can tell he cares about me. Why else would he make me my very own omelet? Something that feels a lot like love rushes into my heart and takes hold of me.

He leans down, and I let go of the towel so I can wrap my arms around his neck and give him the kiss he deserves.

His tongue and mine begin the dance again, the one that we started and perfected last night. His big warm hands span my lower and middle back. It gets hot between us within seconds. I moan as the feelings start to take over. I'm picturing him bending me over the sink and having his way with me when he pulls away.

"Meeting. Gotta go." He leaves me standing there, almost in that sex-mannequin pose again. He's at the door before I can speak again.

"Ozzie?"

"Yeah?"

"I like you."

My chin falls to my chest, and I scoop the towel up off the floor to hold it against me. I totally and completely hate myself for being such a poozer. What the hell, man? Why can't I just keep some of my thoughts to myself? His kisses loosen my willpower and my tongue way too much.

"I like you too, Bo Peep. But don't think for one second that's going to earn you an easier workout today."

I grin really hard into the towel, praying he's not looking at me right now. No way can I check to see. When I have control of myself, I move the towel from my mouth and dry my belly with it. I'm afraid to move it away from my chest and expose myself, silly non-virgin virgin that I am.

"We're working out today?" I ask, aiming for light and casual.

"You'd better believe it."

Flashes of Dev with a sword come to mind. "Is Dev out there waiting to attack me?"

"I guess you're about to find out." He opens the door and walks out, leaving me alone in the bathroom.

My heart leaps. He likes me too! And he's still going to train me and let me be in the company! I throw my arms out to the side and spin around. That was a mistake since my feet are still wet and the floors are marble. I slip and barely catch myself. Now the adrenaline is flowing too. I almost hope Dev will be out there doing another one of his stupid sneak attacks. I will totally be ready for him. Ka-chow! Judo chop!

I finish getting ready in record time, sliding out of the door of his bedroom exactly fifteen minutes after my wake-up call in the bathroom. Yeah, baby. I'm so handling this new life of mine like a boss.

CHAPTER FORTY-FIVE

I sidle down the hall, waiting for the attack. When I reach the entrance to the kitchen, I get the lay of the land. I need to find Dev before I reveal myself.

Everyone's sitting at the table but me, including Mr. Sneak Attack. The omelet's on a plate by the stove, but I leave it there. No way am I going to sit down and dig into my specially prepared breakfast in front of my coworkers. My not-so-sneaky glances at Ozzie are already suspect enough.

"Morning, Bo Peep," Lucky says, grinning at me as I walk up to join them at the table. He looks way too fresh and perky this early in the morning. Is he leaving to do a toothpaste commercial after the meeting? Is that a knowing smile on his face? I think it is. I try to act natural.

"Good morning, Lucky. How's your goldfish?"

"Sunny's great, thanks for asking."

I pull out my chair and sit down, pushing the files around in front of me, trying to appear busy. I can't look at Ozzie. For sure I'll go all goo-goo eyes on him, and then Toni will want to punch me in the face. I have to figure out what to do about her. I need to find out if she likes him or what her issue was with me staying overnight with him. She didn't seem to like the idea much yesterday.

"Morning, everyone," Ozzie says. "Let's start with the Harley Op. As of last night, we have ears on the target. Backyard for now, but I'd like to get inside."

"You should give Bo Peep a try at it," Toni says, sounding a tad bitter. "She handled the Parrot just fine."

"What do you think, May? Willing to give it a shot? Want to try to fly the bug into the house? We can practice with another one we have."

I look up at my boss, all business. "Sure, Ozzie. I'd be happy to." I grin enthusiastically, but realize it's too much when everyone stares at me. My smile falls away to be replaced by embarrassment. *Dammit.* Is the fact that Ozzie and I got seriously naked last night written all over my face or what?

"We added another wrinkle to the Op last night," Ozzie says.

I can't breathe. Is he about to tell everyone that we had sex? *Ack!*

"There was an intruder at May's around nine. Set off the perimeter alarm."

I let out the big breath of air I'd been holding, really slowly so no one will hear it.

"That's not good," Thibault says, looking at me. "Everyone okay?"

I nod. I'm too dizzy from lack of oxygen to trust my voice.

"Yes," Ozzie answers, "but we relocated over here for the night."

I really envy his ability to make that sound so casual. If I had said it, I would have giggled and turned red. As it is, I'm having a hard time keeping a straight face. I seriously need to get a grip on myself. I think a phone call to Jenny is definitely in order. Maybe I can manage a quick one in the bathroom before I start work.

"You'd better stay here until we figure out what's going on," Dev says. He looks across the room and frowns. "Anyone going to eat that omelet?"

I open my mouth to answer, but Ozzie cuts me off.

"Don't touch it. It's not yours."

Dev frowns. "Okay, geez, just asking."

Thibault shakes his head. "Bottomless pit, man."

Dev shoves him with an elbow. "Shut up. I didn't have time for breakfast this morning."

"There's cereal in the pantry," Ozzie says before opening a folder in front of him. "We've gathered about twenty-four hours of data. I'd guess we have about an hour of stuff worth looking at. Any volunteers?"

I raise my hand.

"I don't mind," Toni says, shrugging, "since I've been banned from the site anyway."

"Good. Toni and May, you're on it. Put a report together of anything interesting, and deliver it to me by end of day."

"Done." Toni nods at me and I nod back.

"Dev, workout schedule?"

"I got May this morning," Dev replies. "The rest of you are on the circuit."

Grumbling comes from around the table.

"No whining. I changed it this morning before the meeting. I think you'll like what I've done. Look at the clipboard before you start. Use the timers. No cheating. If I catch you cheating, you'll pay for it."

I have no idea what this circuit is, but it doesn't look like it's very popular.

"I'm going to manage May's workouts for the time being," Ozzie says. His voice sounds a little gruff to me. I look around the table, but I can't tell if anyone else noticed it or not.

"Why?" Dev's clearly not happy. "You think I'm not up to snuff?"

"No, you're up for it. I just want you to focus on combat training. I'll get her cardio where it needs to be. After that we'll work on building muscle."

276

I focus on the papers in front of me. My instinct is to stare at Ozzie and share goofy smiles with him, but even I know that's a bad idea. I don't want to embarrass him and make him hate me before he even has a chance to like me for more than twenty-four hours. That would be a tragedy, considering the amazing sex we had last night. Twice!

"Okay. We'll start with the singlestick."

I'm not going to remind Ozzie that he promised to teach me how to use that weapon. He's doing my workouts. That's enough special attention. I don't want everyone thinking I'm some kind of prima donna.

"What else?" Thibault asks.

"I need someone to chase down the intruder from last night," Ozzie says. He sounds angry.

"I got that," Thibault says. "Not sure what I'll be able to find, but I'll give it a shot."

"We might find something on the tapes," Toni offers.

"Keep your ears open for anything," Ozzie says. He turns his attention to Lucky. "What's going on with the Blue Marine Op?"

"I don't know, actually." Lucky is frustrated. "I sat down and went through their financials, and they seem fine . . . but something's up. They were right to call us."

"What do you mean?" Ozzie stops messing around with folders and stares at Lucky.

"I'm not sure. I need to go on-site and figure some things out."

"Go ahead. Just don't talk to any employees without speaking to our contact first. And obviously, don't identify yourself to anyone there at the site, even our contact."

"No, of course not. I'm going to shop for some fishing tackle."

"And what would Sunny think about that, I wonder?" Dev smiles evilly at Lucky.

"What Sunny doesn't know won't hurt him." Lucky throws his folders to the middle of the table. "We done here? I need to get going."

"Hot date?" Thibault asks, grinning.

"If you must know, I have a doctor's appointment. But thanks for caring about my personal life."

Thibault holds up a hand to the table. "Speaking of which, I need everyone's time sheets by the end of the day. Payroll is Friday, don't forget. If you want to get paid, get me your time sheets. No excuses."

Groans come from around the table. I'm a little worried myself, since I don't know anything about time sheets. Do I need to do one too, or is being on probation somehow exempting me from that?

Thibault rolls his eyes. "I'll say it again, since we have a new hire at the table . . . fill out your sheets every day, *as* you book the hours. That way it isn't a big chore at the end of the week." He points at me. "I'm doing yours for you for now, but after this week, you're on your own."

I nod.

"Booo," Dev says with his thumb pointed down.

Thibault shakes his head. "Jesus, people, grow up. It's a time sheet, not a calculus test."

Ozzie stands. "One more thing before you all leave."

Panic hits me. I know it's irrational and completely contrary to how he's treated me so far, but all I can think is he's going to tell them. He's going to expose me for the slut that I am, revealing that I slept with him just mere days after meeting him for the first time.

"We need a company car for May. I'm open to suggestions about make and model."

I'm too stunned to speak. I get a company car? Does that mean I'm not on probation anymore? Am I the only one noticing how crazy this is?

"How about a minivan?" Toni says, snorting at her own joke.

I glare at her, my misgivings flying out the window. "What . . . you're saying I look like a minivan type? A mom with a bunch of kids? No thanks."

She shrugs. "You're Bo Peep. Might as well work with the cover you've got naturally."

"It's not a bad idea," Ozzie says.

Traitor! I turn on him. "Of course it's a bad idea. It's a horrible idea. I can't drive a minivan! Minivans are for moms. They're for married women, not single ones."

I don't look like a minivan driver, do I? It makes me want to cry. I know they have a lot of headroom and storage space, plus room for eight passengers, but come on . . . I'm single, for God's sake!

"You're worried it'll get in the way of your dating life?" Ozzie waits impassively for my response.

My face contorts itself through several expressions. Frustration. Embarrassment. Sadness. Jealousy. "How come Toni gets to drive an SUV?"

Yes, I'm being childish, but what the hell. She gets to walk around in tight pants and stiletto-heeled boots. I'm in espadrilles and a minivan. I'm calling shenanigans on that. It makes me wonder why Ozzie slept with me in the first place. Is he some kind of weirdo with an Oedipus complex?

"I drive the SUV because it suits me." She smiles at me, and I detect more than a hint of smugness there. *Argh*, she is so begging for a Tasering right now, or at the very least a pee-purse whacking.

I narrow my eyes at her. "A minivan does not suit me at all."

"How about I take her car shopping?" Dev says. "I have time later today."

"Do that." Ozzie nods. "I'll be done with her around nine."

"And I'll be done with her by two," Toni adds. I think she likes speaking for my time schedule a little too much. She and I are going to have to share a few words about that. I can't go running to Ozzie over issues like this, especially now that we're sleeping together. I don't want any special treatment. Yeah, Toni and I are going to have a little convo later this morning, just so we can get some things straight.

"You want to meet me here at two-thirty?" Dev asks me.

"Sure. As long as you don't have a weapon on you that you plan to use against me."

He smiles. "No promises."

I shrug. "Fine. Same goes for me, though."

"Ooooh, baby, that sounds like a threat!" Thibault is laughing. "You opened up a can o' worms with her, Dev. I think you'd better retreat."

"*Retreat* isn't in my vocabulary," he says, standing to his full, almost seven-foot height.

I have to admit, it's pretty impressive. But I'm not going to let anyone know I'm affected by it. I shrug. "Don't worry, Thibault. You know what they say about guys like him." I gesture at Dev with my chin.

Thibault's eyes are practically sparkling with glee. "No, what do they say?"

"The bigger they are, the harder they fall."

Even Ozzie laughs when Dev replies. "Oh, it's on, Bo Peep. It is *so* on right now."

CHAPTER FORTY-SIX

After changing into my workout clothes, I meet Ozzie in the company's gym. He's wearing his workout stuff too, and I have to avert my eyes from his crotch that I swear is growing bigger by the second. It doesn't help to calm me down, though. His chest is massive in the light of day, and I still remember what it felt like beneath my hands and what it looked like naked, hovering above me.

"I'm going to show you Dev's circuit today, so you can do it without me in the future."

My face falls. All sexy thoughts leave my mind immediately. The circuit? Nobody likes the circuit. I don't even know what it is, and I don't like it.

"What's the matter?" he asks me, moving closer.

I back up. "Nothing." I look around at the equipment, acting like I'm not hurt that he's already trying to get out of his promise to work out with me. "Where do we start?"

"We're not starting anything until you tell me what I did wrong." He's looking down at me with an expression that tells me he means business.

"It's nothing. Me being a girl. Silly stuff. Come on, let's work out." I really need to stop being such a wiener. I'm starting to get tired of myself.

He stands still for a few seconds but then moves to my right. "Over here is the famous clipboard." He picks it up from a table and holds it up for me to see. His muscles flex even with just that small movement. *Yums.*

"Dev has a list here of exercises that need to be executed on certain machines. Each one is done for one minute total, as many reps as you can bang out with good form, with a fifteen-second break in between each one. You can't rest for more than that or he blows a gasket."

"How does he know if you followed the plan or not?"

"Because he's a freak. Trust me, he can tell from looking at you if you've been cheating. I don't know if he secretly counts out the seconds from across the room or what, but he knows. Cheating the circuit is cheating yourself, and cheating yourself is cheating the team. So just don't cheat. Follow the rules of the clipboard."

"Sounds ominous," I say, trying to joke about the fact that I have a Nazi war general in charge of my exercises. I'm not as sure now as I was before that I want to get in shape.

"Nah. You'll get used to it. Besides . . . it gets results." He shows me the clipboard. "Here's the first exercise. Dev numbered the machines. This first exercise is done on number eight. You do pull-downs, behind the head. Pictures of how to do the exercise are on the machines themselves, so you can follow them as you work out." He points to the paper and then walks to the machine. "Have a seat."

I sit on the cushioned black mini-bench and wait for Ozzie to do his next thing. He puts a pin in some weights I'll be moving. In front of me I notice the picture he mentioned that describes how to do the exercise. It's a drawing of a person pulling the bar down to the back of his neck, just like he said. I nod. It looks easy enough.

"Grab that bar over your head and pull it down behind your neck. Slow, controlled movements, do as many as you can with your hands spread apart wide." He leans over and presses a button on a timer that's been stuck to the machine with sticky tape. "Timer's set." He presses another button. "Go." Seconds tick down from sixty.

I pull the bar down and smile when I see that the weight he's selected for me is manageable. I can do this. I won't even need to cheat on the seconds.

Ozzie stares at the bar coming down. Then he watches me, focusing on my face.

"You didn't eat your omelet," he says in a lower voice, designed not to carry across the warehouse.

"I know." I wait while I pull the bar down again before continuing. "I didn't want everyone to see." Air hisses out of me as I try to keep the bar from flying back up above my head. Okay, so it's not as easy as I thought.

"Did I embarrass you by making it?"

The weights clang together when I accidentally lose control of the bar.

"Easy," he says.

I hold the bar better and go for another repetition. "No, you didn't embarrass me at all. I like that you did it. I just . . . don't want anyone to know anything you don't want them to know."

"And what would that be?" he asks.

I struggle letting the bar go back up slowly. I think the weights are getting heavier somehow, even though I can see Ozzie hasn't touched them.

"You know." My face turns red, partially from the exertion, but also from his questions. "Don't make me say it."

"You don't want anyone to know we slept together."

I let the bar race back up to its position above me. The weights bang together. "I didn't say that." I have to rub my hands on my shorts to dry them off. I'm already sweating. I'm not sure if it's the workout or our conversation at the root of it.

"If you want to keep everything on the down low, we can do that." Ozzie shrugs.

"I just think that if people know, they'll think badly of me."

"And then they'd have me to deal with," he says. I'm not sure he realizes it, but his chest puffs out a little when he says that.

I smile, seeing that protective instinct coming to the front again. It really is one of his most attractive qualities. "I can fight my own battles, if you don't mind."

"Fine. But you tell me if anyone gives you a hard time."

I shake my head. "No, I'm not going to do that."

"Cheating!" yells a voice from the other side of the warehouse, making me jump.

Ozzie waves the clipboard at me. "Come on, next exercise." He walks over to another machine and points at the seat. "Set the timer. One minute. Then rest for fifteen seconds before you start it."

I push the buttons on this new timer like Ozzie did on the one before and then rest my hands on my legs. I'm actually a little breathless already. How lame.

"Set your weight at sixty pounds."

"Do I do that on all of them?" I lean forward and pull a metal pin from the stack of weights, sliding into the number sixty.

"No. Dev gives us a list of what we should be lifting. Here's yours." Ozzie points to a chart on the top page where everyone's weights for each machine are listed. Ozzie's are big numbers, of course. Huge compared to mine. He's supposed to do one hundred and seventy five pounds on this one. Is that even possible? I look down and see that the weights only go to one-fifty.

"Wow. Is he anal about his workouts or what?"

Ozzie talks in a near whisper. "Let's just say he takes his job seriously."

"I see you cheating over there!" Dev yells. "Fifteen-second rest periods! Not fifteen minutes!"

I press the button on the timer and start the exercise, lacking half the strength I need because I'm trying so hard not to laugh.

Ozzie has to turn away from me to not laugh too.

"So what's Toni's deal?" I ask, feeling stronger now that my mind is focused on her being mad at me for some mysterious reason. The weights practically fly off the stack.

"About what?"

"About you. Did you sleep together?"

Ozzie's face scrunches up. "Toni? And me?"

"Yeah." I pretend not to care, staring at the weights slowly going up and down at my command.

"No. Never."

"Then why is she mad about me being with you overnight?"

"I don't know." He shakes his head. "Maybe she's overprotective."

"Of you?" I snort. "That's funny."

"Toni's loyal. She takes it personally when an outsider messes with her family."

"And I'm the outsider." It makes me sad to hear myself referred to in that sense. I want to belong here more than anything. I haven't thought about wedding portraits in, like, forty-eight hours, when for the past seven years that's all I ever thought about. Freedom! . . . I don't want it taken from me when I've finally gotten a taste for it. I can admit to myself now that I hated what I was doing before. It took Bourbon Street Boys to show me that, to make me be honest with myself.

"I wouldn't say you're an outsider, exactly. You're just on probation in her mind. Don't worry, though. She'll accept you eventually."

"If I measure up."

"You will."

I push the handles in front of me for the tenth time as the beep goes off on the timer. I grunt, pushing the weights that now feel four times heavier than they did when I started. "Eeerrrgh!"

"Get it, girl!" Dev yells from across the room.

I laugh and drop the handles before the rep is finished.

Ozzie rests his hand on my shoulder. "Fifteen seconds. Rest up. You're going to need it."

I look up at him, sweat pouring down my face. "Is the next one hard?"

He grins and drops his voice to a whisper. "No, but I have plans for you tonight."

I cannot for the life of me remember any more of the exercises I did during that workout. I was too distracted, wondering what he was going to do to me and how many orgasms it was going to involve.

CHAPTER FORTY-SEVEN

It's called data mining," Toni says, booting up a computer I hadn't realized existed before, located in a set of cubicles in another part of the warehouse we reached after going through a maze of doors and corridors. "We get all the raw feed in, drop it into folders, and sift through it when we can. Sometimes we use computer programs to help, and sometimes it's just a matter of watching the stuff on fast forward until something interesting pops up."

She opens a folder and clicks on a file. "This is what we got from the Parrot yesterday. This feed file covers through nine this morning." She stands and moves to a cubicle next to the one I'm sitting in. "I'll start with the dragonfly; you start with the Parrot. We'll pick up the Go-Pro action we got after." She sits down at a second computer and clicks on another folder, picking up some earphones from the desk and sliding them onto her head.

I tap her on the shoulder, and she looks over.

"Sooo, what exactly am I supposed to do?"

She grabs her headphones and pulls them off with a sigh. "Watch the video. Write down the time stamp of anything interesting. Screenshot faces if you see any."

She's about to put the headphones back on, but I stop her with another question.

"Talk to me about *interesting*."

She rolls her eyes. "Jesus, Bo Peep, you want me to spoon-feed you lunch too?"

I sit back in my chair and cross my arms. I'm too tired from my workout to have patience for this. Lifting weights drains my body *and* my brain, I guess. "Maybe before you do that, you could tell me what the hell your problem is with me."

Her expression is mutinous. "I don't have a problem with you."

"Of course you do."

She shrugs, going all cool on me. "Paranoid much? Jesus, Bo Peep. Relax. You'll get your minivan later today."

I reach over and knock the headphones out of her hands as she's about to put them on again. Minivan, my butt. I'm not driving a stupid minivan anywhere.

She spins around and glares at me. "You better watch yourself, Bo Peep. Nobody's here to protect you from that smart mouth of yours."

I raise an eyebrow. "And that's supposed to scare me?" Maybe yesterday it would have, but today, knowing Ozzie has my back, not so much. Obviously she has issues, and if I'm ever going to work here permanently, I feel like we're going to need to get them out on the table. It's also possible my workout used up all my fear factor juice and I have none of that chemical left to respond appropriately to Toni's threat. I should probably be scared crapless, but instead I'm antagonizing her.

"If you were smart, it would."

I rest my hands on the arms of the chair. "Let's just say I'm not smart. What are you going to do? Hit me? Tackle me here in the computer room? Teach me a lesson?"

She frowns at me like I'm crazy. "No."

"Then what?" I shrug. "What's your problem? Why are you acting nice to me one second and kicking Thibault under the table the next?"

There. It's out there in the air between us. I pray this isn't a mistake bringing it up.

"What are you talking about?"

"You kicked Thibault in the leg under the table when he suggested I stay overnight with Ozzie."

"I did not."

"Yes, you did. I saw it."

"My foot just slipped. It was an accident."

"Please. Just move on from that BS, and tell me why you did it. Are you in love with Ozzie or something? Are you jealous?"

Her jaw drops open.

"No one would blame you, you know. He's handsome, strong, single, the boss of his own successful business. He's a great catch."

"He's not my type." Toni turns her head away and picks up the headphones.

"I don't believe you."

She shrugs, putting the headphones on her cheeks. "Believe whatever you want. It doesn't matter either way to me." She pushes the ear pads over her ears and presses a button on her computer.

It's on the tip of my tongue to call her the b-word, but I refrain. Instead, I pick up the pen on the desk and slide the legal pad over to the left side of the desk, so I can take notes.

Toni doesn't want to discuss her crush on Ozzie, and neither do I. She's just going to have to accept the fact that he's *mine*. Mine, all mine, all mine. I feel like a greedy Daffy Duck, hoarding a huge pile of gold and freaking out thinking someone's about to steal it. Man, I've got it bad for that man.

I sigh and press the "Start" button on the video, watching as the trees around the house begin to move with the wind. Nothing and nobody is doing anything in this movie except the greenery.

After the first ten minutes of seeing absolutely nothing, I realize what a crap job this data-mining thing is. No wonder everyone seemed happy when we volunteered. I throw my pen down on the table and lean back in the chair, rocking it back and forth, back and forth, back and forth . . .

"Would you quit doing that?" Toni says, pulling her headphones off.

"Doing what?" I keep rocking.

"Moving around." She grabs the arm of my chair and tries to stop me.

I shove her off with my elbow and rock harder. "I can rock if I want to. It's a free country." She doesn't want to talk to me about anything real, but she's going to bitch and whine when I try to stay comfortable in this hard chair? No. I don't think so. I reject that nonsense.

I stare at the computer screen, pretending like it needs all of my concentration. Adrenaline pumps into my bloodstream. I have a very strong suspicion that Toni's going to jump me any second now. If I had my Taser on me, the safety would be off. As it is, I'm thinking about our little area here and anything that might function as a self-defensive-type weapon. Dev would be proud, even though the only thing that comes to mind is her headphones. What am I going to do with those? Bap her about the head and shoulders with the ear pads?

"Do you even hear yourself?" she asks. "It's a free country? Seriously, what are you? Ten years old?"

"Old enough to recognize jealousy when I see it." I roll my eyes, purposely taunting her. Maybe if she gets mad enough she'll admit what her problem is.

"Jealous? Me? You think I'm jealous of *you*?"

"Of course you are. Why else would you be acting like a bitch toward me all the time?"

I have no time to prepare. One second she's sitting in the chair next to me, and the next, she's leaping on top of me.

I'm in headlock a half second later, and my chair has flown out from under me. I'm halfway crouching under her and most of the way to my knees on the floor.

"How dare you call me a bitch!" she yells.

My hands are reaching out for something . . . anything to make her stop.

"You're hurting me!" I yell, grabbing her leg.

She squeezes me harder. "Let go of my leg, Bo Fucking Peep!"

"Stop calling me Bo Peep!"

"Make me!"

"Now who's ten years old!"

"Shut up!"

My fingers scrabble for the headphone cord and I grab onto it, yanking for all I'm worth. I hit her in the shin just as I'm getting my legs under me.

She won't let me go, though. I reach up as high as I can with my free hand and find some of her hair. I latch onto it and yank hard.

"Owwwww!" she screeches. "Let go of my hair!"

"Let go of my neck," I grunt out. My vision is dimming.

"You first." She's breathing like an angry bull.

Screw that. She started this thing, so I'm going to end it. Closing the cord in my fist, I punch her in the thigh.

Her leg collapses as she screams in pain.

Yeah, let me introduce you to a charley horse, bitch. I have an older sister, and I know how to stop a headlock like nobody's business.

Her grip on me falls away, and I stand, shoving her as hard as I can. The adrenaline gives me superpowers, which combined with her featherweight status, send her flying. She lands on her back over the side of her chair. It tips over and dumps her on the floor.

I land next to her ribs on my knees, grabbing one of her hands and wrapping the cord around it super fast. She's like a calf in one of those rodeos. Before she can recover from her charley horse pains, I grab her other hand and tie it up too. The headphones hit my hand as I reach the end of their tether.

"What are you doing?!" she yells, panting after. I think I punched her a little too hard or something. She sounds like she's in serious pain.

"Tying you up until you can settle down."

"You'd better run," she growls, struggling against my lame tying job. I have no way to knot the cord, so it's only a matter of time before she escapes and tries to kill me.

I search the immediate area for a solution. The only things there are the two chairs.

I grab one and flip it over, dropping it over her, the back of the chair on her right side, the arms on her left. It makes a bridge over her tied hands. Leaning over it, using my weight to keep it there, I hang over her beet-red face.

"Say *uncle* and I'll let you up."

"I'll say uncle when I have a knife to your throat, not before." She's practically spitting, she's so mad.

I blink a few times, trying to figure out if she's serious. She sure looks like she is.

"You'd use a knife on me?" I'm kind of hurt by the idea. I feel pretty confident that she wouldn't do that to any of the guys, even if she were this mad at them.

She doesn't answer. She just glares at me while she continues to struggle. She's probably pretty close to getting the cord off, but with me on top of this chair, she's not going to get very far.

"Let me out," she says, her voice calmer. It's kind of a deadly calm, though, so I don't trust it at all.

"Can't. I don't want to die today." I grin at her. This whole thing is too ridiculous. We're two grown women and we're fighting like children. At work! I pray none of the guys comes back here and catches us.

"Then you shouldn't have attacked me."

I frown. "Hey, that's not fair. You moved first. I just defended myself."

"You asked for it."

I shake my head. "Huh-uh. I asked you to explain why you were acting jealous about me being here with Ozzie. It was a fair question."

She stares at me for so long, I'm starting to think she's suffering from lack of oxygen or something.

"Are you going to say anything?" I finally ask.

"I'm not sure I should." Her chin goes up a fraction.

"Why not?"

"Because. You probably won't even be here next week."

"Says who?"

"Says me."

"Wow. Thanks for the vote of confidence."

"You don't belong here."

"Ow." I rub my chest with one hand. "That actually kind of hurt."

"Shut up."

"No, I'm serious."

"See? You're too sensitive. You don't belong here. Why don't you do everyone a favor and just bow out gracefully?"

"Is that what you'd do?"

"No, of course not."

"Then I'm not going to do it either."

"You're not me. We're nothing alike."

Obviously I've insulted her by basically telling her I admire her. How's that for screwed up?

"Maybe I want to be more like you," I say, experimenting with the truth. "Maybe I want to be tougher, more self-reliant."

She searches my face, maybe looking for evidence that I'm not yanking her chain. She's obviously conflicted. I've paid her a pretty high compliment, but will it be enough to break through her anger at me? I'm starting to think I know where her emotion might be coming from.

"We're too different," she finally says.

"Oh, I don't know about that." I ease some of my weight off the chair. "I'm new to the team, but I care about everyone here. I respect all of you a lot. I know how hard you work, how loyal you are to each other. I know you all want to make Ozzie proud and that he's a great boss. I know until I got here, you were the only woman on the team, and now things are going to change with two women being here."

When she looks away, I know I've figured it out. Or at least I've come close.

"But it doesn't have to take anything away from you. From your accomplishments. From your skills."

"You fly the Parrot better than I do," she whispers. Tears gather in the corner of her eyes. I can tell it makes her angry to show that small weakness. Her expression becomes mutinous again.

"So? You kick ass better than I do." I try to smile, but she glares at me anyway.

"Says the girl sitting on me with a chair. You tied me up with my own headphones, May."

"You called me 'May.'" I reach down and poke her on the nose. She's so cute when she's mad. It makes me happy that she left that Bo Peep stuff behind.

"Slip of the tongue." She's trying to hold on to her anger, but I'm not going to let her.

"How about if we make a deal?" I propose.

"What deal?"

"I promise to show you how to fly that stupid thing, and you give me a chance to prove myself worthy of your respect."

She looks anywhere but at me. A tear slips out of her right eye and travels down into her hair.

"I don't need another friend," she finally says. Her eyes move to meet mine, and she's glaring again.

"I'm not asking for your friendship. I'm asking for your respect." It makes me sad to say that, but it's true. If she doesn't want to be my friend, I can't force her to. I'm not sure I've ever been so clearly rejected, though. I wasn't kidding before; it hurts.

"Earn it and you'll have it," she says, letting out a long hiss of air after.

"Just give me one chance."

"Done. Now let me up."

The devil takes control of my mouth again. "Not until you say *uncle*."

She glares, but I just keep on grinning.

Her voice comes out low and threatening. "If you ever tell anyone I said uncle, I will stab you while you sleep."

I laugh. "Say it, or Ozzie's going to be serving you dinner under this chair."

Her teeth grind together for a few seconds before she finally speaks. "Uncle. Now get the hell off me."

I push off the chair and stand back, waiting for the angry mess of a non-friend to get up and attempt to kill me.

But she doesn't do anything to me. She just gets up, rights the chairs, and untangles her headphones from her wrists. When she's done, she sits down, puts the equipment on, and starts the recording again.

I cautiously take my seat and press the button on the video, watching her out of the corner of my eye as I get back to work. The ninja sneak attack that I'm expecting for the next three hours never comes.

CHAPTER FORTY-EIGHT

"A re you ready?" Dev asks, coming across the warehouse and rubbing his hands together.

I put my hand in my purse and wrap my fingers around the Taser inside. "Ready for what?"

"Car shopping." He looks confused. "Isn't that what we're going to do now?"

I pull my hand out of my purse. "Yeah, sure, of course. What did you think I was talking about?"

He points at me and winks. "Mental games. Good. I like your style."

I roll my eyes as we walk over to his car. "I don't have a style."

"Oh, yes you do, Bo Peep. Trust me on this." He's chuckling as he folds his frame into the big old car.

I get in next to him and cringe at how heavy the door is. That circuit workout killed me. I'm going to be sore on top of my already sore spots. At this point, it feels like I'm never going to recover. Everything . . . every muscle, every bone, every *cell* in my body hurts.

He reverses out of the warehouse, and I think about what he said, what Toni said, and how everyone seems to act when I'm around. Even Ozzie.

"You guys keep calling me Bo Peep, and I have to tell you, it really doesn't feel like much of a compliment."

Dev turns the wheel by spinning it around and around on the heel of his hand. It takes about five revolutions to turn the car just ninety degrees.

"It is a compliment. Or maybe it's more just an observation of a really good cover."

"What do you mean?"

He purses his lips. "Hmmm, how to put this in a way you'd appreciate . . ."

"You don't have to worry about offending me," I say. "Toni's already gone there."

"No, I'm just trying to come up with a way to show you . . . I know." He points into the air. "What do you think about when you see Ozzie?" He glances at me, waiting for my response.

My eyes bug out of my head. Is this a trick question? An opener for a conversation about how I slept with the boss? *Ack!*

"What do you mean?" I feign a casualness I do not feel.

"He's standing there in his shirt and jeans, boots, haircut in that military style . . . what comes to mind when you see that?"

Okay, so I can't say *total hotness* in this situation, even though it's the truth. Dev is trying to lead me somewhere else. "Umm, commando?" My face starts burning. "I mean, military guy, not . . . no underwear guy."

Dev laughs. "Excellent." He glances at me and smiles before putting his eyes back on the road. "Exactly. That's what *everyone* sees when they look at him. He sticks out like a sore thumb. He looks threatening, like someone you should keep an eye on. He cannot walk into a situation and be invisible. It's just impossible."

I look at Dev's lanky legs. "Probably hard for you too, huh?"

"Exxxxactly. He's a sore thumb and I'm a sore arm. No way can I go anywhere undercover. I'm only good for when bodies need to

ELLE CASEY

be brought places in trunks or for driving a getaway car. And every once in a while to provide a distraction."

"And you're saying I can go undercover?"

He laughs. "Hell, yeah, you can."

I sigh in defeat. "Are you saying I look like a minivan mom who has nothing going on?"

He frowns. "Uhhh, no. Not exactly."

I look out the window, trying not to be hurt by that. I know being a mom is a greater calling than being a badass, but that doesn't mean I want to be there anytime soon.

"What I meant was that you can blend. If you want to be a minivan mom, you can be one, with the right hairstyle and clothing. But if you want to be a femme fatale, you could be that too."

I look over to see if he's messing with me, but he appears serious.

He continues. "Some leather pants, high heels, different hair . . . easy. Done. And yet, still, no one would see you as a threat."

"Because I'm a woman?"

"Because you have a disarming nature about you." He smiles and reaches over to pat my arm. "Don't sound so sad about it. It's a huge asset in our business."

I shrug, slightly mollified. "I guess being an asset isn't so horrible."

"No, trust me . . . being an asset is *everything*. Ozzie's only cover with this group was the Harley thing. Too many people get around in this town to try going out again too soon. He's out of the game now, for a long time. And I was never in. We just had Thibault, Toni, and Lucky before. Now we have you too."

A little fear trickles into my stomach. "For going undercover?"

He shrugs. "More for just being around and not being obvious about it." Dev drives out toward the main road that will bring us to the area of town known for having lots of car dealerships all grouped together.

I nod. "Okay. I guess I can accept that."

"The minivan is great because you can haul all the surveillance equipment around in it, the dogs, and of course, if we need someone to blend, nothing blends better than a chick in a mom van."

I sigh loudly. "Aaand now we're back to me being the doggie sitter and the soccer mom."

He laughs but doesn't reply.

After a few minutes pass in silence, I realize that this is the best time for me to pry information from an unsuspecting victim. He's trapped in this car with me for at least another fifteen minutes.

"So . . . what's the deal with Toni, anyway?" I ask.

"What do you mean?" He rests his wrist on the top of the steering wheel. The other arm is on the open windowsill.

"Is she in love with Ozzie? Why is she so against me being around?"

"Ozzie?" He snorts. "Hardly. He's not her type."

I frown. "That's what she said, but . . ."

I can see him glancing over at me out of the corner of my eye.

"What?" I ask.

"You don't get it, do you?"

"Get what?" I hate when everyone else is in on a secret and I'm not.

"Why Ozzie isn't her type."

Then it hits me. "Oh. Is she . . . is she a . . . ummm . . ." I can't say it. I feel really stupid now.

"A what?" He's obviously enjoying my discomfort.

The words barely come out. I feel like such a prude. "A lesbian?"

He laughs. Really hard and really loud.

"What?" I'm embarrassed now.

"That was hard for you, I can tell."

"Shut up." I stare out the side window, my face flaming. "I'll have you know I know plenty of gay people. I have several friends who are gay."

299

"Sure you do."

"I *do*." I glare at him. How does he know I have exactly one gay friend? Has he been spying on me?

"Well, that's nice, but Toni's not a lesbian. Not as far as I know, anyway."

I hit him in the side. "Why'd you make me say that if she's not a lesbian then, you idiot?"

He's still laughing as he holds his ribs where I jabbed him. When he finishes he sighs with pleasure. "Oh, man, that was awesome." He glances over at me. "I just like seeing you squirm."

"You're a weirdo." I'm kind of smiling but trying to stop.

He waits until he's done laughing before he tries to speak again. "She's got a past. Ozzie's helping her through that. Regardless, she wouldn't go for a guy like him in a million years."

"A past? What kind of past?"

"I'm not sure she'd want me sharing it. But you could ask her." He sounds way too happy about that idea.

"And get my butt handed to me on a platter? No thanks."

"Word on the street is you can handle it." There's an air of mystery surrounding his tone.

"What's that supposed to mean?"

"Oh, a little bird told me there might have been some hog-tying going on this morning during the data-mining session."

I feel sick to my stomach. "What? Who told you that?"

He snickers. "Not Toni, I'll tell you that much."

"So someone was watching us this morning? How rude."

"Hey, you make a ruckus, and people are going to come investigate." He shrugs.

I drop my face into my hands and leave it there. "Oh my god, Toni's going to kill me."

"Oh, don't worry about Toni. Just make sure you always have a pair of headphones on you, and you'll be fine."

My mind goes around and around that incident as Dev continues to drive. Now what the hell am I going to do? She'll never forgive me for trapping her under that chair if she knows the team saw it happen.

Dev pats me on the shoulder. "Don't worry about it. No one's going to say a word to her."

"She'll hate me forever." I lift my face from my hands. "I'm already on the poo list with her."

"Don't worry. Just keep working hard, and she'll come around."

I snort. "Yeah, right."

"She's tough, but she's not stupid. She'll see you're a good addition to the team, and she'll lighten up."

"What makes you so sure I'm that? A good addition?"

"You got the drop on me twice. On Toni once. No one's ever gotten you yet." He shrugs. "And like I said before, you have the perfect cover. You're a chameleon."

My words come out mumbled. "I prefer that nickname to stupid Bo Peep."

He laughs, chuckling all the way into the used car lot with ten minivans parked right up in front.

CHAPTER FORTY-NINE

Two hours later, after browsing, test-driving, and dickering over prices, I pull into the warehouse in my gently used work vehicle: a gold Toyota Sienna. *Ugh.* I hate this thing. I feel instantly ten years older when I'm sitting behind the wheel. I should probably go trade Felix in for a golden retriever and round out the look.

When I see him racing across the warehouse toward me, so excited he's curved in the shape of a comma, I decide that's a stupid idea. Felix is my little man. Maybe I can get him a little doggie seat to strap into the back. If I'm going to look like a soccer mom, I might as well have a baby seat too, right?

Ozzie comes down the stairs and shuts the driver-side door for me as I bend down to get Felix into my arms. I revel in the happy puppy love for a few seconds, using it to calm my racing heart. Ozzie is trying not to smile at my arrival—I know he is. His face is twitching.

"I like your new ride," he says.

"I hate it."

When I catch the look on his face, I hurry to amend my statement. "I mean, I don't hate it. I just don't like it." Wow. The guy gives me a company car, and I tell him to suck it. Nice.

He raises an eyebrow at me.

I sigh. "I hate looking like a soccer mom when I'm not a soccer mom. I never pictured myself as that person, I guess." The pout that comes out is not faked.

He pats me on the back and takes Felix from me, playing with his tiny ears as the mutt tries to lick him to death. I don't even think he realizes he's doing it. My heart calms and starts to go all gooey. He's forgiven for making me drive a minivan.

"It's just a work vehicle. If you don't want to drive it after hours, that's up to you. But I'd rather you stuck with the van for now, just until we're sure it's all clear at your place."

Dev climbs out of his car and walks over. "You up for the training session, Bo Peep?"

"I guess. I just need to walk Felix first." I reach for the dog, ignoring the thought that driving my red car might be dangerous. I don't want to believe that.

"Already done," Ozzie says, turning so I can't take him. "Go on with the training. I'll join you guys in a few."

I move slowly over to the area where Dev has mats on the floor as Ozzie walks away and puts Felix down by his girlfriend. The two canines trot off to another part of the warehouse, leaving us humans behind.

My body is in full protest over the activity my brain imagines Dev and I are about to engage in. Enough is enough, it's telling me. No more fighting for today. But Ozzie's watching, so I can't wuss out. Besides, if I ever want Toni to trust me and stop being a pain in the butt where I'm concerned, I have to do this. I have to do whatever she would do in my situation, and I'm pretty sure Toni would fight until she was collapsing with exhaustion.

Dev picks up some arm pads. "Put these on."

I'm grateful for the protection. "What about you?" He's just standing there doing nothing.

"I don't need them."

I snort. *We'll see about that.*

He turns to a table behind him and takes two singlesticks from the top of it, handing one to me.

"Okay, so first thing you need to know is you hold it here, on this end, behind the leather hilt."

I roll my eyes. "Yeah, as if I couldn't figure that one out for myself."

"You're a lefty? Okay, fine. Put your right hand behind you. Rest it on your lower back."

I copy his moves, feeling more vulnerable with just one arm out.

"Why like this?" I ask.

"Helps you build your muscles used for balance, and it keeps your other arm from being broken with the stick."

"Oh." Broken? Is he crazy? "I think I'm going to just stop asking questions from now on."

"Scared?" he asks with a twinkle in his eye.

I lift my chin. "No. Are you?" I jab at him with my stick a couple times. Even to my unpracticed eye, it looks less than smooth.

He laughs. "Hardly."

I hold the stick up in front of my face.

"Move your hand up farther. You want some stick exposed at the end so you can use it to butt into someone who gets too close."

"I thought I was going to whack someone who gets too close with the long end."

"It's not always that easy," he says wryly.

I move my hand up the stick a bit.

"Don't hold it too tight. Your hand will cramp."

"Okay, not too tight." The stupid thing sags in my hand.

"Tighter than that, though. Just enough that you can hold it steady. Too tight and you're going to telegraph your moves to me, and you don't want to do that."

"No, definitely not."

"Okay, first rule: Keep your stick moving." His starts swaying around his face, his shoulders, and then his lower body.

My moves are decidedly less graceful. "Why?"

"Because. It's better. You don't want to be caught off guard. Plus your strikes can come faster." He moves his feet a little. "Keep that body moving too. I don't want you falling asleep on me." He reaches out and smacks my stick hard enough to almost knock it out of my hand.

"Hey! I wasn't ready!"

"Always be ready."

He's practically staring holes in me right now, and I'm really glad I have the arm protectors on.

"Remember the acronym B-E-D-S," he says, taking some steps to the side.

I counter his moves in the opposite direction. "Beds?"

"Yes. BEDS. Those are your defensive options. Block. Evade. Deflect. And Strike."

I say them a few times in my head. "Okay. Got it. Beds."

"Readdyyyyyy . . . *block!*" He comes at me with his stick overhead.

"Ack!" I duck down and hold my stick up horizontally without conscious thought. His stick cracks down on top of it, rattling my arm bones.

"Good! Do it again! *Block!*" His stick comes at me once more.

I block him again, only without screaming this time.

"Excellent! *Evade!*" He swings the stick at me sideways and I jump out of the way. He's moving too fast for me to think and decide what to do next. I'm just functioning on instinct right now.

"Perfect! Here I come again!"

I jump again but put the stick down too. His weapon hits it hard.

"Hey! That would have *hurt!*" I yell, getting mad that he's playing so seriously.

"Better not get hit, then." He's prowling around the mat, looking for a chance to come after me.

My heart is beating like crazy as I wave my weapon around. *Keep moving, keep moving, keep moving.* A part of me wants to run out of the warehouse screaming, but the rest of me wants to teach him a lesson. How dare he teach me like this? What happened to the wax-on-wax-off method? The karate kid didn't start off kicking people on his first day.

"What's deflect!" I yell, trying to distract him from the kill.

"A mix of evade and block. Meet the stick but send it off in a nonlethal direction with its own force."

I have no idea what he's talking about. The panic is rising up in me. I'm sure he's about to attack again. If I vomit on my opponent, do I win?

"What about the last one?" I ask, my breath coming in gasps. "Strike?"

"That one's self-explanatory," he growls. And then he comes for me, stick raised.

I step to the side and meet his stick as it comes down, trying to make it bounce off to the side. Instead, it comes the other way and hits my shoulder.

"Owww! That hurt, goddammit!" I nearly trip on myself trying to get away from him. My striking arm feels dead now. I can barely raise my weapon.

"Say goodnight," Dev says, circling around and stepping toward me.

I lift my weapon up to thigh level and put my other hand on top of it, making a big letter T. "Time out!"

"No time outs! Just death to the loser!" He lets out a really loud war cry and comes for me.

I drop my right arm and throw the stick into that hand.

Dev's arm is above him as he prepares to take a swing designed to bring me down.

I swing the singlestick now in my right hand at his ribs as hard as I can.

The look on his face when I make contact is comical.

Shock. Pain. Anger. Pain again.

I jump out of the way as he trips on his own feet and goes down to the mat. His singlestick drops from his hand and rattles across the concrete floor as he curls into a ball.

"Ohhh shit," he moans, "I think you cracked my rib."

I lean on my singlestick, bent over trying to catch my breath. I don't know how much of my inability to breathe is from the workout and how much is from being scared to death. I can't believe I just did that.

"Sorry," I huff out between respirations.

"Don't apologize." He groans a few times. "Dammit, did I see you switch hands?"

"Yes."

"What the hell . . . are you ambidextrous?"

I cringe. "A little?"

He moans and then he starts laughing. Then he moans some more. "Oh, shit, that hurts."

The door above the stairs opens, and Ozzie comes down with Thibault. When they see us below, they pick up the pace, jogging across the floor to where we are.

"What happened?" Thibault asks.

"He says I cracked one of his ribs."

Thibault has to turn around so Dev won't see him smiling.

Ozzie crouches down and puts his hand on Dev's shoulder. "Can you get up?"

"With a little help from my friends," he says. His voice expresses his pain very clearly, making me feel even worse.

"I'm so sorry, Dev. Really. I shouldn't have hit you so hard."

He leans up with Ozzie's help. "Don't apologize." He holds his hand on his ribs. "That was awesome. Told you . . . perfect cover." He winces as he tries to move.

"Hospital?" Thibault asks Ozzie.

"Get him up first. Let me take a look." Together they get Dev on his feet. It's not an easy job since he's at least a full foot taller than Thibault. Ozzie does most of the work. He runs his hands gently over Dev's rib cage.

Dev stands slightly hunched over, still wincing.

"What happened, man?" Thibault asks him.

"She tricked me."

My jaw drops open. "Tricked you? I did no such thing." I point my stick at him. "He just jumped right into the training! No wax on, wax off, *nothing*—just whack, whack, whack! Block, evade, defend . . ."

"Deflect, not defend," Dev says.

"Whatever! You came at me too fast! I didn't have a choice." I drop my gaze to the mat. I feel guilty. Why, I don't know, since I was just defending myself. I'm just glad I didn't have a Taser handy. I would have electrocuted him *and* whacked him with my stick.

"What's going on?" Toni asks from the top of the stairs.

"Bo Peep got the drop on Dev," Thibault explains.

Toni shakes her head in disgust and walks back into the room upstairs.

Great. Just what I needed—Toni pissed at me for this too.

"I don't need to go to the hospital. I'm fine. I think it's just bruised." He stands up straight and then immediately bends a little again. "Maybe."

Ozzie points to the warehouse door. "Get it X-rayed."

Dev shuffles off, but he looks over his shoulder as best he can when he's a few feet away. "Keep the stick. Practice. You won't get so lucky a second time."

"I'll drive him," Thibault says. He walks over to me and puts his hand on my upper arm. "Well done. Don't beat yourself up about it. You won fair and square."

I try to smile, but it comes out more like I have stomach pains. "Thanks, Thibault."

He winks. "Don't mention it. It's not often we see the giant brought to his knees."

I try not to feel proud about being the one who did it, but it's kind of hard when he calls Dev a giant. He is pretty big. Our fight probably looked like the legendary David and Goliath death match.

I catch Ozzie watching me when Thibault is getting into the car with Dev.

"What?" I ask.

He shakes his head, his expression a mystery. "Nothing."

"Can I go home now?" I say, almost pleading. I look over at my Sonic. "I need a shower, I need to change clothes, and I'm tired of all this fighting stuff."

He walks over and puts his hand on the back of my neck, leaning down to look me in the eye. "Your home is here now, remember?"

I blink a few times but don't reply. Mixed emotions overwhelm me. I'm happy, scared, and sad all at the same time. I think it's possible I'm PMS-ing. "Oh, yeah. I forgot."

"Go on up. Do whatever you need to do. The afternoon briefing starts in an hour."

I nod. He's probably going to want to review what I saw on the tapes today, so I guess my day isn't over yet. I walk over to my car, but only to put the singlestick inside. I'll practice later when I'm gone from here. Maybe I'll have time to go see Jenny. She'll get a kick out of the primitive weapon, and I know for a fact that Sammy will want to hit some trees or lawn furniture with it.

Getting up the stairs is an adventure. I have to use the railing to pull myself up. I've definitely overdone it. No sex for me tonight.

How is Ozzie going to feel about that? Does he expect sex from me now? Is he thinking about it too, the way I have been all day? He's probably way cooler about it than I am. I'm sure he can handle working and living with me without losing his mind, unlike me.

Emotions rise up and start to overwhelm me. What in the hell am I doing here? I can't live with Ozzie! I can't get into stick fights with coworkers! This is ridiculous! I'm a wedding photographer, for God's sake!

I pull my phone out of my pocket when I reach the top of the stairs and pull the door open. I need some sister therapy, stat.

Jenny picks up on the second ring, thank goodness. "Hello, little sister! What's up?"

I walk through the kitchen without saying anything to Toni. "Just calling to chat." I wait until I'm in the bedroom with the door shut before I start to cry.

CHAPTER FIFTY

"H ey, hey, hey, what's up with the tears?" she asks, making me cry harder. Whenever she acts like my momma, that's what happens. Total boober baby, every time.

I talk around the weeping. "I don't know. I just needed to hear your voice and have you tell me I'm not being a stupid idiot over here."

"Over where, honey?"

She doesn't know what happened last night and I'm pretty sure I shouldn't tell her. She'll make me move into her house, and I can't do that. If there *is* a threat against me—which I highly doubt there is—I can't bring it into her home. She really is a soccer mom. Or she will be when one of her kids decides to start playing that sport.

"I'm at work," I explain.

"Why are you crying at work? Were they mean to you?"

I laugh through the tears. "No, they weren't mean. They're very nice." Except for Toni, but we won't mention her.

"So what's the deal? Are you on your period?"

"No." I wipe my nose with my hand and then look around for a tissue. I pull one from a box on the nightstand. "I spent the night here and had massive sex with Ozzie."

"Whoa. Massive sex? Is that different than regular sex?"

"Duh. Obviously." She's already got me smiling. Tears are still coming, but at least I'm not sobbing anymore.

"Okay, so why is that making you cry?"

I sigh, trying to push through the sorrow. "Can I be honest with you?"

"Uhhhh, yeah?"

"I mean without you freaking out on me."

There's a three-second pause before she responds. "Did you do anal sex? Is that what this is about?"

"Jennifer Alexandria Wexler! No! That's *not* what this is about!" When I get over my shock, I laugh again. She's nuts.

"Okay, then what is it? Geez." She giggles too.

I can't explain to her why I'm upset if she doesn't know the whole story. I hate that I have to tell her anything that might make her worry, but I don't have a choice. I need advice because I don't trust myself to make the right decision on my own. My heart is biased in favor of Ozzie.

"Last night my house alarm went off. There was an intruder on the property."

"Oh no." Her laughter stops, replaced by concern.

"Ozzie was with me. He handled the call to the alarm company after he made sure no one was there, but he said I needed to come to his place and stay until he could figure out what was going on."

"Sure he did." I can hear the smile in her voice.

"It's not a joke, Jen."

"No, of course not. I'm glad there wasn't anyone trying to break in and that Ozzie was there for you. Continue."

"One thing led to another and we had sex. Twice."

"Hmmm . . ."

"And it was really, really good."

"No anal, though, eh?"

"Stop!" I laugh again. I can't help it. It's way better than crying, anyway.

"I'm sorry, I couldn't help myself."

"Anyway . . . today was just my second day of work. So there I am, working with him, the whole time thinking about what we did last night."

"As I'm sure he was."

"How do you know that?"

"How could he not? Men think about sex over a hundred times a day. Or is it a thousand? I can't remember. Anyway, it's a lot. And you don't think he was reliving those moments with you? Imagining all the ones he wants to have in the future? Please. The guy probably had a raging hard-on all day long."

"I don't know."

"Well, I do. He did. Trust me. He's probably imagining you bent over the toilet right now."

"Wow. That's sexy."

"You have no idea what's sexy to a man. They're sick puppies."

"I'm starting to get scared about how you know all this."

"What can I say? Miles talked too much."

"Ew. Not all men are like Miles."

"Yes, they are. They *all* are. So what else? Why are you crying?"

I shrug. "I'm not sure."

"It's your period. Has to be."

"No, it's not. I think it's just . . . overwhelming. I changed jobs just days ago, started working with a team of really nice but slightly crazy people, I'm sleeping with my new boss—living in his house, for God's sake. My dog is in love with his dog . . . it's crazy! Nuts! Who does this kind of stuff?!"

"That does sound a lot more interesting than my life. You know what I did today?"

"No. What did you do today?" I wipe my nose again and let out a big sigh. I'm feeling better already.

"I removed a hairball from my shower drain that was the size of a baseball."

"Ew." I can totally picture it. My sister has really long, thick hair. "That's disgusting, Jen. I'm so *not* glad you told me that."

"I thought about mailing it to Miles, but then I didn't."

"Probably a good move. We wouldn't want him having you declared legally insane."

"If he doesn't come get these kids from me this weekend, he's going to learn all about legally insane, trust me."

"If he doesn't show, I will." I go all warm thinking about my sister and her kids. At least some things never change. I can always count on them for love bundled up in a whole lot of noise.

"And what does the man in your life think of all this?" Jenny asks.

"The man in my life? What man?"

"Felix."

"Oh." I picture him and Sahara sleeping together. "He's in love with Ozzie's dog. He doesn't even sleep with me anymore."

"Wow. That is serious."

"I know."

"I think you should trust Felix's judgment."

"Really?" It's kind of crazy, but that makes a lot of sense to me. Felix has never let me down.

"I don't know. Don't dogs have a sixth sense about people?"

I think about it for a second. "He does have his preferences."

"He hated that one boyfriend of yours, remember?"

I snort. "How can I forget? The guy was a felon, a fact he neglected to mention when I first met him."

"Good thing your sister is a computer wiz who can do background checks."

I smile. "Saved my butt again."

"Yeah, well, I'm here for you. Always."

"Thanks, sis."

"So you're going to stick this out?" she asks.

I nod, feeling way more confident about it than I was ten minutes ago. "I am. I'm worried I'm going to get my heart destroyed when he figures out we're really not all that compatible, but until then, I guess I'll just enjoy myself."

"Yeah, do that. Great idea. You can't live life always worried about what might happen tomorrow."

"That's pretty much what he said."

"See? He's obviously very smart. When are you going to bring him around to meet the kids?"

"Can I? Should I? Isn't it too soon?"

"I don't see how it can be too soon if you're sleeping with him. I guess it means you're serious about him, and that's what matters."

"Maybe I'm just sleeping with him because I'm wild and free and live life by the seat of my pants."

"Yeah, right. How long did it take your last boyfriend to get in your pants?"

"Four months."

"Exactly. Obviously this Ozzie guy is different. Bring him over tomorrow if you feel like it. I have the lasagna already made."

I chew my lip, considering the offer. "I'll let you know."

"Okay. Listen, Sammy's been quiet too long, so I'd better go. He's probably beheading all his sister's dolls again."

"Wow. That's not freaky at all."

"He's a boy." She sighs. "Boys are so different from girls."

"Okay, better go lock him up. Thanks, Jenny. I really appreciate you putting up with my mania."

"It's not mania. You're just being a girl, and you're allowed to act like one."

"Love you."

"Love you more! Bye!" She hangs up before I can respond.

Dammit. I hate when she wins the love-you-more game so easily.

I send a quick text before shutting my phone off.

Me: *Love you more! Ha!*

CHAPTER FIFTY-ONE

I use a wet washcloth to erase the signs of my breakdown, and then I return to the kitchen with renewed vigor and determination, joining Ozzie and Toni at the table. Lucky comes in as Ozzie starts to talk and sits next to me.

"Did either of you get any data today worth discussing?" Ozzie's addressing Toni.

"Not sure. I wrote a few things down." She pulls a legal pad out of a folder and runs her finger down the page. "I think someone must have opened a window at some point, because I started picking up conversations inside the house too, I think."

"Good." Ozzie nods.

"I heard a lot of the regular BS, people just shooting the breeze and messing around, but then there was some talk about a problem they were having that hadn't been resolved yet."

"Did they say what it was?"

"No, they just kept talking about Petit Rouge. That's who or what their problem is. They talked about shutting it down."

Ozzie nods slowly, his eyes distant.

"What does that mean?" I ask, mystified.

"Gangs use code all the time for just about everything. Petit Rouge could be a shipment of drugs, illegal imports, a rival gang, an operation not paying protection money, a single person . . . until we can put it in context, we won't know what it is." Ozzie returns his focus to Toni. "Any luck with that?"

She shakes her head. "No. I can tell you, though, that most of the talk about it came from one guy. I think he arrived late to the party. I got the impression it was a rival gang member or business they were talking about."

Ozzie's eyes narrow. "What's the time stamp the first time you heard his voice?"

Toni scans the pages in front of her. She stops on the fourth page. "Eleven thirty-three p.m. or around then."

Ozzie looks to me. "Look up that time stamp in your notes. You see anyone coming in just before that?"

My job was easier than Toni's by the looks of our notes. I have less than half as many. "Only seven people went in, and four went out." I look down the page, trying to find a time that matches up with Toni's observations. "There were two people who came in before she heard that conversation." I shuffle through my stack and find the two people I took screenshots of. "You can't see their faces, just their heads and bodies. It was pretty dark."

I hand them over to Ozzie, who studies them carefully. When he gets to the second one, he frowns and turns it around, holding it up so I can see it. "Recognize this one?"

All I can see is a hunched-over figure in a dark coat with a shiny head. His dome is reflecting the light coming from the street lamp nearby.

"Not really." I shrug, feeling like I should apologize. I didn't realize there was going to be a quiz.

Ozzie flips it around and stares at it a few more seconds. "I think this is Doucet."

Toni holds her hand out for it, and Ozzie slides it over the table to her.

"Who's Doucet?" I ask.

Toni nods. "I agree. There are several points of likeness. Shoulder width, stature. Bald head, of course."

Ozzie sighs, looking at me with what appears to be regret. "David Doucet is the man who pulled the gun on us at the bar."

A shiver passes through my body and my mouth goes suddenly dry. "David Doucet is the shooter?" His very name strikes fear into my heart.

"Yes. He's the brother of Guy Doucet, the one who runs the show in this part of town."

"So you think he's the one talking about Petit Rouge?" Toni asks.

"Could be." Ozzie gestures at Toni. "What else you got from him?"

She shrugs. "I could go listen again. Maybe now that I know who the voice belongs to, some of the things he said will make more sense."

"Yeah, why don't you do that. Tomorrow." He looks at me. "What else do you have on arrivals and departures?"

"Let's see . . . I have these guys all coming in,"—I pass over my screenshots—"but only the first four came back out. The last ones to arrive stayed for as long as the tape ran."

"And when did the recording stop?"

I look at my last page of notes. "Two-fourteen in the morning."

Ozzie turns his attention to Toni. "Pull more of the tape from the Parrot. I want to see until six in the morning."

"You got it." She moves to stand.

"Tomorrow. You've done enough today."

"Sure, no problem." Toni sits back down.

"Anything else I should know about?" He looks around the table.

"Bought some tackle today," Lucky says.

"And?"

"And things aren't adding up over there, literally and figuratively."

"How so?"

Lucky scratches his head. "I'm not exactly sure." His expression is pained as he crosses his arms over his chest. "They have the typical expenses of a retail business that also has a service aspect to what they do." He shrugs. "They sell products and they also repair marine engines, usually off site. They have contractors who do some jobs for them, both on and off site. They also pay for services done on and off site by other vendors as a result of the work done by the contractors. But if you run through their financial reports, you see they have an inordinate amount of money being spent in areas that should just be a minor percent of their total business expenses."

"Such as?" Ozzie has all his attention on Lucky, as do Toni and I.

"Well, take, for example, their hazardous waste disposal. They have used oil they have to get rid of when they drain it from marine engines. Most places pay to have it picked up and treated. No big deal. So does Blue Marine. Problem is, that service should be less than one percent of their total expenses. For Blue Marine? It's at almost ten percent."

"That's ridiculous." Ozzie looks pissed.

"I know. And there's more. The janitorial service that's supposed to be worth another ten percent? I went into the store. There're dust bunnies everywhere. The bathrooms haven't been touched in weeks. Employees who work in the store say that the garbage gets emptied and they see someone there at night once in a while, but for what they're paying, everything should be sparkling. They could practically pay a person to be there full-time with what they've spent this year."

"What else?"

"The list goes on and on. Re-machined parts, returns, one-off services—you name it; their numbers are whack."

"So what's our next step?" Ozzie leans back in his chair.

Lucky unfolds his arms and put his hands on the table, palms down. "I need to contact these providers and see what's up. If it's just a matter of a terrible business manager who doesn't know how to shop around, then fine. We can fix that. But I'm afraid it's something more." He shakes his head with disappointment. "You know how hard it is to prove embezzlement without a confession."

"Well, Blue Marine is worried it's something more too. That's why they hired us. Talk to the service providers, and let me know what you find out. If we need a confession after all is said and done, we'll get one. Just get me the evidence to bring to the conversation."

"You got it. You want me on this now?"

"No, tomorrow. Everyone's done for the day." Ozzie stands. "You guys can take off. I'm sure Dev and Thibault will be at the hospital for at least a couple hours. We'll pick this up tomorrow at eight."

All the chairs scrape back at the same time as we get to our feet.

"You're here with me tonight," he says, looking at me. He's talking like my boss, but the look in his eye is coming from my lover. I think Jenny was right; he has been thinking about having sex with me. A whole other kind of shiver is running through me now.

"You mind if I talk to you in private for a minute?" Toni asks him. I get the impression she's specifically not looking at me, even though she wants to. I'm immediately suspicious.

"Sure. I'll walk you out."

I pretend to be busy with paperwork as they all leave the kitchen together.

Felix comes running through the kitchen and jumps up on my lap, trying to reach my chin for a lick attack.

"Where have you been, you little rascal?"

Sahara comes walking into the room behind him, ambling over to sit next to my chair. I scratch her behind the ears a little before I get up and put Felix on the floor. "So, what up, dogs?" I giggle at myself. Lame humor is my specialty. "Have a fun day today smelling each other's butts and eating the same meal you eat every day?"

They both look up at me with stars in their eyes.

"I'm not giving you any treats. Don't look at me like that."

Felix whines.

"Okay, maybe a little treat." I walk over to the pantry and step inside, searching the shelves. It's kind of fascinating seeing inside the heart of Ozzie's kitchen. Everything is lined up with labels pointing out. Canned goods are in one section, boxed goods in another, arranged so that dinner foods and cereals are not together.

I hear noises outside the pantry door that I assume are the dogs messing around, but then I freeze when voices come too, entering the kitchen from the sword room.

"Just let me grab this folder, and I'll walk you out," Ozzie says.

"We might as well talk here," says Toni, sounding frustrated. "The warehouse has too many ears."

"So talk. What's on your mind?"

"I just don't want her in my business."

I'm guessing I'm the *her* she doesn't want around.

"I understand, but I want to assure you that you have nothing to worry about."

She snorts her disbelief. "Listen, I know you want to think you're being third-party removed and all that, but you're not. Everyone knows you're into her."

"What makes you say that?"

"Please. It's obvious. You set her up on a ninety-day probation and the next day buy her a company car? You move her into your apartment? Jesus, Oz, why don't you go buy a fucking ring and ask her to marry you already."

"That's out of line." Ozzie sounds angry.

I take a small step deeper into the pantry. The door is slightly ajar, and I pray they can't see inside it from where they're standing. They'll think I snooped on purpose.

"What, I'm not allowed to speak my mind here anymore?"

"You can speak your mind; I just don't appreciate you getting involved in my personal life. Or what you think is my personal life."

"If it's not your personal life, why don't you explain why she's getting all this special treatment?"

I hate those words. *Special treatment.* I knew it would piss her off that everyone was coddling me so much. Dammit!

"I don't have to explain anything to you. In case you've forgotten, I'm the boss here."

"There was a time when you shared everything with me, Ozzie. What happened to that? What happened to us? It was so good between us for a long time."

My heart collapses in on itself. He said they'd never had sex. He lied! What else could she possibly be talking about?

Tears spring to my eyes. Horrible memories of my father come rushing into my brain. Visions of my mother, sobbing, drinking, trying to erase the pain he caused. His stories that were supposed to be believable. The suffering it brought to all of us. I'll never be able to forget that part of my life, and now it feels like I'm reliving it, only this time I'm my mother and Ozzie is the liar.

Of course Ozzie lied. He was too good to be true. I built him up to be this perfect specimen of a man, a superhero no less, but I should have known better; no man is perfect, including Ozzie. He's just like the rest of them.

I'm devastated. Shattered, just like I predicted I would be. Of course I thought it would take at least a few weeks for that reality to hit me like a ton of bricks, but whatever. It's here now. Thanks a lot, asshole, for getting my hopes up and then slapping me down. Dammit, he was so cute! And fun! And we did have massive sex too. My heart literally aches.

I can put up with a lot of crap, but lying is not one of those things. Not only was my father a lying cheat, but so was Jenny's husband, Miles, which is why his butt got kicked to the curb last year. I hate that I've already slept with Ozzie. Twice. I can't stay here tonight—no way. I'm busy planning my excuse for why I have to leave when he responds.

"You moved on, Toni. You don't need me that way anymore."

"Says who?"

"Says me. And you. You're the one who pulled away, not me. And I think it was the right thing to do."

"Because she's here."

"No, because it just is. It's time to move on from the past. Look to the future."

"My past is my future." Her words sound vicious, even way over here in the back of the pantry. The boots she's wearing strike the floor hard as she walks away.

"Only if you want it to be!" he shouts out after her.

The door to the warehouse slams shut.

"Goddammit." Ozzie sounds totally defeated. His footsteps moving down the hall toward his bedroom fade away as I tiptoe up to the pantry door. I need to get out of here asap, before he has time to find out I'm not in his bedroom and that I was hiding in the pantry the whole time.

CHAPTER FIFTY-TWO

Thank god, I left my purse downstairs in a locker. I race down the stairs and sprint over to it, yanking it out of the metal space. Felix is struggling to get out of my arms, probably because I left Sahara upstairs.

"Stop it, Fee. We have to go. I'm sorry about your girlfriend." The tears want to pour out of my head, but I won't let them. Not here. I'll collapse in a soggy pity party later, when I'm home and drinking copious amounts of wine.

I fish around in my bag for my keys and find them just as I'm getting to my Sonic. Less than a minute later, I'm pulling out of the warehouse, thankful that Toni left the door open. I didn't realize how much Ozzie's home could be like a prison until I remembered I don't have a key fob to use to get in and out of the big door. I could have left through the small door, but that would have meant leaving my car behind, and no way am I taking that stupid minivan. I have to decide if I'm even going to come back to this place.

As I drive down the highway, taking the fastest way home, my mind wanders. Can I work at Bourbon Street Boys if Ozzie and I are no longer together in a sexual way? Can we step back into the boss–employee relationship? I think I can. I want to, anyway.

I'll have to mourn the loss of that almost-relationship first, but it won't take long, right? A couple months, tops? Thinking about going back to wedding photography is positively depressing. At Bourbon Street Boys, I felt like I had an exciting life, for once. People admired me for things that came naturally to me. Every minute of the day, there was something new happening. My muscles are sorer than sore, sure, but soon they'll be strong, and then I'll know how to protect myself out here in a world where things can get pretty damn crazy.

I nod. Ozzie and I can do this. We can decide to be adults about it and acknowledge that things will be better if we're not involved. Then he and Toni can get back together, and I can keep my job. She'll stop hating me when she sees that I'm happy to give him up, and we can maybe even learn to be friends.

I burst out in choking sobs. Why did he lie? Why didn't he just tell the truth? I liked him sooooo much. I probably loved him already. Oh, how I hate myself right now. Why do I have to be so gullible? It makes me angry enough that the tears stop.

Give Ozzie up? How am I going to do that? Can I pretend I never heard about his lie and make myself not care that he did it? When I try to imagine saying the words *Good-bye forever* or hearing the words *Sorry, but it's not going to work out,* I want to bawl like a baby all over again. Why? Why, dammit? Why did he have to be so amazing and such a liar too? Why can't the inside of a man match the outside, like, ever?

I grip the steering really hard and shake it. It's actually my body flying back and forth, but it feels good taking my rage out on the faux-leather cover. I yank the wheel hard to the right, driving up into my driveway way too fast.

I have to slam on the brakes to keep from ramming my garage door. I've for sure left skid marks on the ground. Good. I'll need something to keep me busy for a while after today. I'll get down on my hands and knees and scrub that rubber off for the next week. I'll have the cleanest driveway in New Orleans.

My hair swings into my face with the force of my stop, and Felix flies off the seat and lands on the floor. When he gets his feet under him, he looks up at me, and I swear I can see disappointment there.

"I'm sorry, baby. I'm just upset. You know I drive horribly when I'm in a bad mood."

He's still glaring.

"Don't worry. You'll see Sahara again. I'll work it out . . ."—my voice catches on the last word—"somehow."

Walking up the front sidewalk with Felix under my arm, my feet are practically dragging. I don't want to be here alone, but I don't want to be at work. I can't look at Ozzie right now. I need to calm down before he starts lying to my face. And I can't go to my sister's place. She'll try too hard to cheer me up, and I'm not in the mood. I need to wallow in my pain for a little while. Own it. Live in it like a second skin so that when Ozzie begs for my forgiveness, I won't cave in. I do that too easily. I need to toughen up. Something tells me Ozzie will have amazing powers of persuasion.

I walk in the door and throw my stuff on the ground: my purse, the singlestick Dev told me to keep and practice with, and the folders I had at the table. Felix I lower to the ground gently, of course. He didn't do anything wrong; he's guilty of the same crime I am—loving too much, too fast, too easily.

I don't know why I grabbed all that stuff from work. I guess my heart wants to pretend I'm still working at Bourbon Street Boys, even though my brain is telling me to quit. Stupid heart. Trying to get itself trampled and not just massively bruised.

I've got the wine out and glass of it halfway to my lips when Felix starts barking like a crazy fool.

And then it hits me.

The house alarm never went off when I walked in. What happened to the *beeeep, beeeep, beeeep*?

I lower my glass very slowly to the counter, pricking my ears for any sounds that might explain Felix's agitation. I hear nothing, but he is pissed for sure. If I didn't know better, I'd surmise he's looking out the front door windows that stretch from ceiling to floor. Usually he stands sentry there, so him barking at things like grass moving or a car driving by isn't normally a big deal. It's just that he's so enthusiastic about it this time. He sounds mad, and Felix never sounds mad. And he usually gives up after three or four barks.

Suddenly he yelps really loud and then stops. A whine follows. I've only heard that noise once from my boy, when he pulled a back muscle jumping off the couch as a puppy.

My heart stops beating. I'm pretty sure someone just kicked my dog, and the only someone who would kick an adorable Chihuahua mix like my Felix has to have a black heart and an empty husk for a soul. I want to call the dog to my side and shove him in a cabinet where he can't get hurt, but I don't want to alert the dirtbag who abuses animals to where I am.

I slowly remove a knife from the block on my counter and sidle toward the doorway that leads into my dining room from the other side. Hopefully, whoever is out there will go down the hallway, and I'll be able to run out the door with Felix in my arms before he even sees me.

Please, God, let Felix be okay, and let him still be in the hallway by the front door.

Felix starts growling, and it lightens my heart just a little. If he's mad enough to be angry, that has to mean something good. I follow the sounds that are coming from his tiny throat. He's somewhere in the living room, and hopefully he's alone.

CHAPTER FIFTY-THREE

I'm leaning down to pick Felix up from the rug in the living room when the voice comes.

"Well, well, well . . . if it isn't Petite Rouge," he says with a Creole accent.

My brain does a quick translation.

Petite Rouge. Little Red.

Then it hits me.

Little Red Riding Hood! It's me! I'm Little Red!

Then the second fact hits me.

There's a frigging murderer in my house, and he's going to kill me!

And then the third and final fact hits me.

What is *up* with all the goddamn nursery rhymes being attached to my person, anyway?

I nod once at him, my body language expressing a cool I do not possess more than skin deep. "David." The knife is up by my shoulder, trembling because my entire body feels like it's being overtaken by an earthquake. I'm not ready to die. I have so many unresolved issues to deal with! What will Jenny do without me, and the kids? What about Ozzie? What about Fee?

If this asshole even so much as takes a step toward me, I'm going to bury this knife in the closest part of his body. He has a gun in his hand, though, so I know it's not likely I'll ever get close enough to use my weapon. I should have asked Ozzie to show me that weapon first. Dammit. Now it's too late. It's too late for everything. I never wanted my life to end with this much regret.

"And you know my name," he says. "How nice." The expression on his face is anything but pleased.

"Why are you here?" I ask, hoping that if I keep him talking, maybe someone will come over and find me, rescue me before he makes his move.

"I would have thought that would be obvious. I've been waiting here awhile, actually. Where have you been all day, I wonder?"

I shrug. "I'm a photographer. I'm all over the place."

He stares at me for a long time.

I have to shift my weight to the other foot. My leg is going numb from the stress. I have almost no power left anywhere in my body, thanks to my workouts today. I hate that I'm facing this guy with the strength of a three-year-old. Sammy could beat me in an arm wrestling competition.

"Now what is a photographer doing at Frankie's pub with Harley, I wonder?"

"Harley?" I look as confused as possible. "I have no idea who Harley is. I was there to meet my sister."

I'm probably going to die here tonight, but if I can leave this world restoring Ozzie's cover, maybe he can get to the bottom of what they're doing and help put them all in jail. It's not much in the way of revenge, but it's better than nothing. Maybe they'll put a plaque in the hallway at Bourbon Street Boys with my picture on it, next to the letter from the chief of police.

I try to smile. "The bartender told me your name when I mentioned you were cute." My smile falls apart at the outrageous lie.

He's never going to believe that. He can't be that oblivious to his horribleness could he?

The guy smiles back, lifting his eyebrows a few times for good measure.

Bleh, who am I kidding? He probably thinks he's God's gift to women with that lumpy, bald head of his.

"So, your sister, eh? And who might that be? Maybe I know her."

"It's none of your business who my sister is." Right. Like I'd give that information up to a murderer. He must think I'm Little Bo Peep or something.

He loses his smile and moves toward me slowly. I circle right, trying to get closer to the front door. My purse, my Taser, and my singlestick are waiting for me there. Just ten feet away . . .

"You saw me in the bar," he says, his hand going around his back, taking the gun with it. "You weren't supposed to be there. Frankie's isn't your kind of place, am I right? I had a lot of friends there that night, but you weren't one of them."

"It was kind of hard not to see you, considering you shot a bullet at my face."

"You were with Harley. Don't try to lie and say you weren't. I saw the way he was looking at you. Sending texts to you. I was shooting at him, though, not you."

I act disgusted. "For the last time, I was not there with this *Harley* person. I was there to meet my sister. Some big, hairy Wookiee grabbed me and tried to attack me when I was there in the back room. I figured he was a friend of yours."

His eyebrows go up.

"I tazed him in the alley when he chased after me."

"I was in the alley. I didn't see you do that."

"It wasn't the alley right next to the bar. It was a few blocks over, and I know for a fact we were alone. That idiot ran after me, if you can believe that. Jerk." I fake a self-satisfied laugh. "He probably thought I'd run out of steam and he'd be able to just grab me and have his way with me, but I showed him. Tazed his ass. He fell like a big, hairy rock, right onto his fat, stupid face."

I may still be angry at Ozzie for lying. That could explain why my acting skills have suddenly improved.

"I'll bet he did," David says absently, staring at me hard. His hands come out from behind his back without the gun in them. It's strange, but I'm even more afraid now than when he was holding the weapon out where I could see it. Why is he putting it away? Is he letting me go? Does he believe my lame story?

He takes a step toward me. "You look so innocent." His voice has gone softer. "So . . . pretty in that pink shirt."

I look down at my chest. I'm wearing a polo shirt that I bought last year for my birthday. It reminded me at the time of cake icing.

"Uh, thanks," I say, taking another step to the right. "I think."

"Why don't you put that knife down, and we'll just . . . talk." He holds out his hands like he's innocent. "I put my gun away, see? No harm, no foul." He's smiling at me like I'm Little Red Riding Hood for real, and it's creeping me way the hell out. *What big teeth you have, Grandfather.* He has pointy incisors like a vampire. I can almost believe those monsters are real with him standing there in his black jeans. But in this story they'd be demons, because there is nothing sexy about this vampire with a gun in his waistband. *Ugh.*

"Yeah, okay." I glance at the doorway and then the shelves next to the entrance to the room. "I guess I could put the knife down on the shelves over there." I give him an apologetic smile. "I paid a lot of money for these, so if it's okay with you, I'd rather not put it on the floor."

He gestures to the bookcase. "Go ahead. Be my guest." He smiles again, bigger this time.

I turn my stance into one that doesn't appear as wary, and walk slowly over to the shelves, acting like I'm not watching him out of the corner of my eye. *Just keep your eyes on the pink shirt, psycho. Piiiink shiiiiiirt . . .*

He stands up straighter and moves into position behind me. He's a few feet away when I catch sight of Felix lying in the hallway where he's dragged himself. He's on his side, panting, his head angled up to look at me. He whines when he sees me staring at him.

"Felix!" I yell, putting the knife on the shelf and then running over to bend down by him. Yes, I'm worried for my puppy's life, but I'm also trying to get nearer to my weapons so I can serve up a nice heaping helping of revenge on the man who hurt my baby.

"He's fine. I just tripped on him when I was walking down the hall."

I grind my teeth together to keep from responding how I want to. I touch Felix's little head gingerly, calculating how fast I can jump to the side and grab one of my weapons before David figures out what I'm doing and gets his gun out to shoot me.

Taser or singlestick? Singlestick or foot to the testicles? Decisions, decisions . . .

"Stand up." David's just two feet away, his tone telling me he has plans for me. I'm absolutely sure I do not want to know what those plans are.

"My dog is hurt," I say, panicking. I won't get to my purse in time. That leaves the singlestick, but that's no match against a gun!

"He'll be fine. Stand up."

I point at my purse. "Do you mind if I call my vet really quick? My phone is in my purse."

He laughs. "So's your pepper spray, I'm sure. Stand up. This is the last time I'm going to say it."

I slowly get to my feet, taking a step toward the front door as I do, limping a little and bending down to touch my knee. "Ow, darn it. Leg cramp."

I pretend to have difficulty putting pressure on my leg. I take two half-limping steps to the side. The singlestick beckons.

"Oh, poop, I have a charley horse."

He smiles at my choice of words. Asshole. He really does think I'm Little Bo Peep in a pink shirt. That makes me angrier than that stupid gun he has in his pants. I'm not an airheaded girl standing in a field with nothing better to do than watch a bunch of sheep eating grass, dammit!

"You know, if I had just met you in a different place at a different time . . . ," he says, "I think we could have hit it off." He reaches down and grabs at his crotch, squeezing it.

It's then that I realize he's aroused.

Oh, God. I think I'm going to be sick. He's going to rape me, isn't he?

I smile back, trying like hell to keep all the fear and disgust I'm feeling out of it. "Really? That's so sweet."

No! It's really not! It's really, really, *really* awful, asshole!

My eyes go wide and I gasp with all the drama I can muster. "Oh! My leg!" I fall to the floor and land on the singlestick. Disney would totally recruit me for one of their kids' shows if they could see me now. I'm so not believable *at all*.

He growls and reaches for me. "That's enough fucking around! Get over here!" He has me by the pant leg, and he's dragging me toward him.

The singlestick feels awesome in my hand, like I was born to swing it. I yank it off the floor and bring it around with as much strength as I have left in me.

"Rreeeaahh!" I scream, relishing the strong *thunk* I hear when it makes contact with his leg.

He yells in pain as his knee buckles.

Keep moving, keep moving, keep moving. Dev's instructions race through my head.

I bring the stick up and smack him on the head with it when he bends over to grab me again.

"Eeerph!" He falls forward and lands on my lap.

I emphasize every word that comes out of my mouth with another whack from the stick, hitting him on the head, shoulders, back, and arms.

"Get!" *Whack!*

"Off!" *Whack!*

"Me!" *Whack!*

"You awful!" *Whack!*

"Scumbag!" *Whack!*

He finally stops moving, and I pause the abuse to wriggle out from underneath him.

Scrambling to my knees, I crawl over to my alarm system, using the door handle to get to my feet. All the lights on the keypad are out.

"Of course!" I scream, glancing back at David. "You destroyed my security system, you asshole!"

He's very still.

"Oh, God, please don't let him be dead." I tiptoe over and take the gun from his back where it was tucked into his belt. It's much heavier than I expected it to be. Opening the front door, I throw it out onto the front lawn.

Just as I'm about to close the door, Ozzie's truck pulls into my driveway. I take a step toward him, but then I collapse, my legs going out from under me for real this time. I land on the porch in a puddle of tears.

"Ozzie!" I screech, reaching out a hand to him. Again, very dramatic, but much more believable, so of course Disney won't want me now.

He jumps out of his door and sprints over to me, his face fiery red and his body appearing twice its normal size. Sahara is right behind him, growling, barking, and drooling like a mad hound from hell.

My heroes.

I weep with relief. They've come to save Fee and me. I've never been so happy to see someone in my entire life. I don't care if he loves Toni. I will forgive him anything now.

CHAPTER FIFTY-FOUR

Turns out, there's nothing to forgive. Silly me.

"I'm only telling you this because I don't want you to think I'd lie to you," Ozzie says, holding me in his arms in his bed. We're fully clothed, just coming down from the craziness that was being at the police station, questioned for hours about what happened and then being at the vet to find Felix there just out of surgery to repair a broken leg. He will come home in a couple days when they're sure he can walk on his pinned limb.

"If you want to lie to me, you can," I say, patting his massive chest. "You saved me today." I look at the clock. "Or yesterday, technically."

"First of all, I don't want to lie to you. Ever." He takes my fingers and kisses them. "Lies are not a good foundation for a solid relationship."

I smile like the Cheshire Cat but say nothing. He's on a roll and I don't want to interrupt. A relationship! Wheeee!

"Second of all, I asked Toni if I could discuss something that relates to her, and she gave me her blessing."

"So you didn't have a relationship with her?"

"Not like you're thinking, no. I was her sponsoring employer while she was on parole. She finished that parole a few months ago. She's on her own now."

"Parole?" I nearly sit up at that, but Ozzie's strong arms hold me down.

"Yes, parole. She is a convicted felon."

"Whoa." I probably should have known that before I antagonized her so much. "What did she do?"

"She killed someone. A man."

"I . . . errr . . ." I'm finding it hard to say what I'm thinking. "I can't see her doing that. I mean, she's tough and she's hard, but she never struck me as being so cold-blooded."

"She's not. She was a victim of pretty severe domestic violence that started when she was fifteen. She killed her abuser during one of his attacks. It was self-defense, but she was convicted of manslaughter."

"Why?"

"Because she . . . well . . . she did a really good job of killing him, let's just put it that way."

"Wow." Of course I'm curious as hell about the details, but I'm not going to press for them. I know how much a sacrifice of her privacy this was in the first place. Besides, it doesn't matter. I respect her for sticking up for herself. I'm glad she killed him well.

At the same time, I'm glad I *didn't* kill David Doucet. Giving him a concussion is bad enough. I don't think I could end a person's life without being tortured over it for the rest of my life. Maybe that's why Toni seems so angry. Maybe she's having a tough time with that too. I renew my dedication to become her friend, now that I know I'll definitely be staying here at Bourbon Street Boys and that she didn't sleep with my boyfriend.

"Are you my boyfriend, Ozzie?" I feel silly saying it, but I need to know.

"Do you want me to be?"

"Yes. But it doesn't matter just what I want. We both have to be on board."

He chuckles. "I'm on board."

"But I don't want people at work knowing."

"Fine by me. Either way."

"Because it wouldn't be professional."

"What wouldn't be professional?" he asks, rolling over on top of me.

"Us being intimate. At work." I can't stop smiling up at his handsome face.

He leans down and kisses me ever so gently on the lips. "I agree one hundred percent."

I slide my hands up his back and revel in all the muscles I feel there. "So you should probably stop kissing me, then."

He kisses me on the lips again. "This isn't work. This is my home."

I glance at the door. "I'm pretty sure Dev and Thibault are right outside that door."

"They're in the kitchen, which is thirty feet from that door. And they're not allowed past the kitchen."

"Is that the boundary?" I ask, joking.

"As a matter of fact, it is. No one but you ever comes past the kitchen."

"Not even Toni?" I feel silly asking it, but I do it anyway. I'm still in high school, apparently.

"Even Toni."

I hug him hard, pulling him against me. "I love you, Oswald."

"What if I grow my beard back?"

My face twitches as I try to hold back the giggles. "Let's not test my love so soon, okay?"

He growls and buries his face in my neck. "You're in trouble now, young lady."

I laugh as I try to get away. "No! Not the five o'clock shadow cheek burn!"

He grinds his face against me until I start screaming.

"Shhhh, people are going to think we're being intimate at work," he says in a whisper.

I grab him on either side of the head and try to glare at him. "You're mocking me. Cut that out." The glare slips and I smile instead. I love that he's so playful, but only with me. Everyone else sees him as this big, bad, commando guy who never jokes around, but I know who he really is: a big teddy bear who'll do anything to protect those he loves.

"Do you love me?" I ask him, staring deep into his eyes.

"What do you think?" He grins at me, leaning down to kiss me again.

I turn my head to the side so he can't get to me. "I think you'd better tell me if you don't want me driving home tonight."

He laughs really loudly and flips himself over, dragging me with him. I'm now straddling him on top.

"I love you, Little Bo Peep. Hope you can handle it."

I reach down and press on the cleft in his chin. "Stop calling me that stupid name." I can't be mad at him for real. He just confessed his love for me. A love I already knew was there the minute I saw him racing up my driveway to save my life.

"How about Little Red Riding Hood?" he asks. "Do you like that name instead?"

I reach down and grab one of his nipples, preparing to twist it. "What do you think?"

He holds up his hands at the sides of his head. "Mercy! I beg for mercy. I'll call you whatever you want me to call you, just don't give me a twister."

I loosen my hold and sit back satisfied. "I think I'd like to be called . . ."

He sits up all of a sudden and then flips me onto my back once again. Looming over me he gets that sexy look in his eye that I remember from the other night. Electricity zooms through my body as I wait for his next words.

"I'm going to call you *mine*. May *'Mine'* Wexler."

"I don't think that's going to go over very well with the team."

"Tough. You're mine and I get what I want."

I get a sly look of my own. "And what do you want, boss man?"

He climbs off me and lies on his side, propping his head up with his hand. "I want you . . . to take off all your clothes."

"What if I'm too sore to have sex?"

"I'll be gentle."

"What if I'm too scared?"

"I'll ease your mind."

"What if I'm worried you'll break my heart?"

"I'll show you that you're crazy to think that." He reaches over and puts his hand on my cheek. "I don't tell just anyone I love them, you know."

"You don't?"

"No. Just the girls who I want to stick around. Now get up off this bed and take your clothes off before something bad happens."

I have to bite my lip to keep from smiling too hard. "Something bad? Like what?"

He growls and rolls on top of me. I scream out a laugh that comes from the deepest part of me and wrap my arms around him. I'm going to drown in whatever he's offering me tonight and wake up tomorrow in his arms. I've made my decision. He might have come to me as a wrong number, but he is most definitely the right guy.

AUTHOR'S NOTE

If you enjoyed this book, please take a moment to leave a review on the site where you bought this book, Goodreads, or any book blogs you participate in, and tell your friends! I love interacting with my readers, so if you feel like shooting the breeze or talking about books or your family or pets, please visit me. You can find me at www.ElleCasey.com, www.Facebook.com/ellecaseytheauthor, and www.Twitter.com/ellecasey.

Want to get an email when my next book is released?
Sign up here: http://bit.ly/ellecaseynews

ABOUT THE AUTHOR

Elle Casey, a former attorney and teacher, is a New York Times and USA Today bestselling American author who lives in Southern France with her husband, three kids, and a number of furry friends. She has written books in several genres and publishes an average of one full-length novel per month.